TWILIGHT DESTINY
(Haven's Realm 1)

Tamara Monteau

EROTIC ROMANCE

Secret Cravings Publishing
www.secretcravingspublishing.com

A Secret Cravings Publishing Book
Erotic Romance

TWILIGHT DESTINY (HAVEN'S REALM 1)
Copyright © 2003, 2008, 2011 by Tamara Monteau
Print ISBN: 978-1-61885-080-5

First E-book Publication: July 2011
First Print Publication: October 2011

Cover design by Beth Walker
Edited by Lori Paige
Proofread by Katie Carney
All cover art and logo copyright © 2011 by Secret Cravings Publishing

PUBLISHER
Secret Cravings Publishing
www.secretcravingspublishing.com

Dedication

For Mike, my best friend, partner, lover and soul mate, whose patient support and tolerance over the years enabled me to turn my dream into a reality.
This success belongs to both of us!

TWILIGHT DESTINY (HAVEN'S REALM 1)

Tamara Monteau
Copyright © 2011

Prologue

A gentle breeze stirred among the branches of the mighty evergreens–pines, spruces, and firs that whispered to each other over long-forgotten memories. High above the canopy, a waning moon peeked from behind the scattered clouds, its light casting fleeting silver beams among the shadows to illuminate the mist like specters flitting among the undergrowth. Somewhere in the quiet gloom, a lone owl took flight. Its massive wings softly beat the air as it issued a mournful "who-o-o" that floated on the breeze. Tiny frogs and insects called to each other, adding their songs to the musical harmony of the night.

A solitary figure moved among the shadows in ethereal silence, making note of every sound and smell, every nuance of the dense forest he'd come to call home. He passed unnoticed by the tiny creatures that shared this realm with him, and remembered a time long ago when they fled from him in fear before he knew they were there.

Joshua loved the night. He was deeply attuned to every sound, smell and sight that intertwined to write its own special music–music most creatures dismissed, but he found wonderfully soothing. The rainforests of the Pacific Northwest were not dissimilar to the woods of his native Scotland. Moss hung just as thick and wet from the trees. Mists rolled in just as gently. He sometimes missed the smell of heather on a fine summer's eve, but only occasionally now, for those days were long behind him.

This quiet night was like any other, uneventful and serene, until he heard the sound of raucous laughter from a clearing ahead of him. His sharply tuned senses caught the scents of alcohol, sweat, and burning wood in the air. With the most careful stealth, he moved closer and found the camp with its four drunken occupants. He listened for a few minutes to their bawdy comments and jokes with disgust before moving on.

He had not gotten far from the campsite when he caught a new, elusive scent on the breeze, mildly sweet, like fresh peaches and strawberries covered in cream. He paused to take the scent into himself, savored it, then listened silently until he heard the soft shuffle of feet. With swiftness only he could manage in complete silence, he moved to the source of the sound. What he found brought an unexpected pang to his long-quiet heart.

A little girl, perhaps eight years of age, tripped happily along the poorly used path humming a simple tune. Her dark, unevenly cut hair hung to her collar and floated softly as she moved. A pair of expressive blue-gray eyes sparkled in her delicate, china-doll face. She wore a pair of cotton pants with a flowered print and a hole over one knee, and an undersized sweater. An ill-fitting pair of battered canvas shoes slipped occasionally from her heels.

He opened his mind to her thoughts and instantly regretted the act, for her sweet innocence invaded his mind with unexpected strength. He learned she was on her way home from a day of play with a friend not far down the path while revisiting one of her favorite fantasies, one in which she was a princess, forced to hide in poor exile because her castle was under siege. He smiled at her imagination.

Facts and images flowed over him with the softness of a spring rain, sketching the details of her life while holding him in her tender thrall. She lived in a dirt-floor dwelling barely adequate to shelter herself and her parents. Her father was a lumberjack on a part-time crew. She painted his image in laughter and gentleness, disguising the worry in his eyes, the hard lines on his face. Her mother appeared to have once been a graceful beauty, and in the child's eyes she was the most wonderful woman in the world, but a hard life had put premature care lines on her young face.

The girl turned and headed into the woods, breaking his concentration. Her home was not far from where he now stood, a few short minutes up the path, but he realized with horror she intended to take a shortcut that led straight to the camp of drunken hunters. The thought of what those men might do to such a tender morsel sent an irrational surge of panic through him, overwhelming him with an unsettling and urgent need to protect her.

He knew his appearance would frighten the child, but he had to find a way to avert this tragedy in the making. With his mental prowess, he could sway her from her intended path, but doing so might cause her permanent harm. Tender minds were easily damaged, and his thoughts were far too powerful to force into such a small head. Reluctantly, he opened his mind to her again. The purity of her spirit poured through him, giving him feelings of longing he thought were lost to him forever. He fought against his feelings and focused on her fantasies until he found a way in. Then, with grim determination, he placed himself deliberately in her path.

The girl stopped short with a gasp when she saw him appear before her, but before she could gather herself to scream, he said gently, "Do not be afraid." He knelt down, bowed his head deeply, and said, "I beg your pardon for this intrusion, my lady. Please have no fear. I mean you no harm."

"Wh-h-o are you?" she asked in a tiny, frightened voice. "I'm not supposed to talk to strangers."

He lifted his head, but carefully kept his face shadowed. "I am but a poor knight, my lady, the guardian of this forest. The wood sprites warn of a princess in danger. Tell me, can you be the one of whom they speak?"

"I'm not a princess," she told him uncertainly, but he sensed her guard dropping.

"Indeed? May I be favored with the knowledge of your name?"

She hesitated a moment, then whispered, "It's…Katie."

"Katie?" he repeated in a puzzled tone. "Interesting name. Is it short for something? Let me guess. Katrina?" She shook her head. "No? Caitlin?" Again she shook her head, this time with a giggle. "Catalina, then?"

"No." She laughed, her fear all but gone. "Catherine."

He rose to his full height and nodded. "Ah. Catherine. 'Tis a beautiful name. It suits you well, my lady." He took a step toward her, leaned forward, and shifted his head from side to side in a secretive gesture. "There are monsters about this eve, Lady Catherine. I've been sent to guide you safely home."

Her expression instantly sobered. "There's no such thing as monsters. Daddy told me so."

"Aye, he is correct to a point. But, you see, these monsters are not the kind that hide under wee girls' beds at night. This kind lurks in shadowy woods to attack innocent wanderers such as yourself. The sprites told me they lie in wait beyond yonder trees. I've seen them myself, and they are most unsavory." He straightened again and held his hand to her. "I beg you do me the honor of conducting you safely to your home, Princess Catherine. I swear by the unicorn's heart that no harm will come to you if you place your trust in me."

He watched the play of emotions on her face with amusement. The discomfort in her heart kept company with her strong-willed imagination. It took only the gentlest mental nudge to convince her this was little more than an extension of her fantasies. She reached up slowly to place her small, warm hand in his much larger one. Then, with a regal air that appeared well practiced, she raised her chin and said, "Very well, Sir Knight. You may escort me if you wish."

"Thank you, my lady." He closed his hand over hers and paused for a moment to rub the pad of his thumb across her delicate knuckles. "Now, follow me, and be extra quiet. We don't want to attract attention." He turned and led her through the woods, keeping enough distance between them and the men so her innocent ears would not hear their revelry. When they reached the edge of her property, he knelt to look in her eyes. "Your home lies just beyond, my lady. I thank you again for allowing me to see to your safety."

She performed a proper curtsy. "I thank you for your assistance, Sir Knight." Then, in a sudden gesture as magnanimous as it was unexpected, she flung her arms around his neck. He reluctantly returned the simple show of affection and felt something deep inside him shatter. She whispered a hasty goodbye and ran the rest of the way to her house.

He stood in the shadows and watched as she entered her home. Her mother welcomed the child into her arms and closed the door behind them. He heard her speak excitedly about a forest guardian, and felt relieved to sense the mother's amused dismissal of her daughter's flight of fancy. He turned to continue his nightly patrol of the forest, but now he took little notice of the wonders around him. His thoughts continued to gravitate around the innocent angel that had moved him so strangely.

He grimly resolved to never again cross paths with fair Catherine. He would too easily grow attached to the young mortal, and that was one thing he could not allow himself to do. Not again. Not this time. He'd lived too many years and made too many mistakes to allow himself commit yet another blunder. Trifling with mortals was a dangerous, sometimes deadly, game, and a vampire had to be careful, especially in these modern times. He reminded himself how much he enjoyed his solitary existence while he made his way back to his home on the other side of the woods.

Chapter One

The smell of warm hotcakes woke Katie from her sleep. When she opened her eyes and realized the sun had risen, she groaned and forced herself out of bed. She reached clumsily for her little wind-up alarm clock and saw it was well past eight. "Shoot." She quickly pulled on a pair of jeans, sponged herself off at the old-fashioned washbasin, donned a short-sleeved, button down blouse, and tied sneakers securely to her feet. After brushing her long brown hair and tying it back with a worn bit of dark-blue ribbon, she emerged from the bedroom she shared with her mother.

Natalie waited for her at the kitchen table, a wide smile on her face and a heaping plate steaming in her hands. "Good morning, sweet pea!"

"I overslept, Momma. Sorry. I guess I forgot to set my alarm."

"I turned it off. Here. I made you a special breakfast. Happy birthday!" She set the plate in front of her daughter with a grand flourish. "It's hard to believe you're already seventeen."

"Thanks, Momma! Mmmm. This smells great! Where'd you get the syrup?"

"I traded Mrs. Warren some potatoes for it. Want some coffee?"

"Sure." She sipped at the coffee her mother gave her and stuffed another bite in her mouth. "Why did you let me sleep so long? I'm supposed to meet Dillon and Taska in an hour. They're gonna give me a ride to the fair. I still have my chores to do."

Natalie's smile didn't waver. "I've already taken care of everything that can't wait." She paused to stroke the side of her face affectionately. "Today's your day, and I want you to enjoy it."

"Well, at least let me help with the dishes." She stuffed the last bite in her mouth and rose from her seat. "Don't you have a job today?"

"The Feldman's," Natalie confirmed, working the pump at the sink. "It shouldn't take me too long."

The sound of car engines startled her. She turned quickly to the small front window. "Who could be visiting this early?" she asked, peering outside. "Isn't that your lawyer friend, Carl Foster? Who's that with him?"

While Natalie went to the front door, she watched the familiar, well-dressed gentleman unfold himself from his shiny black Mercedes, a friendly smile on his rugged face. The second car, a white early '80's K-style sedan, pulled alongside, and a young man with a boyish face and short, sand-colored hair stepped out and handed Mr. Foster the keys. She went outside in time to hear her mother say, "I was beginning to think you wouldn't get here in time."

"I'm as good as my word," Carl replied lightly. "Good morning, Katie. Happy birthday." He handed her an envelope. "That's just a little something to help you enjoy the fair," he explained while she opened the envelope and saw the two crisp twenty-dollar bills inside.

"Thank you. So, what's going on?"

In response, Carl tossed the set of car keys in her direction with a wide grin. To Natalie, he said, "The registration and insurance paperwork are in the glove box. I had my mechanic go over it, and he assures me the car is sound."

Shock and confusion held her suspended. "Momma...?"

"Happy birthday," she repeated with a laugh.

"You mean...?" She eyed the sedan suspiciously and cast uncertain glances at Carl and his companion. The young man nudged Carl's arm and made some gestures with his hands, making him chuckle and nod.

A grin lit Natalie's face. "The car is yours. Mr. Foster helped me get it for you."

For a moment, she stared disbelieving at the shiny car and the set of keys in her hand. She felt the corners of her mouth pull upward. "Really?" she whispered.

"All yours," Carl confirmed.

"No way!" She ran excitedly to the driver's door, peered inside at the cream-colored interior, and walked around the Chrysler LeBaron, touching the fenders and the soft landau top reverently. "How...?"

"I've been saving up for it ever since you got your license," Natalie told her. "Mr. Foster helped me find it and took care of all the legal stuff."

She circled the car again, barely noticing when Carl's companion climbed into the passenger side of the Mercedes. "I need to get going," she heard Carl say. "I have an appointment at the office at ten."

She threw her arms around her mother. "Thank you, thank you, thank you!" She turned and did the same to Carl, who returned her embrace somewhat embarrassedly. She smiled at the unknown companion and waved, and the young man returned her smile sheepishly.

"Thank you for your help, Mr. Foster," Natalie said softly. A strange expression swept her face.

"Anything for you, Natalie," Carl replied with equal softness in his deep voice. "And I do wish you'd call me Carl. We've known each other for years, after all."

She wasn't sure, but she thought her mother's face reddened slightly. "I'll...I'll try to remember that...Carl."

He nodded. "Have a great day, Katie."

"Thanks again," she said before he got into his car and brought it to life. She watched while they drove back down the dirt road, and turned her attention back to her own car.

"Well, you gonna stare at it all day, or are you gonna get in?" Natalie asked with a laugh. "I do have other things to do today."

She returned her mother's laugh, gave her another hug, and jumped in. The car fired up without coaxing, and she put it in gear. "I'll be home late," she yelled as she pulled onto the road. "Is that okay?"

"Sure, honey. Enjoy yourself!"

While she drove down the winding dirt road that led to the highway, she smiled at the newfound sense of freedom only owning her own car could bring. "This is going to be the greatest day of my life."

* * * *

The Clark County Fair opened its gates every year during the first week of August, but this was the first time since before her father died that Katie was able to go. When she stepped out of her car in the field that served as the parking lot, warm air and sun-dried grass filled her senses. She took a deep breath and gazed at the fairgrounds with renewed excitement. As she approached the gates, the smells of the fair mingled with that of the field. She knew without looking where the animals would be and what kinds of wonderful food items she might find. With all the activities, random entertainments, and exhibits, there was much more to do and see than can be covered in a day. Nonetheless, she felt determined to experience everything.

She watched a few shows, took in the sights, and visited the barns and the arenas. From vendors in one of the commercial buildings, she purchased a vegetable peeler and slicer set for her mother, and an embroidery kit, complete with floss, needles, and a variety of patterns, for herself.

When twilight crept across the fairgrounds, she made her way to the midway. She'd reserved this part of the fair for last, knowing darkness would make the lights seem magical. As she strolled along the crowded aisles, she noted how music from each of the rides blended into the next.

Carnival barkers filled the air with shouted promises of easy wins and big prizes when she passed.

She stopped to watch one guy not much older than herself throw darts at balloons. His girlfriend squealed in delight when the attendant handed her a prize teddy bear. When the dart thrower put his arm around the girl, and they, laughing, touched their foreheads together, she felt a slight pang. The happy couple reminded her that not all relationships were solely physical in nature. Some day, she hoped to find someone special with whom she could build trust and a lasting friendship. Someday.

She was musing about romance, walking absently through the crowd, when the back of her neck prickled. She suddenly felt absolutely certain she was being watched. She studied the crowd, but didn't see anyone looking her way. Still, the sensation persisted, growing stronger with each step she took. When she turned the corner next to the Tilt-a-Whirl, she saw the silhouette of a man standing in the shadows next to one of the food carts. Although it was dark, she felt his eyes on her. A knot formed in the pit of her stomach that tasted like panic, and she wished she'd insisted on staying with Taska and Dillon, instead of leaving the lovebirds to enjoy the fair alone.

Not wanting to attract undue attention in case this was all her imagination, she let her gaze drift nonchalantly over to the menu on the food booth. After pretending to consider the options at that particular booth, she shook her head and started walking along the midway. She resisted the urge to glance over her shoulder until she had gone several yards and found a good excuse to turn around. At one of the gaming booths, she circled slowly, her gaze lifted to the prizes hanging from the rafters, but she cast quick, furtive glances into the crowd. *There. Is that the shadow of a man next to that ticket booth? Turn away. Now, slowly, look back. Nothing.*

She turned away again and walked farther through the midway, feeling very alone and vulnerable in spite of the pressing crowds. At the next food cart, she stepped in line and made a play at counting the change in her pocket, still watching nervously to see if anyone was behind her. Too soon she was at the window, so she ordered a small bag of popcorn and continued her progress along the midway.

"Too much sugar," she muttered to herself. "Wild imagination." She glanced openly behind her this time while pushing a kernel of popped corn in her mouth. "Trick of the light. Sensory overload." She clamped her mouth shut when she realized she was talking out loud. She turned into yet another aisle of midway still feeling a strange I'm-being-followed sensation.

Brianne and Nicole abruptly appeared in front of her. They were two of the most beautiful girls in school, and the most conniving. They hung out with her when the mood hit them, usually when some new boy cast interested looks her way. She tolerated them most of the time because she wasn't that popular in school and enjoyed the attention. This time, she was instantly grateful for their company. "Katie!" Brianne called.

"Hi. Having fun?"

"As always," Nicole purred. Nicole had the exotic looks and features of a fashion model. Her jet-black hair hung long, straight, and silky smooth. Her body was long and lithe, with just enough curves to make any guy in school flush. She batted her dark, almond shaped eyes at one of the passers-by, and said, "Lots of interesting sights."

Brianne rolled her eyes and laughed. "Sometimes I think you have a one track mind." Katie almost genuinely liked Brianne. Her farm-bred, fresh-faced looks were more wholesome than Nicole's. She usually wore her curly blonde hair in a ponytail, but tonight she'd let it fall unhindered around her shoulders. Standing next to these two, Katie often felt herself even more plain and uninteresting than she knew she was.

"Been on any of the rides yet?" Nicole asked.

"No, I'm just walking around. What about you?"

"We went on that new one over there," Brianne said, pointing to a tall, brightly lit sphere. "It was really wild."

"Can I have some of your popcorn?" Nicole asked.

She handed over the bag. "So, where are you two headed next?"

"Oh, we're hangin' out right now, waiting for the concert," Brianne answered while thrusting her hand into the bag.

"Would you look at that," Nicole said, her voice low and sultry. Brianne looked quickly in the direction Nicole was staring, and her eyes widened. She tapped Katie on the arm and pointed.

She rolled her eyes and turned, and felt a fresh knot form in her stomach. Across the midway stood the finest example of male beauty she'd ever seen. His general height and outline gave her the uncomfortable feeling he was the same man she'd seen minutes before staring at her from the shadows. At the moment, he was busying himself at one of the contest tables, throwing baseballs at stacked bottles. His aim, she noticed, was dead-on perfect.

He appeared to be in his early twenties, twenty-two or twenty-three. He was dressed in a pair of tight fitting blue jeans and a loose linen shirt. The long sleeves were cuffed tightly at his wrists, making them blouse softly. His rich brown-gold hair curled softly around his head and fell to below his shoulders. Those shoulders were broad, and, judging by the way his shirt was tucked trimly into his jeans, muscular. The toes of a pair of snakeskin boots peaked from the hems of his jeans. He accepted his prize, a stuffed Seattle Seahawk, from the attendant and turned to present it to a small boy who happened to walk by at that moment. His face was angular. Low, straight brows topped his eyes, and a straight nose hovered over a set of lips just full enough to look soft and sensual. The slightest hint of a cleft in his chin added more strength and masculinity to his overall appearance.

She swallowed hard and backed up behind Brianne and Nicole, wanting nothing more at the moment than to disappear. Brianne grabbed her arm before she could make good her escape. "Where do you think you're going?"

"I...uh...the popcorn made me thirsty. Anyone want a pop?" To her own ears, her voice sounded higher, weaker, bordering on panic. Luckily, her companions didn't seem to notice.

"I'll bet he's married," Brianne whispered. "No one that gorgeous could possibly be available."

"No," Nicole countered. "If he were, he'd have his wife with him."

"I'll bet I can get his attention," Brianne said with a soft smile.

"No way," Nicole argued. "Look at him. He's more the sultry, seductive type."

"Is anyone hungry?" she asked desperately. Again, her companions ignored her. The knot in her stomach pulsated suspiciously like a heartbeat.

The man turned and walked along the midway toward them. "Look," Nicole said in a voice soft and low. "He's coming this way."

"L-look, I've gotta, uh..." she stammered, trying to pull herself free of Brianne's grasp.

"Come on, Katie, you're in on this too. Let's see who ends up with him."

"No, really, I don't think I..."

"Hi, ladies. Great evening, huh?" the man asked lightly, interrupting her argument. She noticed a slight accent in his smooth tenor voice.

"Couldn't be better," Brianne said, smiling as she extended her hand. "I'm Brianne Anderson."

He accepted her handshake briefly and gave Nicole a questioning look. "Nicole Pierce," she purred. He shook her hand with equal brevity and turned his gaze to Katie. The knot in her stomach climbed up to her throat as if it too wanted to escape.

He sized her up slowly before catching and holding her gaze. "And who might you be?" he asked, his smile softening.

She felt instantly trapped in the depths of his warm-chocolate eyes. There was so much to see in those eyes–self-assuredness that comes from a sense of power, combined with a hint of something she couldn't quite define. The intensity of his gaze made her feel powerless and took the starch out of her knees. It took a nudge from Brianne to snap her out of the spell he'd cast over her. "Katie Mills," she said at last, reluctantly raising her hand to him.

He took her hand, but instead of shaking it as he had the others, he gently rubbed the pad of his thumb across her knuckles. "Katie? Is that short for something? Let me guess. Katrina?" She shook her head. "No? Caitlin?" Again she shook her head, a sudden sense of déjà vu overtaking her and making her dizzy. "Catalina then?"

"No," she answered, her voice trembling. "It's Catherine."

"Catherine," he repeated softly, his eyes pinned to hers intently. "It suits you." Still holding her hand gently, he said, "You may call me Joshua."

The other girls took notice of the unusual attention he was giving her, and broke the spell that had captured her so firmly. "Don't mind her," Brianne said with a laugh. "She's a little shy. Have you been on any of the rides yet?"

"We're going to the concert later. Want to come along?" Nicole offered.

He held her gaze for a moment longer. She thought she saw irritation flicker in his eyes. He turned away to smile at the other girls. "You know, I haven't been on the rides yet. Which ones do you like best?"

"The Ferris wheel," Nicole purred.

"Yeah," Brianne agreed with a sultry smile.

"Well, come on, then. I have plenty of tickets." He put his arms around each of the girls and glanced back to her. "Are you coming, Catherine?"

"I…that is, uh…you guys go on ahead. I'm not crazy about the rides anyway."

"Aw, come on Katie," Brianne called sharply.

"What are you afraid of?" Nicole asked, mischief gleaming in her eyes.

"Losing my stomach," she muttered, looking at the two of them hanging on Joshua's arms like soft taffy.

"It won't be as much fun without you," he coaxed.

She almost asked him if he didn't think he already had his hands full. She desperately wanted to say no, but found herself trailing along anyway. Something about his voice, soft and warm, and yet able to carry so easily over the fair's chaotic atmosphere, pulled at her like a tether. *He can sing.* She watched him walk with her companions and noticed the fluid way he conducted himself. *He's graceful, a dancer, for sure–and rich, no doubt about that.* Rich, to her, meant trouble–rich people couldn't be trusted. Better to leave him to her friends and escape before things got out of hand.

He allowed the girls to lead him along the midway, Katie following behind and watching in disgust while they laughed too loudly at his jests and openly competed for his attention. Desperate for a way to gracefully escape the group, she decided to blend in with the crowd as soon as they boarded one of the rides. With any luck, she would be in her car and on her way home before they noticed she'd gone.

When they reached the Ferris wheel, Joshua handed the attendant enough tickets for the four of them and led the girls to the first gondola. The ride operator quickly stepped in and closed the bar over the two girls' laps. "Hey," Brianne protested. "There's room for one more."

"Two to a car, please," the operator said with practiced curtness.

"Sorry, ladies," he called when the ride swept into motion and they swung over the ground. When the next car came available, he turned and held his hand to her.

Crap. Now what do I do? "N-no thank you. I really don't…"

"Come on," he insisted lightly. "I won't bite." She swallowed her reluctance and accepted his invitation. After all, what else could she do without looking foolish? He seated her in the gondola, sat beside her, and put one arm over her shoulders while the attendant secured the bar.

At first, she sat still and endured the ride while it surged and paused repeatedly to change riders. When the car stopped at the top, she looked across the fairgrounds and lost some of her nervousness to the wonder of the sight. From high above, the lights took on a more magical appearance than they did from the ground. She leaned over the bar, trying to take it all in at once. "First time on a Ferris wheel?" he asked, drawing her attention back to him.

"It's been a long time. I forgot how high it is."

"Does it frighten you, being up this high?"

"No, not really." She turned back to look over the midway. "The view is beautiful."

The tips of his fingers stroked her shoulder lightly, and she turned to him again, her pulse rate suddenly skyrocketing. "Why do you associate yourself with girls like Brianne and Nicole? They're beneath you."

She took a deep breath in an effort to calm her racing heart. "They're not so bad, once you get to know them. When they're not acting like half-crazed…"

"Tavern wenches?"

She almost laughed. "Well, that's one way to put it. Anyway, they let me hang out with them. I don't have many friends."

"I can't believe that. Pretty girl like you? I'll bet all the boys in school trip over themselves to get close to you."

She felt a warm blush rise to her face, and quickly turned away. "They prefer girls like Bri and Nikki."

"Their loss, I suppose," he said, not unkindly. "Don't get me wrong, Brianne and Nicole are two very attractive young ladies, but to be honest, I found their behavior somewhat…obvious. It's a shame, really, that more men don't see through their kind." A soft smile of appreciation pulled at her lips, but fled the instant he touched her chin with the tip of his index finger and guided her face back to his. His eyes had darkened from warm chocolate to hot cocoa. "I am not interested in what they appeared almost desperate to offer."

She felt trapped once more in the power of his gaze. The seriousness in his expression made the bottom drop out of her stomach. "Please don't."

"Forgive me," he begged, lowering his hand. "I've overstepped my bounds."

"No, it's just…" She attempted a lighthearted laugh that sounded as forced as it was. "I barely know you."

The ride pulled to a stop and the operator stepped forward to release the bar so they could disembark. The girls were waiting for them at the gate. Brianne stepped forward instantly and took his arm. "Come on. The Tilt-a-Whirl's next." Katie heard the desperation in her voice.

He smiled brightly and put an arm around each of the girls, leaving her feeling bewildered. After guiding them into motion, he lowered his arms and dipped one hand in his pocket. "That sounds like great fun, ladies. Tell you what though, why don't you go on without me for a while." He handed them a fist-full of ride tickets and took her hand. "Catherine isn't feeling well and needs to sit down." They stared in open-mouthed surprise when he pulled her into the crowd.

She allowed him to guide her along while she regained her bearings. They were halfway through the midway before she laughed, forgetting just for the moment the strange nervousness that had settled uncomfortably in her stomach. "Did you see the looks on their faces?"

His smile was warm and soft. "Took them by surprise, didn't I?"

"I don't think anyone's done that to them before."

After a few moments of silence, he observed, "They follow. No, don't turn to look. They're there."

Maybe that's for the best. "What should we do?"

A spark of amusement lit his eyes. "Come this way." He put his arm around her back and guided her between a food booth and the fence surrounding one of the rides, across the next aisle of midway, and around to the rear of some game stalls. It all happened so fast it made her head spin, and she had to lean against the back of the stall for support. "Quiet now." She heard Brianne and Nicole calling to each other in frustration for a moment, and then their voices were lost in the chaos of other noises around them. "That should do it," he said at last. "Are you all right?"

She took a deep breath and looked up to see the concern in his eyes. "Fine."

"When was the last time you ate?" She thought about the sausage she had for lunch and the two or three bites of popcorn, and realized her diet was not equal to the excitement of the evening. Before she could answer him, he said, "Come. I'll get you something to eat."

She no longer had the will to protest. He took her hand once again and led her through the midway. She noticed for the first time how unusually cool it felt. Who was it that said people with cold hands have warm hearts? *Stop it, Katie.*

When they neared the entrance to the midway, he stopped so suddenly she nearly lost her balance. "Hold on," he said, pulling her to the side. "I want to try this game." He tossed the attendant a twenty and picked up some rings. She watched while he unerringly tossed the rings over the tops of bottles. When he'd tossed his last ring, the attendant shook his head and gathered every one from the necks of the bottles. "Never saw such throwing," he told them. "That was amazing."

"Incredible," she agreed.

"Beginner's luck," Joshua said with a dismissive shrug and a sheepish grin.

"Well," the game attendant said with a wave of his arm, "take your pick."

"Hmmm," he hummed softly, his hand on his chin in consideration. He pointed to a large, fluffy brown and tan bear. "We'll take that one." He accepted his prize and turned to her with amusement in his eyes. "What do you think?"

He put the bear in her arms, and she gave it a firm squeeze. "Wow, he's soft."

"Don't tell me you've never had a teddy bear," he said, chuckling.

"Of course. Oh, well, it was a rabbit, actually. Her name was Carrots." She considered the bear's face for a moment, and said, "He reminds me of a root-beer float. I think I'll call him Soda-pop."

He chuckled again, a soft, easy sound like the flutter of a bird's wings. "All right, well come on then." He gently placed his hand on the small of her back to coax her forward, giving her the uncomfortable feeling he was becoming too familiar. "What would you like to eat?"

Up ahead, mingled with booths offering a wide array of souvenirs, were several food vendors. She scanned the possibilities until her gaze fixed on a garishly painted sign promising fresh-baked pizza. How long had it been, she wondered, since she'd had real pizza, and not the frozen imitation the school offered that tasted like plastic-coated cardboard? "Pizza it is," he declared before she could say a word.

Once he'd seated her at a picnic table nearby, he charged off after the pizza. She watched him go thinking he looked like a knight on an errand. She put her face in her hands and leaned on the tabletop. Part of her wanted to jump up and run away. Another part felt almost compelled to stay put and see what happens. "What am I going to do now?" she wondered out loud. "Lord, don't let me make a fool of myself."

"I would never think you a fool," Joshua said beside her, making her jump.

"That was quick!"

"Short line. Here you go." He placed a thick slice of combination pizza and a cup of Coke in front of her and took the seat opposite hers.

"Wow. Thank you. Where's yours?"

"I ate earlier." He watched her attempt to pick up the slice. "That's New York style. I believe you're meant to fold it." She looked up at him in question, and he reached forward. "Uh, may I?" When she nodded, he took the outside crust and folded the slice lengthwise, then motioned for her to take it. "Now support the other end and take a bite."

She leaned her head over the plate and considered her dinner. How, exactly, *does* one eat pizza daintily? She closed her mouth over the tip of the pizza, and a symphony of flavors exploded in her mouth. After a gasp of surprise, she closed her eyes and savored the richness of the sauce, the spiciness of the meats, the creamy, gooey melted cheese. She opened her eyes to take another bite and saw the astonished look on his face. "What?"

"Nothing," he answered, humor in both his tone and his eyes. "I've never seen anyone eat pizza with so much passion."

After an embarrassed laugh and a quick dab at her mouth with a napkin, she said, "I've never had pizza that tasted this good before. The school's pizza is awful."

"I'm glad you're enjoying it," he said while she stuffed another bite in her mouth and nodded.

"Okay," she said between dabs with her napkin, "I'll eat. You talk. What do you do? Where are you from?"

He chuckled lightly. "Well, let's see. I was born in Scotland to a poor dirt farmer. No, truly," he insisted when she shot him a doubting glance. "I am the fourth of five children. My mother died of a fever when I was but eight years old, and Da followed her less than a year later. Our Laird found a good foster for me, and I learned about financial business. My foster parents died when I was eighteen and left me a little money. I'd lost track of my brothers and sisters years before, and really had nothing to tie me down, so when I heard America was the land of opportunity, I jumped aboard the first ship I could."

"That must've been scary."

"Aye, at first, but I found some interesting business opportunities in New York, made a few rather shrewd investments, and by the time I was twenty-one I could afford to retire."

"Poor boy makes good?"

He chuckled again. "Something like that. When I grew tired of big city life, I moved here. I hired an attorney by the name of Carl Foster to manage my investments, and now I can take things a little easier."

"I know Mr. Foster. He comes around to visit Momma once in a while. I think she likes him more than she wants to admit. Anyway, he helped her buy me a car today for my birthday. Honestly, I don't know how she afforded it. It looks brand new; not a scratch on it." She stopped herself when she realized she was talking too fast, afraid she wasn't making much sense.

He smiled in a strange, secretive way. "Today's your birthday?"

"I'm seventeen today," she told him with a nod after she'd swallowed her last bite of pizza. She blotted her face clean and picked up the Coke. "I'm sure you thought I was older. I get that a lot."

He gathered her trash and rose from his seat. "I'm not much older than you, but 'tis what a person has inside that is more important than their age or outward appearance. I find you to be a very charming young lass."

She was at once disappointed in his acceptance and warmed by his words. "Do you want to go over to the grandstand? The concert's starting."

"I was hoping for someplace quieter. Somewhere we can talk uninterrupted."

Alarms rang loudly in her head at the thought of being alone with him. "I, uh, don't know if I should…"

"I dislike crowds. You're safe with me, Catherine. Don't be afraid."

"I'm not," she lied. "Just careful."

"All right. But I won't hurt you. *Ever.*" His last word was spoken so intently she felt her heart lurch in her chest.

There was conflict in his eyes again—curiosity and reluctance, and a strange desperation, as if he'd found something in her he didn't want to let go of. It struck an impressive amount of nervous anxiety in her chest. "What do you want with me?"

"I would like to know you. That's all. Trust me."

"Why? I mean, why me? I'm nobody special, just a poor hillbilly doing my best to survive. I'm sure there are more interesting people you could be spending your time with. I mean, someone like you, uh, no offence, but…"

"I'm merely curious," he interrupted softly.

She gaped at him for a moment before she realized he hadn't answered her question. "Why?"

He circled her slowly, as if studying her. "To me, women are not unlike flowers. Think of the poppy—it blooms in bright, vibrant colors and promises excitement, but it dies very quickly once picked. Queen Anne's Lace is frilly and fancy, but holds no fragrance and tends to become a nuisance to the unwary gardener. The rose, while often harder to grow, is softer and leaves a more lasting impression on the senses, but the thorns can cut deeply."

He stopped in front of her again and captured her gaze. "You are not unlike the tightly closed bud of a rare and as yet undiscovered blossom, keeping your nature a secret, hidden from the world within a tight cocoon of innocence and mystery."

His explanation was poetic, but almost too proverbial. Suspicion tugged at her brows. "You want me to open myself and let you fly in and take advantage of me."

She wasn't sure, but she thought the expression that came over his face was one of shock. "No, of course not. You misunderstand." He swept his hand through his hair in a gesture of frustration, and took a deep breath. "If one forces a bud to open before its time, the beauty waiting inside would be destroyed. You may be more delicate than an orchid, or sweeter by far than a rose. On the other hand, I may find you are as thorny and unpleasant as a thistle. Only time and patience will yield the answer." She saw the earnestness in his eyes. "It is your uniqueness that makes me curious. That is all. Please believe me."

She didn't want to trust him. His entire being exuded too much power, held too easily in control. She had a feeling he could coerce her into doing anything he wished, and that scared her more than anything else. Still, there was desperation in his eyes that pulled at her, begged her to listen to him. She reluctantly decided to go along, for the moment at least. "All right. Uh…" She licked her lips nervously. "The bleachers over by the exhibition ring should be free."

"Perfect." He took her hand once more and led her toward the animal arena. She sat on one of the bleachers and he seated himself next to her. "This is much better." She held the bear close and fidgeted nervously. "Now, tell me about yourself."

She swallowed hard and took a deep breath. "There really isn't much to tell. Mom and I live in a little house in the woods. It's not much, primitive by today's standards, but it's comfortable. I love living in the woods. It's quiet."

"It must've been hard for you after your father died."

His statement startled her. "How did you know that?"

She thought she saw the slightest hint of a wince touch his face, but he so quickly recovered his usual nonchalance she couldn't be sure. "You didn't mention him so I assume he's not around, and I get the impression you receive no support, so…"

She nodded thoughtfully. "That sounds logical. You're right. He died in a logging accident when I was eleven." She sipped at her Coke thoughtfully for a moment. "Things got better for us after that. Momma got some money, and we bought a nicer place, set up a vegetable garden, and got some chickens."

A hint of a smile touched his eyes. "Do you like school? I'll be willing to bet you get good grades."

"I made the honor roll for the last three years," she confirmed with pride. "I'm hoping this year to get into computer sciences. Graphic arts and web design."

"Sounds interesting. What about friends? Anyone you confide in?"

She shook her head. "Not at school. There's Taska. She lives down the road from me, and I've known her since I was a kid. We used to be closer, but she was accepted into a Christian school, so I don't see her much anymore. Mostly, it's just Mom and me."

"Don't you get lonely?"

"Sometimes," she agreed slowly, "but Mom and I get along very well together."

"I see. What does she do?"

"She has a housecleaning business. I help her as much as I can. It doesn't pay much, but it keeps us going."

"Have you never considered applying for assistance?"

She wasn't sure if she should feel insulted. "You mean welfare? Food stamps? We won't ask for anything more of the government than we absolutely have to. We can take care of ourselves."

"Forgive me, I meant no disrespect, it is just rare to find people these days willing to pull up their own bootstraps, especially when the government makes it so easy to become dependent."

She took another sip of her Coke while she pondered how to take him. "It's not that we're proud. We know we have no rights there. A social worker came once to inspect our living conditions and encouraged Mom to take state assistance, but when she saw all the strings attached, she politely sent the woman on her way."

He looked impressed. "That must have taken a great deal of courage."

She shrugged. "We don't want to become indebted to anyone, especially the government. It gives them too much power over you."

She could tell he heard the warning tone in her voice. "Don't worry, I have absolutely no desire to control you in any way."

His eyes were darkening again. His serious expression and the intent tone in his voice made her desperate to change the subject. "What about you? Friends? Companions?"

His expression instantly brightened. "I live alone, unless you count my servant. I usually don't socialize much."

"Don't you get lonely?" she asked, bouncing his earlier question back at him.

He laughed; a soft, musical sound that belonged to the night. "Sometimes."

She suddenly realized the concert was over. How long had they been talking? "It's getting late. Mom will worry. I should go."

Sorrow touched his eyes for a moment. "May I walk you to your car?"

"I...I guess so."

The smile returned to his face. He helped her to her feet and threaded her hand through the crook of his arm. While they made their way to the front gate, she caught sight of Brianne and Nicole. They noticed her as well, and their mouths dropped open in bald astonishment. Embarrassed and unsure of herself, the best she could think to do was turn her eyes away, but she felt a smile tug at the corners of her mouth. He patted her hand at that moment, and she wondered if he'd also noticed them. She decided it best not to mention it.

When they arrived at her car, she nervously fished her keys out of her pocket. He took her hand and gentled the keys from her grasp, opened the car and tossed the bear on the passenger seat, then turned her to face him, a serious look in his eyes. "Thank you for spending your time with me tonight, Catherine."

She didn't know what to say. She wasn't ready to invite him in with something like, 'Will I see you again.' She wasn't even sure she wanted to. "I had a good time."

A faint smile played on his lips that was in direct conflict with the dark storm gathering in his eyes. "Goodnight."

He backed away and left her to climb into her car, but remained in the parking lot, watching her while she made her way to the exit. Once she was on the highway, and the gaiety of the fair vanished behind her, she had time to think about what had happened between them. "It would never work out. We're from two different worlds." While she drove up the winding dirt road leading to her house, she did her best to dismiss the entire evening as one of those things that happens, briefly, like a strange dream. She felt intense relief when her home came into view.

Chapter Two

Joshua drove his Sebring to its mechanical limits, growing angrier with himself with each passing mile. How could he have allowed himself to be so careless? Why, after all these long years, had he become so self-destructive?

He pulled to a skidding stop on the gravel drive that circled his home, pocketed his keys, then stood a moment on the front walk, hoping the familiar setting would calm him. Nestled deep in the woods, the single-story house featured a wide porch that extended across the front of the house and wrapped around both sides. It was painted in dark, woodland colors to blend in with its surroundings. Moss-colored shingles covered the roof to make it less noticeable to overhead traffic. The one-lane gravel drive circled through the woods, making the house virtually invisible from the road. He'd even had the power and phone lines buried, leaving no hint that a house might lie in that area. The setting gave him a necessary feeling of security.

He walked up the front steps and into his home feeling sullen, and took a moment to scrutinize his surroundings. The overall proportions of the house were generous, the rooms inside spacious. The entire front of the house was open. More than half of that space served as a living room with a fireplace and a crystal chandelier. Three ornate columns were the only divisions between the living room and the dining area and kitchen, providing necessary yet unobtrusive support for the roof. A hallway opened in the center of the rear wall, leading to three bedroom suites and a guest bath. The openness of his home normally gave him a sense of freedom and comfort, but tonight he felt trapped.

He saw his servant standing near the kitchen watching him timidly. The deaf-mute young man slipped uncertainly behind the dining table with a wary expression on his boyish face. Joshua sat down in his easy chair near the fireplace and tried to put a lid on his anger.

Unable to sit still for long, he rose from his chair and paced, slowly at first, but soon with growing agitation much like a tiger in a cage. He cast a quick glance at Alex and noted the concern in his heart. It gave him more to think about while he paced restlessly around the living area. He occasionally shook his head and wrung his hands, scolded himself over and over again for his folly.

He grabbed the poker from the stand and jabbed at the logs in the fireplace, shot a burst of mental energy at it, and the fire came to life with a loud whoosh. He sat again in his chair and studied the flames, but after a few short minutes he resumed his abuse of the thick carpeting. Alex moved furtively around the table, worry deeply engraved on his face. When Joshua cast another glance at him, he quickly signed the question written in his eyes.

"Nothing's wrong," he snapped, making him flinch. "All right," he said more gently, "I made a mistake. A big one."

Alex signed his simple inquiry in response. "I saw her," he told his servant quietly, "and I let her see me." He gave him a quizzical look. "Catherine. The girl I sold the LeBaron to."

The beginnings of understanding swept Alex's face. *She's very pretty,* he signed.

"I can't imagine what possessed me to become so involved with her. I wasn't expecting to see her tonight at the fair, and it took me by such surprise…" He swallowed the unfamiliar lump forming in his throat. "She knows of me now. I don't know what to do about it."

Take control of her.

"No! I can't take her. I won't. It would destroy the best of what she represents."

What's that?

He shook his head. "First off, she's an innocent. You know how I feel about that. And…" he raked his fingers through his hair in frustration, "there's a good chance I'm developing feelings for her. If I take her, I'll never be sure if any feelings she develops for me are genuine. If it goes that far, and I hope to hell it doesn't, I must know she gives her heart to me freely." At Alex's grin, he said, "It's not sex I'm after. I can get all of that I desire, any time I desire it, which isn't that often. If that were all there was to it, I wouldn't be feeling so…out of control." He turned away and started pacing again.

He turned back so Alex could read his lips. "I tried this once before, long ago. Jeanette…" Sorrow and bitterness brought by her memory reopened a hidden wound his heart. "I took her into my home, trusted her. We were together less than a year before she betrayed me." He shook his head again. "I lost everything that day. It took me months to recover the physical consequences of her treachery. I can't do that again. I can't place my existence on the line for some tender mortal with a sweet face."

Then don't see her again.

Unreleased sobs cramped his chest. Anguish rose like bile in his throat. "I wish it were that simple! There's something different about her, something I can't quite put my finger on, but it attracts me, draws me in like no other, and I fear I can no longer resist her pull."

How did this happen?

With a heavy sigh, Joshua returned to his chair and motioned for Alex to sit on the sofa. After a moment, he told Alex how he'd first met Catherine. "A sympathetic bond formed between us that night. I don't know how or why, but I've found it unshakable. At first, I felt overwhelmingly driven to protect her. I became aware whenever she was in trouble or need, and was drawn of necessity that was almost painful to aid her any way I could. I watched over her the night her father died, helped her through Carl every way I could without getting directly involved. Over the years, I've protected her from wild animals and rapists; influenced the path of her life much more than I should have, but I never again placed myself deliberately in her path, until tonight when I saw her at the fair.

"I was so taken by surprise I forgot to veil my presence from her. When she saw me, I don't know. I had to introduce myself. I thought if I could face her, I might understand this strange power she seems to have over me." He leaned his head back against the chair. "It was a mistake," he said, more to himself than to Alex.

"She was frightened of me," he continued after a few minutes had passed, "just as I knew she would be, just as all innocent creatures are frightened, on some primitive level, of beings such as I. It was only my rampaging pheromones that prevented her from fleeing the moment I showed interest.

"But it was as if I were under a spell, as if she'd bewitched me somehow. Meeting her was not enough. I had to spend time with her. Talk with her. And I...somehow, I *wanted* her to see me, know me, in spite of the danger to us both. I've stopped seeing her as a child, Alex. Tonight I met a young woman I could very easily fall in love with, and I know too well what that would cost.

"I don't want to see her again," he concluded, feeling doomed. "I want to pull up stakes and move away from this place. Never look back. I've been fighting this from the moment I laid eyes on her. I wish I'd never opened my mind to her thoughts nine years ago. Now I'm powerless against her."

What are you going to do? Deep concern weighed Alex's eyes.

"I don't know." He rose from the chair and paced again, but this time more thoughtfully. "I moved too quickly with Jeanette. Perhaps if I had been more careful, I might've seen the deception in her heart, recognized her treachery before things got out of hand. I was young, then. Naïve. I've learned a few things since."

Do you love her?

"Yes. No!" He sighed and thrust his fingers through his hair again. "I don't know. There's a part of me, deep down inside, that refuses to let this one pass. Do you think, if I'm careful, if I move slowly enough…do you think it possible? Can any mortal truly learn to trust a vampire? Love one?"

Alex's expression softened.

"Yes, I know you care for me. I feel your concern. I wonder, though, if you would feel the same had I not taken you under my control. The bond we share is based on that power."

Alex smiled and shook his head. *You're a good man. You never mistreat me.*

Joshua smiled himself. "I've never mistreated anyone who didn't deserve it. When I do hunt, my victims are always repaid for what I take from them. The women…" he did smile at his forming thought. "The women enjoy my company. I always make sure they wake in the morning believing themselves victims of scandalously erotic dreams, nothing more."

Alex did something then he'd never done before. He gave his master a stern look of determination and issued what, to him, amounted to an order. *Give her a chance. Let her get to know you. Give her the chance to show you what's in her heart. She might surprise you.*

"What if she turns against me? What if, once I reveal myself to her, once she knows it is a vampire she's involved with, it's more than she can handle?"

Alex shook his head sadly. *You have the power to make her forget.*

He considered the idea for a few moments. "Yes," he said at last, "but who will make me forget?"

* * * *

When Katie pulled up in front of her house, she saw the light of the oil lamp in the window and knew immediately her mom had waited up for her. She shut down the engine and sat for a minute to think. It had been a very eventful day, she thought to herself, looking around at the interior of her car. *Her* car. The idea still filled her with wonder. She glanced at the bear seated beside her and reviewed once again the evening's events. If there was one thing she was certain she'd learned, it was that there were at least a few men out there who might be interested in more than her body. It gave her a renewed feeling of hope for the future.

She gathered the bear and her purchases and got out of the car. Before she could take three steps toward her front door, though, her stomach delivered a sharp, painful lurch. She barely made it to the edge of the woods before she lost control, spilling the contents of her stomach into a crop of fern. Dizzy, she dropped to her hands and knees while her stomach continued to purge itself. Before she was finished, she felt the soft, supportive hand of her mother on her back. "Are you okay, baby?"

"Sorry, Momma." She picked herself off the ground with effort. "I'm all right."

Natalie helped her gather her belongings and led her into the house. She dropped, exhausted, onto the love seat while her mother scrutinized her with loving concern. "Nerves?" She put the bear on one of the kitchen chairs and went to the kitchen.

"Probably."

"Do you want to tell me about him?" she asked, handing her a glass of water.

She accepted the water and drank half of it, not the least surprised at her mother's perceptiveness. She'd always had a sixth sense where her daughter was concerned. "There's not much to tell," she fibbed. "Just some guy I met tonight."

"It takes more than that to make you lose your stomach."

She sighed and took another long drink of water. "Just a man," she insisted. "I was talking to Brianne and Nicole in the midway when we saw him. He introduced himself and took us on some rides."

"Uh huh," Natalie said coaxingly, "and then what?"

"Oh, you know. Bri and Nikki were their usual, flirty selves, and I was, well, scared, I think. I wanted to leave him with them, but he insisted on spending time with me instead. You should've seen the looks on their faces."

"Go on."

"He's beautiful, Momma," she said softly. "Polite and old-fashioned. His name is Joshua."

"Joshua, huh? Is he a student?"

She shook her head. "No, he's older."

"Hmmm. What did you do?"

"Talked, mostly. He's from Scotland. I think he's rich. He said he hired that lawyer friend of yours to help manage his investments."

"He knows Carl?" Natalie thought quietly for a moment. "I know we never talked about, well, you know. Are you sure this guy wasn't after your body?"

"He just wanted to talk. If all he wanted was sex, I think he would've gone after Bri or Nikki."

"Well, some men are like that, you know. It's no fun if the prize is handed to you. Sometimes they prefer the challenge."

"He wasn't that way at all. He held my hand while we walked. That's all he did. He didn't even try to kiss me." She sighed softly and sank deeper into the couch, "I think he's kinda sad. He doesn't have any real friends, just a servant. He must be awful lonely."

"Well, he sounds nice. Do you think I'll get to meet him?"

"No," she answered with a yawn. "I don't think I want see him again. There was something about him that made me feel out of place. He had a way of looking at things that was almost, I don't know, poetic, as if he's had several lifetimes to think about the world. I'd be in way over my head if I got involved with him. He was kinda scary, in a way."

"How do you mean?"

"I can't explain. I just…I felt like a rabbit cornered by a fox. Now that I think about it, he didn't do anything threatening, but I felt…"

"Nervous?" Natalie offered.

"Drawn to him," she finished. "The more I wanted to get away from him, the more I needed to stay. I didn't feel like I was in control, like maybe he had some kind of power over me. Does that make sense?"

Natalie smiled gently. "Maybe you're attracted to him. It happens, you know."

"Not to me, it doesn't," she grumbled. "I have other priorities right now."

"Well, the heart is a strange thing. You can't always predict or control with your mind the direction your heart wants to lead you." She leaned over and kissed her cheek. "You look tired. Maybe you'd better head off to bed."

"Yes, Momma." She kissed her mother back, and yawned again. "G'night."

* * * *

Carl Foster set his briefcase down and studied the stack of messages left by his secretary. His caseload was full, and he didn't have the time to answer every call. He was sorting the slips of paper by priority when the intercom on his desk beeped.

"Mr. Foster, you have a call on line two. The woman says she's a friend of yours. Say's it's urgent."

"Thanks Nell." He picked up the telephone and voiced his usual greeting.

"Mister, uh, Carl? Hi. This is Natalie."

"Good morning, Natalie. What's wrong? Car not working out?"

"Oh no, the car is perfect. Thank you for helping me with it."

"Oh, it was my pleasure. So, what can I do for you?"

"Well," there was a nervous tone in her voice, "Katie met someone at the fair last night. She said he's a client of yours. I was wondering if you could tell me about him."

"Hmmm. I'll try, what's his name?"

"Joshua. I don't know his last name. She says he's Scottish."

He felt as if someone punched a fist in his chest. "That would be Joshua MacAaron," he managed when he could draw breath. "What would you like to know?"

"Well, I know this probably sounds silly, but you see, she's never taken an interest in guys, and I've never seen her so worked up about anyone. Joshua sounds a little too far out of her league, if you know what I mean. I'm just...well...."

"Concerned for her? I understand your meaning, Natalie. If she were my daughter, I might be equally concerned if an older man took an interest in her."

"Is he...I mean...?" She cleared her throat. "I just want to know...."

"If he's dangerous?" Carl asked.

"Something like that," Natalie answered, relief in her voice.

"I've known Mr. MacAaron for quite some time. He's a very gentle man. I've never known him to give in to anger. In fact, when one of his investments went flat last year I was afraid to tell him, but he took it all in stride and moved on to other interests." He leaned forward in his chair and fiddled with a pencil. "If he has taken an interest in Katie, you can rest assured he would never mistreat her."

"He sounds like he's awful old for her," Natalie said doubtfully.

"Not really. I've had dealings with couples with much greater age differences than theirs who got along together perfectly. And if this does become more than a passing interest, she'll be well cared for. He has more money than he knows what to do with." He offered his last statement with a slight chuckle.

Natalie hesitated a moment before asking her next question. "Carl, Katie is not experienced with men. Would Joshua take advantage of that?"

"Not a chance," Carl replied firmly. "He's an old fashioned sort, almost eccentric. Always conducts his business affairs correctly. I can only assume he'd handle his personal affairs, if you'll pardon the use of the word, with equal correctness. It wouldn't surprise me one bit if he paid you a visit. Men of his class usually ask permission of the parents before courting their daughter." He jabbed the point of his pencil through the center of a gum eraser and felt the tip break on his blotter. "Now, I can't say for sure he's that interested. He rarely speaks to me of personal matters."

"I see. Well, I won't take up any more of your time. I know how busy you are."

"Not at all. Call on me any time."

"Thank you," she said before hanging up the phone.

He put his receiver down and took a deep breath. He had to remind himself his favorite client was not only his friend– he was his master. If he had dared, he would've offered a prayer for Katie's soul. After congratulating himself for keeping his cool with Natalie, he picked his messages up and grimly resumed the task of sorting them.

Chapter Three

Joshua kept to his home for the next two weeks, trying desperately to put his meeting with Catherine behind him to no avail. Dreams of her haunted his rest, where no dreams had ever invaded before. During his waking hours, he paced the confines of his home restlessly, fed only when the need became too great, and argued with himself back and forth on whether or not it would be in both their best interests if he left Washington. Just when he thought he'd made up his mind to leave, a sharp pain surged through his heart, forcing him once again to reconsider the matter.

He felt Alex watching him struggle against his conflicting feelings. On occasion, the boy gave him quiet encouragement, apparently hoping he'd give in and explore a relationship with her. While tensions grew, Alex bore up to his volatile moods with cautious patience. One night he left a florist's flier on the dining room table featuring a photograph of a vase filled with roses. Joshua found the flier and carried it in his pocket for the next three nights. Every so often, he pulled it out and studied it thoughtfully. In an angry moment, he wadded the paper in his fist and threw it into the fireplace. Alex looked on with deep sorrow in his eyes.

On the evening marking the second week since their encounter at the fair, Joshua donned a white, tailored shirt and a pair of brown trousers, combed his hair carefully, and left the house while Alex watched in hopeful surprise.

He drove to town and pulled into the parking lot at the mall without knowing why he was there. He decided the crowds and anonymity would do him some good, and walked the mall, watching the people who were entertaining themselves by gazing at the wares artfully displayed in each of the storefronts. Couples walked arm in arm or hand in hand, smiling and chatting with each other. Others sipped cappuccino at the coffee bar or shared an evening's repast at the food court. He looked down the corridor and saw himself walking with Catherine, laughing and talking naturally, holding hands. He blinked and the couple he saw before him became strangers. "Hellfire."

He turned down another corridor and tried to distract himself by gazing at the storefronts. It seemed everywhere he looked, he saw her instead of some stranger walking along the mall, or saw some article of clothing or jewelry that would look good on her. There was nowhere he could turn his gaze where thoughts of the girl didn't invade the privacy of his mind. When the sight of a florist shop appeared before him, displaying a colorful array of freshly cut roses, the thought of Alex's flier came to mind. "Bloody hell." He fished his wallet out of his back pocket and entered the store.

* * * *

Natalie pulled the last of the laundry from the line behind the house and sighed. The past two weeks had been difficult ones for her and her daughter. School would be starting in a week, she mused while she carried the basket into the house. They still had to shop for the clothes and supplies she would need.

She picked up the dishes on the drain board and put them away, and began folding the laundry on the loveseat. When she heard the sound of a car engine pull up to the house and die, she frowned. *That wasn't Katie's car.* She moved cautiously to the front window. The sight of a sleek convertible confirmed her suspicions. The satin blue Sebring glowed in the moonlight. A young man with long hair stepped out of the car, looked around anxiously, then lifted a vase full of roses from the back seat. With one hand, he adjusted the front of his tailored shirt and squared his shoulders. He stepped up to the front door, paused, and knocked gently.

Natalie opened the door slightly and looked out. "Yes?"

"Mrs. Mills?"

"I'm Natalie Mills," she confirmed.

"My name is Joshua MacAaron," he said, smiling shyly. "I met your daughter at the county fair."

"Yes." She opened the door a little wider. "She told me about you. I'm afraid she's not in at the moment. She's babysitting tonight."

His smile dropped in disappointment. "I see. Do you expect her to return soon?"

"Not for a couple of hours, at least."

He stood in contemplative silence for a moment, cleared his throat and offered the roses. "Would you mind giving these to her? There's a card…"

"They're lovely," she said, accepting the vase. "Uh, would you like to come in? I can make some coffee."

"Thank you. As a matter of fact, I would like a word or two, if you have the time. I expect," he added with a slight smile, "that you have a question or two for me as well."

"I suppose I do." She indicated the kitchen chairs, and turned to the wood stove to put the coffee pot on while he took his seat. "So, you're the man Katie's all worked up over," Natalie stated after she joined him at the table and studied him. Katie was right–the man was certainly handsome, though his skin was awful pale. She wondered if he'd been recently ill.

He raised an aristocratic eyebrow. "I hope I haven't frightened the lass."

"I wouldn't say that, exactly," she answered, smiling cautiously. "Well, on the other hand, maybe you did, a little anyway. May I be candid, Mr. MacAaron? Katie's never expressed a personal interest in anyone. I think she's feeling confused. She's spent the better part of the last two weeks trying to convince herself it never happened. She hasn't spoken of you since the fair, but I can tell you're all she's thought about. She's thrown herself into her chores and kept herself busy, but...I don't know, there's this look she gets in her eyes. I've never seen her so distracted."

"I must confess that I, too, have been feeling distracted of late. I don't know how much Catherine told you about me, but I usually don't socialize much. I have a tendency to keep to myself, something Alex often criticizes me for."

"Alex?" She rose to pour two mugs of coffee.

"My servant. He's a good man, if sometimes a bit presumptuous." He accepted his mug and lifted to his lips. "He's been doing everything in his power these last two weeks to convince me to take this chance. I'm afraid it has me at a loss."

She set the mugs on the table. "Cream or sugar?"

"Black is fine." He lifted one of the mugs to his lips and took a casual sip while she resumed her seat.

"No offence, Mr. MacAaron..."

"Joshua, please. 'Mr. MacAaron' is too formal. It makes me feel as if I must live up to the title."

"All right, Joshua. If we're on a first-name basis, you may as well call me Natalie." He nodded once in acceptance. "Don't you think you're out of her league?"

He set the mug down carefully and met her gaze. "I hope you won't let the fact that I have a little money turn you against me. Or is it my age that troubles you?"

"You have more than a little money," she accused.

"Aye, Carl told me you called to inquire about me."

"And you are older than she is. Someone of your sophistication…"

He held up a hand in polite interruption. "Natalie, I started life on a poor dirt farm in Scotland. What wealth I've accumulated is the result of hard work and determination. Deep down, I'm still that dirt farmer's son. And while 'tis true five years is a bit of a stretch at this time in her life, when she's twenty-five and I'm thirty, the difference will seem more slight." He lifted the mug to his lips again and frowned, making her wonder whether he disliked the coffee, or if some deep thought troubled his mind. "I've met a few women you might consider more my status," he continued at last. "Most I've found to be shallow, selfish, and totally untrustworthy. I've made it a habit to stay away from the fairer sex, until two weeks ago. To be honest, the moment I saw Catherine, I felt she was different somehow. There is something about her I find fascinating."

"She's a very private child. Ever since her father died, she's found it hard to let anyone close to her. I think she grew up overnight. She took it upon herself to do all the things James did for me. She tends the garden, earns money any way she can to help, and even fixed a leak in the roof last winter. She faces every day with too much severity." She paused to shake her head. "She doesn't socialize much. I guess the two of you have at least that much in common." Sobering, she added, "What are your intentions toward her?"

He leaned forward, folded his arms on the table in front of him, and met her concerned gaze earnestly. "I feel something happened between us that night at the fair, something I've tried very hard to dismiss. Perhaps it was all just a dream. Perhaps nothing will come of it. But there is also a chance more will develop. I would like your permission to explore that possibility with her."

She felt herself warming up to the gentleman who was looking at her with hope in his eyes. "What if she's not interested? She was pretty upset when she got home from the fair."

He winced as if she'd slapped him in the face. "If that is the case, this is all in my mind. I'll not trouble her further."

"She's awful young yet. It will be another year before she graduates high school."

"I won't interfere with her studies," he offered quickly. "In fact, there are some subjects I may be able to help her with."

She felt a lump forming in her throat. "She's so innocent of the ways of the world. You're obviously a man who's been…"

"I want to be honest with you, Natalie. I've seen much of this world and its people. I've involved myself with women a time or two. My associations have never lasted long, and I've grown weary of disappointments and one-night stands. If feelings do develop between Catherine and myself, I fully intend to handle them appropriately. I would never take advantage of her."

"Is that a promise?"

He rose to his feet, a desperately serious look in his soft brown eyes. "I give you my word as a gentleman, I won't bed the lass unless and until she allows me to place my ring on her finger. I don't know if it will come to that. If it does, it won't be for a long time, not until we both know beyond doubt it is what we want. And," he added shyly, "not without your blessing."

She stood up to face him. "All right, Joshua. If she wants to spend time with you, I won't object."

His warm smile lit his entire being. "I thank you, ma'am. Well, I won't take up any more of your time. My phone number is on the card with the flowers. Tell Catherine she may call if she likes. I've, uh, developed an unfortunate allergy to sunlight, so I sleep during the day, but I have an answering machine. Alex is deaf. He won't be able to answer should she call." He took her hand in his and looked deeply into her eyes. "Thank you for tolerating my company."

"Come by any time," she found herself saying. With another nod, he left the house. She watched him drive away thoughtfully, then turned to the vase of flowers and shook her head. A dozen pale pink roses, arranged carefully among ferns and baby's breath, rested in a vase of heavy, hand cut crystal trimmed in gold, obviously worth much more than the flowers it held. "What has she gotten herself into?"

* * * *

When Katie returned home from babysitting, she couldn't help but notice the vase of roses on the table before she saw anything else. "Oh, my," she whispered. She sniffed each blossom. "Where'd they come from, Momma?"

"Read the card," she suggested, her voice noticeably tight with suspense.

She nervously opened the small envelope, but had a strong feeling she knew who the flowers were from. "'*Thank you for an enjoyable evening. Let's do it again soon. Yours, Joshua.*' Joshua sent these?" she asked, disbelief in her eyes.

"He came by to see you tonight. We had quite a talk."

She sat on one of the kitchen chairs in shock. "He was here?"

"Apparently, you made an impression on him. He asked my permission to court you."

Her heart began hammering in her chest. "Court me? You mean, go on dates? With me? Why?"

She sat down and chuckled softly. "He likes you. Come on, don't look so surprised."

"But he's…" She shook her head. "He scares me." She shook her head once more while tears filled her eyes. "I can't."

"He seems nice to me. Carl says he's a good man, and I trust his judgment."

"You checked up on him?" she asked, unable to hide her shock.

"I have to protect my only child."

She swiped at the tear that dripped down her cheek with the back of her hand. "I still don't understand what he can see in someone like me. I don't have much to offer."

"Don't sell yourself short. He told me he finds you fascinating." Humor tinged her mother's voice. "He wants to spend time with you. Get to know you better. Let you get to know him. Baby, I've thought about this a lot since he left. I don't think there's any harm in seeing him. If nothing comes of it, well, you'll have a good time. Maybe this will give you a chance to come out of your shell. If things become more serious…" Her smile and her mood softened. "If the two of you fall in love, I suppose a mother couldn't hope for a better match for her child. He seems gentle and kind. A little old fashioned, but maybe that's because he's Scottish. I don't think he'll ever hurt you."

"I suppose it doesn't hurt that he has money," she said bitterly.

"Does that bother you? It did me at first," she confided. "Rich people are normally so, well, rich. I've never trusted them. Joshua…" She shook her head. "I don't know why, but I want to trust him. He isn't like any rich man I've ever met. He seems sincere."

She felt a slight smile tugging at her lips. "He's good looking, don't you think?"

At that, Natalie laughed lightly. "Beautiful," she quoted. "He's everything you described." She stroked an errant strand of hair from her daughter's face. "I don't have an appointment tomorrow. How about we make a day of it? We'll visit the thrift shops and see what they have in the way of clothes, pick up your school supplies, and maybe go see the sights at the mall. I'll even spring for a couple of corndogs. We haven't done that in a long time."

With an easier smile, she said, "That sounds great!"

"All right, then." She rose up to put the two freshly washed coffee mugs away and clean the pot. "Go to bed. You look tired. I'll be there in a minute. We'll head out right after breakfast."

Chapter Four

Joshua belted his black slacks and picked up a comb. A week had passed since his visit with Natalie, a week filled with anxious anticipation, but Catherine had yet to call. He could no longer stand the suspense. After smoothing his hair into soft waves, he pulled the top back and fastened it with a black band. Alex watched him take extra care with his appearance, a look of satisfaction on his face. "Don't look so smug," he groused. "You knew this would come the moment you insisted I give the girl a chance." He closed the top of his white linen shirt, fastened a black lariat in place, and toyed nervously with the silver clasp. "Do I look presentable?"

Alex held up a finger in response, turned and left the room, to return moments later with a bottle of cologne. "Is that really necessary?" he moaned while Alex splashed the liquid on his face. "All right, that's enough." He picked up his jacket and started to put it on, but Alex stopped him. "You don't think so? Well, all right." He tossed the jacket onto the bed he never used. Alex adjusted the lariat clasp, stood back and nodded his approval. With a heavy sigh, Joshua pocketed his keys and headed for the garage.

During the half-hour drive to her home, he contemplated the prospect of seeing her again. He almost turned the car around more than once, feeling strongly he was making a mistake. "Why am I doing this?" he asked himself out loud. "I'm not that lonely." He knew full well that wasn't the truth. In fact, he realized how lonely his existence had become the moment he'd laid eyes on her.

An unexpected pang of anxiety struck him in the chest with all the force and pain of a wooden stake when he turned up the dirt road to her home. He slammed on the brake, skidded to a stop on the soft shoulder and killed the engine. He didn't have to look in the mirror to know his eyes were glowing red–the urgent need to feed and the sudden sharpness of his fangs told him that much, as did the feral growl that escaped through his clenched teeth.

He jumped from the car, moved to sit on its hood, and slumped over until his head was level with his knees. Still, the pain in his heart persisted, giving him the unreasonable urge to draw in breath he didn't need. Even the sighs that escaped him on occasion were mere affectations–some of his mortal habits had refused to die.

"I've never seen you this out of control, brother." He was on his feet in an instant at the sound of the familiar voice. Vincent stepped from the shadows and leaned casually against a nearby tree. "It must be a woman," he observed evenly. "Some tender mortal has drawn your attention again."

"What are you doing here?" To his own ears, his voice sounded rough and menacing.

"I was in the neighborhood," he replied smoothly, moving to stand beside him and place a familiar hand on his arm. "I sensed your presence and thought I'd pay you a visit. I had no idea you'd be so…entertaining."

"I don't need this right now." He turned away sharply and glared into the woods.

"Sorry," Vincent offered half-heartedly. "I know what you're going through. I've been there too many times myself."

"I know you have," he said, not without sympathy. He felt himself calming and affected a long sigh in relief.

"I know you're unwilling to repeat past mistakes. Still, you've been alone too long. You really should consider returning to Haven. We've missed you."

He snorted his disgust. "Antonia no doubt has plenty of other toys to play with."

"Our Mother in Darkness has her appetites, but once she takes a creature to heart, he stays there."

"Well, I'm not interested in her kind of affection."

"No, you were always the serious, devoted type," he reflected, offering his own sigh. "Do you intend to pursue this new mortal?"

"Are you asking as my brother and oldest friend, or as a member of the Council of Elders?"

Caution and sorrow dimmed his sapphire eyes. "That all depends upon who you need me to be."

He closed his eyes, drew in a deep breath, and pushed it out along with more of his anxiety. He knew too well Vincent's responsibilities. It would never do to lose control in front of a Council representative, friend or no. "What I do here does not concern the Council. I won't endanger the Community. I'll take the girl before I let that happen." He put his hands on the roof of the car and lowered his head. "I remember too well what happened last time."

Vincent put a supportive hand on his shoulder. The familiar gesture evaporated what was left of his inner turmoil. "Don't worry, Josh. I won't tell the others about the girl. No Enforcers will be hounding your movements. Just promise me you'll be careful."

He turned around and rested against the car door. With his fangs safely retracted, he felt much more like his usual, calm self. "You know I will."

Vincent smiled. "I'll be in the area for a while. I don't plan to return to Haven until next month. Perhaps I can stop by your home later. We could share a drink and catch up."

He returned his old friend's smile and felt more calm flow through him. "I'd like that." With a nod, Vincent took flight, leaving him alone to slide behind the steering wheel of his Sebring. He sat there for a moment, gripping the wheel tightly with both hands. "If you're not going to go through with this, now is the time to turn back." He waited, but the urge to return home didn't come. No, he had to move forward, see this through to the end. For good or ill, he'd give it his best effort, to Hell with the consequences. He turned the key and gunned the engine, letting the sudden roar express for him his frustration before continuing his journey to her home.

* * * *

Katie sat on the love seat, leaning forward in concentration over an attempt to embroider a floral pattern on the open end of a pillowcase. The tip of her tongue occasionally stuck out over her upper lip while she worked her needle, and she cursed softly when the thread knotted and she had to stop and detangle it. She glanced up at her mother, who was sitting beside her, lost in a romance novel a friend had loaned her. The occasional giggle or grunt that issued from Natalie's lips brought a gentle smile to her face.

She knotted her thread and clipped the end, then sat back with a sigh. "School starts tomorrow. I probably should go to bed early tonight."

"Are you planning to drive to school this year?"

She thought for a minute and shook her head. "No, I probably should keep taking the bus. Gas costs."

"That it does."

"Besides, I thought maybe I should teach you how to drive. Then you wouldn't have to rely on the bus system to keep your housekeeping appointments."

"You know I don't like to drive," she scolded. "Traffic makes me jittery."

"It doesn't bother me a bit. I like the freedom." She cocked her head toward the window. "Do you hear...?" She leaned over to peek outside. "What kind of car does Joshua drive?"

"A light blue convertible."

She jumped up and backed against the wall. "Oh, my God."

Natalie put the book down and rose to her feet. "Go brush your hair. I'll answer the door."

"Tell him I'm not home," she cried softly. "I'm...No! I can't."

"You can't put him off forever, baby. If you don't want to see him, you'll have to tell him yourself. He won't hear it from me."

Tears pooled in her eyes as she struggled against the panic welling up in her chest. "I'm not ready," she whispered. She shot a frightened glance at the front door when she heard the sound of Joshua's tentative knock.

"What is it you're afraid of?" Natalie asked, impatience in her voice. "Do you think he'll hurt you, or are you afraid you'll find out you like him after all?"

"I don't know," she answered when he knocked again.

Natalie shrugged. "I'm opening the door. If you don't want him to see you with tears on your face, you'd better go straighten yourself up."

She moved so fast her shoulder struck the doorsill. She leaned against the door for a moment, listening while her mother opened the front door and welcomed him inside. She quickly brushed her hair, splashed some water on her face, and studied her reflection in the mirror. When her mother called to her, she straightened her clothes, swallowed hard, and opened the bedroom door.

"Good evening, Catherine. It's good to see you again." He reached for her hand, she took it reluctantly and felt the pad of his thumb rub gently along the tops of her knuckles.

"Hi, Joshua," she said, feeling her face grow warm. "Uh, thank you for the roses. They were beautiful."

"You cut your hair," he observed with an appraising frown.

"Yeah." She nervously fingered a lock resting on her shoulder. "Mom's idea. It's not that much shorter."

He released her hand and looked embarrassed at having held it so long. "I like it. It brings out some of the natural curl."

His compliment brought a strange warmth to her chest. "I've had my ears pierced, too."

She held her breath as he lifted her hair with his fingers to inspect one inflamed lobe. A brief flash of sympathy and discomfort flickered in his eyes. "This looks painful."

"It wasn't that bad."

"She screamed at the top of her lungs," Natalie countered with a laugh. "Katie doesn't do well with pain. It took me over an hour to talk her into it."

He smiled softly, bringing the warmth in her chest to her face. "They look good, and your discomfort will end soon enough. It's a pleasant evening. Would you like to go for a walk?"

She shot a nervous glance at her mother, who frowned and nodded sharply. "O-okay. A short one."

He opened the door and allowed her to precede him into the night. She watched him lean, half sitting, on the hood of his car, then climbed up on the trunk of her own and crossed her legs. After several minutes of silence, he said softly, "I haven't been able to put you out of my mind since the fair."

"I've been thinking about you, too."

"Pleasant thoughts, I hope. Your mother said you were quite upset when you returned home that night."

"No, just nerves." She adjusted her position so her heels were supported on the bumper and rested her crossed arms on her knees.

"No doubt your mother told you of my visit last week."

She nodded slowly. "I was surprised. How did you find me?"

With an abashed smile, he said, "Carl can be very helpful at times."

She rolled her eyes. "Of course. I should've known."

"I'm sure she told you I'm interested in you."

"I think 'fascinated' was more the word she used. I still don't understand what I could possibly have to offer you. I'm no one special."

"I don't agree, Catherine. Some of the greatest gifts in the world are often wrapped in the simplest packages."

She wanted to argue that she had no special "gifts," but the look on his face stopped her. "You don't know me very well."

"I'd like to," he countered. "Do you feel the same? Are you at all interested in who I am, or was I imagining the attraction I felt between us?"

She sat there, studying him in the darkness, wondering how she should answer his question. No, he hadn't imagined it. Something had happened between them, but she still didn't know what it was. At the moment, he didn't seem as threatening as he had at the fair. Or maybe the quieter setting had softened his approach. Whatever it was, he looked more vulnerable, maybe more lost than he had before. "That all depends on what you expect from me."

He stood up and started circling his car slowly. "This is not easy for me. I'm usually the one in control, the one who always knows what to say. I find myself uncertain as to how I can make you understand what I've been thinking of these past weeks."

"Then say what's on your mind, and if I have any questions, I'll ask."

He paused his pacing to glance at her in surprise, then leaned against the car door with a sigh. "I've been involved in relationships that ended badly. You can't know how painful it is to give your heart to someone and have it crushed through deceit or betrayal. I vowed never to put myself in a position where I can be hurt like that again. You're different from any woman I've ever known. I'm afraid I was angry with myself that night for even considering getting involved again, but…"

"So you think you want to 'get involved' with me?"

"Not in the way you're thinking."

"How do you know what I'm thinking?" she asked sharply.

"I can see the mistrust in your eyes, the suspicion. I sense you believe my intentions are less than honorable."

"You're very perceptive," she said, feeling reluctantly impressed by his insight. "All the guys I've met have one thing in mind when it comes to girls, and right now I'm not interested."

He circled the car again, and she watched him wring his hands in agitation. Finally, he half-sat on the hood of his car again and looked at her with the same powerful gaze that had captured her so fiercely before. "If I'd wanted only your body, I could've taken you easily enough, and am fully capable of making you believe you want me to. No," he raised a hand when she opened her mouth to protest, her anger building. "You don't believe I know you that well, but, trust me on this, you know less about me. I'm attracted to you, yes, but having pointless sex with you is the farthest thing from my mind."

"I'm supposed to take your word on that?"

He shrugged and relieved her of his powerful gaze, turning instead to look past her into the woods. "Carl knows me well enough. Ask him if you doubt me."

"I just might." She saw him wince at the sharp tone in her voice. "So what *do* you want?"

He looked at the ground and prodded a pinecone with the toe of his shoe. "I've had enough of cake and ice cream affairs. I want the meat and potatoes."

"I don't follow you."

The pinecone skidded several feet before he said more. "All my life,

I've hoped to find someone who touched my mind and my heart, someone I can be at ease with. I want a relationship based on mutual respect and trust. Tenderness, affection, intimacy; those are things that should come in their own time, and like dessert, only after the main course has been completed."

For a moment, she felt like he'd been reading her mind. How can he have known what she'd been thinking of minutes before they met? "Trust isn't something you can buy," she observed tightly.

"Aye, I know well the cost of trust, and I know the risks. I've worked hard for everything I've ever achieved in my life. Do you not believe me capable of putting at least that much effort into a friendship? I'm willing to invest all the time necessary to earn your trust, and to learn to trust you."

She felt an unexpected knot forming in her throat, and had to swallow hard before she asked, "What if I decide you're not right for me? I mean, well, we're from two different worlds. And what if, after all that time, you decide I'm not what you're hoping for? I don't want to be hurt either."

He approached her, gently took her hands, and guided her to her feet. "We cannot take this chance without risking pain, but I'll do my best not to push you any further than you're willing to go. If I should overstep my bounds, I trust you'll let me know."

She licked her lips nervously and tried hard to think of something intelligent to say. He seemed to assume she would agree to go out with him, and that assumption tempted her anger. Still, he seemed so genuinely interested in her, so open and earnest, that she couldn't deny the fact that she was beginning to feel the same way. "Okay."

He smiled and threaded her hand around the crook of his arm, and turned to walk them along the road. "I walk these woods often. When I need to think, I enjoy the quiet." He paused. "Listen."

She strained her ears, but couldn't hear anything. She looked up at him in question. "Do you not hear it?" he asked softly. "There is a special music in the woods at night. If you're quiet, you can hear the trees whispering to each other. There. Did you hear the owl?"

She turned her head toward the woods and listened more carefully. "I hear frogs, crickets," she whispered. "Oh! I do hear an owl. Funny, I never noticed before."

He patted her hand and resumed their walk. "The sounds of the night are soothing to me, and these woods remind me of home."

"I'd like to visit Scotland someday. I hear it's really pretty in the summertime."

"Aye," he breathed. "On a warm summer's eve, you can smell the heather. 'Tis very fine. When the mists roll in from the moors, the woods become almost magical."

"Sounds like a fairy tale," she mused. "Do you miss it?"

He looked at her with a soft smile. "Sometimes."

They walked together in silence for a few minutes. "Mom tells me you're allergic to sunlight."

"It was unexpected," he confirmed, "and happened very quickly. It was one of the reasons I left New York. I needed a place to stay where I wouldn't become accidentally exposed."

"Do you burn easily?" she asked carefully, hoping she wasn't prying.

"You might say that," he responded lightly. "My reaction to the sun is instantaneous. 'Tis not a pleasant sight."

"I've heard of people like that," she said sympathetically. "Is it difficult for you?"

"No more than I've learned to handle," he responded in a dismissive tone. "I don't view it as a disability. In fact I find I prefer living by night. The daylight world can be far too hectic."

"I know what you mean."

He turned them around and started back to her house. "I think I can become quite fond of you, Catherine."

"I like you too, Joshua," she confided slowly. "I didn't think I would. I mean, well, I was a little afraid of you at first, but now, I think I'd like, you know, hanging out for a while."

The soft smile that swept his face curled her toes. "Does this mean you're willing to take a chance on me?"

She answered his smile with a nervous one of her own. "We can see how things work out."

When they reached her home, he opened the door for her and followed her inside. He nodded his respect to Natalie and said, "I'm glad we had this chance to talk."

"So am I," she said, feeling unsure and embarrassed.

He touched her hair briefly. "Perhaps you'll allow me to visit again soon."

"I'd like that." She watched him slide behind the wheel of the Sebring and bring the car to life, and closed the door with a sigh.

"You're not going to throw up again, are you?" Natalie asked.

She looked at her mother in surprise, and saw the humor on her face. "Not this time, Momma," she answered with a laugh.

Chapter Five

"I think you'll enjoy this," Vincent said, handing a corked beer bottle to Joshua. "I got it from a young network donor in Gresham."

Joshua pulled the cork and tasted the contents with all the finesse of a connoisseur. "A musician," he commented softly. He sat in his chair and motioned his visitor to take the sofa, took another sip, and smiled. "This one has potential. I'd like to hear him sometime."

"I might be able to arrange that," Vincent responded, opening his own bottle and sinking into the sofa cushions. They sat in companionable silence, sipping their drinks and gazing at the flames playing in the fireplace. "You look much better than you did the last time I saw you," he commented at last.

"I've had some time to adjust. It hasn't been easy."

"So what's she like, this new infatuation of yours?"

"I wouldn't call Catherine an infatuation, but I am attracted to her." He drained his bottle and leaned his head back. "She's intelligent, sensitive…sophisticated well beyond her years, and has absolutely no understanding of her own worth."

"Beautiful?"

He felt a smile play at his lips. "Not in an elegant, high-bred way. No, hers is natural, simple beauty. Her eyes are blue-gray, with little specks of gold that flash when she gets excited or angry. She's delicate, fragile, and she possesses an innocent purity that is almost frightening."

"I didn't know you'd developed a taste for innocents." Vincent's surprise was evident in his voice.

"I wasn't planning to make a meal of her," he answered sharply.

Vincent gave a dismissive gesture with his empty bottle. "So it's romance you seek."

"To be honest, I don't know what will come of this. If it comes down to romance…love, so be it. I'll do whatever I feel is necessary when the time comes. If not, she'll not have learned enough about me to be dangerous. I intend to take this one step at a time."

He chuckled softly. "So you did learn something all those years ago."

"'Twas a lesson hard-learned," he recalled bitterly. "So tell me, what news of Haven?"

"Oh, you know, the usual trouble with rogues, Stephan's penchant for stirring up discontent, Trey and Jason holding things together the best they can. Antonia's gone to the old country to meet with our Southern European Coven, and without her and Jason's amusing verbal sparring matches to lighten our hearts, it gets positively boring. Devon's still in England, presiding over Northern European affairs, and Bastian's had his hands full lately. He's training three new recruits into the Enforcement League."

An involuntary shudder rippled through him. "I remember him–a warrior in a child's body, at once playfully irreverent and dangerously serious. And that was while he was under Trey's tutelage. I can only imagine what he must be like now."

Vincent chuckled softly. "Playfully irreverent and dangerously serious, and a whole lot more powerful. I almost wish something would happen to stir things up. Haven has settled into a somewhat tedious routine. A little action to get the blood pumping would do us all a world of good."

"In other words, nothing ever changes."

* * * *

Katie stacked her homework and stretched her arms over her head. "Got that report done," she declared as she reached toward a plate of fried oat cookies.

"I'm glad," Natalie said with a smile. "You look tired."

"Nah, just stiff. I've been sitting for too long." The sound of a car engine brought an instant flutter to her stomach. "Joshua?"

Natalie glanced out the front window. "Yep." She admitted him with a smile the moment he knocked on the door. "Hello, Joshua. Come on in."

"Good evening, ladies," he said, the smile on his face slight, but warm. He stepped beside the table. "Did I come at a bad time?" he asked, his eyes scanning the contents of the table.

"No. I just finished a report for agriculture. It's due Monday."

He picked up one of the books and glanced at it. "Beekeeping? I knew a man once who kept bees. He made a lot of money selling the wax and honey they produced."

She smiled at the thought. "I like honey, but it's too spendy."

"Why don't you try making your own?"

"Uh, no thanks," she said with a nervous laugh. "I don't handle pain well. One sting, and I'd be burning the whole lot. Would you like a cookie? Mom makes the best fried oat cookies in the state."

Joshua glanced at the plate of cookies with an expression that looked like embarrassment. "I'm sure they're delicious, but I'm afraid I'll have to decline."

"Oh, okay," she said uncertainly.

"I, uh, suppose I should explain."

"No, that's all right."

"I must," he insisted. "I had forgotten this sort of thing would come up. You see, I'm on a restricted diet."

"Are you diabetic?" Natalie asked.

"No," he answered slowly, embarrassment clearly visible on his face. "Before I left Scotland, I became deathly ill. I spent several weeks in the hospital, but the doctors never determined what was wrong. By the time I recovered, I found my stomach no longer had the ability to process solid foods. Eating makes me violently ill."

"That's terrible," Katie said as gently as she could.

"Have you tried seeing a specialist?" Natalie asked.

"The best in the world, once I had the funds to seek them." he confirmed. "Unfortunately, by that time, my system had atrophied. There's naught they can do."

After a long, uncomfortable pause, Natalie observed, "You don't look sickly. How do you survive?"

"I take a liquid diet of protein and nutrients. It took a while to get used to, but it sustains me adequately. Have no concern, 'twill not kill me. In fact, I'm told I'll likely live longer than Methuselah."

Katie stood silently, observing the shock on her mother's face and the discomfort on Joshua's, and offered a smile to break the tension. "Okay, got it. We won't invite you to dinner."

He looked surprised. "This doesn't bother you? I've found my condition offends most women's delicate sensibilities."

"Well, if it doesn't bother Katie…" Natalie said doubtfully.

"No, it's all right," she insisted.

He smiled his relief. "Thank you. I was worried you wouldn't understand."

"No problem," she assured him, and was surprised she really meant it. "Do you want to go for a walk?"

He clasped his hands over his heart and sighed theatrically. "Ah, the lady fair deems to favor me with her company. How shall I endure it?"

"You're crazy," she laughed, offering her hand.

"I'm honored," he replied formally, taking her hand and threading it around his arm.

"So, do you have any other problems I need to know about?" she asked after they'd walked in silence for several minutes.

"What more do you imagine can be wrong with me?"

"Oh, I don't know," she answered slowly, feeling unusually playful. "Epileptic fits, split personality, impotency..."

"I can assure you that part of me functions just fine," he cut in with humor in his voice.

"Oh, that's good," she blurted, and bit her tongue when he laughed.

"Take care, young Catherine, before I find myself tempted to demonstrate."

She shot him a startled glance. "You wouldn't!"

His laughter seemed to float in the air like soap bubbles. "I might."

She shoved at him playfully, bringing even more laughter from him. He stopped to study one of the trees beside the road. "Will you walk with me into the woods?" he asked.

A sudden nervous flutter took hold of her stomach. "I guess so."

He smiled gently. "I know this forest well. Come, there's something I want to show you." He took her hand and led her off the path. He pushed through the underbrush, helped her when she lost her footing, then held back a branch and allowed her to precede him. The woods opened onto a moss-carpeted clearing, thirty-odd feet wide and almost perfectly round. Along the opposite side, she saw a steep rock face, where the hill reached upward toward the Cascade Range. Moonlight spilled through the hole in the canopy and sparkled on a small stream that cut through one corner of the clearing. When she stepped closer, she saw the stream was fed by a tiny waterfall.

"Oh, my," she said in awe. "I never saw this before."

"'Tis not easy to find."

She turned slowly around and looked at the wall of forest that enclosed the clearing. "It's like in a story book." She knelt and tasted the sweet, icy water. "How did you find this place?"

He chuckled and sat on the ground, leaned back against a tree, and stretched his legs in front of him. "Stumbled upon it, I did. 'Bout a year ago. It's especially nice when the moon shines full on it."

She sat down beside him and folded her legs Indian style. "It's wonderful."

"You really like it?" he asked softly.

"Yeah, I do."

"This can be our private place. Somewhere we can be alone together, to share our secrets and our dreams. You can talk to me about anything you wish here. Anything we confide to each other while in this place will remain ours alone."

"You make it sound so romantic."

"Do I?" She heard amusement in his voice. "Strange. I've never given much thought to romance. I've always thought myself too…pragmatic."

"Neither have I."

"You've never fancied yourself being rescued by some handsome knight and living happily ever after?"

"Oh, well, sure, when I was a kid. Then I grew up and learned about the real world. It can be cold and cruel to someone who doesn't stand against it." She shifted her position and plucked a pinecone from under her left hip.

He pulled his knees up and leaned on them. "Aye, 'tis true, and the people living in it can be unkind at times."

She saw a flicker of unpleasant emotion bring a slight frown to his face. "What were they like?"

"Who?"

"Those women who hurt you."

He chuckled, but there was a hint of discomfort in his eyes. "There were only two I've ever been seriously involved with. The first one, well, let's just say she was too flighty. I held her interest only briefly before another led her away."

"And the other?"

"She was young and pretty, and I was far too eager. She led me to believe she loved me, and I think I convinced myself I was in love with her. We never really shared anything, except, perhaps, a bed."

She heard the sorrow in his voice. "So what happened?"

"'Twas my money she was after," he said, his voice turning bitter. "One day she had two of her accomplices try to kill me. I got away, barely. I daresay I gave almost as good as I got. She made it impossible for me to return. She kept the house, for whatever good it did her."

"Didn't you call the police?"

"I suppose I could have," he answered, his voice changing to sad resignation. "The house caught fire that very night. She died in her sleep, or so the story goes. I guess I figured she'd gotten what she deserved."

"How terrible."

"Ah, well," he said dismissively, "'Twas a long time ago. I took the insurance settlement, cut my losses, and moved on."

She thought about that for a while. "You've lived alone ever since?"

"Oh, there've been occasions since when the need for female companionship became too great, and I can always find a woman interested enough to share an evening or two with me. I've accepted their comforts and given them pleasure, but I've never again let one in here," he said with his hand over his heart. "I have Alex, my servant, to keep me company, and my investments keep me occupied. 'Tis enough. Or at least," he added more softly, "I thought it was."

She felt herself blush at his honesty. Compared to his life, hers seemed even more unremarkable. He stared at her with an "It's your turn" look in his eyes until she cleared her throat and nodded. "I was interested in a guy once in my sophomore year. He took me to the homecoming dance, and we went to dinner once, but I never went out with him again."

"What happened?"

She lowered her eyes to her hands, an embarrassing, true-confessions feeling rising inside her. "He took me down to the Columbia where we could watch the yachts. It was a long drive, but I really wanted to see the river, so I agreed to go with him. After we got there, he…"

"He took advantage of you?"

"He tried. When I told him to stop he got mad, yelled at me, called me a tease, you know, stuff like that. I ended up running to the nearest public place I could find. After that, I didn't know what else to do, so I called Mr. Foster. He was more than happy to come and take me home. He wanted to go find the guy and beat some sense into him, but I told him to forget it."

"I'm glad Carl could help."

"He's real nice. Anyway, the next day at school I found out he'd been talking about me. The word was all over school that I was a cold fish and a tease."

"I'm glad you stuck to your principles. Peer pressure can be an irresistible force."

"I can handle it."

"Of that, I have little doubt," he commented with a chuckle. "So, now, where do you suppose we should go from here?"

"I don't know what you mean," she said, her voice faltering.

"I've told you what I'm looking for in a relationship. I'd like to know what you want. Have you given that much thought?"

She thought for a long time before answering. "I guess I'm looking for the same things you are. Do you remember me telling you about Taska? Her boyfriend, Dillon, graduated last year, and just found a job. Taska will graduate this year. They've been close friends for as long as I can remember." She paused to gather her thoughts. "Last week, Dillon asked Taska to marry him. I wish you could've seen the look in her eyes when she told me. She's so happy." She sighed deeply at the thought. "I think I'd like to find someone like that, someone I can be friends with. A lot of the kids at school date around, and I think they take sex way too lightly." She felt herself blushing, this time at her own bluntness.

"I'd like very much to be your friend. I'd like us to take the time to get to know each other. There's plenty of time yet before we need think of taking this further."

She felt relieved. "I agree. I mean, I think I'd like that a lot."

"Good, then," he said, a sudden down-to-business tone in his voice. "What kinds of things do you like to do?"

"I've never thought about it. I don't go out much. I went to the movies with Taska a couple of times, and one night Mr. Foster took us to dinner to celebrate when he won a really big case."

"Surely there are things you've heard of that you'd like to try," he coaxed. "We can take in a movie from time to time. Perhaps you might enjoy attending school dances, or garden golfing. I can take you out to dinner if you like."

"That wouldn't be fair," she said gently. "If you can't eat…"

"'Tis your company I'd savor more than the food. I'd like you to experience some of what life has to offer."

"Well, maybe," she said doubtfully.

He shrugged. "Whatever you're comfortable with." He took her hand, once again rubbing the pad of his thumb across her knuckles and bringing a smile to her lips. "We can do whatever you want to do." He rose to his feet and pulled her after him. "Come. I'll walk you home."

"All right." She wondered why, all of a sudden, he sounded tense. He helped her back to the main path, and released her.

When they reached her front door, he opened if for her and motioned for her to precede him. He nodded at Natalie and said, "Pick out a movie for next Saturday night. Give me a call when you decide. We'll need to take in a late showing," he looked at Natalie, "if that's all right with your mother, of course."

"That sounds fine with me," Natalie said with a smile.

He nodded, the faintest hint of a smile softening his face. "Good night, ladies."

* * * *

"So, what does one do at a bonfire?" Joshua asked Catherine one evening more than a month later while they were returning to her home from a curiously decorated garden golf establishment. They'd spent every weekend together, and had quickly become, much to his satisfaction, the best of friends.

"Just hang. It's kind of, um, tradition. I think it's based on some medieval practice where they burned the likeness of the enemy before a major battle to boost morale."

"An effigy."

"Yeah. That's it. All the kids will be there. Most of the teachers, too. I thought you'd like to meet some of them."

"All right." He found it hard to deny her any request. "Do you want me to pick you up next Thursday?"

"Sure. There's a game on Friday, and a dance Saturday night." She lowered her eyes, an attractive blush rising to her cheeks. "We don't have to go."

"Perhaps not the game. I don't care much for sporting events. But I would be proud to escort you to the dance."

"I don't…know how to dance."

"You're afraid you'll make a fool of yourself." She shrugged her shoulders. He felt her embarrassment as well as her longing to go. "Perhaps I can teach you. We can practice in our clearing. I'll bring a radio. No one will notice if you miss a step or two."

She nodded reluctantly. Two nights later, he appeared, radio in hand, to take her into the woods. He'd also brought with him a couple of lanterns, which he hung from the trees to light their steps. He explained some of the modern dances to her, made up steps of his own, and they ended up laughing more than dancing. "You know," he told her, "I don't think I've had this much fun in years. I can't remember the last time I laughed so hard."

The happy light in her eyes stunned him. "Me too."

A slow love song came on the radio. He held his hand to her. "Come here." He pulled her close, looked into her eyes, and read the sudden nervousness there. "Now, don't be afraid. Balance on your toes and relax your knees. Follow my lead."

She closed her eyes. While they moved to the slow rhythm, he gently drew her nearer until she was close enough to rest her cheek on his shoulder. They fit together well, he thought with a smile. She trembled in his arms with the virginal nervousness that came with new and unexplored sensations. She was so like the timid creatures that dwelled in the forest, exploring new territory with a mixture of curiosity and fear. He needed to guide her carefully into this new world, or risk frightening her away. When she sighed, he drew her still closer, held her tenderly against him and pressed his face in her hair. The warmth of her, the soft scent of her hair, filled his senses and renewed the longing in his heart. He felt her relax against him and turn her face to his neck, and thought she was feeling the same.

He opened his mind to her thoughts for the first time since she was a child, careful not to pry for fear she would sense the intrusion, and let her feed him whatever her subconscious was willing to share. He instantly experienced her wonder at his closeness, mingled with fear, not of him, he noted, but of the strange new sensations overtaking her and the ill ease of uncertainty. *It's too soon for this*, he told himself with regret. *I mustn't push too far.* When the song ended, he stepped away from her and forced a smile. "You did that very well."

"Thank you. So did you."

He cleared his throat and gave himself a mental shake. "Right. Well, I'd say we've got the basics down. Shall we call it a night?"

"Yes," she answered, looking both relieved and disappointed. She helped him gather the lanterns, and they walked back to the house.

After loading his equipment in the trunk of his car, he turned to face her and gently rubbed the backs of his fingers along her cheek. "I had a good time tonight. Thank you."

She blushed so hard he thought she might catch fire. "You're welcome. Me too. I…"

"You'd better go now," he cut in, glad it was too dark for her to see the passion he knew was burning in his eyes. "I'll pick you up Thursday for the bonfire."

She nodded and backed away. Without another word, he climbed in his car and drove away. He saw her watching until he drove around the corner and out of sight.

"Did you have a good time?" Natalie asked when Katie entered the house, and frowned at the strange look on her daughter's face. "Something wrong?"

"Not exactly," she said, her voice sounding distracted. "Just…different. Goodnight, Momma," she said, going into the bedroom with a deeply thoughtful look in her eyes.

"Good night, baby," Natalie whispered after the door was closed. She smiled a sad, knowing smile and turned her attention back to the magazine she was reading.

Chapter Six

"I've a gift for you, lass," Joshua said after the bonfire. He climbed out of the car and walked around to the trunk.

"What?" she asked, curiosity sparkling in her eyes. She watched him open the trunk and pull out a large flat box. "Chamberlain's," she whispered when she saw the markings on the box. "You really didn't have to…"

"Open it," he begged softly.

She nervously untied the ribbon bow and lifted the lid to reveal a silvery blue party dress. "Oh, my."

"I hope it fits. I had to guess at your size."

She lifted the dress and held it in front of her. "It's beautiful."

"I look forward to seeing you in it. I'll pick you up at seven on Saturday. Is that all right?"

"Yeah, that'll be great." Her nervous smile told him she wanted him to kiss her good night, and that knowledge gave him a warm feeling deep in his chest. Just friends, he reminded himself sternly. He purposefully put the slightest additional distance between them and took her hand, and rubbed his thumb gently across her knuckles in what had become a habitual gesture. "Good night, lassie. I'll see you on Saturday."

* * * *

Katie closed the front door and leaned against it, and listened while Joshua's car pulled down the road. When the sound of the engine faded beyond her hearing, she sat down on the love seat to think. He'd been true to their agreement, keeping their relationship as casual as any friendship could be, with the exception of that one incredibly intimate moment the other night. Was it her imagination that led her to believe he was attracted to her? He'd shown no sign tonight of wanting to repeat that contact, and she had been careful not to show the feelings building up inside of her.

"We're just friends," she reminded herself.

"What's that, baby?" Natalie stepped away from the kitchen, a dishtowel in her hands and a smile on her face.

"Nothing, Momma. I was thinking out loud."

Natalie nodded thoughtfully and tossed the towel onto the drain board. "How are things going between you and Joshua?"

She forced a smile. "Fine," she told her, though she didn't think she sounded convincing enough. "He's becoming a real good friend. I like being with him. It's like I've known him all my life."

"Sounds like you're comfortable around him," Natalie observed, her tone sounding doubtful. "What has you so pensive?"

She felt herself flush. She'd forgotten how well her mother knew her. "Momma, what was it like when you met Daddy?"

Natalie smiled in surprise at the question and sat beside her daughter. "You haven't asked about your father in years. What brings that up now?"

"Just curious. I would really like to know."

"All right. Well, I met your father in town one day. I guess I was about your age. Actually, bumped into him would probably be more accurate," she amended with a laugh. "I was coming out of a restaurant with your grandma. I had a milkshake in my hand. I stopped to hold the door open for her, and turned around too fast. He was going in at the same time, and, well, we both ended up wearing the milkshake."

She appreciated the humor in her story. "Sounds romantic."

"My mother was mortified. You never knew your grandma. She was always so proper. Anyway, we stared at each other, and when the surprise wore off we both started laughing so hard we caused a scene. Neither of us could apologize to the other enough." She paused for a moment as if to reflect on memories she'd held back for years. "We started dating the next day. He came to my house with a rose and a candy bar, and we went to the movies."

"Did you date for a long time?"

"No. In fact, we were married inside of two months. Oh, my mother was beside herself, against the whole thing from the start, but, I don't know, it felt like the right thing to do."

She thought quietly for a few moments. "Momma, what's it like to fall in love?"

She laughed gently, but there was a cautious look in her eyes. "Philosophers have been pondering that question since the beginning of time." She paused to take her hand. "It's a feeling you get, deep down inside, like he's the most important thing in your life. There's no way to describe it. It just happens. Do you think you're falling in love with Joshua?"

She took in a deep breath and let it out slowly. "I don't know," she answered truthfully. "I like him. A lot. We have a great time together. We talk to each other. I mean, we *really* talk, about a lot of things. He calls himself a pragmatist, but some of the things he says sound so romantic. The way he looks at me at times makes the bottom drop right out of my stomach, and when he touches me…"

"Does he make you nervous?"

"Sometimes," she admitted. "The other night, we practiced for the homecoming dance. We were making up new steps and laughing. It was a lot of fun–but then a slow song came on the radio. He held his hand out to me, and I felt like running away. He held me close, Momma, and so gently; I think he was afraid of breaking me." She paused to meet her mother's worried gaze. "It felt right, but strange, too."

"So that's what you looked so worried about," Natalie said, nodding in understanding. "You're attracted to him. You're starting to look at him with a woman's eyes. That's not a bad thing, but if you're not careful it might get out of hand. Take things extra slow for now. You still have a long way to go before graduation."

"I know." She sat back tiredly. "Do you think…I mean, how do I know if he's feeling the same way?"

Natalie smiled. "He'll let you know. Maybe he won't say the words. Then again," she added thoughtfully, "maybe he will. I wouldn't be one bit surprised if he asked your permission before he tried to kiss you."

"Yeah," she said with a smile. "That sounds like him."

* * * *

"There. That's the dress he bought me," Katie told Taska the following afternoon while they walked the mall.

"Chamberlain's. Wow. He's got good taste," her friend said in awe. "I'll bet it cost a small fortune." She started for the entrance to the designer store.

She pulled her arm, stopping her from going farther. "I don't want to know," she said with a firmness that made her friend look at her in surprise.

She cast one more brief glance at the dress in the display case. "Do you have any jewelry to go with it?"

"I don't wear jewelry."

"You don't wear it because you don't have it," she countered. "Got any money?"

"Not much. Just my potato money."

"Well, you need something," her best friend said with a twinkle in her eyes. "Tell you what, I'll buy. I missed your birthday anyway. Let's go pick out something from Charlie's."

Taska selected a beaded necklace and earring set in clear, soft blue that would complement the dress, while Katie picked out a pair of matching barrettes. With their purchases in-hand, they headed to the food court for a snack. "So, what are your plans?" Taska asked once they were seated. "Do you think you and Joshua will get serious?"

She shrugged. "He's been doing his best to make us friends. I really like him a lot."

"It sure took you long enough to find a boyfriend," Taska said with a laugh. "I was beginning to wonder about you."

"I wouldn't call Joshua a boyfriend." She felt a frown pull at her brows while she considered their relationship. "He feels like more than just a friend, though. You know what's funny? Right before we met, I was wishing for someone like Dillon, someone I can be friends with. I kinda thought maybe I'd find someone after school, after I got a job, moved to town, you know. None of the guys in school are, well, you know."

"Yeah. I guess they can't all be like Dillon," Taska agreed happily. "Do you think you and Joshua…?"

"What? That we'll end up married? Settle down and have a boatload of kids? Live happily ever after?"

"You always did believe in fairy tales."

"Yeah, well, that was a long time ago."

"You were a lot more fun back then, too. You made my Barbie dolls come to life. You were always making up stories and wanting to play make believe. After your dad died…"

"Well, it was hard then."

"I think you grew up too fast. You've never been the same."

"You were still my best friend."

"Someone had to stand by you, but it wasn't always easy. Some days I'd think I couldn't deal with you anymore, but my mom reminded me you didn't have anyone else to talk to, so I gave you whatever support I could. I miss the old Katie."

"I felt like part of me died that day. I'm not the happily-ever-after type anymore."

"Uh huh." Taska leaned forward and looked more closely into her eyes. "Why do I have a feeling the old you is still in there somewhere?"

She lowered her eyes to her drink. "I don't know what you're talking about."

"You don't think I see the way you look whenever we talk about Joshua? You've got some of your old spark back, Kate. It's good to see."

She shrugged. "It's too soon to tell if I'll stick with him."

"How'd you meet, anyway? You never told me."

"We met at the fair. God, I think he actually scared me to death. He looked so...I don't know. Powerful, I guess, but under control, like a big waterfall that doesn't break at the bottom. He made me feel just the opposite. Powerless. A feather on the wind kind of powerless." She shrugged again and tried to smile away the tears she felt pushing at the back of her eyes. "I guess I've been embarrassed to admit that."

"You didn't feel that way when you told me about him later."

"No. When he came to the house, I don't know, it felt different. He was different, like he wasn't sure he wanted to be there. But we talked, and decided to, you know, see each other for a while."

"Yeah, okay, and you started going out."

"And it was friendship," she said. "Just friendship. Fun times, long talks. Friendship. Until..."

"Go on," Taska prompted.

"Until the other night, when he held me. It felt..."

"Natural," Taska finished for her. "Like the two of you were made for each other."

"Yeah. I haven't been able to think about him in quite the same way since."

"And that worries you."

Tears that had threatened before dripped hotly down her cheeks. "It scares me. What if he doesn't feel the same way? What if he does? Maybe it's too soon. Maybe I'm taking too long. I've never felt so unsure in my life."

"Well calm down, people are staring. Here," she handed her a napkin and paused while she blew her nose and blotted her eyes. "I wish we were going to the dance tonight. I really want to meet him."

"I want you to meet him too. I've got an idea. He usually comes to pick me up for a date on Saturday nights. How about if you drop by early next Saturday evening, just after sunset."

"That'll work," Taska said with a smile.

She glanced at her watch. "Oh, snap! It's getting late. I gotta get home and get ready for the dance."

"Okay, see you next week." Taska gave her a quick hug before she turned at a run for the parking lot.

Chapter Seven

The Homecoming dance was held in Katie's school gymnasium. Since she'd wasted time on these events only once before, she had a hard time shaking the out-of-place feeling she had as she walked among her fellow classmates. Joshua's eyes had practically sparkled when he saw her wearing his gift, which had warmed her face and put amusement on her mother's. It was the most beautiful dress she'd ever worn, and it made her feel self-conscious and uncomfortable.

Or was it Joshua who made her so unsure? Since their dance in the clearing, he'd been acting almost remote at times…distracted. She stepped into his arms nervously every time the disc jockey played a slow song, but he held himself reserved and her at arm's length. At times she caught him studying her face in the dim lighting, and the uncertainty she thought she saw in his eyes made her count the moments until it was time to leave, though why she suddenly felt anxious for the evening to conclude she could never explain.

She sat silently in the Sebring's firm bucket seat while Joshua drove her home. Tension was building between them, and she hoped her own uncertainty was the cause. He was still holding himself closed to her. Finally, he broke the silence between them by getting to the heart of the problem. "You've been pensive tonight, Catherine. Did you not enjoy the dance?"

"No. I mean, yeah, it was fun. I'm all right, really."

He pulled the Sebring to a stop beside her LeBaron and killed the engine. "What troubles you, lass?"

She forced herself to meet his gaze. "Joshua, I know we haven't known each other for too long, but I feel like we're, uh…I mean, I'm really starting to like you."

"The friendship we share is special to me, Catherine. For now, this is enough." She lowered her eyes, but he hooked her chin with his finger and guided her back to him. "There may come a time when I'll ask for more. My feelings for you grow stronger with every moment we are together."

"Mine too. I just wanted to know how you feel."

The look on his face softened. "You are a bonny lass, but I want to take the time to get to know you more fully before we think of becoming...serious. The moment my lips come in contact with yours, our relationship will change dramatically. I...we...are not ready for that just yet."

"Fair enough," she said, imitating his accent the best she could. She was rewarded with a soft chuckle. He led her to her front door and bid her goodnight, taking her hand the way he had so many times in the past and holding it briefly before leaving her.

* * * *

It was Christmas Eve, and the tiny Mills household was brightly lit. A small tree Natalie had cut was sitting in the corner behind the table, festooned in popcorn and construction paper ornaments Katie had made as a child. A holiday candle burned on the table, surrounded by a variety of snacks for the women to munch on while they enjoyed the coming festivities. A few gifts were carefully placed under the tree, lying in wait.

Katie stood at the window, watching for signs of headlights coming up the road. "He's here!"

Natalie took the cue and started the cassette player, filling the house with the soft, instrumental sounds of old holiday favorites, while she opened the door in time to see Joshua lift several packages from the trunk of his car. "Need any help?" she called from the door.

"Nay, I've got it." He juggled the boxes and closed the trunk lid.

"You can put those under the tree," Natalie suggested, her eyes wide at the size of his burden. "I bought some Chablis. Would you like to open it?"

"I'd be delighted." His musical voice rang through the room gaily. "Merry Christmas, ladies."

"Merry Christmas," they responded in unison.

After he'd opened the bottle and dispensed the wine, he lifted his glass in a toast. "To the two most beautiful women in all the world."

Katie felt her face grow warm while she raised her glass. Natalie returned with, "To the kindest Scotsman ever to grace American shores."

"Well, open your gifts," he said anxiously. "I never was very good at suspense."

"Neither was I." Katie hastily set her wine glass on the table and dove for the tree, his soft laughter following her.

The largest packages were first, revealing warm wool coats for the women, which they both modeled gratefully for their guest. Next Natalie opened two large boxes containing a stovetop oven and a set of baking dishes and trays. A temperature gauge was set in the front, and a series of vents in the hinged lid provided for temperature adjustment. "I can bake again! Thank you."

"'Tis not near enough," he stated softly. "I wish, some day, to do more."

Katie was busying herself with a flat box. "A book?"

"Longfellow. I love poetry. That is a very old volume, containing the story of Camelot. Perhaps you will grant me the pleasure of hearing you read it." He handed her the last package with a grin. "Now this one."

She ripped open the last box and gasped. "A cell phone?"

"Aye. There's a car charger in there so you can keep it working. I thought you ladies might appreciate having ready communication at hand." He took the phone and turned it on for her. "I've coded my number into its memory for you, as well as Carl's, in case there's an emergency. Don't worry about the bill. I've taken care of the network charges for you."

"I don't know what to say," she said, feeling embarrassed at the poor selection remaining under the tree. "You're too generous."

He leaned forward and touched his lips briefly to her forehead. "Think nothing of it."

She jumped from the love seat and to the tree before her companions saw the blush she felt rising to her cheeks. To her mother, she presented a set of bedding embroidered with lilies and fern leaves. "So that's what you wouldn't show me," Natalie said with a smile. "It's beautiful."

"This is for you," she said, turning to Joshua nervously. She watched him open the simple package and withdraw the scarf it had taken her over a month to crochet. The soft brown wool closely matched his eyes, and while he fingered the shell pattern she saw the softest smile spread over his face.

"'Tis the finest scarf I've ever owned," he said reverently. "You made this yourself?" She nodded silently. "I'll treasure it always. Gifts of this sort mean so much more than store-bought trinkets."

"I'm glad you like it."

They laughed and talked away the evening easily, as companionable as the dearest of friends, and Katie felt suddenly sad when midnight neared and Joshua rose to his feet. "Well, 'tis getting late. I should leave you ladies to your rest. I've had the most enjoyable evening."

Katie picked up his scarf. "I've never had a better Christmas," she said while tenderly wrapping it around his neck. "Thank you for coming," she added as she embraced him briefly and felt his arms surround her and pull her tight.

"'Twas a pleasure beyond words," he said before he released her, a warm expression on his face.

"For all of us," Natalie said before offering him a hug of her own. He slipped his coat on, bowed his head slowly and stepped silently into the night.

* * * *

At long last, winter gave way to spring, and all of nature was preparing to wake from its long slumber. The earliest wildflowers were making their presence known. Pale green shoots appeared on the tips of the evergreens. Joshua walked among the trees with a smile on his face, memories of his long forgotten childhood flitting through his thoughts like echoes. Catherine should be here. Their special place had come to life virtually overnight. Tiny purple and white blossoms were peeking from the moss floor, and Queen Anne's lace lined the outer boundary.

He was at her house in moments, moving almost as quickly as the thought that drew him to her. He knocked gently on the door, but when Natalie opened it, the worried look on her face made his smile disappear instantly. "Natalie, what's wrong?"

"Joshua, I'm sorry. Katie can't see you tonight. She's sick."

"Sick? Natalie…" He reached in to take her gently by the shoulder when she tried to close the door. "Tell me."

A tear crept down her cheek, and she quickly brushed it away. "She started getting sick two days ago. I thought she just had a cold. But today…"

"Let me see her," he said urgently. "Please." She reluctantly let him in. He crossed the small room and reached her bedside in less than a heartbeat. He knelt quietly beside her bed and touched his hand to her damp face. "She's burning with fever." He opened his mind to her and gently called her name, using a mental tone of command in an attempt to reach her, but found her mind too clouded by phantom imagery. He looked up at Natalie, all too aware that he was unable to keep his distress from showing in his eyes. "How long has she been like this?"

"A few hours," she answered, her voice trembling. "She won't wake up, Joshua. I don't know what to do. She's never been this sick before."

He smoothed the sweat-soaked hair from her neck. "Get your purse. I walked here. We'll have to take her car. Where are the keys?" He looked up at her again, and found her still standing beside him, wringing her hands anxiously. He rose to his feet to gain her attention. "Natalie, she needs a doctor."

Another tear dropped unhindered down her cheek. "I can't afford..."

"I'll take care of it." Although he tried to keep his voice calm and measured, there was a sharp undertone that betrayed his feelings. He lifted her limp body tenderly, blanket and all, and held her tightly against him. "Where are her keys?" he asked again.

She opened her mouth to speak, but he sent a quick but gentle command for her compliance. She turned and pulled Catherine's car keys out of her coat pocket, then moved quickly for her own coat and purse. She turned out the lamp, followed him to the car, opened the passenger door, and watched while he put her inside and carefully fastened the belt around her.

He wasted no time getting to the hospital. Thankfully, no police stood in their way. "We need help," he announced loudly as he rushed through the emergency room entrance with Catherine in his arms.

A young nurse picked up a clipboard from a stack at the end of the counter and approached them. "What's the problem?"

"This young lady is ill," he told her, barely holding back his impatience. "She has a very high fever."

She led them to a treatment room and motioned for him to put her on the gurney. "How long has she been sick," she asked, holding the clipboard and a pen ready.

"Two days," Natalie told her. "I'm her mother. The high fever started a few hours ago."

"All right." She sized Natalie up with a quick, appraising glance. "Do you have insurance?"

"I'll cover the charges," Joshua said, growing annoyed. "Help her."

The nurse met his gaze uncertainly, but he lacked the patience for lengthy discussion. A hint of mental energy was sufficient to facilitate her cooperation. "You'll need to fill out a few forms. Let me call the doctor first. If you'll have a seat in the waiting room, I'll bring them to you."

He felt as if elephants couldn't drag him from her side, but Natalie, with the softest touch, got him to comply. They worked together to complete the forms the nurse brought, then waited impatiently for the doctor to make his appearance.

"What's taking them so long?" he grumbled as he rose to his feet and paced the waiting area. He felt Natalie watching him, tracking his movements with her eyes. He sighed sharply, thrust his fingers through his hair and sat down again.

"The doctor will be out soon, I'm sure," she offered quietly. "Katie's going to be all right."

"I hope you're right," he said, his face buried in his hands. "I lost my mother to a fever when I was young. I remember how pale she was, how her skin glistened with sweat. We didn't have the money for medicine that might've saved her. I can't lose Catherine that way."

After a long pause, she asked softly, "You're in love with her, aren't you?"

He looked up at her in astonishment, but quickly pulled himself under control. After a moment, he whispered, "I care for her. She has become very important to me."

"She loves you too. You should tell her how you feel."

Before he could think of a response, a man approached them wearing a long white lab coat and black slacks. A stethoscope hung loosely from his neck. The badge clipped to his pocket identified him as Dr. Lambert. They instantly rose to their feet when he stopped in front of them. "Mrs. Mills?"

"Yes," she responded, nervously wringing her hands. "What's wrong with Katie?"

"We found a tick in her scalp. I've sent it to the lab for analysis. We're not sure which disease it was carrying, but it's a vicious one. Her lungs are clear, so we aren't worried about pneumonia. I've put her on a broad-based antibiotic and an IV. Her condition is stable, but serious. I'd like to keep her for a couple of days."

"She's all right?" Joshua asked quietly.

"She should be fine," the doctor told him. "It's a good thing you brought her in when you did."

"Can we see her?" Natalie asked.

"We're assigning her a room. As soon as she gets settled, you can see her for a few minutes. Visiting hours ended at nine."

"Natalie will be staying with her," Joshua said sternly.

"I'm afraid I can't permit that," the doctor explained gently. "Hospital policy…"

"It's all right for us to stay with her," he said evenly, pinning the doctor's eyes with his intense gaze. "You will arrange a private room for Catherine."

The doctor's eyes widened and his face grew pale. "I'll get her a private room," he echoed softly. "You can stay with her if you like." He turned and walked away slowly.

"How did you do that?"

"What?" he asked innocently.

"Get him to let us stay."

He shrugged noncommittally. "I guess I have a way with people."

Within the hour, they were taken to a room where they found her hooked up to an IV bag. He moved to the head of the bed and touched her forehead. "Her fever is still high," he commented. He took her hand and held it in his own for a moment, then turned to Natalie. "I'll sit up with her for a while. Why don't you take that other bed and get some rest. I'll wake you if she comes around."

She nodded reluctantly and pressed her lips to Catherine's damp forehead. "She's so still," she whispered.

"Natalie," he said sternly, nodding his head in the direction of the other bed. She sighed and curled up on the other bed. Once she'd closed her eyes, he sent a gentle yet firm mental command that sent the woman into a deep and restful sleep. Then he returned his attention to Catherine. She was still. Too still. Her breaths were coming too infrequently and far too shallow. He opened his mind to her, and found nothing but a deep, foggy void. "Come back to me." He rubbed her cheek with the back of his index finger and fought the tears that threatened his careful control.

He held her hand and kept his vigil as the long hours passed, her body growing weaker with each passing moment. He watched her struggle against the infection that had taken complete control over her body, knowing at any time she could take a turn for the worse. Nurses came in at intervals to take their medical readings and draw blood. They nodded in uncomfortable silence at him each time.

Her heart faltered, skipped too rapidly over the unsteady rhythm that kept her alive, and he knew he was losing her. A painful weight pressed down on his chest. "I could bring you across," he whispered. "Would you welcome what I can offer? Will you only end up hating me for forcing your change?" He felt his voice thicken with unshed tears. "If I could reach you somehow. Just for a moment. Just long enough to give you a choice."

Her heart slowed, and he realized the time had come for him to act. "I can't do it," he whispered. "I cannot rob you of your immortal soul." He pulled up the sleeve of his cable-knit sweater, closed his eyes and let his fangs lengthen. "I don't know if this will help, love. I'm not certain what it will do to you, but I must try." He bit deep into the underside of his wrist and gently slid his other arm under her shoulders. "Drink," he commanded softly, pressing his bleeding wrist against her slackened lips. "Take my strength into yourself and let it heal you." Her breathing faltered and her heart skipped a beat. He shook her sharply. "No, Catherine. Drink," he commanded more desperately. He tipped her head back and sensed his blood moving down her throat. She sputtered, gave a weak cough, and the muscles of her throat constricted.

She began suckling weakly at his wrist, like a newborn babe taking its first tentative sips at its mother's breast. "That's it, my darling one. Take me. Feel my power flow through you." He closed his eyes and dared to offer a prayer. "Please let this be enough." Soon she was drinking in earnest. He felt a surge of grim satisfaction when he sensed his power taking hold, strengthening her heart and boosting her will to live. He stopped when his own strength faltered, gently wiped his blood from her lips with his handkerchief, and firmly tied it around his wrist and pulled the sweater sleeve back in place.

Her fever broke, and healthy color returned to her pale cheeks. An hour before dawn, she stirred, drew in a deep breath, and opened her eyes. "Joshua?"

Overwhelming relief swept through him. "Aye, lassie. I'm here."

"Where am I?"

"You're in the hospital," he explained gently. "I...we thought we were going to lose you."

"Where's Momma?"

He quickly sent a sharp mental command to Natalie, bringing her out of her spell and to her feet. "Natalie, she's awake," he said gently.

"Katie, baby," she said, taking her other hand. "Thank God you're all right. I was so worried."

Her tongue worked at the strange taste he knew she found in her mouth. "Thirsty," she said weakly. Natalie quickly filled a cup with water and held the straw to her lips. She took a few sips and drifted back to sleep.

Reluctantly, he released her hand. "'Tis nearly dawn. I must go."

Natalie frowned. "I wish you could stay."

He smiled apologetically. "Catherine means more to me than you can know," he said softly. "If it were possible for me to stay, I would, please believe that. I need to find adequate shelter before the sun rises." He touched Catherine's cheek with the back of his fingers. "She'll sleep through the day. I'll return as quickly as I can this evening."

She nodded reluctantly. "Have you been up all night?"

"Aye. I couldn't rest, not when she was in danger. I think that danger has passed." He pressed a number of bills into her hand. "If the doctor releases her before I return, take a cab back to your house. Don't...don't speak of my feelings for her. I will tell her when she's ready to hear the words."

"All right, Joshua," she said doubtfully. She turned her attention back to her daughter before Joshua left the room.

He took Catherine's car and drove up the highway and into the woods. He hoped to reach his lair before it was too late, but dawn was too close. The sun was already peeking over the horizon, painting the sky in shades of deep pink and coral by the time he reached her house. His eyes were stinging from the light. Fine prickles of heat nipped at every part of his body. Smoke seeped through his clothing when he jumped from the relative shelter of the front seat and surged around to the rear. He climbed into the trunk and closed the lid as the sun chased the first shadows away and shone its warm beams over the car.

Chapter Eight

When the last shades of purple faded and stars were once again prominent in the sky, Joshua stepped through his own front door carrying a bag full of women's clothing. Alex was so overwhelmed by relief he barely understood his master's explanation of the night's events. "Catherine has taken ill," he said while he quickly changed into fresh clothes. "She nearly died last night at the hospital." Alex stared, too stunned to think of a reply. He went quickly to the refrigerator and drained a full gallon of fresh cow blood, not taking the time to bother with a glass, then cuffed his servant gently on the arm. "I'll return before dawn. Try not to worry." He snatched up his keys and headed to the garage while Alex looked on with worry in his eyes.

He hurried back to the hospital, and found her sitting up in bed. "You're awake," he commented in happy surprise.

"The doctor says her recovery is nothing short of miraculous," Natalie told him.

Catherine swung her legs around to the side of the bed, looking at him in confusion. He did his best to hide the secret concerns growing in his heart. "They're letting me go," she said weakly.

"How are you feeling?" he asked, sitting next to her.

She looked at him in silence for almost a minute before she answered, "Hungry."

He chuckled softly. "Oh, well, I think I can fix that."

After taking the women to a restaurant, he drove them home and insisted on carrying Catherine all the way to the love seat, where he propped her up with pillows and saw to her comfort. He felt Natalie's suspicious, watchful gaze and realized he could no longer hold his feelings secret. He could only hope she'd respect his confidence.

* * * *

"You've been unusually pensive," Joshua commented. Catherine sat quietly watching the landscape pass. More than a week passed since her release from the hospital, and cabin fever had her acting jittery. He thought a movie might perk her spirits. "Is there something troubling you?" he asked, studying her while he waited for a traffic light to change.

"No, not really. I've been feeling...strange. Maybe I'm still recovering."

"Strange how?" he asked cautiously.

She glanced at him after the light changed and he was once more concentrating on traffic. "It's hard to describe. Everything looks different. I can hear noises at night I never noticed before. And you..."

"I what?" he asked when she paused too long. A curious tug wrenched at his stomach as he prepared himself to answer questions he knew might come.

"I think I can feel you, in here," she said, pointing at her head. "It's like I can tell when you're thinking about me. I feel like I can tell when you're coming to visit. It's almost...I don't know, it's probably nothing."

Joshua tried to chuckle, but what came from his throat sounded hollow. "They say when a person suffers a high fever, it can do strange things to the mind. Mental talents once latent can sometimes come to the fore." He held his mental breath in hopes she'd accept his explanation.

"I suppose that makes sense."

He heard the doubt in her voice, but was unwilling to press the issue. Instead, he asked, "What is this movie we're seeing tonight?"

"It's about vampires," she said more lightly.

His head snapped up instantly. "Vampires?"

"Yeah. I've heard it's exciting."

He nodded reluctantly. "All right." He sat through the movie, in which vampires were portrayed as evil creatures being hunted down and slaughtered by a vigilante warrior, and did his best not to betray the emotions stirred by the scenes being played out before him. What distressed him more were the reactions those scenes stirred in his companion. Her anxiety became a palpable force during the more violent parts of the movie, and he realized she was waiting for the 'happy ending' when all the vampires were extinguished.

"You didn't like the movie, did you?" she asked on their way back.

He took a deep breath and held it for a moment. "I didn't find it very believable."

She laughed. "Of course it's not," she argued. "It's just a movie. There's no such thing as vampires."

He pulled the car to a stop in front of her house, but didn't move to get out. He studied his hands for a few moments and thought about how close he'd come to introducing her to the truth when she hovered so near death in the hospital. "Do you believe in the supernatural, Catherine?"

"That's an odd question, coming from you. I thought you were a pragmatist." She sounded surprised.

He raised his eyes to study the landscape in front of the windshield. "It's a valid question."

"Well, I don't know," she answered slowly. "I never gave it much thought."

"You believe in God, don't you?"

"Of course."

"Is He not a supernatural being?"

"Hmmm. I suppose you could think of Him that way," she said thoughtfully.

"You believe in the teachings of His Bible." She nodded her head. "Therefore, such beings as angels and demons exist. Surely they might be considered supernatural."

"I guess so."

"If beings like those exist, wouldn't it follow that other creatures might exist?"

"You mean like ghosts, witches, werewolves...?"

"And vampires. Yes. Couldn't they also exist?"

"Well, if you put it that way...I don't know," she answered, shaking her head. "It's too hard for me to believe."

"The old countries are filled with legends of all sorts of fantastic creatures. Most of the tales are based on fear and speculation. I find they have little bearing on the truth, but I cannot dismiss their foundations out-of-hand."

She appeared to consider his words for a moment. "Are you saying you believe in those things? That ghosts, and...and vampires, are real?"

"If they were," he said, purposely evading a direct answer, "do you suppose they would all be as evil as those we saw on that screen tonight?"

"Well, wouldn't they be?"

"Consider this, Catherine." He folded his arms on the steering wheel and rested his head against them to hide any feelings his eyes might betray. "Vampires, to quote the legend, were once mortal creatures such as yourself. Human beings are neither good nor evil altogether. Some perhaps are worse than others, but not all human beings are inherently bad. Wouldn't you agree?"

"Well, sure."

"Okay, so," he continued carefully, "if a mortal of good character chose to become a vampire, would that automatically make him, or her, evil?"

"Why would anyone want to be a...I mean...having to drink blood..."

"There are obvious downsides, of course, but suppose for a moment that person had nothing left in the world to hold them. Suppose he'd become involved with a vampire who treated him well. Imagine the possibilities–to watch eternity unfold, witness the marvels engineered by mankind's ingenuity; to love someone deeply, and never have to fear the pain of losing that person to death's final victory."

He watched her consider the possibility, and realized he was once again mentally holding his breath. "Well, in that case, maybe not."

"I don't think so either," he said. He got out, circled the car and opened her door. "That's why I didn't like tonight's movie. If they did exist in this world, they'd deserve to be considered as fairly as any other race. Society has a tendency to cast people they don't understand into stereotypes. That's where prejudices begin." He paused to study her for any hint of acceptance. "Don't let yourself fear the things you do not understand. Not all forces in this world exist to do you harm."

She shook her head and smiled. "Maybe you should have been a lawyer. You present cases very well. I want to believe you."

"I want you to look at things from a different perspective, that's all. Everyone deserves the chance to be judged on his own merits."

"Even vampires?"

He smiled softly. "Yes. Even vampires."

As they walked to the house, she said, "I'll be graduating soon. It's hard to believe school is almost over for good."

"Will you miss it?"

"No," she said, her tone definitive. "That's too much like looking behind me. I need to move forward with my life."

"Do you have any plans?"

"Well, when I finish with high school, I'll have a good understanding of basic web designing and office automation. I thought I'd try to get a job, and move Mom and me into a nicer house or apartment in town."

He nodded. "Things have not been easy for you here in the sticks, as they say."

"Oh, we get by. Still, Momma works awful hard. I think it's time she took things easier. Let me take care of her for a change."

He chuckled. "You're something else, lass, always with your thoughts to others." When they reached the house, he asked, "Isn't there one more dance before too long?"

"Yes, the senior prom," she answered reluctantly. "I wasn't going to tell you about it."

He raised an eyebrow. "Why not?"

"It's a formal affair. I…it would be expensive."

He put his fingers to his chin and feigned concentration. "I suppose you will be needing a gown. Do I wear top hat and tails?"

She laughed nervously. "No, most guys rent tuxedoes."

"A limousine too, I expect," he added, humor shining in his eyes.

"Sometimes. Look, really, we don't have to go."

"Catherine, this sounds like it is meant to be the most important evening of your entire school career. A rite of passage, as it were. How could I not take you?" He put a hand on each of her shoulders and smiled softly. "I have an account opened for you at Chamberlain's. I want you to buy something spectacular. I'll make it an evening you'll never forget."

Tears welled up in her eyes, giving him the sudden urge to kiss them away. "Why?"

He gently touched her cheek with the backs of his fingers. "I care about you. You've been a good friend. I enjoy making you happy."

She wrapped her arms around him and hugged him briefly. "Thank you," she whispered.

He returned her quick embrace, and opened her front door. "Now, young lassie," he said more sternly. "To bed with ye. I'll not be having you getting sick on me again."

She smiled and sniffed back a tear. "Good night, Joshua," she whispered.

Chapter Nine

Joshua stood on the highest peak of Mt. Hood and gazed at the low clouds below his feet. From this great height, the stars were too numerous to distinguish, filling the sky until the dark velvet dome could hold no more. Thoughts of Catherine filled his head and his heart until he felt they would tear him apart. Soon he wept, softly at first, but then with great sobs that shook him to the core of his being. He sat on the icy ridge and let his tears spill forth, hoping to purge himself of his pain.

He sensed the presence long before Vincent appeared on the ridge beside him. "Leave me," he begged when he found his voice.

"You require counsel," he answered in a soft and sympathetic tone. "Let me help."

He glanced at his friend, who was now seated beside him. "I thought you returned to Haven."

"I did. I returned only to see how you were doing. Not well, I see."

"In other words, you're checking up on me."

He shrugged marginally. "I can't dismiss my responsibilities. Still, I should think my support would be more welcome to you than Bastian's interference."

He tried to call forth his anger, hoping it would give him the strength to argue, but all that erupted from him was yet another round of sobs. "I've made a mistake," he said when he again found his voice.

"Catherine?"

He nodded silently. The two sat on the ridge for some time before he confessed, "I gave her my blood." He took a deep, unnecessary breath. "Her life was at risk. I sustained her."

"This distresses you?"

"Yes. I fear there were…complications."

"You knew there would be."

"No," he said sadly. "I only suspected."

"How far has it gone?"

He looked up at the myriad stars, wishing for the oblivion they enjoyed. "An increase in visual acuity, especially, I suspect, at night. Sharpened hearing. Judging by the way she toyed with her clothing the other night, a heightened sense of touch, perhaps changes in taste and smell as well."

"That isn't the worst of it."

"No. If that were all…" He turned his attention to his hands, studying the smooth, pale skin absently. "A sympathetic bond formed between us years ago, one I alone was sensitive to. That bond has strengthened, and she's becoming more and more aware of it."

"I see." After a long, intense silence, he asked, "Are you in love with her?"

It took several tries for Joshua to release his response. "Aye."

"Does she return the sentiment?"

"I believe she was moving in that direction."

"I don't understand the problem. Take her into your confidence."

"I'm afraid she might not be as open to certain…possibilities as I had hoped."

"If she resists, you can always take control of her."

"No. I value her freedom of thought, her ability to choose. I can't take that from her. You of all people should understand that." He rose to his feet, slowly and gracefully unfolding himself until he felt he could reach out to the stars and surrender to their embrace. "Her love for me cannot grow on its own. I've influenced things far more than I intended. I'll never know if she gives her heart to me freely. I must…" he choked on another sob. "I intend to release her right after her senior prom."

"And then what?" Vincent's voice had a tight, irritated edge to it.

"I don't know. Go to ground. Move on. Block myself from her perceptions until she no longer feels my pull."

"I hear your feelings much more loudly than your words. You would choose suicide rather than see this through." He snorted in irritation. "Antonia did not teach you very well."

"Just what is that supposed to mean?" he asked, his anger at long last beginning to boil.

"Joshua, do you understand so little of what you are? The girl's heart was yours long before you gave her your gift. Otherwise, she would not have willingly grasped the bond you so greatly fear." More calmly, he advised, "Continue on as you have been. Block your mind from her if you feel you must to prevent yourself from unduly influencing her. Guide her carefully, and she'll accept your secrets. Unless you intentionally interfere with her will, she will do as her heart directs."

His words poured over Joshua's heart like a soothing balm. "If you're certain…"

"Young Catherine belongs to you, my friend. I look forward to the time when you can introduce her to me as your bride."

* * * *

Natalie applied the finishing touches to Katie's face and stepped back to look at her appraisingly. She didn't need to say a word; the look of astonished approval shone brightly in her eyes. "When did you grow up on me?" she whispered.

She studied her reflection in the mirror in disbelief. Her mother used only enough makeup to enhance her exceptionally expressive eyes without making them look made-up, and carefully arranged her hair in a bounty of curls that toppled off her head and down her back. "Is that me?" She turned back to her mother. "Do…do you think he'll like it?"

"If he doesn't, there's something wrong with him," Natalie answered with a laugh. "Now, there's something I want to give you." She pulled a box from of the corner of their room, and dug her hand in until she found a small velvet pouch. "I've been hanging onto these until you were ready," she said, producing a short strand of pearls and a pair of matching studs. "They belonged to your grandmother." She fastened the choker to her daughter's neck.

She tenderly fingered the delicate white beads. "They're beautiful." They heard the sound of a car's engine as they went to the front room. She shot a nervous glance at the front door. "He's here," she whispered, unable to move.

Natalie peeked out the window and gasped. "Oh, my God," she whispered and moved quickly to the front door. She opened it when Joshua knocked, and Katie watched her mother stare speechlessly at the man standing in front of her. He was wearing an exquisite deep green tuxedo, trimmed in rich velvet, which looked as if it had been tailored especially for him. The pale green shirt underneath was finished off with what appeared to be genuine emerald cufflinks. His hair was pulled back severely and tied off at the back of his neck, giving him the most formal, and handsome, appearance she could've imagined.

"May I come in?" he asked, a hint of amusement in his voice.

"Of course. I'm sorry," Natalie stuttered, stepping back to admit him.

When he saw her, it was his turn to stare. She'd chosen a gown of deep blue satin that was all the more elegant for its simplicity. It rested on one shoulder, where a sheer sleeve flared partway down her arm. Her other shoulder and bow-arm were bare. From the waist, it was fell gracefully in shimmering waves to the floor. The pearls hanging above her collarbone and from her ears emphasized the simple elegance she had hoped to achieve.

His eyes returned to her face after a moment, stunned surprise evident in his eyes. When Natalie chuckled and pushed his jaw in place with her index finger, he pulled himself together and stepped inside. He took her hand in his, but instead of the simple gesture she'd become accustomed to, he raised it gently and pressed his soft lips to her knuckles. "I've never in my life seen anything so exquisite," he said softly, making her blush.

"You look wonderful." She turned her eyes away shyly. "I feel like Cinderella."

"You look the part. Here, this is for you." He produced a corsage featuring a perfect white orchid. While he carefully pinned it to her gown, she felt the touch of his fingers on the skin above her breast. Her eyes shot to his in surprise and felt her blush deepening. He smiled softly and backed away, but there was, deep in his eyes, recognition and uncertainty that belied his calm appearance.

Natalie stepped forward and handed her a white carnation, which she tried to pin to his lapel. Her hands were trembling so hard she had to give up and let Natalie take over before she drove the pin into her fingers. Then he took her gently by the hand, nodded his respect to her mother, and led her out the front door.

She stopped short when she saw the car parked in front of her. The silver-on-black stretch limousine shimmered in the moonlight. Its driver stood at the ready beside the rear passenger door. "How did you get that thing up here?"

"It wasn't easy. I had to offer the driver extra to make the attempt." He placed his hand gently on the small of her back and conducted her to the car. The driver stoically opened the door for them to enter, and once they were settled, started the slow and careful journey down the road to the highway.

"Are you nervous?" he asked once they'd entered the highway.

"A little," she admitted. "I'm not sure what to expect tonight."

"You sound troubled. Is there something wrong?"

"No. Well, I don't think so. It's just, well, the kids at school have been acting strange toward me lately. Maybe it's my imagination."

"I'm sure this is going to be a wonderful evening."

She sighed and relaxed against the soft leather seat. "It already is."

He slid closer, put his arm over her shoulder and moved her toward him, close enough she could rest her head on his shoulder. "You're trembling. Does it bother you that I hold you like this?"

She looked in his eyes, and was instantly trapped in his gaze. His face, his lips, were so close to hers she felt the heat rise in her cheeks again. Her breath caught in her throat when she thought of how soft those lips had felt on her hand. "It feels strange," she admitted breathlessly. "You've never held me this close before."

He traced her jaw line gently with his index finger, starting below her ear and pausing at the end of her chin. A thrill she didn't recognize surged through her. "Do you want me to stop?"

After a moment, she whispered, "No."

A soft smile played across his lips. She thought for a moment he might cross that short distance between them and kiss her. Instead, he took her hand and turned his head to look out the window at the passing traffic. The lights of the hotel where the prom was being held soon came into view. The driver swung the car around a long drive in front of the building and pulled to a stop, then got out and opened their door. He tucked her hand in the crook of his arm and smiled. "Ready?" She nodded and allowed him to lead her inside.

* * * *

They followed the strains of music to a darkened ballroom to the rear of the main floor. Her eyes opened wide in wonder at the decorations and lights. Mirrored balls were suspended from the ceiling, spotlights cast fleeting colored reflections around the room like fireflies. More lights projected soft images of stars on the walls. "It's so beautiful," she said in awe.

He looked over the ballroom as well, but his focus was on its occupants. He noted grimly they were being watched as they passed through the room. Some of the students cast furtive glances in their direction while others studied them openly. He opened his awareness to their thoughts, a survival tactic he'd practiced to perfection long before his first century concluded, and found mixed feelings of curiosity and disdain. Rumors regarding the two of them had been circulating, rumors that could spoil the festive mood of his companion. He did his best to prevent her from becoming aware of the crowd's attitude, hoping to make the evening as special for her as possible.

He led her to the buffet and helped her select a few of the delicacies, and they found a table. The disc jockey played a combination of new rock tunes and some old and sentimental favorites. He took advantage of every slower song played and pulled her onto the dance floor. As the evening progressed he held her closer, and smiled his satisfaction when she grew more accustomed to his nearness. "Are you having a good time?"

"Wonderful," she told him with a smile. "If you'll excuse me for a moment, I need to go to the ladies room."

"I'll get some more punch while you're gone. Hurry back." She nodded and left the room. As he watched her go, the strangest feeling came over him that he should've followed her. He shrugged it off and headed for the buffet. Despite his earlier misgivings, the evening was going smoothly. The other students, for the most part, seemed content to keep to themselves, and Catherine showed no sign of noticing anything amiss. He hoped his luck held.

He refilled her cup, and was replacing the dipper when Brianne sauntered up to him. "Hi, Joshua," she said with a smile. "Having a good time?"

He recognized her instantly, and took uncomfortable note of the predatory gleam in her eyes. "Uh, Brianne, isn't it? Brianne Anderson. Yes. We met at the fair."

She smiled sweetly. "I knew you'd remember me. Nikki and I tried to catch up with you that night, but the crowds were so..." she paused, lowered her eyelids, "I mean, I didn't want you to think I'd run off on you."

He smiled cautiously. "Don't give it another thought."

She opened her eyes wide in feigned surprise. "Really? I thought you'd be upset. Do you want to say hi to Nikki?"

He took a purposeful stride in the direction of his table. "Perhaps another time."

She put her hand on his arm and tugged gently. "This will only take a sec. Come on."

He was becoming more than annoyed. He didn't need his vampire senses to recognize her obvious advances, but her thoughts were so loud a moderately skilled human could hear. She was desperate to distract him, and he knew why. He shrugged off her grasp. "Another time, Brianne."

"Oh, come on, Joshua. I don't see Katie around. You've got a minute to..."

He closed his eyes an instant before she would notice the change he knew was imminent. He drew in a breath and held it for almost too long while he grappled at his control. He released that breath in a tightly controlled statement he hoped she would understand. "I'm not interested in you. I thought I made that clear the night of the fair."

She stared at him, obviously stunned by his words, scrambling mentally for a way to regroup without missing her opportunity. When the scheming gleam returned to her eyes, he almost showed his disappointment. "You never had the chance to get to know me. You let Katie drag you away. Don't you know she's only taking advantage of you?"

His rage once again threatened his control. The power swirling around him was so tangible it amazed him that she, standing so close, didn't feel it. He held himself rigid, frowned hard against the pressure in his eyes. Through clenched teeth, he asked, "What do you mean by that?"

"Everyone knows she's only after you for your money. Poor girls like her always are."

"You don't know what you're talking about," he said as he turned away.

"Don't I?" she asked, following him closely. "Just wait. You'll see I'm telling the truth."

He stopped and gave her a hard look. "Leave this alone, Brianne. I don't want to hurt you, but I will if I must." He started to turn away again when the sudden sense of Catherine's distress hit him with the force of a lightning bolt. He looked back at Brianne with genuine anger. His darker nature begged for release. He stepped closer, pinned her with his feral gaze, and warned her mind to ignore his nature as he growled low, "What have you done to her?"

Her eyes widened innocently. "Me? Nothing." He released her abruptly and left the ballroom at a run, the sound of Brianne's spiteful laughter following him into the hallway.

* * * *

Katie went into one of the stalls and sat down with a sigh. Things were going very well between her and Joshua. She wondered if he felt the things he was making her feel. Was it wishful thinking that led her to believe he was beginning to have romantic feelings for her? She hoped not. Tonight felt truly magical. She hated to see it end.

She was finishing her business with the bathroom when some girls entered. They were laughing secretively and talking amongst themselves. Something she thought she heard made her pause. She held her breath and listened.

"Did you see that dress she's wearing?" one of the girls said. "I saw that one at the mall. There's no way she could've afforded it."

"I'll bet he gave her those pearls, too," another speculated. "It's no wonder she's stayed with him so long. If I had a rich man giving me presents like that, I'd stay with him too, even if he is older. Of course, Joshua is awful good looking."

"She must be good to him," another said, distain in her voice. "No man is gonna hang around that long unless he's getting something out of it, if you know what I mean."

"It's funny, though," the first girl added, "Katie never really seemed the type, you know? I guess you never know about someone."

"Well, you know how white trash girls like her are," yet another girl countered. "They smell opportunity and take advantage of it any way they can. Brianne told me she met him at the fair. He was getting along real well with her and Nicole before Katie horned in and made him go with her. Bri told me she saw her leaving with him later that night. She was hanging on his arm like she owned him."

She sat in silent shock and listened to the growing list of lies. When they left the room a few minutes later, she sat and digested all she'd heard. She couldn't return to the ballroom after all she'd heard. Did everyone think she was that way? Had they been watching her with Joshua all evening, speculating on what was going on between them? The thought made her stomach turn. Her chest grew tighter as her mind replayed the girls' comments, shock giving way to severe emotional distress. Tears pressed hard against her eyes while her throat constricted painfully. She clenched herself tightly and gave in to her tears.

* * * *

Joshua exited to the outer corridor and swept his heated gaze past the few students congregating there. Catherine's distress called to him, and while he had yet to discover the cause, he suspected the group of girls who cast him brief glances before retreating into the ballroom from the opposite door. He opened his mind to her, and discovered that she had firmly blocked herself. Surprised, he walked with measured steps along the corridor and listened with his heart. Her distress was loudest within the ladies' lounge. A moment in deeper concentration told him she was sobbing silently, her mind accidentally blocked from his perceptions in her efforts to silence her tears.

He pushed the door open cautiously and peered inside. Her sobs were coming from deep within the room. He called her name softly, and heard her hiccup and swallow her tears. Still, he couldn't sense her drawing nearer. "Catherine, if you don't come out, I'll come in after you."

He listened to her slow, hesitant steps and sniffles until he saw her, makeup running down her cheeks, her eyes red-rimmed and swollen. "My poor darling." He pushed his way into the room and took her by the shoulders. "Come now, no more tears." He pulled out his handkerchief and gently wiped the mascara from her cheeks. "You're all right."

"They think…"

"I know. Brianne told a few stories. Rumors started milling about. I can't help but feel this is all my fault."

"Take me out of here." Her voice hitched with as yet unresolved sobs.

"I can't do that." He moistened the end of his handkerchief at the sink and finished cleaning her face. "This isn't something you can run away from, Catherine. Sometimes you have to stand up for yourself, no matter how hard it is."

"I can't go in there," she protested weakly. "Not when they think I…that we…"

"Listen to me," he said, holding her chin in his hand. "We've done absolutely nothing to be ashamed of. Those kids are like sharks. If they smell blood, they'll go into a feeding frenzy. You can't let them know they cut you. Do you understand?"

She looked in his eyes and nodded reluctantly. "I think so."

"That's my girl," he said with a smile. "Hold your head high and smile as if nothing has happened. We'll go in and dance a bit more. Once we've made a brave showing of it, we can leave. Ready?" She nodded and forced a smile.

He tucked her hand in the crook of his arm and led her into the ballroom, seated her at their table and handed her the cup of punch. She sipped at it nervously while her eyes flitted from one curious face to the next. He followed the progress of her gaze, and noted when she paused at the sight of Brianne, who was standing near the buffet and glaring at her openly.

When he sensed her resolve crumbling, he took her hand, drawing her attention back to him so she could see his supportive smile. At that moment, the disc jockey chose to play *Knights in White Satin*, the old Moody Blues tune just as beautiful and timely as when it was new. He pulled her gently to her feet and onto the dance floor, where he held her closer than he'd ever before dared. He began humming along to the tune, and when she softened against him and he was sure he had her full attention, he softly sang the refrain in her ear, and felt strongly how the words 'I love you' affected the most private places in her heart. It gave him the greatest satisfaction to know Vincent's council was proving to be true.

They returned to their table slowly once the song ended. She toyed with her cup for a full minute before she lifted her gaze to his, where he saw tenderness that had never been there before. Before either of them said a word, Brianne showed up to spoil the mood. "Hey, Katie. You've got yourself a pretty good racket here, don't ya?" She put her palms on the table and leaned toward Catherine to continue in a stage whisper, "I wish I could find a sugar daddy of my own." She swept her gaze over her in open appraisal. "*I* certainly couldn't have afforded that gown. He sure does take good care of you."

Catherine's face went pale, but she never had a chance to protest. Joshua rose to face her, holding his deepest anger at bay with extreme difficulty. "You will apologize for that, Brianne."

"Why? Everyone knows the truth. Well, go on Katie. Tell him. You're only interested in his money."

Her face reflected her own growing anger. "Why are you doing this?"

"Because she's jealous, lass," he said tightly. "She's never had a relationship that was honest or decent as ours is." He stepped forward and pinned Brianne with his angry gaze, silently thanking the stars that Catherine was close enough to help him maintain his control. "Brianne is a misguided young lady," he said loudly enough for everyone to hear over the music, though it was clear he was still addressing Catherine. "Do you know, she tried to distract me from your side tonight? She was quite obvious in her actions. I believe she doesn't know who fathered the child she carries and was hoping she could trick me into going with her, and then taking responsibility."

If the music hadn't been playing, the room would've become deathly silent. Brianne's face took on an unhealthy pallor. "How did you know?" she whispered. All the students who had been looking with sarcasm at Catherine were now staring at Brianne in shock. Catherine's eyes were on him. Astonishment had replaced the anger on her face.

Joshua sensed a deep and festering wound opening in Brianne's heart. Although she didn't deserve his mercy, he felt inclined to help her, but needed to do so in a way Catherine wouldn't see. He held her gaze while he forced her mind to listen to him. "Your search for acceptance has led you down a troubled path, Brianne," he said, his voice smooth and hypnotic. "Do yourself and that innocent babe you carry a favor. Go home. Have a long talk with your parents and work this out. Stop making life miserable for yourself and everyone else who comes in contact with you."

When he released her mind, she burst into tears and ran from the room. He cast his mind after her for a moment longer, to assure himself she would do no harm to herself or the babe, then turned his angry gaze at the rest of the crowd. They were regarding him with new respect. "The rest of you should be ashamed of yourselves. You've been led by that poor, misguided girl, and have hurt someone who's never had a hateful or dishonest thought in her life. Catherine and I have done nothing to deserve the animosity you've shown tonight."

The students murmured uncomfortably to each other. Most of them backed away from the area in embarrassment. He returned to the table and took Catherine's hand. "Are you all right?"

She nodded her head. "How did you know? About Brianne, I mean. Is she really pregnant?"

"You couldn't tell?" he asked, feigning surprise. "I thought it was rather obvious, myself. We may leave now. That is, if you still want to."

"Yes," she said, though not as urgently as she might have minutes before. "I'm getting tired." He nodded and led her out of the ballroom. He noticed with satisfaction the mood of the room's occupants had changed drastically. Most of the students were hiding their faces from him in shame as he swept his gaze over the crowd. He felt well assured Catherine would receive no further ill treatment when she returned to her classes.

Limousines were lined up outside the hotel. The drivers stood waiting for their passengers to return. Their driver opened the door when they approached, and Joshua held her hand while she stepped inside. Once the car was moving, and the lights of town gave way to the less invasive lights of the highway, he put his arm around her and encouraged her to sit closer. This time, she rested her head on his shoulder and breathed a tender sigh. He took her hand and held it tenderly. "You're quiet."

"Thinking," she said tiredly. "Do you think Brianne will be all right?"

He chuckled. "Still thinking of everyone but yourself," he accused gently. "Yes, she'll be fine. She just has some growing up to do."

"I had a good time tonight. It's too bad she had to spoil it for us."

"Don't think about it," he said as he softly stroked an errant lock of hair behind her ear. "Remember only that we had a wonderful time together." The limo pulled off the highway and started its perilous climb to her house. When it came to a stop and the driver opened the door, he reluctantly pulled himself away from her and helped her out of the car.

At the front door, he turned her to face him and gently led her into his arms. He wanted to tell her how beautiful she was in the moonlight. He wanted to say he'd had the most wonderful evening of his entire existence. He touched her face gently with the tips of his fingers, and she lifted it to look into his eyes. The trust he saw in hers sent shockwaves rocketing through his system.

When he slid his hand along her cheek and into her hair, he felt her tremble in anticipation. There was so much he wanted to say to her at that moment, but all that came from his lips was her name, spoken so softly the sound blended with the breeze. He moved slowly closer, then touched his lips to hers.

Her breath caught with that first tentative contact, and he sensed something important and undeniable pass between them. He paused for a moment, waiting to sense if she would accept the change sweeping over them. When she didn't move away, he kissed her again with tenderness that spoke of all the love in his heart. When his lips closed over hers the third time, he felt her arms move around his waist. He held her there, suspended in the moment, his lips playing softly with hers, until he felt the sweetness of her sigh. With the greatest reluctance, he pulled himself away from her and saw wonder glowing in her eyes. "Good night, love." He turned from her before the temptation to take her home with him became too great.

Chapter Ten

"It's been two weeks, Momma. Why hasn't he come by?" Katie flopped down on the love seat and heaved a heavy, frustrated sigh. "Why hasn't he called?"

Natalie smiled in understanding. "He'll be here, baby. He's probably been busy. Maybe he got called out of town. Or maybe," she added, her smile fading, "he needed to give both of you time to think things through."

She leaned her head back and closed her eyes. "We had such a good time at the prom. When he kissed me goodnight…"

"When he kissed you, everything changed," she finished for her. "You're too young and inexperienced to know how powerful a kiss can be. My guess is, he didn't see it coming and he's afraid it happened too quickly. Either that, or he's afraid you weren't ready."

"I am ready. I've been ready. I want…" A hot blush rose to her cheeks.

"What do you want, baby? Do you love him?"

After a moment, she nodded. "Yes, I guess I do. I…I want to be with him. I hate it when we're apart. Is that wrong?"

"Not if you handle it right. I like Joshua. I didn't think he was an appropriate match for you at first, but I've watched him with you, watched the two of you together. He cares for you more than he's ready to admit. Give him time. Be patient."

"That's not going to be easy. I keep thinking about the way he made me feel when he held me. I felt so…"

"I know exactly what you felt, baby. At first, the excitement you felt the moment you realized he was going to kiss you took you by storm. Your breath caught in your throat when his lips touched yours. Your body trembled. Strange new feelings flooded your heart. Then, as his arms closed around you, and his lips played tenderly over yours, warmth filled you from somewhere deep inside. You felt safe, sheltered. You felt loved."

"Yes. How did you know?"

She smiled sadly. "I felt all those things the first time James kissed me." The cell phone rang, making both women jump in surprise. Natalie smiled again. "There, you see? I told you he'd call."

She picked up the phone with trembling hands, pressed the call button, and slowly raised it to her ear. "Joshua?"

"Aye, love. Have you missed me?"

"Yes," she whispered.

"Can you meet me? I think we need to talk."

She shot a nervous glance at her mother and nodded. "Okay."

"Come to the clearing," he said softly. "I'll be waiting."

She put the phone down on the table slowly. "He wants me to meet him. He says we need to talk." She looked up at her mother with tears in her eyes. "Momma, I'm scared. What if it was all a mistake? What if he...he doesn't...?"

Natalie put her hands on her shoulders. The smile she offered looked like encouragement. "Go to him. Listen to what he has to say. I'm sure everything will be okay." She sniffed and nodded her head reluctantly. "Wear your sweater," she added. "It's cool tonight."

* * * *

The night was especially dark. Thick clouds had rolled in, and thunder rumbled in the distance. She found her way easily through the woods to the clearing in spite of the lack of light, but this time her nervous anticipation kept her from wondering at how well her eyes had adjusted to the night. Wild thoughts and fears were running through her head like phantoms, making her pause at the border of the clearing. She took a deep, calming breath in an attempt to draw on the courage she felt had abandoned her and stepped through the brush. He stood near the center, a shadow among shadows, yet she could see his face as clearly as if the moon were shining brightly on their special place. She stood still, ready at any moment to burst into tears. When he held his arm to her, she rushed to him and felt his arms surround her and hold her tight.

"Hush now, love. Why the tears?"

"I was worried that...that you'd..."

"Sh-sh-sh. I'm here. I'm sorry I didn't come sooner. I needed time." He lifted her face and looked into her eyes. "So did you." He brushed the tears from her face and touched his lips to hers, easing the doubts from her mind. "Come sit with me. Let me hold you." He led her to the rock face, pulled her gently down with him, and cradled her against his chest with his strong arms. He gentled her head against his shoulder, and she breathed a tender sigh.

"You're trembling," she said, her voice reflecting her wonder.

"Aye. So are you." He held her for a few minutes before he spoke again. "Are you afraid?"

"No. I…It feels right."

"I wasn't expecting to kiss you, Catherine. Truly, it was not what I intended, but the need took me so much by surprise that I couldn't help myself."

"Momma told me it might've surprised you."

"Your mother is a wise woman," he responded with a chuckle. "What else did she tell you?"

"That you might be afraid things are happening too fast."

"Your friendship has been my greatest joy. I find myself experiencing feelings I never believed I could have, ever again." He pressed his face gently into her hair and whispered, "I care deeply for you, lass. I'm afraid of frightening you away."

She turned her head to look up at him, a nervous smile tugging at the corners of her mouth. "I'm not afraid. I trust you."

"I don't believe I can trust myself. If I lose control…"

"You won't," she interrupted softly.

"You sound so sure, for one with so little experience in these matters," he said in amusement. Then a serious look passed over his face like a storm cloud. "I don't ever want to hurt you."

"You won't," she repeated. "I trust you. And…" She paused to lick the dryness from her upper lip. "…I'm ready to move forward."

"Catherine, are you sure?"

She turned in his arms and met his gaze. The passion she saw burning in his eyes brought a fluttery feeling to the pit of her stomach and filled her with a strange, warm-pudding feeling. How far would it go, she wondered, if she surrendered to the power of that passion? Was she ready to lose herself in his embrace? Or would he be able to control what developed between them, stop himself before they both went too far? She decided the risk was well worth the taking. "Yes. I'm sure."

"Come then." He put his hand on her face, guided her gently to him. His lips touched hers as tentatively as they had the first time they'd made contact, sending a thrill of suspense through her. His arms closed around her, drawing her easily onto his lap. While he moved his mouth tenderly over hers, she slid her arm along his and buried her fingers in his hair. He moaned, strengthened his kisses and held her more closely to him. She felt his hand cradle the back of her neck and allowed her head to rest against it, surrendering herself to the powerful feelings that swept through her.

When she felt the tip of his tongue graze her lower lip, she gasped her surprise and let her lips part in invitation. His tongue touched her again to find hers there waiting, and a groan that sounded deep and rusty rumbled in his throat. He shifted her in his arms until he was positioned over her and she was completely under his control. He nipped at her lips playfully, teased the tip of her tongue with his own, spread his fingers into her hair. Her heart pounded a trip-hammer beat in response to the intense and heady power of her own surrender. In that moment, she wanted him in ways she didn't understand.

As thunder rolled over the tops of the trees, he pulled himself away, raised them both to a more upright position, and pressed her head against his shoulder. She was breathless and trembling, lost to the wonder of feelings she liked too much. "I can't feel your heart beat," she commented when she trusted herself to speak.

"Perhaps that is because it is keeping perfect time with your own." His voice sounded strained. "You should go home now. A storm approaches."

"Will you walk with me?"

"Not this time." She heard a strangely dark quality in his voice that whispered to her mind of foreboding. He pulled her to her feet and caressed her cheek lightly. "You feel too good in my arms. My need of you is too great just now. Do you understand?"

She felt her face flush as instinctive, forbidden knowledge swept her understanding. "I think so." He led her as far as the road to her house. "Will it be another two weeks before I see you again?"

The smile he gave her was filled, oddly, with sorrow. "No. I don't think I can keep myself away from you if I try." He bent to touch her lips gently with his own in parting. "Go now," he said, his whisper sounding husky.

She nodded silently and turned for home. When she walked through the front door, Natalie looked up from her magazine and studied her daughter appraisingly. "I take it things went well," she commented quietly.

The blush that rose to her face felt hot and furious. "Yes," she answered self-consciously. "Very well."

* * * *

Katie pulled her car alongside the house, stepped out and smoothed her dress before closing the door. It had been another long and frustrating day. She didn't know how to face her mother with the news that she had once again failed in her task.

She went in the front door and smiled, but she couldn't hide the troubled look in her eyes. "No luck again?" Natalie asked sympathetically.

"It's the same story I've heard all summer." She dropped onto the love seat with a sigh. "No one wants to hire me until I get more experience." Tears brimmed her eyes as she asked, "How can I get the experience if no one will hire me?"

"I'm sure something will come up," Natalie offered in encouragement. "Have you checked with the state office?"

"I have an appointment with a counselor next week. There are programs that can help." She kicked off her shoes, leaned her head back and closed her eyes. "This is all so frustrating."

Natalie sat down next to her daughter and took one of her hands. "Have you considered marrying Joshua?" When she looked up in surprise, Natalie smiled. "It's no secret you're in love with him. If the two of you were to be married, you wouldn't have to worry about getting a job. He'll take care of you."

"I'd marry him tonight, if he asked me," she confessed softly. "Lately he's been acting so…distant. I'm not sure he feels the same anymore. And I don't want to ask him. If he thought I was only interested in his money…"

"I'm sure he knows better than that. Tell me what's been going on between you."

She studied her hands thoughtfully. "That night, after the prom, when I met him to talk?" She glanced questioningly at her mother to confirm she remembered, and when Natalie nodded she continued. "He held me close and kissed me so very…" She paused to release an embarrassingly tender sigh. "I think he wanted me. I wanted him too." She lowered her eyes, embarrassed by her own admission. More quietly, she said, "Ever since that night, he's been…I don't know, different. He doesn't hold me as tight, doesn't kiss me like that anymore. I'm not sure why."

Natalie smiled. "I know why, baby." She gave her mother a hopeful look. "When I met him last year, I made him promise to behave himself with you. He vowed he wouldn't let things get out of hand until the two of you were properly married. I think, that night, he came too close to breaking that vow, and it scared him."

"You really think that's all it is?" she asked softly.

"I'm sure it is. That only proves to me his feelings for you are strong. He's an honorable man. He'll make you a good husband, and unless I miss my guess, a gentle and passionate lover."

Her blush deepened. "I'm tired of waiting for it to happen. I want to spend the rest of my life with him. I don't know how to tell him how I feel."

"Then show him." She gaped at her mother in shock. She laughed gently and took her hand. "I'm not a prude. I trust your judgment. If something does happen between you, I'm sure he'll do the right thing afterwards. I want you to know I'd understand. Next time you see him, encourage him. Make yourself open to him, and see where it leads."

"I can't believe you're saying that to me."

"You've been a good girl, Katie. Most girls your age have already experimented with sex. No, it's not a dirty word. I'm just saying if it does happen, I'll understand." She stroked her daughter's hair gently. "I want you to be happy."

She returned her eyes to her hands nervously, shock and wonder bringing strange feelings to her heart. "You don't think he'll believe I'm trying to trick him into marrying me?"

"No, I don't think so. Now, you don't have to be obvious about it. I'm not telling you to throw yourself at him. I think he needs a gentle push in the right direction. I have a feeling that's all it will take."

After a long, nervous pause, she asked, "Does it hurt much, the first time?"

"If he's careful, and takes his time, it shouldn't be too bad. If he's the kind of man I think he is, he'll make it up to you in ways you can't possibly imagine."

She felt herself blush again, as much over her mother's frank talk as from the feelings growing inside her. "You've given me a lot to think about."

"Are you planning to see him tonight?"

She shook her head. "We don't have any plans. That doesn't mean he won't show up, though. He's kinda unpredictable."

After supper, she slipped her shoes back on. "I need to go for a walk. I need some time alone to think." She hesitated at the door, then turned and threw her arms around her mother and hugged her tightly. "I love you, Momma."

"I love you too, baby," Natalie replied, returning her hug. "I always will. I'm very proud of you."

She smiled and left the house. Her smile quickly faded as she walked down the road. She fingered her grandmother's pearls absently and went over everything her mother had said. Was she right? Was Joshua behaving like a gentleman because he wanted her too much? The idea made her heart ache. She wondered if she could bring herself to be more aggressive with him if the situation called for it. She always felt so timid when he was near, so unsure.

Before she knew where she was headed, she found herself crossing the threshold to their clearing. It looked much different in the waning daylight, she thought. Pretty, yet lonely, as if it refused to come to life without his presence. She smoothed her dress and sat down against the rock face where they'd shared that brief moment of passion, and let herself remember how she felt cradled in his arms and under his control. She wanted that feeling again, she decided. It was good and right. It had to be.

She curled up on her side, cradled her head on one arm, and let her mind drift along the paths of her imagination. She wondered what it would be like to live with the man she'd come to know and trust so deeply. She drifted off to sleep without realizing that was where she was headed.

* * * *

Joshua walked through the woods, as was his want of late, deep in thought. His mind continued to return to that night in the clearing when his relationship with Catherine had so drastically changed. The passion they'd shared that night nearly drove him insane. He'd almost given in to that passion before she was ready, long before he was ready to face the consequences of becoming intimate with her. It frightened him more than he wanted to admit to himself. Keeping distance between them had been the hardest thing he'd ever endured.

She was in love with him, deeply. Her longing sang to him constantly, making his dilemma all the more difficult. She was waiting for him to declare for her, but every time he attempted to work up the courage to bring her into his confidence, the words refused to come. He berated himself on a nightly basis for his own cowardice. Still, he couldn't bring himself to face the possibility of her fear, her rejection.

With a heavy sigh, he opened his mind to her, as he had done covertly over the past months, to savor the thoughts and feelings she was unknowingly broadcasting. She was dreaming of him…a passionate dream, judging by its intensity. He paused when his mental compass told him she was not in her bed, as she should have been. No, she was in the clearing, reliving in her dreams the passion he could not himself dismiss.

In the space of a heartbeat, he was there. He knelt beside her, laid a hand gently on her arm and felt her trembling sigh. "Catherine," he whispered. She mumbled softly, but didn't wake. He shook her gently and called her name again, bringing her out of her dream with a start. "Are you all right?" he asked softly, helping her to her feet.

She busied herself with brushing off her dress, too flustered and embarrassed to do little more than nod. "Guess I fell asleep. What time is it?"

"It's after two in the morning. What are you doing out here alone?"

"I was thinking about us," she told him shyly.

"Oh?" He gently lifted her face and studied her. He saw the longing in her eyes, the uncertainty. She nodded again and reached up to smooth a strand of hair from his eyes. When her fingers brushed his ear, he caught her hand and pressed her knuckles to his lips. He pulled her into his arms and held her tightly against him while his own feelings waged a war within him. When she raised her face to his, his lips found hers of their own accord. He couldn't give her the tender kisses he'd held himself to. Instead, all the feelings he'd held tightly at bay broke free of their bonds. She returned his kisses hungrily and clung to him as if she were drowning.

He wanted her. God help him, he did. He sensed her passion rising, and when he realized she intended to let him take her as far as he would go, his tenuous control nearly snapped. She touched her tongue to his lips in a tentative gesture, igniting his passion into a raging storm that demanded answer. He took possession of her mouth, drank in her sweet, warm depths until her knees weakened. In another moment, he'd have her on the ground, exploring every inch of her, making her his own. It was only with the greatest difficulty that he managed to stop before he did just that. He pulled her tightly against him and held her while he did his best to bring his mutinous body back in line. "Oh, Catherine," he said at last, his voice strained.

She trembled with frustration and need. "Joshua..." Her voice sounded like a sob. She tried to push away, but he held her more firmly. "Joshua, I..."

He pressed his fingers against her lips so suddenly it took her by surprise. "No, love. Be still." When her sobs started bubbling their way to the surface, he stroked her hair and tried hard to soothe her. "I know how you feel," he said softly. "I know what you want. We mustn't. Not yet."

She pushed against him until he reluctantly allowed her to leave his arms. The look on her face spoke to him of the pain and frustration in her heart. "I'm in love with you." Her statement sounded like a desperate challenge.

He felt a lump growing in his throat. "Aye."

"You…you love me too."

"More than I can tell you."

"I know you want me as much as I want you."

"So much so it's killing me," he confirmed, his voice growing thick with anguish.

"Then, why…?"

He turned from her, unable to face the strength of her pain for another moment. "There are things you need to know first. Things I haven't been ready to tell you. Things that…" he paused to swallow the lump in his throat, "things that may frighten you."

She moved to stand in front of him, tears spilling down her cheeks. "I don't understand."

"I have secrets, Catherine. There are facts concerning my life I've not shared with you. I can't let us go any further than this until I know you can accept the truth about me."

"You're being awful mysterious," she accused. "What can be more important than how we feel?"

He brushed the tears gently from her cheeks. "The knowledge I must share with you is dangerous. I can't tell you without risking both our lives." When she frowned and shook her head, he added, "There is more at stake than you realize. I can't explain it simply. It will take time for me to help you understand." He turned away again and swept his fingers through his hair. "Do you trust me?"

"You know I do."

He turned to look at her again, this time with a seriousness in his eyes he knew was frightening her. "Do you believe I could never cause you harm?" When she nodded voicelessly, he added, "Can I trust you?"

"Of course you can. I'd never do anything to destroy what we have."

He pulled her close and drew in a pained breath. "Let me take you to my home. Plan to spend this weekend with me." When she looked up at him in surprise, he gave her a sad smile. "Nothing will happen between us. I've prepared my guest room for you. That will give me the time I need to explain things to you."

"All right," she said, nodding slowly.

He touched her hair gently. "I'll pick you up Friday evening. You can tell your mother whatever you wish. If you still want me after this weekend, after I tell you everything, well, we'll see."

She reached up and touched his face with the tips of her fingers. He closed his eyes tightly against his own tears. "Nothing will change the way I feel," she insisted. "Nothing can."

He felt the strength of her declaration force its way into the shattered remains of his heart. "I can only hope you are right," he told her sadly. "Go home now. I'll see you on Friday."

She nodded and backed slowly away from him. "Friday," she agreed. He watched her leave feeling as though he was about to lose the most precious thing he'd ever held in his hands.

Chapter Eleven

Katie walked slowly, at first doing nothing more than focusing on bringing her feelings under control. She pondered the mystery of Joshua's actions over and over in her mind. What was this terrible secret he felt she needed to know? She had grown comfortable around him. How can anything make her fear him? Impossible. "Whatever it is," she muttered to herself, "it's not as important to me as the way I feel. Nothing will change that."

Friday was only two days away, but it felt like an eternity. She wished she'd insisted on going now. Why would he want to wait, when he'd admitted how much he wanted her? Why would he wish to prolong the agony they were both feeling? Maybe he wanted a chance to pull himself under control first. Maybe this terrible secret of his was something he needed to think about a little longer. Maybe…

How would she tell her mother what she planned? The loyalty she felt for him now prevented her from giving her mother any uncomfortable details. She kicked a pinecone out of her path with the tip of one shoe and watched it skitter under a fern. Her mother had told her to give in to him, hadn't she? Wasn't that the same as giving her blessing? So what if the trip ended less innocently than it began? Her mother had said she would understand. She decided half the truth will serve her better than full disclosure.

When she opened the front door of her home, all thoughts of Joshua fled in one terrible instant. The sudden shock of the scene before her held her frozen in stunned disbelief. Her mother was on the floor, her clothes ripped and scattered around the room, and a strange man was looming over her with a knife at her throat. A scream of pure terror ripped its way out of her chest.

"Katie, run!" her mother called. The man poised on top of her grunted and slid his knife neatly across her throat. She managed one horrible gurgling sound and reached one last time to her daughter, then fell terribly still.

She screamed again, paralyzed by the horror before her. Blood ran thick and heavy across the wood floor. Her mother's killer jumped to his feet, made a grab for her and broke her out of her paralysis, but not before he'd caught the hem of her dress. Her feet slipped in the growing pool of blood and she slammed heavily to the floor.

"Hold still, damn you!" the man cursed. While he struggled to gain control of his newest prey, she fought him, kicked with her feet in a desperate attempt to break free. One of her shoes left her foot, and she heard it strike the far wall. What traction it had provided her was lost, and she squirmed and slipped in an effort to break free of her attacker's grasp. She felt her ankle come in sharp contact with the table by the front window. It clattered to the floor, and along with it the oil lamp that provided the only light in the room. Darkness instantly closed over her. One of his hands found the top of her dress and jerked at it violently, ripping the bodice down to the waist. She screamed again and renewed her efforts to free herself. Then the cold tip of his knife touched her throat.

"Move again, bitch." He leered greedily at her. "Looks like Ricky gets a two-for-one tonight." His high, nasal voice grated against her nerves.

She lay frozen, paralyzed by panic. "Don't..." An orange glow blossomed behind him as he yanked her dress up, but he was too intent on her to notice and she was too terrified to wonder at its meaning. He pressed his mouth over hers while he ripped at her stockings and panties, then maneuvered himself over her and grabbed roughly for her leg. She turned her face toward the door and stared up at the stars while she braced herself for his brutal assault.

* * * *

Joshua walked home slowly, moving with soundless steps through the thick underbrush that had become so familiar to him. The air was fragrant with the smells of the season. Soon the forest would accept the long and restless sleep of winter with little more than a sigh. As he walked through the silent realm of the night, he reviewed in his mind all the times he had shared with Catherine. He'd waited a long time for the words she insisted he hear, but he couldn't allow her to commit herself to him until she knew the truth.

Her love for him had deepened beyond anything he had allowed himself to imagine. Their relationship had grown to the end of its current boundaries, like a flower bud straining against the need to burst open. He had to take the next step or watch their love die. "The time has come," he told himself softly. His voice held the tone of regret.

How should he tell her? How can he make her understand? There had to be a way. If he were patient in the telling, gave her only what she could absorb, led her carefully each step of the way, perhaps her love for him would be enough. His hope lie in not allowing her to give in to the fear he knew the truth would cause her.

Bringing her to his home was necessary. There, and only there, would he be sure of keeping his secrets safe. If she rejected him, and he prayed with all his being she wouldn't, he would be forced to make her forget. The safety of the Community was hinged on that one very uncomfortable fact. He realized with mounting sorrow that, if it came to that, he would need her in a position where he could deal with her uninterrupted. The possibility of having to force her mind sent a quick surge of dread through his heart.

What if she resisted? The question popped into his mind with the lightning fast and painful speed of a bullet, making him pause in his journey. There are mortals who possess the strength of will to resist the power of a vampire's mind. He pondered that question while he watched a snake slither undisturbed under a thick crop of fern. She had a strong mind. She held within her the potential to develop the power to resist, and even to block herself from immortal discovery.

He forced himself onward while he chewed on these new thoughts. The answer was a simple one, but one that would cause him the greatest agony. Taking the girl in thrall would solve all his problems. The Community would leave them alone then, assured that she would never pose a threat. Although he'd never taken a mortal against his will, he'd seen it done. His imagination played out the deed in his mind as clearly as if it had already happened. She would fight at first, of that he was certain. In her eyes there would first be anger, then fear, then at last blank compliance. It was that last expression he hoped he'd never have to see.

He didn't hear her scream. He felt it. The sudden shock of her terror froze him in his tracks. In the next instant he was in the air and racing to her home, hoping desperately he wasn't too late. As he skirted over the tops of the trees, he focused his senses on her house. He heard the nasal twang in a stranger's voice, felt the menace. As he grew closer, he saw her lying inside the door, staring outward in wide-eyed terror while a stranger poised to take what he considered his. Flames were licking at the doorsill, seemingly unobserved.

With a feral growl that didn't sound human, he surged to her defense. The smell of freshly spilled blood called to his senses, feeding the rage growing in his heart. Shock joined the stark terror on her face as he flew through her door, his eyes glowing and fangs bared. That she should thusly be exposed to his secrets multiplied his rage. With another fierce growl, he lifted the attacker from her, carrying him with his own momentum. His fangs were in the man's throat in the next instant, his fury robbing him of all reason. The pathetic creature he held never had time to scream, but he did sense, with the man's last heartbeat, a final, terrified realization. He dropped the carcass and wiped his face on his sleeve in disgust, and turned to kneel by Natalie's still body.

A look of terror was frozen on the woman's pale face. He winced at the sight of the ugly gash that had opened her throat, and gently closed her eyes with a sweep of his hand. He knew if he'd only had the courage to take Catherine into his confidence, he'd likely have had both women in his home, under his protection, and this would never have happened. Profound sorrow swelled in his chest. "Forgive me," he murmured softly.

Fire was climbing rapidly up the walls of the house. The ceiling was obscured by a thick blanket of black smoke that streamed through the open door while simultaneously drawing fresh air in to feed the flames. The heat and light was searing his eyes, but he still saw Natalie's spirit shimmering above her body. It sparked angrily at him, as if trying desperately to warn him off. *Be at peace,* he told her, speaking with his mind in a language only such beings can understand. *I'll never harm her. I swear it.* The specter faded reluctantly and drifted out of the house.

He turned to see Catherine still on the floor, pressed in a huddled position against the far wall. Her face was expressionless. Her ruined dress hung in shreds over her shoulders, and her entire body was covered in blood. He heard the timbers overhead crackle as the flames ate through the poor roof. He went to her with inhuman speed, snagged her around the waist and rushed for the door. The ceiling collapsed just as they cleared the threshold. The house exhaled a great gust of heat and flame. He surged away, pulling her in front of him so he could bear the brunt of the fire, and felt his back ignite.

He dropped her to the ground, where she lay staring blankly at the flames while he did his best to extinguish himself. He quickly turned his attention back to her, noticed the hem of her dress burning, and stomped out the flame. Then he lifted her to her feet.

"Catherine. Catherine! Are you hurt?"

As her eyes slowly came back into focus, her intense terror returned. She backed away from him, shaking her head. "No," she whispered, her voice hoarse from the smoke. Her gaze shifted to the house, now a blazing inferno. Its heat was tearing into his back. "Momma?"

"She's gone, Catherine," he said as gently as he knew how. "I'm sorry. I wasn't in time to save her."

Her eyes shifted slowly back to him. She was rapidly going into shock. "No."

"Catherine." He took a step toward her. When she shook her head and stepped back, he felt an intense pain shoot through him greater than the severe burns to his back. "Please." His throat was growing thick with emotions he couldn't suppress. "Don't be afraid."

She opened her mouth to speak, but no sound came out. Her eyes drifted back to the burning remains of her home. "No…"

His sharp hearing picked up the distant sounds of emergency vehicle sirens. Someone had noticed the fire and called for help. They were running out of time. "Come with me, Catherine," he begged. "There's nothing for you here."

Her head snapped back to him. "No."

The windows of her car shattered and the interior burst into flames. In less than an instant, his arm was once again around her waist. He hauled her unwillingly away from the car, and managed to get to the edge of the woods before it exploded. He thrust her in front of him and onto the ground, and covered her as much as he could with his own body as another wave of intense heat swept over him. The pain to his back was intense. Nerves all ready laid bare screamed in agony. He hauled himself weakly to his hands and knees, and barely noticed when she scampered out from under him.

"Stay away from me," she croaked, her voice quickly leaving her. "Don't touch me."

"Catherine." His voice was so weak from the pain he was barely audible over the roar of the flames. "I'm not going to hurt you." He pulled himself slowly to his feet, braced himself against the nearest tree, and struggled to draw on his remaining strength. The sirens were coming closer. "You have to come with me. I won't hurt you." The pain in his back was growing more intense by the moment. His flesh cracked under the continued, radiant heat, his blood seeped from the wounds, dripping with increasing speed down his back. He'd need help soon, or his own life would be forfeited.

She backed up against a tree, her eyes wide with terror and grief. "You're…"

"You must give me a chance to explain," he said, trying hard to sound patient. "You don't have to stay with me. After I explain everything, if you still want to leave me, you'll be free to go. If you chose to stay here now, you'll never see me again."

She had gone too far into shock to understand. "Momma…"

"Listen to me," he said more sternly, sending her the briefest mental nudge, and nodded at the slight refocusing of her eyes. "Your mother is gone. The life you've known has come to an end. 'Tis time for you to move on." She shook her head slowly and pressed herself against the tree behind her. "The fire department will be here in moments. I can't be here when they arrive."

He took a step closer and saw her press herself more firmly against the tree. The fear in her eyes burned a hole in his chest. "I can protect you, provide for you. Catherine, I love you. Please…" The sirens were closer still. The lights of the vehicles were becoming visible. He had only a few moments remaining to make his escape. "Let me help you."

She glanced down the road, her gaze flicking to the red lights flashing above the trees. Her head turned to her house again, now reduced to a pile of burning timbers. Her mother's body lay somewhere in the ashes, likely burned beyond recognition. Her car was a melted heap of twisted metal. Some of the nearby trees had caught fire. She looked again at him, and he listened to the scattered thoughts flickering through her mind. She was trying to reconcile herself between thoughts of the man she loved and the monster who had flown to her rescue. The oppressive weight of her conflicting feelings was more than her mind could handle.

When she fainted, he caught her and cradled her in his arms. He wasted no time in taking flight. He cleared the tops of the mighty evergreens while the first headlights shone on the very spot where they had been standing. He hovered beyond sight and took a moment to study her slackened face. He'd caused her to fear him. That alone was more than he could bear. Now he was forced to take her unwilling into his lair, the one place he knew he could protect his secrets and keep her safe from the Community. He hoped with all his being he could make her understand. "Forgive me," he said as he turned for home.

* * * *

Joshua surged through the front door of his home, the unconscious Catherine hanging limply in his arms, startling Alex into dropping the magazine he was reading. He headed for the sofa and paused. Her dress was soaked in blood and dirt. The stains would never come out of the velvet upholstery, and he would be forced to replace the furniture rather than have a lasting reminder of the night's events in his home. He cast a quick thought to one of the chairs under the kitchen table. It moved as if on its own, and he placed her in it gently. He folded her arms on the table and laid her head on them. Only then did he sink to his knees.

Alex was by his side in an instant, a thousand questions glistened in his eyes. Without a word, he gingerly peeled the remains of his burnt shirt from his body. When Alex saw the condition of his back, he ran to the guest bathroom for first aid supplies, then spent the next half hour gently cleansing and dressing the badly burned flesh. When he finished and helped his master into a fresh shirt, Joshua pulled himself onto one of the other chairs while he went in the kitchen. He returned with a gallon jug full of crimson fluid and a glass.

Joshua didn't bother with the glass. He upended the jug and drained it of its contents in under a minute. Alex looked at the girl sitting unconscious at the table, shaking his head in horror at all the blood that covered every inch of her. "Catherine," Joshua confirmed voicelessly. "She doesn't yet know I've brought her here."

Alex stared at his master in shock. *You brought her against her will?*

"I had no choice." He explained briefly the tragic events that had just taken place. Alex's expression went from shock and horror to deep sympathy. "I couldn't leave her there," he concluded. "There was no time. I have to explain things to her and hope she can understand. If she doesn't," he shook his head. The pain of overwhelming sorrow did battle with the pain in his flesh. "If I can't regain her trust in me, I'll remove her memories and return her to what's left of her home."

Alex looked as if he were about to cry. He took the empty plastic jug back into the kitchen without comment. Reluctantly, Joshua focused his mental energy on her and brought her around. She moaned softly at first, and struggled against the compulsion to wake, as if unwilling to once again face the horror she'd witnessed, then raised her head with a start and gasped. She jumped from the chair in panic and stepped back against the wall, her eyes on his. "Where am I?" she asked, her voice almost non-existent from smoke damage.

"My home."

She gaped at him while her panic swelled to fear. "No."

He could not hide all the pain he was feeling, so he didn't try. "Catherine, please. You're in no danger. I won't touch you again. Let me explain."

She swept a lock of sodden hair away from her face, and stared at the blood on her palm in disbelief. Her gaze quickly swept her body, taking in all the blood, then shot him another fearful glance. He heard instantly what she was thinking, and winced inwardly. *How can a vampire possibly control himself in the presence of so much sustenance?* "No...."

He sighed heavily. "Alex will show you your room. There's a shower and a robe there. Get cleaned up and come back out here. Then we'll talk."

Her attention snapped to Alex, she stared at him for a moment, then recognition and suspicion joined the panic in her eyes. "Alex," she whispered over her tender throat. "My...my car...? But...but that was before we..." Her fear turned to dread as she returned her gaze to him. The vilest of speculations swept her thoughts while she struggled to put the puzzle together.

"I'll answer all your questions, love. Go clean up." He gestured to Alex, and watched his servant gently take her by the arm and lead her down the hall. Only then, and only briefly, did he allow himself the comfort of tears.

* * * *

Katie allowed Alex to lead her to the first bedroom down the hall, too stunned to think beyond the simple need to move. He took her around to the bathroom and pointed mutely at the soaps, shampoos, and other supplies stored under the sink along with the washcloths and towels, and the white terrycloth robe hanging from a hook behind the door. She nodded dumbly at him and caught sight of herself in the mirror. Thick crimson smudges covered her face. Her hair was matted and caked with dirt and blood. Her mother's blood. Shock gave way to realization, and the first tears dripped from her eyes, leaving pale traces down her dirty cheeks.

He gestured mutely at her, deep concern etched on his face. It took him several tries to make her understand he wanted to help her unzip what was left of her dress. When she nodded, he blushed slightly, performed the deed, and quickly left the room. She allowed her ruined dress to fall to the floor, peeled her undergarments off, and opened the glass shower door. After she turned on the water and adjusted the temperature, she took what she needed from the sink cabinet and stepped under the steaming spray.

She'd taken showers in school, but in large, communal chambers open to everyone in gym class. Having a private shower was something very different. She reluctantly gave in to the simple pleasure and allowed the evidence of the evening's tragedy to flow down the drain and out of sight. She lathered her hair three times, scrubbed herself until her skin was raw, and leaned her head back and let the steaming water run down her body. She wished soap and water had the power to wash more than physical evidence down the drain.

After a few minutes, she felt her mind clear enough to take in her surroundings. White marble tile gleamed brightly all around her, spattered here and there with blood and dirt. The fixtures appeared gold-plated. She splashed water on the tile, desperate to erase every reminder of her mother's gruesome death, and turned off the water. She dried herself with a towel that was thicker and softer than anything she'd ever held in her hands.

She scooped up her ruined clothes and pushed them into the trash basket next to the toilet, winced and rinsed her hands off in the sink. She used her washcloth to wipe up the stains left on the floor by her clothes, then put on the robe that was as soft and thick as the towel. Its weight made her feel almost safely clothed.

Soft, thick carpeting greeted her bare feet when she stepped out into the spacious bedroom. She thought her whole house could fit inside it. A big bed occupied one wall, flanked by wooden tables and lamps. On the bed, a white satin comforter shimmered under the soft light of the chandelier overhead. A large, mirrored dresser occupied the opposite wall. One overstuffed chair sat in the corner, covered in rich green velvet.

She studied herself in the mirror. Her face was pale, but unmarked. She pulled back the robe and winced at the deep bruises on her arms where her attacker had grabbed her. More bruises were on her leg, and her ankle was swollen where she'd kicked the table over. What amazed her was the fact she felt no pain. Even her back and the back of her head, where she'd slammed hard to the floor, didn't hurt. She decided she was probably too much in shock.

A hairbrush rested on the dresser beside a fine porcelain dish. She took off her grandmother's pearl jewelry and dropped it into the dish, then picked up the hairbrush and studied it thoughtfully.

I've prepared my guest room for you.

How long had he been planning to bring her here? Why did Alex bring her the LeBaron before she and Joshua had ever met? That question brought more she wasn't ready to entertain. She sat reluctantly on the foot of the bed and worked at her hair, slowly at first, then with increasing effort, until she'd worked out all the knots and her scalp ached. Then she knotted the robe tightly around her, sighed heavily in an attempt to relieve the anxiety cramping her chest, and reluctantly opened the bedroom door.

She found Joshua standing before the fireplace in the living room, adjusting firebrands with a pair of polished brass tongs. He turned his attention to her when she stepped away from the hall. "Come sit down," he told her, his voice gentle but firm. She felt the tone of command in his voice. She eyed him warily while she sat on the farther end of the deep blue, velvet sofa and pulled her legs under the robe. He took his seat in the matching easy chair, moving curiously slow and lacking his usual easy grace. He studied her for a moment, took in a deep breath, released it slowly, and closed his eyes.

"I was going to explain everything to you this weekend," he began, his voice much softer and more apologetic. "I didn't want you to be frightened of me." He opened his eyes to look at her again, and seemed to see the fear and disbelief she was feeling. "I'm sorry."

She struggled to find the will to speak. "I saw…" she squeaked, then winced at the growing pain in her throat.

"I know. Please try to understand. I would never have allowed you to witness such a thing. There was no time for subtleties. Your life was in danger. I had to act."

She let her eyes roam around the spacious living room. "Why…?"

"Why did I bring you here?" he asked for her. When she nodded, he said, "I know it wasn't your choice, and I can't apologize to you enough for acting without your consent. It was necessary. There wasn't time to handle the situation properly at your house." She gave him a look she hoped plainly said she didn't understand. "Catherine, true knowledge of the existence of vampires is forbidden to mortals. You know now. It is my responsibility to protect others like me from any harm that might result. If one of the others found I let you go uncontrolled, they'd destroy me, and kill you."

She shook her head and tried to speak. "Don't talk, Catherine. Listen." He made a few quick gestures to Alex, who quickly filled a glass and offered it to her. "Take it," he coaxed. "It is very old brandy. I've had that bottle for many years. You should find it quite mellow. It will help reduce the pain in your throat." She accepted it, nodded her thanks to the concerned looking servant, and took a cautious sip. The warmth of the brandy quickly spread to her stomach.

"I sense your efforts to deny what you saw. Vampires are real, and I really am one of them. Let's not waste time debating that fact. I'm not a cold-blooded killer–the truth is, I rarely drink from humans. A meat processing plant provides me with all the cow blood I need. I'm willing to pay for something they usually throw out, so no questions are ever asked. It sustains me well enough."

She took another, larger sip of the brandy, more to bolster her courage than for any other reason, and whispered, "What are you going to do to me?"

"I hope I don't have to do anything to you, love." Some more of his Scottish brogue came through in his voice, a habit she'd noticed in him when his feelings were too near the surface. "As you Americans say, the ball is in your court. If I can be certain you won't act on your newfound knowledge, I'll leave you be. For now, at least."

"And later?" she managed.

He sighed deeply. "I want you to take the time to think this through. Too much has happened tonight for you to make sense of it all. You need time to grieve for your mother. You may stay here as long as you wish. I'll help attend to your affairs as best I can. Concentrate first on putting that part of your life behind you. Then, after you've had a chance to calm down, I want you to think about us.

"We've only just begun to explore our love for each other, I know. If I haven't totally destroyed that tonight, if you decide you want to continue our relationship, everything will proceed as it has. I won't force anything on you unless you give me no other choice. I don't intend to drink from you," he added quickly when she widened her eyes, "but I will cause you to forget me, if the need arises. If you decide to leave, which you may do at any time, I will release you only after I've ensured the safety of the others."

He leaned forward to look at her more seriously. "I'll leave you back at your house with no memory of what happened. If you remember me at all, you'll have a vague recollection of a man you once knew, and the knowledge that it didn't work out between us. You'll be left to make a life for yourself on your own, as you might've done had we never met." He shook his head at the deep sorrow and confusion she knew he saw in her eyes. "I have no choice in this, Catherine. I'm treading dangerous ground. I find myself torn between the feelings I have for you and my duty to the others. Please believe me when I tell you this whole situation is causing me great pain."

She stared down at her empty glass for several moments. Tears brimmed her eyes and spilled down her cheeks. "I don't know what to do." She looked up to meet his eyes, and saw her pain mirrored in them. "I want this all to be a really intense nightmare. I want to wake up to the feelings I had before all this happened. I was happy. Now..." Her shoulders shook with unreleased sobs.

He rose from his chair and moved to kneel down beside her. When she pushed herself back into the sofa cushions, her eyes raised to his in panic, he held up a hand in a conciliatory gesture and stepped back. A tear dripped from his face and left a wet stain on his shirt that drew her gaze. "Stay," he whispered softly. "At least for a day. You're safe here. We can talk again tomorrow night. I'll tell you everything." He winced suddenly, groaned and quickly moved to sit stiffly on the edge of his chair.

"You're hurt."

He looked at her with pain burning in his eyes. "Protecting you from the fire was no small task," he said, a tight edge in his voice. "Vampires are as susceptible to flame as to sunlight. I'm badly burned."

She raised a hand to her mouth while more tears streamed down her cheeks. "I'm sorry."

He forced a smile. "'Twas not your fault. This will heal with rest and time. I'll recover from my burns much more quickly, I think, than I will the pain of losing you. I saved your life. I can bear anything knowing I protected you when you needed me."

Her eyes dropped to her empty glass again. "I don't know what to say."

"Just say you'll stay," he begged. "Give me a chance to make things right again. That's all I ask."

She looked up at him again and saw the intense hope in his eyes. "You won't hurt me."

"Never."

"I won't be forced to do anything I don't want to do."

"No, of course not."

She slowly nodded her head. Her tender throat choked on the sobs she was desperately trying to hold back. He nodded to Alex, who silently appeared beside her. "Go with Alex. He'll help you settle in for the night. Try and get some sleep."

She nodded again, rose, and followed Alex toward the hallway. She turned and looked back at him, feeling like she needed to say more, but the right words didn't come to mind. She turned away again and headed for the bedroom.

* * * *

Alex returned moments later to collect his master and help him to the back room. He helped Joshua out of his shirt and checked his bandages, then pressed a spot on the wallpaper next to the closet. A secret panel swung open silently to reveal a hidden chamber not much larger than the twin bed it contained. Joshua turned to Alex, captured his gaze, and mentally gave him instructions for the next day. He nodded his understanding and motioned for his ailing master to take his rest. Without a word, Joshua stretched himself face down on the bed, curled his arm around the scarf Catherine had made for him, and allowed the deep, healing rest he desperately needed take him beyond the pain. He barely noticed when Alex closed the panel behind him.

Chapter Twelve

Katie didn't believe she could sleep, but she climbed into the huge, soft bed anyway, still too much in shock to release her tears. She closed her eyes as the sun began to lighten the sky. Much to her surprise, it was mid-afternoon before she opened them again and winced at the bright sunlight streaming in through the window. The unmistakable smells of bacon and eggs wafted in to her, bringing a growl to her stomach. She reluctantly pulled herself into a sitting position and groaned at the stiff pains in her back and ankle. She was glad her head didn't hurt as well.

She got out of bed and stretched, then noticed a pair of jeans and a t-shirt lying across the arm of the chair. "Well, you can't run around in a robe all day," she chided herself softly, noticing with relief that the smoke she'd taken in the night before had not left lasting damage to her vocal chords. After she'd donned the clothes and cinched a belt tightly around her waist, she picked up the brush and smoothed her hair, then warily left her room and followed her nose to the kitchen.

Alex looked up and smiled when she rounded the corner, and finished dishing up breakfast. He put hers on the table and motioned for her to sit, and quickly produced a glass of orange juice. "Thank you," she said nervously. Alex gave a gesture and seated himself near her with his own plate. She ate her breakfast in silence. Under the circumstances, she didn't know what else to do. When she was done, he picked up her dish with another bright smile and headed for the kitchen.

While he cleaned up after breakfast, she looked around at the details she'd been too frightened and confused to notice before. The layout of the house was simple, but spacious. The floor under her feet was marble tile similar to that which adorned the bathroom. A graceful arc was cut around the solid oak table, and where the tile left off, thick, eggshell-colored carpeting took over.

The living room was furnished in deep blue velvet and polished oak. The walls were also eggshell in color, and bore only the most essential adornments–a painting, an oak and brass wall clock, a few candle sconces bearing crystal votive cups. A beautiful yet unpretentious crystal chandelier hung in the center. Everywhere she looked, she saw details that lent themselves to solid comfort, reflecting a great deal of wealth and taste without looking overdone and stuffy. Her new surroundings were so far removed from anything she'd ever known, so foreign, it added to the sensation that she'd stepped into a dream, like Alice falling through the rabbit hole. The problem was, this wonderland was fraught with dangers still far too incredible to fathom.

Alex appeared in front of her, gesturing, an inquisitive look on his face. "I'm sorry," she offered gently, hoping he could read lips. "I don't understand sign language." He understood, to her relief, but he pointed at her again and gestured. Then he tugged at her clothes and gestured again. "Yes, thank you for the clothes." When he shook his head in frustration, she realized she'd misunderstood. "Can you write?" she asked hopefully.

He rolled his eyes and slapped his forehead, dashed away, and returned a moment later with a pad and pencil. He quickly scribbled on the pad and handed the top sheet to her. After she'd read his hastily written note, she nodded her understanding. "I see. Okay, we're going shopping." He nodded. "Did he tell you to take me? Buy me things?" He nodded again and quickly wrote he was to buy her anything and everything she needed. She decided she had no choice but to accept whatever charity Joshua wished to offer. She couldn't go around without basic clothing, after all. "All right," she agreed slowly. "First, I want you to take me to my house." He shook his head, and she raised her hand to get his attention.

"Alex, the neighbors need to see me coming up the road and leaving. I have to go there for appearance's sake. How would it look if I never showed up? Then we need to visit the fire department, and probably the police. I don't think, under the circumstances, I should show up there in new clothes." At the word police, his face went pale and he emphatically shook his head again. She studied him thoughtfully for a moment. "He told you to keep an eye on me, didn't he?"

He slowly nodded, looking embarrassed. "Listen. I have to find out what happened to Momma. I need to…to claim…" She had to close her eyes for a moment to force back her tears. "Arrangements need to be made. The police will expect me to come looking for her. Do you understand?" He nodded again, a worried look in his eyes. "Don't worry, I won't tell them about Joshua. I won't even mention his name unless I have to. As far as they're concerned, I…I spent the night with friends. That's at least partly true. Besides, who would believe me?" She paused to think some more, surprised at how clear headed she felt, how logically ordered her thoughts were. She felt numb from the neck down, as if her heart had shifted into neutral. "I think I should pay Carl Foster a visit. Joshua said he'd help me. I assume that means providing for Momma's funeral. I think Mr. Foster can take care of that."

He nodded again, sat down in front of her, and laid a compassionate hand on her arm. "I'm okay," she said, guessing at his feelings. She looked around the room again, then back at Alex. "Where is he?" He made a simple gesture. "Sleeping? Here in the house?" He nodded, but then his eyes widened. "No, I'm not going to look for him," she assured him. "Are you…are you afraid of him?" He smiled softly and pressed both hands to his chest, and slowly shook his head. "You…like him? Love him maybe?" He nodded, picked up the pad and wrote again. "He's always been gentle with me, too," she said sadly. "But I'm afraid. Scared to death, in fact. What were his plans for me? Did he tell you anything?"

He nodded and wrote again. She shook her head. "That's not what I mean, Alex. I know he loves me. At least, I thought I did." She closed her eyes for a moment, and asked, "Was he planning on turning me into a vampire?" He saw the fear in her words, and smiled reassuringly while shaking his head. "Well, what, then? If I agree to stay with him…damn it! I'm mortal! I'll get old. Die some day. He'll always be…" She shook her head sadly. "This could never work out."

He put his hand on her sleeve to draw her attention and gestured, rolled his eyes and wrote on the pad again. "You're right," she said with a sigh. "I'll hear him out. I'm already in this up to my neck. Uh, no pun intended," she added, bringing a smile of amusement to his face. "Okay, do you have any shoes I can borrow?"

He gave her a pair of his old shoes, which were only a little too big for her. An extra pair of socks made them fit passably. Then they left on their errands. The first stop, of course, was to her house. When she saw the neighbors watching them travel up the road in the Sebring, a car they were sure to recognize, she smiled and waved at them. She did her best to act as if she didn't know what she would find. She didn't have to fake the troubled look on her face when they left a short time later.

The nearest fire station pointed her in the direction of the police station in town. When she inquired at the front desk, the officer led her to Lieutenant Hawkins' office. The lieutenant greeted her uncomfortably and motioned for her to sit down. "Your mother's body is in the county morgue," he said gently. "Did you see what happened?"

"No," she told him, "I spent the night with friends."

The lieutenant gave her a curious look. "Your car was found at the scene, Miss Mills."

"I went for a walk. I've been having trouble finding a job, and needed time to clear my head. I walked through the woods for a while, and found my way to their house. It was late by the time I got there, so I decided to spend the night."

"Uh huh," Hawkins said. "This your friend?"

She looked at Alex and nodded nervously. "One of them," she answered. "Am I under suspicion for anything?"

He relaxed in his chair. "No, of course not." He fingered the file on his desk. "There was a man in the house with her. Do you know who that might be?"

She did her best to act surprised. "A man? No. Momma never had any visitors. Well, one, but he didn't come by too often. I don't think she was expecting him last night."

"Does this man have a name," Hawkins asked in an annoyed tone.

"Carl Foster. He's an attorney."

Hawkins wrote the name down on his pad and nodded, then lifted a photograph from his file and slid it toward her. "Ever see this man before?"

She mentally braced herself and glanced at the photo, doing her best to keep from reacting to the face on the paper. It wasn't easy; she was afraid the terror she'd felt would show in her eyes the moment she saw the image of the pockmarked, leering man who had killed her mother. "No."

He withdrew the photo and placed it back in the file folder. "Richard Connor, age thirty-two, convicted in his teens for molesting his neighbor's eight-year-old girl. His body was found beside your mother's. We identified his remains through dentals."

"Never heard of him," she said carefully.

"Okay, here's what we think happened. The coroner's report says your mother's throat was slashed." He paused to hand her a box of tissues and looked more sympathetic. "Connor was found with a knife in his hand. We think he–I'm sorry–raped her, slit her throat, and slipped in her blood while trying to leave the scene. Maybe knocked himself out. He kicked over the oil lamp that started the fire."

Her tears flowed in earnest. "Oh, Momma…"

"Miss Mills, for what it's worth, I am sorry. We believe this is the same man we've been trying to track down for months. The evidence matches other cases we're investigating. Once we get a DNA match on him, we'll know for sure. The stories have been in all the papers."

"We don't get the paper," she said between sobs.

"Well, if it is him, your mother was his last victim." He paused for a moment while she blew her nose. "Is there any way we can reach you if we need more information?"

She hiccupped and blotted her eyes. "I've got nowhere to go." Her voice sounded hopelessly pathetically. "I'll probably stay with one friend or another until I figure out what to do. I'll keep in touch with Mr. Foster. He'll know where to reach me."

He stared at her for a moment or two, then added that information to his notes. "Very well, Miss Mills. Uh, about your mother's, er, remains…"

"I'll ask Mr. Foster to handle the arrangements."

"All right." He rose to his feet. "Thank you for coming by."

She nodded and left the station with Alex. When they reached the car, she asked, "Do you know where Mr. Foster's office is?" He nodded uncomfortably and started the car.

Carl Foster's office was located in a brick office building near the courthouse. A prim-looking secretary with a pinched face studied Katie through her thin spectacles. "Do you have an appointment?"

"No," she answered with as much bluster as she could manage. "Tell him Katie Mills is here to see him. Tell him it's an emergency."

The secretary picked up her phone and relayed the message to her boss doubtfully. The surprised look that came to her face told Katie what she needed to know. Carl appeared a moment later. "Katie! It's good to see you." He stopped abruptly when he saw the look on her face and Alex standing beside her, then, in a quieter tone, said, "Come into my office."

They followed him in silence, watched him close his inner door, flip the lock and move to his desk. He pressed a button on his phone, and said, "Nell, hold my calls please." Then he looked at her, a grim look clouding his handsome features. "Something must've gone terribly wrong if you're here with Alex," he observed while she seated herself in one of the two plush leather chairs in front of the massive mahogany desk. Alex silently took the other.

"I'm in trouble," she confirmed before Carl sat behind the desk. "Momma's d-dead."

His mouth dropped open as he sank into his chair. "Oh, Katie. I'm so sorry. Are you all right?"

"Of course I'm not all right."

He drew in a breath and held it for a moment. "I'm assuming Joshua was involved somehow."

She gave him the slightest nod. "I'm staying at his house…for now."

He nodded knowingly. "I see. Maybe you'd better tell me what happened." She opened her mouth, but closed it again, unsure how much she should tell him. "It's all right, Katie," he said when he saw her hesitate. "I've been in his service for a great number of years. Rest assured you can trust me with any details the police don't need to hear about. I'll need to know in case something should come up I need to derail."

She shot an uncertain glance at Alex, who nodded his silent confirmation. "I guess I should've known. How long...?"

"You first," he said in a gentle, but firm voice.

"There was a man...a rapist. He..."

A sob choked off her statement, but Carl seemed to understand instantly. "I heard the report on the radio this morning. I didn't realize it was your house. I'm so sorry."

"I guess Joshua sensed my terror. When I saw him flying down from the trees, when I saw his eyes...his..." She gave herself a sharp mental shake, and told Carl everything that happened from the moment Joshua arrived. It made her feel better to know she could talk to someone about what really happened. Letting it all out helped her to come to grips with the reality of it, and started at last the process of accepting the painful details.

He listened patiently and handed her a box of tissues when she broke down. While she pulled herself together, he wrote notes on his legal pad. "I'll make arrangements for your mother right away. Do you know where you want her buried?"

"Next to Daddy, if it's possible. I think she would've wanted that."

He nodded, his face holding a well-practiced, business-like expression. "I'll take care of everything. I'll let you know when her body is released and the service is scheduled. I assume a simple graveside ceremony will be sufficient, perhaps after sunset?"

She started to say it didn't matter, but when she considered Joshua's feelings, she nodded. He had, after all, been very fond of her. "That will work."

"You say the police will contact me if they need to talk to you? I'll look after your interests, of course. As well as Joshua's," he added, offering her a reassuring smile. She blew her nose and tried to smile bravely, and knew she'd failed when she saw the sympathy on the older man's face. "I think I understand what you're going through. Learning the truth about Joshua the way you did must have come as quite a shock."

"You could say that," she said, her voice trembling. "Personally, I think the word 'terrified' comes closer to describing my feelings at this point."

He sat back in his chair and laced his fingers together on his desk. "He's a kind man. In all the years I've known him, I've never witnessed the anger you describe. His feelings for you must be strong if he lost control that way."

She wadded her tissue into a tight ball in her fist while she studied the assurance in Carl's eyes. "How did you meet him?" she asked, her voice barely a whisper. "Help me understand how anyone could...would want to..."

"It's a simple story," he interrupted gently, "though the telling is difficult. It was, oh, I'd say, fifty years ago, give or take."

She gaped at him for a moment in shock. "You don't look older than...forty?"

At that, he smiled. "Thank you. Longevity is one of the benefits of service. I was twenty-six when I met him. My life to that point was, well, let's call it an unqualified disaster. I lost an important case, and an apprenticeship, with a law firm in Olympia. I took to drinking, which drove my fiancé to leave me not long after. I was, as they say, on a slippery skid to a messy end the night he found me."

He looked embarrassed as he leaned forward on his desk. "I sat alone in a dive on the outskirts of town, drank as much as I thought I could hold and still walk, then bought the rest of the whisky bottle from a greasy bartender and headed for my pickup and the loaded thirty-eight I kept in the glove box. I fully intended to finish off the bottle and put a bullet through my head."

"You never made it to your truck," she guessed.

"Oh, I got to the truck, all right. Pulled out my gun and checked the ammo. My hands were shaking so bad I had to set it down on the dashboard. He was in the passenger side so quickly, and so silently, I dropped the bottle and spilled whisky all in the carpet. He told me he knew what I was planning, understood my despair, and that he could help me in ways I could never imagine." He laughed softly at the memory. "I thought he was from some mission or public service office until he...revealed himself. I'll admit I thought I was hallucinating at first, and then I was scared right down to my socks, but he spoke softly of his need for my service, assured me he would treat me well. He led me patiently into believing in him. I never once felt he was trying to force my cooperation. Giving myself over to him was a hell of a lot easier than eating a bullet."

"Did...didn't it hurt when he...?"

"Not at all," Carl said with a genuine smile. "Once I'd given my consent, I felt his will come over me. A wave of calm washed over me, erasing my apprehension. He had my loyalty, and my blood, before I realized it happened. Ah, Katie, he's given me so much more than I could ever have given him through the years. I owe him everything, and will do anything he asks without hesitation, even if I were not compelled to do so."

She felt her own blood drain from her face at the thought of his graphic account. "I don't think I can be that brave."

"Then it will surprise you to learn I've allowed him to feed from me on a number of occasions since." He smiled at her shock. "He always asks my permission, though I know he could easily demand it if he chose and I would be powerless to resist, and he's always more than gentle."

She looked down at her lap and studied the wadded tissue in her hand. First Alex, and now Carl, had spoken of Joshua's kind and gentle nature, reminding her once again of how well he had treated her since they met. He'd guided her carefully through difficult times, uncertain friendship, and finally to trust and love, seemingly without skipping a beat. Facing the truth of his existence was a greater difficulty than anything she'd ever experienced. She had a hard time believing he would be able to guide her into this new reality as easily. "I guess I have a lot to think about."

He rose to his feet and rounded his desk. By the time he'd come to her chair, she was standing. He put his hands on her shoulders gently. "He'll give you all the time you need to adjust, I'm sure of that. In the mean time, if there's anything else I can do…"

"Thank you." She fought to hold back fresh tears when he put his arms around her.

Once they were again in the Sebring, she looked at Alex, sniffed, and said, "Okay, now we can go shopping." He smiled boyishly and brought the car to life with a roar.

It was early evening by the time they returned to Joshua's home, an embarrassing load of packages filling the trunk and spilling into the back seat. Although she'd begged him to shop at a discount store, he'd taken her to the mall. By the time they left, she had everything from clothing, socks and underwear, to accessories, personal products, and even a blow drier. Her every conceivable need had been seen to. She complained more than once that Alex was spending far too much on her, but he kept on smiling in the boyish way he had and pointing to something new. She spent the next hour removing tags and putting her new possessions away with the uncomfortable feeling she was moving in for good.

Twilight was near at hand by the time she finished and returned to the dining room, where Alex was setting out a simple dinner of soup and sandwiches. She sat down and ate anxiously, knowing with the setting sun

Joshua would make his appearance. He took longer than she expected to emerge, so her dinner was almost gone before she felt him watching her from the hallway. When her head turned sharply in his direction, Alex jumped from his seat. He was leaning heavily against the wall, looking pale, weak and exhausted. Alex helped him to the nearest chair as carefully as he could.

He offered her a weak smile. "Are you settling in okay?"

She lowered her eyes uncomfortably. "Yes. Thank you for...Alex took me shopping today. He told me you..."

"I instructed him to see to your needs."

"He was awful generous."

"Less than you deserve," he said dismissively. Alex laid out fresh bandages and began seeing to his back. "Tell me what you did today. I want to hear everything."

She shot a nervous look his way. "I didn't tell anyone what happened. Except Mr. Foster–I thought he should know."

He winced when Alex pulled too hard at his bandages. "A wise precaution. Still, I'd like you to tell me. I need to listen to the sound of your voice. It will distract me from what Alex must do."

A sudden surge of sympathy swept through her at the thought of the painful wounds he'd suffered on her account. She drew in a nervous breath and reviewed the day's events. She paused when he grunted and closed his eyes tightly, and looked to see what Alex was doing. The bandages had bonded to the wounds on his back, and when he pulled them loose he caused fresh bleeding. She put her hand on his to gain his attention, and said, "You should wet that down first. It will soften the bandages." She looked doubtfully at Joshua's back. "I wish we had sterile saline or something. That could become infected."

"I won't suffer infection," Joshua assured her quietly.

She nodded reluctantly and sent Alex after some towels while she filled a bowl with tepid water from the kitchen tap. She reluctantly took over the job when she saw Alex handling it too roughly, and sympathy battled her fear while she concentrated on the task at hand and her continued narrative instead of the subject of her labor. Joshua rested his head on his arms against the table, and kept himself still while she worked. By the time she'd finished removing the bandages, she had reported all of the day's events.

She stepped back to look at his wounds. "This doesn't look too bad." Alex gestured to her, and wrote quickly on his pad that it had been much worse the night before. She did see, around the edges of the remaining scabs, evidence of newly formed flesh.

"I heal quickly," Joshua told her. "Another day or two, and that should clear up."

She nodded thoughtfully. "Well, I hate to put more bandages on it like that, but I can't leave it open to the air. You don't want it to dry out and crack." She scratched her head for a moment, then turned to Alex. "Do you have any ointment? Petroleum jelly maybe?" Alex nodded and left for the bathroom. He returned a few moments later with a jar of ointment.

She opened the jar and poised herself behind Joshua. "This might hurt a little," she said nervously. As tenderly as she could, she applied the ointment to his raw back, and coated gauze with more ointment before covering the wounds. She taped another thick layer over that and took a moment to survey her work. She rested one hand on the table and said, "That should do it."

"Thank you. You have a tender touch." He moved his hand to gently cover hers. She jerked away and stepped back abruptly, instantly filled with irrational fear. He looked up at her, and the deep pain in his eyes made her turn away.

"I'm sorry. I can't help it."

He sighed and lowered his head back onto his arms. "I won't hurt you."

She seated herself at the far end of the table and stared at him in silence. He pulled himself slowly upright and closed his eyes, his face as pale as old ashes. Alex studied his master in silent empathy, then solemnly rolled up his sleeve and offered the ailing vampire his wrist. Her anxiety leveled jumped ten notches.

"No, my friend," he said, brushing his arm away. "The contents of the refrigerator will suffice." He shook his head and thrust his arm back. He pushed it away again and shot an uncomfortable glance by way of gesture to her. Alex slapped the table a couple of times and gestured sharply. "Are you yelling at me?"

He responded by holding his arm to him again, his fist clenched in defiance, a stern look firmly set in his aquamarine eyes. Reluctantly, he took his servant's wrist in hand and rubbed his thumb lightly across the underside. "You don't have to watch," he said to her.

She stared, mesmerized by fear and morbid curiosity, while his eyes changed from soft, chocolate brown to a feral yellow/red color; not the hot red she'd seen the night before. The expression on his face was soft, tender, as he put his lips to Alex's wrist. Alex stroked his master's head lovingly while he drank. There was not even a trace of pain or fear on his face. He leaned against the table for support, and when Joshua released him, he dropped heavily onto the nearest chair.

She jumped up and ran to the refrigerator, and brought Alex a tall glass of orange juice, which he accepted and drank gratefully. Then she turned angry eyes to Joshua. "Why?"

He returned her gaze with one of patient tolerance. His eyes had returned to normal, and color was returning to his cheeks. "I needed it. I don't expect you to understand."

"Then explain it to me." She returned to her chair on the opposite side of the table, where she felt she could study him in relative safety.

He sighed heavily and shook his head. "Animal blood can sustain me for a long time, but it is substandard nutrition. Healing wounds this severe requires a lot of energy. Alex's gift, along with your tender mercies, will allow me to heal all the more quickly." He smiled affectionately and tousled Alex's short blond hair, bringing an equal smile to his servant's face. "Alex knows my needs well. He cares for me too much, I think. This is the first time I've taken blood from him since the night we met."

She gave Alex an appraising glance, afraid to speculate on how old the young man really was. "Mr. Foster told me about the night you…How you…"

"It's all right, Catherine. It does not embarrass me to speak of such things. Carl was the first. I took control of Alex perhaps two years later."

"Are there others?"

"There have been in the past, though none alive today. Once I release a person from their service, the benefits they enjoy come to an end. They accepted their servitude willingly. I didn't force it on any of them. Most, like Carl and Alex, had little or nothing in their normal lives to hold them. Thralls can live up to three times their expected remaining lifespan, and are remarkably resistant to illness."

Alex was gazing at her with a look that begged her to understand. "Where did you find him?"

"I came across Alex when he was a lad of fourteen, a wild animal in a child's body, living on the streets and eating from garbage cans. He was sitting in a dark alley chewing on the crumbs from someone else's plate, and I guess I felt sorry for him. I took him to a nearby hotel and got him cleaned up, though it was all I could do to hold him still long enough to wash the grime out of his hair. If there is one constant in this world, it is a boy's inherent dislike of soap and water." Alex gave his master a rueful smile. "I bought him a decent meal and watched him devour every bite as if it were his last, then ordered all the chocolate cake he could hold. Once he'd eaten his fill, I gave him all the money in my wallet and tried to send him on his way.

"He followed me to my car, though I tried several times to make him leave. You see, he was innocent. I didn't want him involved with me. I even let him see my fangs in hopes I might frighten him away." He gave a shrug, and winced at the tug to his bandages. "Who could he tell? He had no concept of language, didn't even know his own name."

"What made you, uh, take him?"

His expression gently transformed to one of deep fondness. "The lad stood there, staring at me for the longest time, studying me. Perhaps he saw in me the loneliness I refused to acknowledge. Perhaps he was only considering his own. I saw in his eyes such need, such trust. It was then I realized my kindness to him was the first he'd ever received. He surrendered himself to me completely and without fear, but also without the understanding I normally require. I accepted his loyalty with the greatest reluctance.

"It took two years to teach him the basics of language. Rather like teaching a baby, I'd imagine. Carl helped me adopt the lad, an easy process in those days. I gave him a name, took him into my home, and now he attends to my needs. His devotion to me is beyond measure. It's been a mutually satisfactory arrangement."

She studied the two men uncomfortably for a moment. "How long have you been a vampire?" she asked quietly.

His smile lifted a little more. "Most of what I told you a year ago had basis in truth, though I may've glossed over some of the details for the sake of mortal understanding. I was born in 1714 in an obscure little village on the Scottish moors–a lowlander. My parents were both dead before I was a lad of nine. Our Laird fostered me to his accountant, and I learned a great deal from him with regards to financial matters. I stayed in his service well into my adult life.

"Just after my twenty-second birthday, I met an extraordinary creature by the name of Antonia." His gaze softened at the memory. "She was an exotic woman, much like your friend Nicole, and she had me captivated from the moment her eyes locked with mine. She was traveling with a band of merchants; gypsies, I suppose you'd call them. I watched her dance in the light of their campfire. Her every movement enticed me to thoughts both dark and erotic. She made me feel as if she was dancing for me alone, and when the evening was over she led me to her bed and taught me pleasures a man can die from." His smile broadened when she felt her face redden.

"They stayed a week, and I visited Antonia's tent nightly. While they were preparing to leave, she offered me the opportunity to join her. I believed myself in love with her, and accepted her dark gift believing she felt the same. When she brought me across, I felt the most incredible pleasure a mortal can experience. It was so sensual; so erotically seductive."

"Weren't you scared?"

"Perhaps a little, at first, but my feelings were strong. I couldn't bear to part from her. She taught me how to care for myself, taught me how to use my powers and relish what I had become. We stayed together for little more than a year. When I found her sporting with another mortal, I was crushed. I left her that night, and never visited her bed again."

"How sad."

He shrugged. "I quickly discovered it wasn't love I felt for Antonia. We're still friends, after a fashion. She is, after all, my master. I haven't seen her since I moved here."

"What's it like? Being a vampire, I mean. Is it anything like in the legends?"

"Legends usually bear little resemblance to truth. Human supposition adds half-truths and sensationalism to anything it cannot explain logically. Although I must avoid contact with the sun, I do not have to sleep when the sun rises. Most of us prefer to, because the nighttime suits us and it is more convenient. Older vampires are said to have the ability to resist the powers of the sun for short periods. I do not require a coffin to take my rest, though there are some with a more morose sense of humor who seem to prefer it.

"My body is very much like your own, with a few exceptions. My normal temperature is lower than yours. My hair and beard will grow if I don't expend the energy to prevent it. Many vampires do just that, but I prefer to care for myself as I did when I was mortal." He paused to shrug again. "Some habits are hard to break. I can survive for long periods in an airless environment. My lungs do not crave oxygen as yours do. My heart still functions, but with much more grace than a mortal's, its beat imperceptible to casual notice, which is what probably spawned the popular assumption that vampire hearts are dead and still.

"I have an aggressive and persistent physiology. I heal quickly and am virtually immortal, since my body regenerates itself each time I rest. I must drink blood to survive; that much is true. My stomach will not tolerate solid foods, though I've forced myself to eat with mortals for appearance sake. The shared consumption of meals is an integral part of your culture and rather irritatingly expected, especially during business functions. In those cases, I've had to purge myself when the first opportunity presented itself, which is why I avoid eating whenever possible. I do take a glass of wine or scotch from time to time. Alcohol, sadly, does not affect me in the way it does mortals, but I still enjoy the flavor.

"I feel everything, pain, pleasure, emotion, much more intensely than mortals do. I see and hear with sharper clarity. I am a solid entity, reflecting light and casting shadows as you do, and can, therefore, be photographed and seen in mirrors. There is very little supernatural magic involved."

"You have supernatural powers."

"My mental disciplines are sharpened. I can probe and even force the minds of lesser creatures; bend them to my will. I can mask my presence from mortals to avoid notice. I am able to cause fires and move objects with the slightest thought. I can move with much greater speed and agility than any other creature on earth, and when the situation requires it, I can fly." When her eyebrows shot up in surprise, he added, "No, you didn't imagine it. It's a simple manipulation of the elements. I don't turn into a bat."

She studied her hands thoughtfully for a moment. "You're not invincible."

"No. Even momentary exposure to the sun causes severe burns. I'm extremely susceptible to the heat and radiation. Within minutes, I can become burned beyond the ability to protect myself. 'Tis, as I understand it, a very painful death, lingering in the soul long after the body ceases to exist. A stake through my heart can kill me, just as it will any other living thing, but I can assure you I wouldn't be likely to lie still and let it happen. It's been tried before. I am not affected by religious symbolism, garlic or silver, but I do bleed freely. I can become quickly drained beyond my ability to recover if I were cut badly enough."

"You kill people," she said with nervous conviction.

He winced. "Only when the need arises. In fact, in my entire existence, I've taken the lives of only a handful of souls. When I do feed, I never take more than my prey can afford."

She nodded slowly. "Now I understand your reaction to that movie we went to see. Okay, what did you do after you left Antonia?"

"I traveled Europe for a few months, wandering aimlessly, you might say, trying to get a handle on what I had become, how I should spend eternity. I acquired a home deep in the woods near the Seine, and not long after that I met Jeanette."

"She's the one who betrayed you."

He nodded, some of the pain from that memory reflected in his eyes. "She hurt me deeply."

She did some quick calculations in her head. "You've been alone for…for almost three centuries?"

"Aye. After what happened with Jeanette, I couldn't bring myself to trust another mortal. I've traveled from town to town, country to country, living the life of a recluse. I had convinced myself it was the life I was meant to live. I even believed I enjoyed it…until I found you."

He must've sensed her dwelling on Jeanette's fate, comparing it to her own. "It wasn't I who killed her," he said, interrupting her thoughts. "There are those who jealously guard our secrets. Enforcers. When they learned what happened, they killed Jeanette and her accomplices. They would have destroyed me as well, but as I was a fledgling, and the immediate threat posed by my carelessness had been eliminated, they let me go with a warning." He looked at her with deep concern in his eyes. "That's why I found it so hard to tell you the truth. If anyone discovers I've left you uncontrolled, with knowledge that can pose a serious threat to the vampire Community, both of our lives will be forfeited."

The weight of his words sank uncomfortably to the pit of her stomach. "What made you decide I was worth the risk?"

"'Twas a twist of fate that put me in your path. You yourself were the direct cause of my involvement with you."

"Me?"

"Aye." He looked abashed. "You put your arms around me in simple affection and trust one night long ago. I lost myself to you at that moment."

She shook her head with a frown. "I only met you a year ago."

"No, love," he said sadly. "We met for the first time when you were eight years old, walking home from a friend's house. I had just left a campsite full of drunken hunters—a most unscrupulous lot. I sensed in you such innocent joy and strength, I felt compelled, somehow, to protect you from them."

The memory of that long-forgotten night abruptly jumped to her mind's eye. The shadowy image of her forest guardian appeared with crystal clarity, an image, she realized, that closely resembled the man she had come to know. "That was you?" she asked, her voice barely above a whisper.

He nodded. "You offered your trust to me so completely that night.

When you gave me that hug, you captured my heart. I tried to stay away from you, but I was unable to resist. You initiated a bond between us I could not break. It wasn't physical attraction that drew me to you, nothing that sinister, I assure you, but something deeper; something I can't put a name to. I found myself assisting in your life whenever you had need of me. 'Twas I who sent Carl to you when your father died with money meant to appear as a legitimate insurance benefit. I made arrangements with the man who sold your mother his house at a fraction of what it was worth. I protected you from a lurking rapist when you were fifteen, scared away any wild predators that picked up your scent."

She glanced at Alex, and back at Joshua, feeling the unsettling beginnings of belief. "So that *was* your car."

He nodded in confirmation. "I sold it to your mother through Carl when I learned of your desire for it, and for less than it was worth, so you would have something of mine, even if you couldn't know where it came from." He paused to study her, as if assessing her reaction. "It wasn't until I saw you at the fair last year, and saw what an exceptionally beautiful young woman you'd become, that my thoughts and feelings for you changed. I became attracted to you. I fought it. Alex can tell you how upset, how angry I was with myself for allowing you to have such an effect on me, but I had no choice. With that one, simple, innocent embrace, you changed my world irrevocably."

She sat in silent contemplation for several minutes. "What did you plan to do with me?"

He gave her a desperately hopeful look. "I wanted only your love. I hoped, if I were careful, if I explained my situation to you in a way you could understand, you would accept what I am, learn to trust me and…agree to become my wife."

She shot him a surprised glance. Any doubts she might've had regarding his feelings for her fled with his last word, which he spoke so softly it brought a lump to her throat that she swallowed hard to control. "Were you going to turn me into a vampire?"

"I would never have asked it of you. All I wanted was a brief moment in time I could cherish for the rest of eternity."

She shook her head. "I'll get older, and one day I'll die. You'll always be as you are now–young and…and handsome."

"And I would give you my love every day for the rest of your life, even when you become old enough to be my grandmother."

She worked her mouth silently before she asked, "What about children?"

He looked down at his hands for a moment. She thought she saw regret in his eyes. "I cannot give you children, love. I had hoped what I do have to offer you would be enough."

She felt his sorrow. It raised her own. "What happens now? You can't let me leave here, knowing what I know."

"Have your feelings for me changed?"

The sorrow in his voice brought yet another lump to her throat, one she had a hard time breathing around. "I don't know. Maybe this is still too much of a shock. Maybe everything is too new, too wild. A part of me wants to accept all this, to trust you in spite of what I saw. I promised myself last night that nothing was more important than the way I felt about you. But now…"

"Now I've caused you to fear me," he finished for her. "Even the touch of my hand brings you terror. Do you think it will always be so?"

"I don't know. Maybe, if you're patient with me, I can learn to trust you again. I want to, I really do. I can't control how I feel. I don't want to be afraid. I know how much it hurts you."

He smiled and shook his head. "Let's give it time. You may stay as long as you like. I won't push. My feelings for you haven't changed, and never will. When you're ready, I'll still be here for you." He rose painfully to his feet. "Now, my dear, I'm afraid I need to retire. My injuries have weakened me greatly. We can talk again tomorrow night."

"I'll be here, Joshua," she said with resolve. "We can try to work this out. And I promise you can trust me. Alex doesn't need to guard me, your secrets are safe."

"I know. I trust you, but I'd prefer it if you had Alex with you, just the same. He might be able to protect you. Please don't leave the house at night without me. If one of the others were to find you," he shook his head. "I don't want to think what will happen."

She found herself wanting to smile at his concern. "All right," she agreed solemnly. He nodded his satisfaction and disappeared down the hall.

She rose and paced the living room thoughtfully. She'd promised herself she would accept his secrets, no matter the cost, and make him know how much she loved him. She never dreamed the cost would be so high, or that her love for him could ever be in doubt.

She sank onto the sofa and closed her eyes. Did she still love him? She wasn't sure anymore, and that realization brought tears to her eyes. She recalled the feelings she had during their last moments in the clearing. In her mind, she pictured him holding her close, kissing her passionately, and taking her further than he was willing to go last night. Then, against her will, she saw him pull back, eyes glowing red, fangs gleaming in the moonlight. With a startled gasp, she opened her eyes and jumped from the sofa.

Alex was watching her from the kitchen. When she jumped up in panic, he rushed to her side and put a comforting hand on her arm. "Oh, Alex. What am I going to do?"

He shook his head slowly in mute response.

"I want to trust him, but I'm so afraid." She took his hand and studied the wrist he had offered to his master. Thinking she'd chosen the wrong one, she took the other and touched it gently. "There's no mark. He bit you. I saw it. How can that kind of wound heal so quickly?" Alex shrugged and shook his head.

"Did it...did it hurt?" Again he shook his head. "Why?" He held her gaze silently with an expression of profound trust and devotion for the man who was his master. She sank back down onto the sofa and shook her own head. "I don't understand any of this." She buried her face in her hands and repeated to herself, "What am I going to do?"

Alex put his hand on her shoulder, and when she looked up at him, he smiled softly and gestured in the direction of her bedroom. "Yeah." She rose to her feet with a heavy sigh. "I guess you're right. It's been a long day." She returned to her room, stripped her clothes, slid beneath the heavy covers, and surrendered herself to sleep she hoped would not be plagued by the nightmares she felt almost certain would come.

Chapter Thirteen

"Catherine, it's time to go," Joshua said softly. She sat beside the mound, seemingly oblivious to anything but her own thoughts. He reached down to touch her shoulder lightly in an attempt to draw her attention. She shrugged away from his hand and continued to stare silently at the freshly laid turf covering Natalie's grave.

He turned away quietly, took Carl by the arm and led him a short distance from the gravesite. "I'm at a loss," he confided with a sigh. "Catherine has spoken nary a word in the past two days."

"She's in a lot of pain," the older man said, glancing at her in sympathy.

"Aye, but so am I." He could no longer hide the anguish in his voice. "I wish to share this with her, help her through it. Let her help me. She won't let anyone, even Alex, near her."

Carl considered for a moment. "Is she still afraid?"

"She will come to me when her nature requires it, but only to aid me with my injuries. Her touch is soft and tender while she treats my wounds, and I sense the caring in her heart. If I remain still..." he paused to shake his head. "The moment I reach out to her, she turns from me. Her fear is a palpable force."

"Maybe she needs more time. She'll come around eventually."

"I've been patient, but even I have my limits. I don't know what I can do to help her."

"Sometimes a firmer hand is called for at times like this," Carl advised.

"I won't force her into my arms," he replied sharply, still keeping his voice low.

"There are kinds of force that do not require supernatural powers," Carl said just as sharply. He went to her, put his hand on her shoulder and said firmly, "Katie, let's go."

"Leave me alone," she said quietly, shrugging from his grasp.

"Come, now," he insisted, lifting her to her feet and turning her to him. "Your mother is at rest. It's time to let her go and move on."

She raised her eyes to his for a moment, her face a dull, lifeless masque, then lowered her head in silent submission. He put his arm gently around her shoulders and guided her back to Joshua's car.

Tears came later that night as she lay in her bed. Joshua went to her at once, entering her room so stealthily she didn't notice his presence until he spoke. "I'm here for you, love," he said thickly. "Let me help." She opened her eyes for the briefest glance, rolled away and sobbed harder while the grief inside her swelled. He rounded the bed, knelt until his face was level with hers, and whispered, "I share your sorrow. Don't shut me out." His heart shattered when she pulled herself into a tight ball, painful sobs wracking her body.

With a silent sob of his own, he sat in the corner chair, closed his eyes and gently opened his mind to her. His need to share her pain, if only in that small way, was too great to ignore. The profound, searing despair in her heart tore through him like unseen claws, but he bore her misery and listened to the random memories than flickered in her mind. Foremost, at first, were scenes of her mother, her home–scenes filled with comfort and love lost forever, things he expected to find as she dwelled on her loss.

When her thoughts turned to him, he stiffened in surprise. Only his image was there in her mind, surrounded by memories of her feelings and dawning hopes. "That man loves you still." His gentle voice brought another cry of despair, and he watched her mind's eye paint him in shades of gray and black, the only color being the shocking red fire of his anger. Fear and the sense of love both newly born and tragically lost swept through her, and so into him, tasting as bitter and dry as an unripe persimmon. He kept silent vigil, hoping his presence would be enough, until at last she'd cried herself to sleep. He placed a gentle kiss on her forehead before retreating to his lair.

* * * *

She stayed in her room, passing each day in retreat, drawing herself farther and farther into a world of her own making. When hunger drove her too firmly, she crept out of her self-made prison to pilfer snacks from the refrigerator, which she consumed while standing over the sink with little more than mechanical indifference. Then she'd retreat once again, usually slipping back to bed to take solace in the relative oblivion of sleep. If the other occupants of the house made any sounds at all, she didn't hear or care. In fact, she lacked all curiosity of people and events passing around her.

On a night little more than a week after the funeral, she woke to the quiet ringing of the phone in the kitchen and the mellow tones of Joshua's voice. She closed her eyes again, drawing on the bland numbness that had settled firmly inside her like a heavy blanket that protected her from feeling anything at all. She heard his voice again, less than an hour later, and was taken by surprise by the voice that accompanied him.

Her door opened and footsteps moved to her bed, but she ignored them until a deep voice demanded, "Get up."

"Go away, Carl. I don't feel good."

She tried to roll away from him, but he grabbed her firmly by both upper arms and jerked her roughly to her feet. "Oh, no, young lady, you're coming with me." She looked at him in surprise at his irritated tone. His eyes swept over her, taking in her rumpled clothing and tangled hair with a look of growing anger. Without another word, he took her by the wrist and propelled her, stumbling and uncooperative, out of the house and into the woods.

After he had spun her around and deposited her none too gently onto a long-dead log, she managed to sputter, "What's this all about?"

"You. This," he said, sweeping his hand to indicate her disheveled condition. "How long has it been since you even bothered to take a shower? It's not doing you any good, sequestering yourself in your room day and night." He put his fists on his hips and glowered. "So help me, I should turn you over my knee and put a hand to your scrawny rear."

She lowered her head and whispered, "It doesn't matter anymore."

"Like hell it doesn't! Okay, you lost your mother. I'm sorry to sound cold about this, but that's life. Natalie would hate to see you like this. She wanted you to be happy."

"Would she have wanted me to live with a vampire?"

"She thought the world of Joshua, and you know it." He took a deep breath in an obvious effort to calm himself. "You're not the only one suffering. This morbid depression you're surrendering to is only making a bad situation worse." He sat down beside her and pulled her hand into his. "You lost a mother, and faith in the man you loved. Joshua believes he's lost the most precious gift that ever entered his lonely existence. The difference between the two of you and what I've lost is you still have each other, if you can bring yourself to accept it."

A frown tugged at her eyebrows. "What are you talking about?"

He rose abruptly and took two quick steps away, then stopped and put a hand against a tree. She was surprised when his shoulders shook with silent sobs. "Your mother was...we were lovers."

"I'm sorry. I never...she never told me."

"We didn't want you to know. Not until you and Joshua were married. I thought, once the two of you were settled, I could ask him how he wanted to deal with our feelings for each other."

She thought about the difficulties he'd have faced, loving a normal woman when he aged more slowly and served a man who didn't age at all. Her thoughts turned to the difficulties she herself would've faced, maintaining a relationship with her mother while being married to an immortal. A belated feeling of dread settled in the pit of her stomach. "What would he have done, do you think?"

"I'm not sure. I intended to ask him to release me, so I could live out a normal life with her."

"He'd have had to make you both forget about him, wouldn't he?"

"Likely," he said, leaving her to think of consequences.

"It wouldn't have worked," she decided. "Momma wouldn't have willingly surrendered her memories of me, and if I was with Joshua…."

"Yeah," he interrupted with understanding in his voice. "In the end, how he dealt with your mother would've had little to do with my feelings for her."

"He would've had to take her," she realized. "Oh, this gets more complicated the more I think about it."

He sighed heavily and returned to sit on the log. "Well, none of that matters now, does it? We can sit here and speculate on what might have been all night, and not accomplish a thing. The best we can do is let go of the past and move on. Natalie would have wanted it that way."

"It's not that easy."

"No, young lady, it's not." His irritation was returning. "Let me ask you a question, and I want a straight, from-the-heart answer. Are you still in love with him?" She hesitated over his question, finally answering with a slow nod. "Then pull out that strong character of yours, and do something about it."

"I don't think I can be that brave."

He took her chin in his hand and forced her to look at him. "You have a lot of courage in you, if you can find it. I love you like the daughter I never had but always wanted. I want what's best for you, and, my loyalty to Joshua aside, I'd like to see you settle in with him. He's…you're good for each other."

She tried to smile, but had to settle for a weak nod. "I'll try," she promised.

He followed her silently back into the house, and she glanced uncertainly at Joshua, who stood near the fireplace with a stoic expression on his face. She looked back at Carl, who was standing inside the still-open front door, and saw him watching her with a frown on his face. After raising a hand to her tangled hair, she headed for her room. Just before she closed the door, she heard Carl's stern voice say, "Now it's your turn," and wondered what he had to be irritated at Joshua about.

Could it be Joshua had been too patient with her? He had been leaving her alone, seemingly unwilling to interfere with her need for solitude. She'd thought maybe he'd been giving her time to sort things out in her head, but after her talk with Carl she realized what she'd really been doing was giving in to the kind of depression that would've probably killed her. She heard Joshua make a sharp comment, and though she couldn't make out his words, she felt his growing agitation. For a moment, she was tempted to return to the living room and intervene, but decided she didn't want to witness any more of Joshua's anger. Instead, she headed for the bathroom and a quick shower.

While she leaned her head under the hot spray to rinse out the shampoo, she thought she heard a loud thud, as of something heavy falling. She poked her head out of the shower stall, water and shampoo running into her eyes, and listened intently, but heard only the sound of the water. She shrugged and finished her shower. She was drying her hair when she thought she heard a muffled crash, and quickly turned the dryer off to listen. Again, silence. With a frown, she pulled on a pair of jeans, laid a sweater beside her on the foot of the bed, and started brushing her hair. A loud bang against her wall, followed by the sound of shattering glass and a male voice grunting in protest, made her jump to her feet. She grabbed her sweater and pulled it over her head as she dashed for her door.

The living room was in shambles. Cushions rested half on the floor and half on the sofa in disarray. Joshua's easy chair had tumbled backward and lay beside the overturned side table. By the window, she saw the remains of a once beautiful dish garden, the foliage crushed beyond hope, the container no more than a shattered pile of ceramic and potting soil. The beautiful wood stand that had supported it could only serve now as kindling. On the back wall, outside her bedroom, the antique oak bar was unscathed, but the objects normally arranged on it were scattered across the carpet. The fine crystal decanter containing very old Scottish whisky–how old was very old to a vampire?–lay in shards, the amber fluid a puddle in the pale carpet.

Alex was kneeling on the carpet picking up the broken glass. He glanced up to give her a frightened and confused look. "Alex, what...?" She heard Carl let out a yelp, followed by a loud wooden crashing sound, and ran outside the front door. She discovered him lying on his back, half on and half off the porch, bloodied, bruised and breathless, amid scattered broken railing. Joshua, his eyes displaying a vicious yellow hue, was perched over him holding his arms firmly to the ground.

Before she could think to say a word, she heard Carl ask in a breathless yet strangely calm voice, "Have you had enough yet?" Almost a minute of tense silence preceded Joshua's soft laughter as he helped the older man to his feet. "Good," he said, sounding relieved. "I wasn't sure how much more of that I could take."

She gaped at Carl in shock. "You…you started this?"

He straightened his torn shirt while Joshua adjusted his trousers. "Someone had to." She watched in disbelief as the two men walked amiably into the house and sat at the dining table. Alex stopped his clean-up efforts long enough to bring the men a fresh bottle of scotch and two glasses.

"Catherine, love, I believe Carl and I need seeing to." Joshua winced and reached around his side. "I think this was part of the planter." He dropped a sharp ceramic shard edged in blood onto the table and chuckled.

Carl touched the bruised side of his face gingerly. "You have a wicked left hook." He picked a piece of glass from his hair and studied it thoughtfully. "I think I have some glass in my shoulder. Good thing scotch is a good antiseptic."

"I believe you've broken some of my ribs," Joshua countered, one hand on his ribs and the other massaging the side of his thigh. "You wrestle like an alligator and kick like a mule."

"Well, I'm not as strong as you are. I had to use every tactic I had to bust through that thick skull of yours." Both men laughed softly and raised their glasses to each other.

"I don't believe you two!" She looked at the deepening bruise on Carl's face and shook her head, feeling the beginnings of anger. "You could've killed him!" She turned to the kitchen to prepare an ice pack.

"I was merely defending myself."

"I should let both of you suffer," she said in disgust. She handed a cloth-wrapped bag to Carl, who placed it against his face with a wince.

"Ah, Catherine, have mercy. 'Twas naught but a minor disagreement."

"I'd hate to see what you'd look like if you'd been serious." She snorted and turned to retrieve the first aid kit from the guest bathroom. "I should knock both your heads together." She heard Joshua repeat her words, and both men roared with laughter.

* * * *

An uncomfortable truce settled between them. Joshua's quiet control returned to him, along with the easy way he'd always handled himself. Katie did her best, but even speaking to him often left her feeling exhausted and brought frustration to her companion. She noticed him watching her one night with a contemplative look in his eyes and wondered at it, but couldn't bring herself to ask. Late the next afternoon she came out of her room to find a strange array of objects lying on the kitchen table. Closer examination revealed them to be a plastic-wrapped block of clay, an idea book, several tools, paints, and a stack of newspaper.

She glanced at the objects in curiosity while she made herself breakfast, long past the novelty of eating her first meal so late in the day. She ate quietly, occasionally returning brief attention to the supplies. She lifted the cover of the book and felt herself being drawn in to artistic possibilities.

By the time Joshua rose that evening, the table was covered in newspaper, and she was consumed in her efforts to model the clay in front of her. He sat down opposite her, accepted a glass from Alex, and gave her a look that was half frown, half smile. "What's all this?"

"I'm making something." She felt ridiculous with her hands covered in clay and an unidentifiable blob sitting in front of her.

"Mind if I have a go at it? It looks interesting."

She studied him for a moment, suspicious of the expectation in his voice, and gestured to the block of clay now opened and covered with a wet towel. "Help yourself." He rolled up his sleeves and pinched off a bit of clay, a look of victory gleaming in his eyes.

When the clay was exhausted, other projects or games appeared. While autumn faded into winter, they worked nightly on crafts or played games. On weekends, when Carl came to visit, the four of them competed in one game or another. When she took to calling Carl "Dad", the pleasure on his face brought a warm feeling to her heart. Alex worked patiently with her during daylight hours, teaching her basic sign language so they could more easily communicate with each other.

Joshua took great pleasure in spending interactive time with her, but she sensed his reluctance to reach out, to touch her and thus risk driving her away. Instead, he kept a casual distance between them and waited for her to decide when the time was right.

They were becoming friends again, but the happiness of that fact was muted by the uncomfortable reality of her fear, which never diminished, no matter how hard she fought it. The invisible wall that had risen between them strained their tenuous friendship. As time passed and the snow outside melted, the tension between them grew until she sensed his sorrow giving way to resolve. The uncomfortable feeling she was losing him robbed her of many days' sleep.

Spring finally came, and with the renewing of life in the forest came a renewed sense of longing that gnawed at her heart. She woke up early and walked through the silent house, deeply lost in troubling thoughts. Unable to remain cooped up in the house any longer, she took the keys Joshua kept in the kitchen and went for a drive. Getting out on her own felt good. It gave her a chance to air out the stuffy attic that had become her mind. With the Sebring's top down, she cruised through town, stopped to buy some red roses, and visited the cemetery. "I'm sorry, Momma." She sat beside the grave now blending in with the ground surrounding it. "I miss you. I wish you were here to tell me what to do."

After a long while, she picked herself up, dusted herself off with a sigh, and got back in the car. When she stopped in front of her former home an hour later, she looked at it in surprise, realizing she'd driven there automatically. The sight of the rotting timbers and twisted remains of her car brought back some of the terror she'd witnessed. She decided she had to face it and get it out of her system once and for all.

With one last rose in her hand, she crossed the threshold and surveyed what had once been a place of comfort. Nothing remained that held any resemblance to the home she'd known, as if her former life had been eradicated from human memory, leaving in its wake an impossibly small, charred patch of earth. The sight left her feeling hollow and alone. The partial remains of police tape still marked the place where her mother had drawn her last breath. She swallowed the lump forming in her throat, laid the rose where her mother's heart had been, and turned away.

Her back to the rubble, she walked the winding road, reliving past moments, happier times, and, most of all, her relationship with Joshua. She picked her way back to the clearing she hadn't seen in half a year, wishing she would find him there, waiting as he often had to share time with her in their special place.

She sat against the rock face, where the memory of their intimacy was the strongest. Instead of finding comfort there, she felt the aching need to feel his arms come around her once again. With her knees drawn tight to her chest, she cradled her head in her arms and cried for the love she once had.

She'd almost forgotten the bond between them, a bond she noticed immediately when she woke in the hospital, a year, and a lifetime, ago. She had, in fact, begun to take it for granted, like the beating of her heart. So when the sense of his alarm hit her, she clenched herself in surprise. She raised her head when his alarm quickly changed to panic, and understood instantly why he seemed so desperate to find her. The sun had set without her realizing it, and she was sitting alone and unprotected in the darkness. She reached out along the force of their bond when she sensed him calling to her, and felt him anchor his perceptions on her. His relief swept through her mind.

Within moments, she watched him drop to the ground in the center of the clearing where he studied her in growing relief. "I was concerned," he chided softly. "I warned you against being abroad after dark. 'Tis not safe here for you now."

"I'm sorry," she said, climbing to her feet. "I lost track of time." The feeling of longing hit her again and she wanted nothing more at that moment than to run for his arms, but the fear still controlling her had glued her feet to the soft ground. "You're not mad at me, are you?"

"You know that I am not," he said matter-of-factly, confirming her belief he knew all too well about their bond and how sensitive she'd become to it. She also sensed he was aware of her fear and how hard she struggled to control it. Slowly, his expression change from relief to profound sorrow. "We cannot allow this conflict between us to continue."

"No," she agreed softly.

He nodded once, slowly, and said, "Come to me, Catherine."

His sorrow swept over her along with his will, his mental tone of command compelling her while the sudden knowledge of his intent stuck a knife through her chest. She shook off his control with all the courage she could muster. "No, Joshua."

A light drizzle filtered down around them. Her improved perceptions registered each tiny droplet as it drifted between them, sparkling in the darkness. It transformed the tiny clearing into an enchanted realm, yet accentuated the way he seemed to shrink into himself when she refused him. "You've taught yourself to resist," he said, his voice so thick and deep it sounded foreign. "That is…unfortunate. It makes what I must do more difficult to bear." He took a step toward her, and she instantly took a timid step back. The pain that overcame his features sent tears pouring down her cheeks. "You cannot escape me, Catherine. Please don't try."

"You're going to make me forget."

He paused, looking surprised at her intuition, while the drizzle around them quickened. "I must."

"I don't want you to."

"'Tis for the best, love." She felt the hypnotic tone in his voice. The power he was broadcasting sent her senses reeling. "I can no longer bear up to your pain. 'Twill destroy us both."

The pain in his eyes tore at her heart; pain and the need to console him became as strong as her uncontrollable fear. An intense war raged in her mind, threatening her tenuous control. "You can't make me forget you," she insisted, grappling to keep a grip on her will in a desperate effort to shake off his control.

"Can I not?" His pull on her increased as he took yet another step toward her.

She felt herself losing their battle of wills. "Okay, maybe you can. But you can't tell my heart to forget. No matter what you do to me, even if I don't consciously know the reason, I'll never love another man as long as I live."

Her words stopped him short while the rain came down in earnest. A drop of water trickled from her scalp and down her face, mingling with her tears. "You cannot know what you do," he said, his tone deadly serious. "You do not understand the power behind your words."

"I understand we love each other." Another drop of water trickled down the back of her neck and under her shirt collar, sending an icy chill down her back. "I don't want to lose that."

He raised an eyebrow aristocratically. "What, then, do you suggest? 'Tis your fear that keeps us apart."

She thought of the passion he'd taught her, the needs he'd awakened with his touch. The memory of his rage sent shockwaves through her heart. Her conflicts poured down her cheeks in hot drops that blended with the chill rain. "I don't know," she admitted with a shiver. "I…I'll think of something."

He studied her silently, seemingly oblivious to the heavy downpour that had them both soaked to the skin. "Very well. One way or another, we will resolve this. Tonight." She nodded in agreement. "We cannot talk here. This cold rain will make you ill." He paused to hold his hand to her. "Come."

She looked at his hand and told herself it was a test of the strength of her resolve. With determination, she forced herself to put her hand in his, and saw the look in his eyes soften. "I left the car by my…." It wasn't a house anymore, she realized while handing him the keys. "I think I left the top down."

With the slightest hint of amusement, he said simply, "It will dry."

They returned to his house in silence, heat from the Sebring's vents raising the humidity until she felt uncomfortably sticky. He gave her a terse command to clean herself up, and disappeared into his own room. She took a shower, dried her hair, and studied herself in the mirror. The woman who stared back looked haunted and desperate. After considering the contents of her closet thoughtfully, she selected a pair of black slacks and a cobalt blouse of soft, brushed silk that had, on more than one occasion, brought heated longing to his eyes.

She found him waiting for her in the living room. The fireplace was alight, casting its welcoming warmth into the room. His gaze swept her briefly, and she felt him take note of the blouse. He watched expectantly while she crossed the room. "You didn't ask me why I went out alone today," she commented, hating the nervous tremor in her voice.

"No." He perched himself on the arm of the sofa and crossed his arms.

She sat on his chair with a sigh. "I needed time to think, time to…sort things out in my head." She rose and moved to the window. The rain continued, leaving the forest as dark as green/black velvet. Her own reflection in the glass stood out starkly against the darkness, accentuating the haunted look in her eyes. "I want to stay with you, Joshua, but I can't help being afraid. I've tried so hard. I just…I'm not sure what to do, but somehow…" Her eyes focused on his reflection behind her pleadingly.

"What would you ask of me, Catherine?"

She turned to face him again, although it cost her every ounce of courage to do so. "I need you to help me. You've taught me so much, Joshua. Teach me not to be afraid."

He raised an eyebrow, but betrayed no other emotional response. After a moment, he asked softly, "What is it you most fear?" She didn't have to say a word. The night her mother was killed rose instantly to the forefront of her mind. He shook his head sadly. "What you saw that night was a vampire angered beyond the point of outrage. My anger was not, and could never be, directed at you." He paused to offer a reassuringly smile. "I will never hurt you that way."

She gave him a frustrated nod, trying hard to take his words to heart. Okay, she told herself, get on with it. She took in a deep breath and chose what she considered the easiest of her ideas. "Can…can you force me to forget my fear?"

"If you were to submit yourself to me, open your mind to my will, I could force you to accept what I am, if that's what you're asking," he confirmed carefully, "but the results might not be as satisfying for either of us as you hope. Somewhere deep inside of you, your fear of me would remain. It could rise again to the surface of your heart unexpectedly."

"I see." She nodded to herself in an attempt to force down her growing dread. "Take control of me, like you did Carl and Alex."

"No!" His sharp response made her look at him in surprise. "I will not rob you of your freedom in that way."

"You have my consent."

"But not your trust. If I take away your ability to choose, I will never be certain you gave yourself to me freely. I will have your love given without any implied coercion, or not at all."

"All right," she said, feeling herself trip nervously over her next, and final, suggestion. "Bring me across."

He studied her for a moment in silence before responding, "I can't."

"If I were a vampire too, I wouldn't have to be afraid, and I'd still be free to make up my own mind."

"No, Catherine. I cannot," he repeated softly.

"Why not? Do you know how?"

He unfolded his arms and resettled himself on the sofa arm. "I know the trick of it well enough. Again, it comes to a matter of trust. To bring you into immortality, I must first take from you your mortal life. You must be completely prepared to make the change. If there is any doubt in your mind, any trace of fear either conscious or unconscious, you could easily slip from this world to the next, and I'll have ended your life to no avail. I cannot take that risk."

The weight of his words sank to the pit of her stomach. She lowered herself slowly into his chair and hung her head. "That's it then. I'm out of ideas."

"Catherine, in the clearing you spoke a Vow sacred among my kind. Are you so deeply in love with me?"

"Yes." She stood up and met his all-too-serious gaze. "Yes I am."

"You wish us to become…" He paused to size her up with growing heat that warmed her face and curled her toes. "…intimate?"

The power of his gaze became more intense as the memory of his touch swept over her, weakening her knees and bringing a flutter to her heart. "Yes," she admitted breathlessly.

"Then come to me. Face down your fear."

She felt her heart leap to her throat. She took a step toward him and hesitated. "What…" she paused to swallow her heart back into place.

"What are you going to do?"

"Give you what you want most. Help you to understand and accept what I am, what I can be to you." He reached out to her, his gaze at once as dark and intense as it was hopeful. "All you have to do is take my hand."

She studied him nervously while she made herself remember the man she'd fallen in love with, the man she had once been so eager to surrender herself to. He didn't look like the same gentle man she'd known. Instead, what she saw in his eyes was power easily contained and seriousness that was almost frightening. She stood on the threshold between her world and his, and he was prepared to help her cross. She closed her eyes and pulled in a deep breath in an attempt to calm her racing heartbeat, swallowed hard at the lump of sheer terror that was closing her throat, and placed her trembling hand in his.

He closed his fingers over hers, and the pad of his thumb swept across the top of her knuckles in his familiar and comforting gesture. As he pulled her closer, a strange feeling swept over her like the calm Carl had described. She struggled to accept the comfort he was broadcasting her way. He rose to his feet, his hands sliding slowly up her arms to her shoulders. "Silk of this type was made for a woman's tender skin." His voice was low and soft, like the sigh of an evening breeze. He stroked the side of her face and captured her gaze with his while he pulled her more fully into his embrace. With his lips brushing lightly against hers, he whispered, "Try not to resist me."

His kisses came softly, patiently, coaxing her response. His mind continued to invade hers, probing deeper, easing her anxiety. When she relaxed into his arms, he held her closer and touched her with the tip of his tongue. He moistened and teased her lips, pressed persuasively against her teeth, and with a trembling sigh she opened herself to him, allowed him to explore her until her breath came in short gasps and what starch she had left in her knees evaporated. His arms tightened around her, and his mind took hold of her last spark of fear. *Now surrender.*

His passion swept through her, dissolving her fear and igniting her senses in ways she'd never before known. A soft moan whispered in her throat and she let her head rest against his waiting palm. She melted completely into his strong support and felt the evidence of his desire press hard against her. Her body instinctively responded to that secret knowledge. The warmth building in her belly became an urgent, unrelenting fire. With one final, trembling sigh she surrendered to his power.

When his mouth moved away from hers to kiss a path to her ear, she let her head fall back to give him access. Slowly, he kissed his way from her ear toward the pulse-point at the base of her throat, playing his lips and tongue along her skin while thrills danced over her entire body. He moistened the soft skin under his lips and pressed his kiss more firmly against her flesh. Heat blossomed in the center of that kiss and spread quickly through her, sending her senses spiraling out of control. She became nothing but sensation; passion filling every ounce of her being, and she could give thought to nothing else.

After a moment or two, he straightened and folded her into his firm embrace. "Now you understand."

She struggled to bring her breathing under control, her body still alive with needs yet unmet. "What just happened?"

His head dipped to nuzzle her gently. "A demonstration. If I pressed my advantage too far, it was only to help you release your fear of me." It was then she became aware he was trembling, and realized his desire had also not been answered. When she pulled away to look up at him in mute inquiry, she saw more than desire and need glistening in his eyes, a feeling so intense, so unusual for him, that she couldn't give it a name.

On his lower lip, a thin red smudge stood in confession of what had passed between them. She raised her fingers to her throat and gingerly explored the place he had given so much attention to moments before. Although it was tender, she found no trace of broken skin. When she looked to his eyes for an answer, he pulled his lip into his mouth to clean off that last drop and said softly, "By morning, you will find no evidence that I've taken you." He turned away from her abruptly and leaned heavily against the back of the sofa. He kept his feelings closed to her, but his body language suggested distress. "Forgive me, Catherine. I should not have…I'm sorry."

"It's okay, Joshua. Really." She raised her hand to touch his shoulder, but paused uncertainly. "Are you all right?" When he straightened but didn't otherwise respond, she moved around him and looked in his eyes. A single tear fell unchecked down his cheek before he pulled her back into his arms.

"I see the questions in your eyes. I don't think I can explain this in a way you can understand. If you'll give me a few moments," he paused to press his face into her hair, "…a moment to…" His voice failed him. He pulled her around to the front of the sofa, where he sat and gathered her on his lap. She allowed him to cradle her in his arms and settled her head on his shoulder. Her sudden transition from fear to affection had a strangely unbalancing effect on her equilibrium, but the feel of his arms surrounding her was a welcoming balm to her tormented heart.

Silence fell over the room, broken only by the soft crackling of the fire. It seemed like a small eternity before he lifted a hand to smooth her hair. "Forgive me," he said at last. "I wasn't quite prepared for...." he paused and shook his head. A soft chuckle shook his chest. "I should have known."

"Known...what?"

"You are a very dynamic young lady. Your innocence runs deeper than the purity of your body. Your heart and soul are untouched. But there is so much more to you than simple, profound innocence. You view the world and all its intricacies with wonder. You have the ability to face any challenge as an adventure in which you can, if you're willing, become a participant instead of a victim. Your potential for strength and courage is like none I've ever seen. Your capacity to love, to give with complete selflessness, is greater than even an Angel can boast." He smiled at her in sad wonder. "Yours is a destiny I have not the right to interfere with."

"You got all that from a taste of my blood?"

He nodded slowly. "Blood is much more than mere sustenance. All that you are, all that you know and can become, is written there, like a blueprint for your life. We take that knowledge into ourselves every time we drink. It is the need to feel the lives around us, perhaps to share a part of the mortality we left behind, that draws a vampire to drink." He traced a fingertip along her jaw line. "The power of your innocence, your loving spirit, flows through me still. Your effect on me is quite...overwhelming."

She sat in silent contemplation for several minutes. "This vow you said I made. Explain it to me."

He rested his head against the sofa and drew in a deep breath. "Immortal beings have very little use for mortal laws. We have our own rules we must abide by, laws far more binding than those written by men. These rules have been in place for centuries, and exist to protect both mortals and immortals alike. They are the cornerstones that support the vampire Community. In some ways, our rites have a measure of magic attached to them. The Vow you offered me is a rite far more permanent than any mortal wedding ritual."

"So, I was really repeating a wedding vow in your culture without realizing it?"

"Aye, but you do not understand how serious this is. For us, it is a thing that cannot ever be dissolved so long as both live. It is deeply engrained into Community lore. All who identify with them are susceptible to its power. The strength of the law was meant as a deterrent. Eternity can be a terrible burden to bear should love grow cold." She heard a hint of sorrow in his voice when he added, "I forgive you the Vow you made without understanding. You didn't know what you were doing."

"Then I'll offer it again. If a mortal ceremony doesn't mean anything to your culture, then I'll accept whatever laws your Community imposes on me."

"You still do not understand. I cannot deny the strength of your power to love; your need to give it. I cannot ask you to commit those gifts to me alone."

"I do understand," she argued solemnly. "You and I are alike. Carl and Alex are evidence of your need to reach out to those in need of what you can provide. We'll share our charity with others, our friendship, but keep our love just for ourselves. I know it will be okay."

He considered her words carefully, the possibilities of her suggestion bringing one tiny ray of hope to his eyes. "Catherine, are you certain this is what you want?"

She sighed her frustration, turned until she was straddling him, put her hands on his shoulders, and looked him square in the eyes. "I'm not Antonia, to leave you if temptation comes my way. I don't want your house or your money, unless I can have you along with it. I'll never betray your love or your secrets. If what I am is in my blood as you say, you know that's true." She sat straighter, meeting his gaze with solemn certainty. "If I initiated a bond between us when I was a kid, some force greater than both of us wanted it to happen. Maybe you were written into my destiny before I was born. Who can say? The only thing I'm absolutely sure of is I want to be your wife, no matter what that means."

"What of your culture? Have you never dreamed of the things only another mortal can offer you?"

"I never gave it much thought," she answered honestly. "Oh, sure, when I was a kid I used to dream of fairy-tale endings and white weddings, a home and a family of my own, but after Dad died, I was too busy surviving to think about things like that." She thought for a minute, and added, "This is no different than if I'd fallen in love with someone from another country, who did not believe in the whole "white wedding" thing. I'd have had to accept their laws in order to fit into my husband's culture."

It was as if she'd lifted an eternal weight from his soul. The warmth growing in his eyes spoke more loudly than words ever could of the love and gratitude in his heart. "'Tis enough. I must ask that we wait one more day. I wish to arrange a compromise between our worlds. No formal ritual is required on my part beyond the sharing of the Vow, no minister or witnesses are needed, but I want to make this a special event for your sake."

Disappointment settled inside her like a lead weight. All the desire she'd felt earlier at his touch returned to reassert itself. The unanswered passion between them begged for release. She thought maybe he was reading her thoughts, or maybe he felt the same way. The soft chocolate in his eyes darkened until it looked more like molten cocoa when she whispered, "I don't want to wait."

"I'm afraid we must, love," he said, stroking her hair with an air of regret. "I made a promise I intend to keep." He kissed her tenderly. She sensed he was holding himself back with the greatest difficulty. "We've waited this long. One more day is a small sacrifice. Get some rest. I have some thinking to do."

She left his arms reluctantly and headed for the hallway. At the entrance, she turned and said, "I won't change my mind."

He gave her a decidedly lewd grin. "If you don't go to your room right now, I'll break my own promise, and end up hating myself in the morning."

With a smile, she retreated to her room to make her own plans for the following night.

Chapter Fourteen

Katie woke early the next afternoon and gazed at the sunlight streaming in through her bedroom window with the happy realization that this was her wedding day. She jumped from the bed, took a quick shower, dressed in a cream-colored silk blouse and a pair of dark brown slacks, and went to the kitchen for breakfast. Alex was at the table, eating toasted bagels with cream cheese and fruit spread. Her mouth watered while she toasted some of her own and joined him. She smiled at the cautious look in his eyes while he watched her slather spreads onto them.

"I need to run an errand this afternoon," she told him between hasty sips of coffee. When he nodded and headed for the car keys, she stopped him. "This is something I need to do by myself. Don't worry," she added when alarm spread over his face. "I'll be back long before sunset. I promise." Alex nodded reluctantly, worry etched in his eyes.

She returned two hours later with a shopping bag and a dress box. She laid her purchases on the bed, fingered the dress reverently and smiled at the surprise she expected when Joshua saw her in the white satin and lace. It wasn't a traditional wedding gown, but more like the compromise he'd suggested. The dress was knee length and of a casual style more appropriate to a night on the town, but the fine, white lace stockings, satin garter, and frilly underwear she'd gotten to go with it made the outfit special enough in her own mind. She smiled softly and hung the dress in the closet to await the setting sun.

She returned to the kitchen for more coffee and a snack to calm the nervousness in her stomach, and sat at the table with Alex to wait for Joshua. Before the sun had fully set, she sensed him awaken and watched the hallway in anticipation. She felt Alex's tension as he waited with her for the sky to darken. Her hand started trembling when the quiet sound of Joshua's bedroom door opening announced his approach, and she had to set the cup it held on the table before its remaining contents spilled on her lap. Alex went to the kitchen to prepare his breakfast when he appeared, looking more casual and relaxed than ever in his unbelted brown slacks and half-buttoned shirt.

She felt her heart skip a beat when he moved to her silently, took her hand, and guided her to his arms. She nuzzled his cool chest with a shaky sigh as he held her close, and when his hand stroked her face and moved to the back of her neck, she raised her head to receive his tender, playful kisses. He pressed his forehead against hers for a moment while his hands moved gently down her back, then released her and took a seat at the table.

It was at that moment she remembered Alex. Joshua's adoptive son was standing frozen at the kitchen counter, a glass in one hand and a jug in the other, a look of shock and astonishment on his face that made her want to laugh.

"Alex, how long do you intend to tease me with my breakfast?" Joshua asked with great humor. He shook himself and quickly handed him the glass, his eyes wide with dawning understanding. She watched his expression slowly turn to one of joy so extreme he laughed in that cute, voiceless way he had. Finally unable to contain the joy building inside him, he flung his arms around Joshua, and shook his hand enthusiastically in congratulations. Then he gave her an equal hug and a loud, brotherly kiss on the cheek.

"I believe Alex is happy for us, Catherine."

"Do you really think so?" she asked with a laugh. Alex stood looking from one to the other of them with his hands clasped tight against his stomach in an obvious effort to control himself.

"Yes," he said, his expression softening. "As am I." A warm blush crept to her cheeks. He drained his glass and rose to his feet. "I want you to throw a few things together. I have a phone call to make, and then we are going away for the weekend."

"Away? Where?" she asked, excited at the prospect of an outing.

"You'll see. You deserve your traditional wedding trip, and we need to be away from the house for a while." She didn't need her special senses to know he was planning something. The look on his face was too secretive.

"All right. What's going on?"

"If I tell you, it will spoil the surprise. Now, go get ready. We have much to do."

It took her a few minutes to gather enough things for the weekend and stuff them into a shopping bag. She gently folded the dress and laid it back in the box it came in, and put her undergarments on underneath her street clothes, preparing for a quick-change act for whatever he had planned. After stashing her things in the trunk of the car, she returned to the front of the house in time to hear him conclude his telephone call. "That's right," he said in a business-like tone. "Yes. Yes, whatever you feel is necessary.

No, and I don't want her to. It's a wedding gift for both of us." He laughed briefly. "Yes. Thank you. Yes, we'll be leaving shortly. I'll have Alex begin preparations here. See that the job is completed before we return."

"Joshua, what's going on?" she asked when he hung up the phone. "What are you planning?"

"A surprise, love," he answered, sweeping her happily into his arms. He hugged her tight and gave her a brief kiss, then released her. "Come, Alex. I need to have a word with you while I pack."

Katie sat anxiously in the passenger seat of the Sebring while Joshua drove them into town. "What are we doing at the mall?" she asked when he parked the car.

He smiled another secretive smile. "There is something I need to give to you before we leave town."

"Joshua, you've already given me so much. I don't need..."

"Ah, but you do," he insisted after he'd opened the mall door for her to enter. He took her by the hand and led her to the finest jewelry store in the mall and straight to the case displaying a wide and extravagant array of diamond rings. "Only the finest will do. The ring you wear as my wife must speak to all the world of our love for each other."

"Oh, Joshua. They're beautiful!" She gazed at the selections, and when the shock wore off, she more carefully scrutinized each one while he gestured to a saleswoman. Most of the rings were large and showy, and not to her taste. The relationship she had with Joshua had always been much more reserved, she thought her wedding ring should be equally reserved, and thus more comfortable to wear. She pointed to a modest band with one medium-sized diamond flanked by two smaller ones in an offset pattern of yellow gold. "This one is nice."

He looked surprised. "You do not wish for something larger?"

She shook her head. "The cost and size of the ring I wear for you is not as important as its meaning. Besides, I don't want to be stuck wearing one of those gaudy monstrosities for the rest of my life."

The pleasure she saw in his eyes when he nodded to the saleswoman made her think she'd passed an important test. If he'd had any doubt his wealth was unimportant to her, she knew at that moment she'd proven to him her devotion was real. The saleswoman, wearing a badge identifying her as Becky, dutifully withdrew the ring she'd indicated, and he took it from her to examine it closely through the jeweler's loop chained to the case. He studied each of the stones and handed the ring back to Becky with a shake of his head. "No, this stone is flawed and does not befit the love I bear her."

She smiled, obviously impressed by his sentiment. "I may have just what you're looking for in the vault. Wait a moment." She hustled away, and returned five minutes later with a small white pouch. "This is one of our finest," she said, withdrawing a ring for their consideration. The setting featured a pair of perfectly matched heart-shaped blue diamonds arranged with their tops touching and flanked at the tips with long-cut white diamonds, all set in shimmering platinum.

She held her breath while he studied the stones. "Does it fit?" he asked, handing it to her for inspection.

She slipped it on her trembling finger, and stood for a moment admiring the simple elegance of the piece, so like the simplicity and style of Joshua's home. "Perfectly," she managed to answer over the lump in her throat.

He took the ring from her and returned it to Becky with a smile. "We'll take it." While she slipped the ring into a velvet box, he said to Katie, "Now I wish for you to select one for me."

Becky led her to a display of men's rings, and she saw instantly the ring that suited him best. "That one," she said.

He once again scrutinized the stones in the ring–a brilliant emerald flanked by the same long-cut style diamonds in her ring and set, also, in platinum. "The emerald is indeed rare. Too many times jewelers put fillers in them to hide flaws from unwary patrons."

"You have a discriminating eye." Becky said as she slipped the second ring into the box.

They were walking arm-in-arm toward the mall exit when he asked, "Isn't that your friend Taska?"

"Katie!" Taska exclaimed. She squealed and rushed into her friend's arms. "Oh, it's good to see you! I was so worried about you."

"Oh, my goodness," she said, pulling away to place a hand on Taska's swollen belly. "How long?"

"Five months," Taska said as she took Dillon's hand. "It happened on our honeymoon."

"Hi, Dillon." She gave the man a brief hug. "I'm sorry I missed your wedding. I really wanted to be there for you."

"We understood," Taska said more soberly. "When we heard what happened to your mom, we knew you wouldn't be up to it."

"I had a rough time for a while," she admitted. "I guess I suffered a nervous breakdown. I was a real basket case for a while, but Joshua was there for me. I don't know what I'd have done without him. Oh!" she exclaimed when she realized the two men hadn't met. "Dillon, this is my fiancé, Joshua MacAaron. Joshua, Dillon Ward."

"A pleasure," Joshua said with a smile while they shook hands.

"You are so lucky," Katie said to her friend.

"So are you," Taska replied, gazing appreciatively at Joshua. "So, when's the wedding?"

"Tonight," Joshua told them.

"So soon? Aw, I really wanted to go," Taska moaned. "We have to be back at his parents' house in an hour. They're throwing a baby shower."

"Sorry," she said sadly. "This was a last minute thing. I didn't have time to make any plans. We're gonna, you know, do it."

"Eloping, huh? Oh, how romantic! Well, okay. In that case, I guess I understand."

"When I get back, I'll take you to lunch, how about that? We can play catch-up."

"That sounds great!"

"Darling, we should be going if we're to reach our destination before sun-up," Joshua said softly.

"Going on a honeymoon, huh?" Dillon asked with a laugh. "Be careful not to get too carried away, unless you're ready for a family of your own."

"Dillon!" Taska exclaimed. "Oh, don't let him kid you. I think he was more excited than I was when we found out." She gave Katie another firm hug. "Congratulations," she whispered before she pulled away.

She sat back in the Sebring and enjoyed the feel of the wind softly tossing her hair while he drove them back into the woods with a loving smile on his face. When they pulled to a stop on the side of the dirt road she knew too well, she looked at him in surprise. "The clearing?"

"Aye. 'Twas here we first discovered our love for each other. I thought it appropriate our special place should bear witness to this important event."

"Okay. You go ahead of me. There's something I need to do first."

He touched her face and kissed her tenderly. "Promise you won't be long."

"Just a couple of minutes," she promised. "I want to get ready." He nodded, looking amused at her secretive tone, and turned away.

It took her less than a minute to change, and she carefully picked her way to the clearing, doing her best not to snag her delicate stockings on the prickly underbrush. She paused at the threshold for a moment longer to relish her own suspense, then stepped through and gasped her surprise.

Somehow, Joshua had managed to transform their clearing into a natural chapel. There were white flowers arranged all over the rocky wall and floating in the tiny stream, and a tall candelabrum stood on the one spot she knew better than any for its significance.

Joshua stood under the soft glow, a look of pure astonishment and delight on his face as he gazed at her. He held his hand to her and she walked with solemn dignity to his side. "Oh, Catherine."

"Do you like it?"

He pulled her easily into his arms and captured her eyes with his own. "Never have I attended a more beautiful wedding, nor seen a more exquisite bride." He bent to give her a kiss filled with reverence and love.

"Now this is indeed a tender site."

She spun around in surprise as a man stepped lightly out of the woods, moving with the same exaggerated grace she'd noticed in Joshua. His dark, chestnut hair could best be described as a mane that curled softly around his head and hovered above his shoulders. The seriousness in his sparkling sapphire eyes sent a surge of panic through her chest. "Don't be alarmed, love, he will not harm you. Vincent is an old and trusted friend. He has come at my summons to stand for us as a member of the Community."

She kept her eyes warily on Vincent and whispered, "I thought we didn't need a witness."

"True enough," Vincent replied for him. His voice was soft and musical, filled with power that prickled her senses. "But it is a prudent request in this case, and one I am more than honored to fulfill." When he reached for her face, she instinctively shrank away, but Joshua's reassuring touch at the small of her back made her submit herself to the new vampire's scrutiny. He lifted her chin with one cool finger and studied her, his eyes moving studiously from her face down the length of her body and back again. "She is all you described and more, brother." Then he lowered his hand and added, "Are you absolutely certain you want to do this?"

Joshua pulled the velvet box from his pocket and handed it to him with a nod. "I told you I would do what was necessary when the time comes. Taking Catherine to heart is as necessary to me as the blood I must consume."

"And what about you, young woman?" he asked sternly. "One lifetime is not so much to sacrifice, but if you should choose, in the future, to come across, you'll be stuck with this joker for all time."

She cocked her head slightly, uncertain of the levity she heard in his warning that was in direct conflict with the hard seriousness in his eyes. "He can be a challenge sometimes," she admitted cautiously, "but I can handle him."

He laughed, his entire being relaxing into a much friendlier posture. "You've sure got your hands full, my friend." He opened the box and gave the smaller ring to Joshua.

"Don't I well know it." He positioned the ring to place it on her finger, and with a brand of seriousness she'd seen in his eyes only a few times before, said softly, "For as long as you walk this earth, I shall love no other." Then he lifted her hand to his lips and sealed the ring to her finger with a tender kiss. "My wife," he whispered.

She felt herself being captured by the power in his gaze, and only responded after Vincent spoke her name. With a deep breath, she accepted the ring from him, her hand trembling so hard she almost dropped the precious symbol. "I will love only you for the rest of my life," she whispered, sliding the ring onto his finger. She lifted it to her lips, mimicking his actions, and sealed their Vow with a kiss and the words, "My husband." She met his gaze and saw tears pooling in his eyes as she added softly, "My love."

A strange, frightening power surged through her at the completion of their Vow, strengthening their bond into something much more compelling. She knew without asking it came from the rite Joshua had described as being a powerful part of his culture, sent to her through their already undeniable connection. "It is done," she heard Vincent say, confirming verbally the feelings coursing through her. "I will take my leave of you, Joshua, and leave this delightful creature in your capable hands. There are urgent matters at home requiring my attention."

"Vincent," he said, his voice thick with emotion, his eyes turned sharply to his friend. "Speak naught of this to the others. The Community will be tempted to interfere in matters that are none of their concern. I will protect her from their meddling as much as I am able."

"I'll respect your privacy. Rest assured I will offer testimony to the Council only if it becomes necessary to Catherine's survival." He glanced up at the sky, and said in parting, "I wish you both the best of luck. I think you'll need it." He surged into the sky, leaving her to stare after him in stunned surprise.

"I told you we can fly," he said with a chuckle. He pulled her tight against him and buried his face in her hair. "Never have I felt such happiness." Then he pulled away, kissed the tear dripping down her cheek, and said regretfully, "We cannot stay, though right at this moment, I wish we had more time." He took a deep breath. "Come."

He led her back to the car, and in no time at all they were headed west. "Where are you taking me?"

"A little place I know of near North Cove."

"What's in North Cove?"

The look he gave her set her on fire, so intense was the passion in his eyes. "The beach."

"You mean the ocean?" she asked excitedly. "We're going to the ocean? Oh, Joshua! I've always wanted to see it!"

He laughed gently at her excitement. "The Community has a network that stretches around the world. I learned of a contact there who owns a shelter overlooking a private beach, which is suitable to my needs. He's expecting us."

"Oh, I can't wait! How long 'till we get there?"

"A couple of hours, love." He took her hand and held it tenderly. She felt his fingers exploring her ring. She sat back and did her best to contain her excitement and anticipation.

* * * *

The shelter Joshua mentioned turned out to be a log cabin, situated at the end of a long, single lane drive that followed the coastline. He pulled alongside the cabin and helped her out of the car, and she felt the heels of her shoes sink in the soft sand. She tried to walk on her toes to the porch extending across the front of the cabin, but the dry sand shifted too much, and she felt in danger of toppling over. He chuckled and carried her up the steps. She saw a bench swing hanging on one side of the porch, and on the other side of the single door there was a window covered by heavy wooden shutters. He seemed unwilling to release her long enough to unlock the door, and she was too comfortable to protest, so he shifted her weight in his arms long enough to slip the key he'd gotten from the owner into the lock, then kicked the door in and carried her through.

The inside of the cabin was divided by a rough-cut wall with a door on one side. The first section was modestly furnished very much like her former home, containing a sofa and a table with chairs, though this house lacked both kitchen and stove. He backed against the door, bringing it to a close, and used his mental discipline instead of his hand to push the security bolt in place.

He nuzzled her neck and carried her wordlessly to the bedroom containing little more than a double bed. He set her gently to her feet and closed the door behind them, his eyes never leaving hers, and sent one last flicker of thought at a lamp hanging on the rear wall. Its light cast a dim yellow glow around the windowless room. She felt the intense power of his passion when he turned his full attention to her. The effect his gaze had on her awakening body sent nervous tremors coursing through her.

When he slid his hands gently along her face and into her hair, she closed her eyes. He guided her to him and took possession of her mouth. The urgency of his kisses quickly took her breath away and set her body trembling harder. He moved his hands slowly down her neck and onto the satin fabric of her dress, caressing her as if she were a great and fragile treasure.

She felt her dress loosen under his touch, then it slid softly to the floor along with her undergarments, leaving her top half naked to his gaze. His eyes darkened hungrily when he found the satin garter supporting her stockings. He knelt reverently to unfasten the stockings and push them slowly down her legs, caressing her skin as he moved while her hands fluttered nervously at her side. She felt like she was being unwrapped like a Christmas present. The sensation brought a nervous giggle to her lips.

He stepped back to look at her, his eyes moving up and down her body in obvious appreciation, and she felt rewarded for the hard work she'd endured most of her life that had resulted in her firm, slender curves. "You are more beautiful than I could ever have imagined."

She felt hot color rush to her cheeks. "I don't know what to do."

He guided her hands to the front of his shirt. "Follow my lead, love. I'll teach you, and then we can learn from each other." She swallowed hard and plucked at the buttons of his shirt. When she found she couldn't manage the task, he chuckled softly and helped her. Now it was her turn to look at him. His pale skin stretched tightly over well-defined muscles. She touched his chest and found him only slightly cooler than herself. His skin was as smooth as fine silk, the muscles beneath firm. The patch of soft-looking golden curls in the center of his chest was even softer to the touch. When her eyes found his manhood, she felt a sudden surge of doubt. He chuckled again and pulled her against him. "That part of me exists now only for your pleasure."

"It's so...big. I might be too..."

He picked her up and lowered her onto the bed. "We'll fit together nicely," he assured her before taking her mouth once more. He moved his hands slowly over her body, exploring every inch of her skin he could reach. She let her hands roam over him as well, tentatively at first, then more boldly when her touch brought soft moans from his throat. When he cupped her breast and teased it with the pad of his thumb, she pulled in a sharp breath and arched her back. His mouth left hers to close over the tip and she moaned her surprise. With his teeth and tongue, he teased her sensitive flesh until it stood up hard and proud, then turned his attention to its mate.

She felt his hand move down her belly and brush the nest of curls at the crux of her thighs. He put his hand inside her trembling thigh and gently parted her legs, moving slowly upward. When his fingers penetrated those curls and found the nubbin of flesh hiding within, an urgent moan escaped her lips. His mouth left her breast to kiss a hot path down her belly. She found herself torn between the pleasure he was bringing and a sense of embarrassment. That embarrassment faded with the first touch of his tongue, and she surrendered herself to the magic he was performing on her body.

Her pleasure came quickly and brought a startled cry to her lips. He moved over her, looked deeply into her eyes, and gently lifted one of her legs over his hip, an expectant gleam burning in his eyes. She followed suit with the other and felt him press himself into her. As her flesh stretched around him, she braced herself for what came next.

He paused in an obvious effort to restrain himself and closed his eyes. "Your body is ready for me. Relax and let me in," he instructed, his voice tight. "Take a deep breath and hold very still." She nodded, remembering her mother's assuring words as she met his gaze in trust. He surged inward and a quick, sharp pain preceded the incredible fullness as he buried himself deep inside her. She gasped and felt the hot burn of tears pooling in her eyes.

He paused again to let her adjust to him. "Did I hurt you?" he asked gently. The look in his eyes was a mixture of concern and hot desire.

"I'm okay," she answered breathlessly, uncertain herself if she was telling the truth. "You?" she asked when she saw the hint of discomfort on his face.

"Oh, you're a snug fit," he teased. "I'll manage."

"M-manage...what?" With a rumbling laugh that came from deep inside him, he demonstrated, pulling slowly away and surging forward again, this time going deeper inside her. "Oh!"

He slid a hand under her hips and taught her the ancient movements that followed. She quickly learned his rhythm and countered with growing enthusiasm. With each of his thrusts, she felt a surge of pleasure that increased at an alarming rate until she thought she might explode at any moment. "Johsua...?"

"Let it happen," he whispered in her ear. He lengthened his thrusts, changed his rhythm, and in less than a heartbeat the pleasure he was bringing overtook her. She cried out, her entire body singing with sensation, and he quickly covered her mouth with his and took her impassioned cry into himself, while with one final thrust his body answered hers. He held her suspended in that moment, suddenly still while he pulsated deep inside her. A long, soft, almost musical hum floated from his lips as he collapsed into her arms.

She accepted his weight easily and strove to catch her breath and calm her racing heart. When, at last, he raised himself up to look into her eyes, she saw in them wonder and happiness she'd never found there before. She returned his gaze lovingly, squirmed under him, and felt him still buried deep inside her. Her body recognized his presence and shamelessly begged for more, and when he chuckled softly with that knowledge, another bright blush flooded her cheeks. Without a word, he answered the demands her body was making on him, this time with tenderness that brought tears of joy to her eyes.

Chapter Fifteen

Joshua gazed in wonder at the sight of Catherine curled against him on the small bed, sleeping contentedly. Her disheveled hair covered the pillow in an array of glistening waves, looking so soft he couldn't resist touching them with the tips of his fingers. He lifted one tendril from her face and pressed it to his nose to take in her scent. When he slid his arm back under the covers and caressed the soft skin of her back, she moaned in her sleep and stretched one leg down between his, the warm contact bringing an involuntary surge of passion to his senses.

A mere forty-eight hours ago, her fear of him had made this moment impossible to imagine. He was amazed at how easily her fear had evaporated with the awakening of her passion, how eagerly she had surrendered to the power of his embrace. But nothing in his experience had prepared him for the pleasure he found in her enthusiastic response to his lovemaking, and no sound had ever been sweeter to his ears than his own name, wrung from her lips in passionate cries each time he'd brought her to completion.

He moved his hand to cup her breast, weighed tenderly the pleasing handful. She moaned again and opened her eyes. His lips were on hers instantly, bringing her to full wakefulness with gentle, languid kisses. "What time is it?" she asked against his skin as he held her close.

"Nearly sundown. Did you sleep well?"

"Mmmm…" She traced one finger through the golden curls on his chest. He took her hand and held it still against him. "Last night was incredible."

"That was only the beginning," he said in quiet humor. "'Twas little more than normal lovemaking, except, perhaps, for stamina no mortal man can match."

"You mean there's more?"

He laughed at her nervous surprise. "When you're ready, I'll show you what I can really do when I put my mind to the task." He pressed his face against the top of her head. "I do not wish to wear you out before our honeymoon ends."

She wiggled her slight body against his. "I thought maybe I'd worn you out. How long were we at it?"

"Several hours." He moved his hand to her side and held her firmly. "Lie still, love. Are you not sore?"

She pressed her hips against his thigh, nearly driving him mad. "Terribly."

He swallowed the groan he felt rising from his chest and held her more tightly against him. "I can pleasure you all night, every night, but that will be harmful. You need to eat, and I don't intend to keep you from enjoying the ocean, no matter how tempting you are at this moment." He looked at her and was taken in by the love he found lighting those tiny bits of gold in her eyes. "I want you to go outside and watch the sun setting into the ocean. 'Tis a rare sight."

"Mmmm," she said with a slow shake of her head. "It wouldn't be much fun without you to share it with me."

"I can share it, if you'll permit me."

"What do you mean?"

He smiled at the innocence that was still so much a part of her. "There is much you have yet to learn of my abilities, and much I can teach you. While it is true I cannot face the sun directly, if you allow me to borrow your senses, I can watch the sun set through your eyes, feel the warmth of the breeze, hear the cries of the seagulls, without suffering the consequences. And you will be able to feel my response to your perceptions and know I am there with you."

Her eyes were wide, astonishment and trepidation evident on her face, but she nodded in complete trust at his suggestion. "What do I have to do?"

He tucked a loose strand of hair behind her ear with the tip of his index finger. "Relax your mind and let me in. 'Tis not hard, just don't let yourself resist. I will observe whatever you wish to show me."

"All right." She rolled reluctantly out of bed. "Ah! It's cold out here!" She pulled the bedspread around her for warmth and went to the door, her bare legs peeking from the front of her makeshift gown as she walked, making him regret sending her on this errand and out of his bed.

"Hurry now, the sun sets." He watched her leave the bedroom, trailing the bedspread behind her like a train, and when she'd closed the door, he rested his head back and closed his eyes. Although he'd spoken confidently of his abilities, he'd never tried this particular trick before. Projecting himself into her mind was easy. Teaching her to accept his presence proved to be more of a challenge. He watched her grope dizzily through the dark outer room and reach for the bolt on the door, felt the metal press cold against her palm as she pushed it back, then she paused to rest her head against the wood in an attempt to stop the world from spinning out from under her.

Your mind resists. Take a deep breath, and it will pass. He felt her head nodding against the door and tasted the coolness of oxygen rich air rushing into her supple lungs. He struggled against the unexpected pang he felt at the sensation of life he drew from her. She opened the front door and felt the warmth of the sun on her face. He felt her muscles work as she moved along the porch, and sensed the gentle creek and sway when that lovely bottom of hers came to rest in the swing. It took him a minute to realize the odd throbbing sensation coursing through his own body was an echo of her pulse.

She raised a foot in the air and wiggled her toes in the sun's warming glow, then tapped it against the railing to set the swing in motion. She looked up at the fluffy clouds dotting the remarkably blue sky, their undersides tinted in pinks and golds they reflected from the sun's waning light. A pair of seagulls swooped and played along the sandy shore, their calls providing sharp counterpoint to the soft swell of the ocean waves. Her eyes followed the progress of the gulls for a moment, and he felt a smile of wonder tug at her lips.

She turned her eyes to the setting sun and he lost himself in the spectacle playing out before her. A thin band of cloud stretched across the farthest horizon, carving a bright golden band across the sun. The fiery ball changed color, transforming itself from hot yellow to a more mellow gold, then to orange as it touched the sea. He half expected the water to boil and spew forth in a hot rush of steam the moment the sun dipped the horizon, but the ocean welcomed the sun into its embrace. The clouds changed their hue from one moment to the next, the pale pinks and golds deepening to salmon, deep mauve and cinnamon, and lavender and brown as the sun took its last look at the day and passed from view.

She was unaware of his physical presence, too wrapped up in the sensation of feeling him in her mind, until he seated himself beside her, released his mental hold and rested his arm around her shoulders. She pulled some of the bedspread over his naked skin, and they sat together in silence while the sky finished its transformation, the deep blue giving in to the dark velvet curtain of night. He pulled her against him and rested his head on top of hers. "Thank you, Catherine."

"I will remember that for the rest of my life," she whispered.

"The sunset was indeed beautiful."

"No, I mean having you inside my head. It was a feeling I'm not likely to ever forget."

"Was it unpleasant for you?"

"Oh, no. Well, at first, I guess, until I got my bearings. But I felt you, in here," she said, pressing her hand to her heart. "I wasn't expecting it to be so…intimate."

"It pleases me to know you can accept me so easily into your life. You've opened yourself so quickly to the possibilities I can offer. I am truly amazed."

She nuzzled her face against the hollow of his shoulder. "I hope the newness of this lasts. I think I like this feeling of discovery."

He chuckled and pulled her to her feet. "Ah, love, there is so much more. I won't let you get bored." He kissed her and patted her gently on the rear. "Let's get dressed, and we'll find you something to break your fast."

"W-what about you? Aren't you…thirsty?"

He sensed she was preparing to offer herself to him, and turned her to face him–too sharply, he realized, when he saw the look of alarm in her eyes. He softened his reaction by placing a gentle hand on her face. "I'll never feed from you, Catherine," he said firmly. "I may ask to taste you on occasion. My passions can become somewhat intense at times. I demonstrated some of that intensity to you the other night, and I don't believe you objected. Never will I take you without your consent, and never, ever, will I endanger your health in that way."

Her mouth moved nervously for a moment before she whispered, "I thought…I mean, you'll need blood. I don't see any cows in the area."

Suddenly the entire situation became comical to him, and he couldn't help the deep laugh that surged out of him. "Ah, Catherine my love, this is a network sanctuary. My needs will be met adequately, I assure you." He felt her relax in his arms, sensed the relief in her heart, and laughed again. "Go back inside. I'll get our things out of the car."

* * * *

As much as Katie enjoyed a weekend at the beach with Joshua, she was happy to be heading home. She smiled at the landscape sweeping past the car windows, and reviewed in her mind all the wonders she had seen. She discovered quickly that sand was best traversed barefoot, and enjoyed the sensation of sun-warmed sand sifting between her toes. The water was ice cold and salty, but she endured it long enough to explore the strange feeling of sand washing from under her feet as waves rolled over her ankles. Calls of seagulls still echoed in her mind.

Joshua had done his best to make the trip a memorable experience. Her mouth still watered at the memory of Dungeness crab and clam chowder. Her fingers absently explored the cockleshell she held in her lap while she recalled the long, relaxing walks along the beach followed by even longer sessions of sensual exploration. The memory of chill water lapping at her toes while they made love on the beach sent a shiver of remembered goose bumps crawling up her legs.

She felt the soft smile on her lips broaden when she thought of the passion that had heated their nights. The first time her hand brushed his manhood, his reflexive jump made her pull away uncertainly, but he had gently guided her hand back to him, and his hoarse whisper, "Yes, love. Touch me," still resonated in her mind. When she'd closed her hand around him and given him a gentle squeeze, he had lifted her over him, planted her firmly and accurately over his need, and taught her the heady pleasure of taking control.

"If you don't cease your train of thought, we'll never make it home," he complained, breaking her out of her musings and bringing her mind back to the present.

"Sorry," she said with a laugh. "I didn't realize I was thinking out loud." She turned her thoughts homeward. "I wonder what Alex has been up to."

He drew in a deep breath and let it out slowly. "Keeping busy, I'm sure."

"It'll be good to be home."

She thought she saw a sly smile pass briefly over his face. "Aye."

"How many more places are there like that one at the beach?"

"Too many for me to tell you. They're all over the world." He gave her a genuine smile and said, "I can take you anywhere, show you anything you can imagine, and many things you can't. Just ask."

She rested her head against the seat. "I wouldn't know where to begin."

"We could explore America, for a start. Not just the United States. We can walk the shores of Mexico. Head farther south and visit Rio. Would you like to explore ancient Aztec and Incan ruins? Tour the great castles of Europe? Discover secret chambers in the pyramids of Giza or ride camels across the Sahara? All this and more I want to share with you."

She thought silently for several minutes. "Scotland."

His smile brightened. "Oh, aye. 'Twould be a pleasure to show you my homeland."

He exited the freeway onto the county road leading through the woods, and she sat back and watched the trees pass by, deep in thought. After a while, she drew in a deep breath and asked, "Could we just stay here for a while?"

He slowed to turn up the narrow drive to the house. "Getting tired already?"

"No, I thought maybe we could take some time to get used to each other first." She caught a glimpse of an old pickup parked in front of the house. "What's Carl doing here?"

He pulled the Sebring to a stop, and she jumped out to look at the odd array of objects in the bed of the truck. There were various sized scraps of lumber, used paint cans, painting tools, chunks of drywall, an electric saw, and several other things half buried in the rubble. Carl came out the front door, whistling tunelessly and carrying an old-fashioned tool caddy. "All finished, sir." He dropped the caddy in the passenger seat with a decidedly noisy clunk.

"Okay, what's going on?"

"Let's take a look," Joshua said in Carl's direction. He stepped lightly up the porch steps and around to the side of the house where her bedroom was. She followed closely behind. "Looks good here," he said to Carl.

"The clapboards gave us a bit of a bother. We had to cut into the existing panels to stagger the seams for a better seal."

"Where's my window?"

"You matched the paint well."

"W-well, we actually painted the entire side, so it would blend in better."

"Where's my window?" she asked again.

Alex appeared around the corner and handed a screwdriver to Carl. *The hardware is finished.*

"We had a little trouble with the door, too. We had to take the entire wall apart and reframe it," Carl added. "I'm afraid it still smells of fresh paint, but the mess is cleaned up."

"What's going on?" she asked. "Joshua?"

He laughed lightly and put his arm around her waist. "Were you able to find the painting I wanted?"

"Yeah, that was the biggest trick," Carl said, his eyes showing his growing humor. "I called around all night Friday, and finally found one like what you described in a gallery in Edinburgh. A courier delivered it to my office this afternoon."

"Joshua!"

He gave her an innocent look, his eyes twinkling merrily. "Are you ready to go inside, love?"

"If you don't tell me..." She almost punched him when he laughed again and led her to the front door.

He swept her into his arms to carry her across the threshold. "Welcome home, Mrs. MacAaron."

Once her feet touched the floor, she looked around and quickly noticed the change to the hall entrance. "A pocket door? Why did you put a pocket door on the hall?"

"To keep out the sunlight," Joshua explained as if it should be obvious, his voice reflecting barely contained excitement.

"Sunlight?" She felt a frown pull at her eyebrows, and then realization sank in. "Sunlight!" She dashed down the hall and through her bedroom door, where she skidded to a stop and stared in disbelief. The outside wall looked as if it had never had a window in it. In its place, a beautiful painting hung on the wall, flanked by a pair of mirrored sconces. Joshua's chest of drawers had been moved in and placed next to the closet door. She didn't have to look to know his clothes were hanging inside.

She stepped forward slowly to study the artwork, which featured a young woman with raven hair and an angelic face, wearing a full-length, old-fashioned gown and sitting in a field dotted with heather and wild flowers, a small wooden harp resting on her lap. Her fingers were poised over the strings, and her lips were parted softly as if in song. A man with brown hair Joshua's length was seated near her, wearing a blue and green kilt and a rapt look on his face. She could almost hear the music that must've inspired the scene.

Joshua's arms slid around her from behind, and his chin came to rest on her shoulder. "Are you pleased, my wife?"

"You did this for me?" she asked, her voice barely a whisper.

"For both of us," he answered, turning her to face him and stroking her face. "I believe a man should have the privilege of waking each day with his wife at his side."

The tenderness in his eyes brought a lump to her throat. "You can sleep with me now," she said, understanding filling her heart.

"My shelter was inadequate. You would not have found it as comfortable." He kissed the tear that dripped onto her cheek and smiled. "The outer door will allow you to leave the room without admitting the sun, should you wake early and desire food."

"Oh, Joshua!" She flung her arms around him and felt his close firmly around her. "Thank you!"

Carl cleared his throat, drawing her attention. She pulled herself away from Joshua to give both Carl and Alex grateful hugs. "You guys did a great job."

"Thanks," Carl answered happily. "If you'll come to the front, we've arranged a celebration."

Alex placed a small white cake decorated in red rosebuds on the table while Carl drew a bottle of champagne from the refrigerator and popped the cork. After he'd poured four glasses and handed them around, he said, "I'd like to propose a toast. May your lives be forever filled with all the joy you're feeling at this moment."

Joshua turned to Katie and linked his arm around hers, and she sipped the bubbling liquid while he tipped his glass to his lips, his eyes capturing hers and filled with happiness. Then Alex handed her a cake knife and motioned for her to cut the cake. Joshua put his hand over hers and helped her guide the knife and lifted a piece to her waiting mouth. She knew she could not return the favor, but he surprised her when he bent to lick the frosting from her lips. "Mmmm. Tasty," he said, his eyes darkening. She almost forgot Alex and Carl were in the room.

Chapter Sixteen

Nothing about Katie's new life with Joshua could be described as normal or routine. During the weeks following their wedding, each night had been nothing less than an adventure. She had a lot to learn, and did her best to take his lessons to heart. For the most part, he was a gentle and patient teacher. His soft voice guided her thoughts and helped her turn the chaos in her mind into a more ordered discipline ranging from simple vampire resistance to blocking herself from notice, and even sensing the presence of and recognizing vampires among normal humankind.

He told her of the Community, their Enforcers and the Council of Elders, answered all her questions regarding vampire lore, societal relationships and clan differences, and firmly warned her on the proper way to face one, in case her knowledge should ever be challenged. Vampires, he advised, are attracted to fear. It sweetens the blood. Her only defense to a vampire's scrutiny is to endure it unflinchingly, and hope a show of courage impresses the creature. After what she'd already been through, she hoped never to need his advice.

Learning to reach out to him with her mind had been easier than she'd imagined, given that they were so closely bonded. After several practice sessions, accepting his presence in her mind became almost automatic.

When it came to exploring sexuality, he seemed to have an inexhaustible repertoire. Some of the positions he'd introduced her to were way beyond her wildest imaginings. Yet he always held back, keeping their sessions within the realm of normal. She sat on the sofa, working on an embroidery project and thinking back over all the ways they'd explored. She wondered if he'd been teasing her about having special abilities to draw on. Okay, so he was inhumanly insatiable, always ready to continue even into the early hours of dawn until she fell asleep in his arms exhausted and deeply satisfied. In all the conversations she'd ever overheard in school, from all the giggling, hormone crazed girls she'd ever known, she'd never heard of anything that compared to Joshua's appetite for lovemaking.

He sat in his chair reviewing the financial section of the evening paper. At the moment, he looked the way any normal husband might, turning to the next page and folding it over the way the average man would. If not for the fact they started their day when most of the world was preparing to end theirs, she might've believed it to be true. She smiled softly and returned to her embroidery, but her mind had drifted too far away from the pattern, and she pricked her finger more than once while pulling back a few stray stitches.

She wasn't sure when she first became aware of the fact the room had gotten hotter. Or was it her own body temperature that climbed as her most sensitive areas came to life? She took a deep breath and felt her tightening breasts strain against her blouse. That breath threatened to come out as a moan when her nether region suddenly ached with the need to be touched. She swallowed hard and changed the position of her legs, and a thrill swept over her.

With a gasp of surprise, she looked up to find that Joshua had rested his paper in his lap and was looking at her with heated concentration in his eyes and the slightest smile on his lips. "Are you doing this?" she asked breathlessly. His only response was a knowing smile before he shifted his gaze back to his paper, but she could tell by the hot gleam in his eyes he was not focusing his attention on the newsprint. "You!" she cried, jumping from the couch and over to his chair. He quickly dropped the paper to accept her onto his lap, where she straddled him and playfully punched at his chest.

He caught her hands easily and held her still. "Now you do not doubt my abilities," he said with a smile."

"H-how far can you take it?"

His voice took on a dangerous edge when he answered. "I'm not yet certain you can take it, were I to show you the full extent of my love for you. I've been told mortals, especially women, can die from such pleasure."

She felt all the blood drain from her face. "Wow. What a way to go." He chuckled softly and put his hands behind her back. "Was this what you meant about…when you were with Antonia?"

He smiled again. "She was overwhelming, but I had a strong heart, and proved to be, even then, equal to the challenge." He slipped his hands tenderly down her back to cup her bottom, and she felt his fingers curl toward her more sensitive flesh. "This is an interesting idea," he commented, that hot gleam returning to his eyes.

"In your chair?" she asked, trying to sound shocked. "What if Alex…?"

"Alex has gone into town this evening to seek his own amusement."

This time she was shocked. "You're kidding!"

"He may look and act shy and innocent," he countered with a laugh, "but he knows well the pleasures to be found in a woman's arms." He lifted her from his lap long enough to divest her of her slacks, and pulled her back to her former position. "Now, let's see if I can relieve some of the tension I've caused you."

* * * *

"Are you coming, Catherine?" Joshua called from the hallway.

"Yeah, just a sec." She adjusted the blue ribbon bow on the wicker basket sitting on the table. "Do you think Taska will like it?" she asked, carrying the basket filled with assorted baby toys and newborn clothing.

"She'd better," he answered with a smile of amused annoyance. "You took enough care in selecting your gifts."

"I can't believe it's August already," she said on the way to the hospital.

"Well, you know what they say about time passing quickly when you're having fun," he replied, his eyebrows raised suggestively.

She laughed. "You're incorrigible!"

"No love. Where you are concerned, I'm downright insatiable."

"Do you think they'll let us in?" she whispered nervously as they approached the maternity ward entrance.

"I'm sure of it. Leave it to me." She watched curiously while he approached the guard, saw the uncomfortable look on the poor man's face when Joshua made his request, then smiled when he motioned for her to follow him inside.

"Hi, Momma," she said softly when they entered Taska's room.

"Katie! Hi. Hi, Joshua." She smiled at the tiny bundle in her arms and said, "Wake up, Mathew. We have visitors. Guys, meet my son, Mathew Kyle Ward."

"Oh, Taska," she whispered, gazing at the sleeping cherub wrapped in a tiny hospital blanket. "He's precious. Can I hold him?"

"Sure," Taska answered, lifting the infant into her waiting arms. She accepted the bundle and rocked him tenderly. "He's so tiny. How much did he weigh?"

"Six pounds, eleven and a half ounces," Taska replied.

"Just look at him, Joshua. Isn't he the sweetest thing?"

"Aye, love. That he is." She looked up at him in time to see the hint of regret in his eyes. He caressed the tiny cheek with the tip of one finger, then turned away to sit in a chair. She could tell he was making an attempt at casualness, but sensed more going on deep in his soul.

"I've got some bad news for you. Dillon got a job offer in Sacramento. We're moving as soon as I'm well enough to travel."

"Oh, no! That's such a long way away."

"Perhaps we can go to visit them sometime," Joshua suggested quietly.

"Oh, I'd love that," Taska said with a smile.

They stayed a few minutes longer, visiting until Taska looked too tired to stay awake any longer. They drove silently back to the house, and sat together on the sofa. He sent his usual burst of thought to the fireplace, and they sat for a long time, gazing silently at the flames. "Seeing the baby bothered you," she said finally.

"No, love. Seeing you holding the baby bothered me. I regret not being able to give you such a precious gift."

She took in a deep breath and nestled herself more comfortably in his arms. "I'm okay with it. I've never been happier in my life."

She felt the smile that came to his lips deep in her own heart. He stroked her hair tenderly for a few minutes, then asked, "Do you want a child of your own, Catherine?"

She sat up to look at him, a frown pulling at her brows. "What do you mean?"

"Modern medicine has ways of compensating for my inabilities. There are fertility clinics where you can receive the cells you'd need. I can ask Carl to help make the arrangements, if you wish. We can select a donor who closely resembles me, so the child will grow to look like one of us."

She shook her head and settled back into his arms. "I've heard of those clinics. The baby I'd conceive from them would not be yours. Besides, I hear it's painful. I don't know if I want to put myself through it."

He smiled softly and rested his head on hers. "If you change your mind, I'm willing to help. The child would be yours, and I would love it as much as its mother. I want you to be happy."

She hugged him tightly. "I am happy, Joshua. You're so good to me, and I love you very much. I don't need two-o'clock feedings and messy diapers to make me happier." He returned her firm embrace, and she felt silent laughter shake his chest.

* * * *

For her nineteenth birthday, Joshua presented Katie with a beautifully sculpted candle stand for the bedroom. Graceful brass stems rose from the simple base, each topped with fine cut crystal shapes layered and artfully arranged to resemble lotus blossoms. She reverently lit each of the six votives and smiled at the softly refracted light they cast around the room.

He put his arms around her and gazed lovingly into her eyes. "You're even more beautiful by candlelight," he whispered. He touched his lips to hers so tenderly she thought she might melt.

"Joshua," she said, moving away to look at him. "Don't hold back tonight. Teach me how to handle your love. All of it."

"No, Catherine," he said tightly. "If I should end your life...."

"I won't let it go that far," she insisted, pulling his hands to her waist. "Neither will you." She reached up to put her hand on his face, and watched him close his eyes tight. "I have faith in you."

"I could lose control. We both could. I can't take that chance."

"Start slow," she said quietly. "Take it one small step at a time and give me a chance to get used to it. I'll be all right. I know you won't let me die."

He stroked her face tenderly. "If you're certain this is what you want." She nodded, and closed her eyes when his lips touched hers. He laid her gently on the bed, captured her eyes with a gaze both dark and powerful, and she surrendered as he moved into the deepest parts of her mind. Her body nearly exploded on contact, her senses reeling. He seemed to be everywhere around her at once. Every nerve ending sang at his slightest touch. At first, it was all she could do to withstand the sheer strength of him. Her heart raced, her body trembled, until she found the ability to respond to sensations both physical and spiritual.

By the time he moved over her, her heart was pounding a crazy, uncontrolled beat in her chest. His entry brought a frightening surge of power through her, and she started wondering if she really did have the strength to live through it. He held her close while he moved inside her, and she sensed his vague awareness of her struggles to control her own responses. Wordlessly, he guided her hand to his lips and kissed the tips of her fingers, sending shock waves skittering up her arm. Then he rose up to look at her, his eyes glowing with ferocious yellow heat. He closed her fingers into a fist and positioned her thumbnail over the pulse point at his throat, and said in a quiet voice that was almost a growl, "Take me."

She wasn't sure what he meant until his grip on her hand tightened, and her nail broke the surface of his skin with an unsettling pop. He quickly pulled her tight against him again, his hand guiding her face to the wound now open and dripping blood. "Take me," he whispered again. When she nervously licked at the blood running down to his collar, she heard him moan and felt the word "Yesss" blow against her skin. She closed her lips over his wound and pulled gently at it, and felt his blood rush into her mouth and down her throat.

Overwhelming sensual chaos swept through them both. What tenuous control he had snapped the moment she drew her first taste of his blood. With a feral cry, he pressed her body tighter against him until she could barely breathe, drove himself deeper than he'd ever gone before, his movements becoming pure, fluid urgency. She was only vaguely aware that her body was reacting in kind, and that her mouth was still drawing at his throat. A strange sense of exhilaration overtook her, giving her the strength she needed to withstand his unrestrained passion.

She felt his body stiffen, and with two long, violent thrusts, he launched them both into completion so intense they both cried out, their voices blending and reverberating around the room like a victory cry. Before her pleasure had a chance to ebb his fangs were in her throat and she cried out once more, her body giving the last of its strength to a reaction that sent her tumbling over the abyss.

* * * *

He slowly returned to his senses an hour later, the taste of her blood still fresh on his tongue and their impassioned cries still echoing loudly in his mind. Gradually, the events of the evening filtered back to his mind. He'd lost control. Completely. Not since his time with Antonia had he felt such soul-deep, unbridled pleasure. Shame poured through him when he recalled how uncontrolled he had become, how quickly he had succumbed to the power of his own passion. He vaguely recalled the sense that she was losing her struggle to survive under the torrent of feelings he'd sent her. Her heart had almost burst with the strain, and he'd been relieved when she gave in and took his blood. Now, as he lay beside her still body and struggled to regain his own strength, he wondered if he'd only prolonged the inevitable, if he'd sustained her long enough to quench his own needs, but not enough to save her.

He raised himself up on one elbow the moment he found the strength to move, afraid of what he might find when he looked at her, and was deeply relieved to see her sleeping soundly and still very much alive. He sobbed silently at the sight of her lying beside him, so warm and trusting, too eager to please. The thought of her enthusiasm and strength during this trial returned to him, and with the memory of her courage came a final and lasting hope they will be together, happily together, for many long years to come. He settled himself back against the pillow and pulled her limp body against his, felt her unconscious, trembling sigh, and let himself drift into much needed rest.

Chapter Seventeen

Katie woke and stretched languidly under the rumpled bedding. She yawned deeply and reached for Joshua, and felt mildly confused when she found he wasn't there. She sat up feeling oddly spent and shaky, and wondered how long she'd slept. With effort, she managed to swing her legs around to the side of the bed, and had to put her head down against an unexpected wave of dizziness. When her head settled, she made use of the bathroom, where she found evidence he'd been up at least long enough to shower and shave.

Last night had been a wild ride, by far more intense than she'd anticipated. She knew almost from the moment they began she would have trouble adjusting to the sheer power at his command, but she'd been sure she could handle it, and felt so trusting in his ability to protect her. When he lost control and let his fullest passion overwhelm her, she thought for a moment she was going to die. "He tried to warn you," she scolded herself weakly.

A smudge of his blood still clung to the corner of her mouth. The face in the mirror frowned back at her while she tried to remember what happened after he'd insisted she drink from him. Once she'd closed her lips over his skin and tasted his blood, all rational thought had fled in a wave of passion too overwhelming to be believed, ending in completion so intense the world could've exploded and gone into oblivion without her ever noticing. She reached weakly for the shower controls and advised herself sternly, "Next time, be careful what you ask for."

Once she'd gotten cleaned up, she thought she felt better. She sat on the foot of the bed and brushed her hair, then reached out her mind in an attempt to discover what had happened to him. It didn't take much effort to learn he was sitting in the living room, and the sensation he was not alone, that there was another vampire in the house, took her by surprise. After a minute of concentration, she learned their otherworldly visitor was Vincent, which would've set her mind more at ease if it wasn't for the strange sense of urgency and grief she received from Joshua's mind.

She dressed quickly and went to join Joshua in the living room and greet their visitor. She found him standing at the fireplace, one hand braced on the mantle, his head hung as if in deep thought or despair. Vincent was no longer present. "I thought Vincent was here."

He turned to look at her, deep pain in his eyes. "He had to go," he said, his voice oddly deep and strained. "Are you well, Catherine?"

"I'm a little tired, that's all. Last night was...."

"I should never have allowed you to talk me into it. I warned you we might lose control."

She forced a weak smile. "I survived it. Next time, I'll know what to expect."

"It will be a long time before I allow myself to indulge again in that fashion, if it happens at all. I almost lost you."

"It was harder to take than I thought, but I can get used to it in time. I never realized how...intense our lovemaking could be." She looked up at him and smiled. "There will be a next time, Joshua, and I'll be better prepared for it."

He threaded his fingers through her hair and gave her a sad smile. "You need to learn to temper your courage with a bit of common sense, love. Don't sacrifice yourself for the sake of my pleasure, 'tis not necessary."

Something in the way he looked at her, as if he were holding her for the last time, sent a surge of dread through her heart. "What's wrong, Joshua? What did Vincent want?"

His distress deepened instantly. "Sit down. We need to talk." He led her to the sofa and pulled her tight against him. "I'm afraid I must leave you for a time, love, though the timing is not best. You will have questions about last night I don't have the time to explain."

"Leave? Why?"

He drew in a deep breath and held it for a moment, and released it in what sounded like a resigned sigh. "The Community is threatened. A call-to-arms has been issued. I must go to Haven and aid in its defense."

"What's Haven?" she asked, trying hard to control the lump growing painfully in her throat.

"I'm sorry. I thought I explained that to you. 'Tis this country's central base, or headquarters, if you will," he explained. "It's hidden deep in the mountains of northern Georgia. Its location has been a closely guarded secret since long before your country was born. The Council meets there when important issues arise, and it provides shelter for those in the process of relocating. There are usually around a dozen vampires in residence at any given time, as well as a host of servants. I have not visited there in a very long time but I can't imagine it's changed much."

"Kind of like vampire central?"

"Aye, you may think of it thus," he answered with a strained chuckle. "Two months ago, they discovered a rogue lying in the woods not far from the stronghold. He had an arrow in his heart. Since that time, more dead have been found. Some were killed in the same manner, others were found in a condition not easy to conceive, their bodies seemingly ravaged from within."

"What's a rogue?"

"Rogues are fashioned differently than more civilized clans. They are little more than mindless killing machines. We leave them alone, for the most part, unless their savagery threatens to expose vampire existence."

"Well, if someone's taking them out…"

"There's more to it, love," he added, his voice thickening. "About three weeks ago, a vampire by the name of Devin, an Englishman I knew well and respected, took an arrow south of Haven. Little more than a week later, another was found, destroyed in the same curious manner they've yet to identify."

He pulled in a deep, shaky breath. "Two nights ago, another member of our kind was struck down. He lives, but appears to be suffering that same strange affliction. His name is Jason, and he's the oldest and wisest creature in modern knowledge. Some have gone so far as to call him our King, though not within his hearing. He managed to tell his woman he'd been poisoned before he lost consciousness. He's been in the vampire equivalent of a coma ever since." He pulled her close and held her tightly against him. "I have to go, love. My kind are being slaughtered without discretion. Attacks are growing closer to Haven. It is uncertain yet whether this is the work of one hunter acting alone, or if there are more waging a war bent on destroying us all. Every vampire in the country is being called in to assist in Haven's defense."

She clung to him fiercely. "When do you have to leave?"

"Right away."

"Can…" she paused to choke back a sob, "can I go with you?"

"No, lass, you can't. It's too dangerous for you right now."

"Why? We're bound to each other. The others won't hurt me if they know how close we are."

"It's not entirely the Community I'm concerned about, though not all of them are predictable enough where you're concerned. I have not taken you under my control, as is required of me before I can take you there unannounced. There are a few who might take exception to that, at least at first. But there are other dangers present which could put your life in jeopardy."

"I'm not afraid of anything but losing you."

"I feel the same, love, but this situation is no different than any other war in your mortal history. I am uncertain what I will learn once I get there. If Haven falls, all who reside there may be destroyed. If it will help you to understand, think of yourself as the wife of a soldier being called to battle. You wouldn't have expected your husband to allow you to charge the hill at Iwo Jima or storm the beaches of Normandy at his side, now would you?"

"No, I guess not," she whispered against his shoulder. "I don't want you to go."

"I cannot turn my back to the need of the others, not at a time like this, although it pains me deeply to become so far removed from you. I will be able to focus better on my mission knowing you're here, safe and waiting for my return." He rose from the sofa, pulled her with him, and kissed her gently before pulling away. "I need to pack and get moving. I'll have to hurry if I'm to reach Haven before sunrise. Explain the situation to Alex. He will look after you in my absence. Call Carl and let him know as well. Lean on them for support until I return."

She followed him to their room and watched him quickly stuff a few basic items into a sports bag. She took his scarf from the top of his chest of drawers and looped it tenderly around his neck. "Promise me you'll be careful," she said, her voice sounding like a plea. "Keep your head down."

He kissed her deeply, brushed more tears from her cheeks and did his best to smile. "I will. Now give me a smile, love. Let me remember your smile until I can return to you." She gave him a smile trembling with grief and fear, and watched him leave the house and fly into the night. She sank onto the sofa, buried her face in the soft velvet, and released her distress in a flood of hot tears.

Alex did his best to console her when she told him the news. She placed a call to Carl while Alex prepared dinner, and did her best to assure him she'd be all right. Alex watched her pick silently at her dinner, the look on his face mirroring her own deep concern. "I'm sorry," she said at last, pushing her plate away. "I guess I'm just not hungry. My stomach is upset. It's probably because I already miss him so much. I think I'll go back to bed." She went to her room, slid under her covers and closed her eyes, but sleep didn't come until almost daybreak.

* * * *

The miles flowed past Joshua without notice. The way Catherine looked worried him, nagged at the deepest reaches of his heart, and more than once made him consider returning to her and forsaking his duty to the Community. He couldn't help but think there was something wrong. He resolved to bring the problems at Haven to a close as quickly as possible, and hoped with all his heart for her health and safety. He set himself on the grounds of Haven an hour before sunrise.

He stood for a moment and gazed at the forbidding fortress, its rough-cut stone exterior standing out darkly against the forest pressing close around it. It looked just as he remembered it, though the wooden porch had been replaced since his last visit. As he stepped slowly to the heavy double doors in the front, he steeled his heart against the memories he would encounter inside.

As he expected, when he opened the door and entered the grand hall, he found Antonia waiting to greet him. He gave her a carefully closed look as she smiled and approached him. "Good morning, Antonia," he said tightly.

"Joshua MacAaron! How good it is to see you again," she said happily as she moved to put her arms around him. When he didn't respond to her embrace, she backed away to study him closely. "You've changed, my darling," she said, losing some of her smile. "What happened to the carefree boy I used to know?"

"I am no longer your darling, Antonia. You well know this."

She pretended a pout as she eyed him suspiciously. "Have you no care left for the one who gave you life eternal?"

An involuntary stab of old pain and anger came over him, and he nearly let his careful control slip. "I desired your love once," he answered tightly. "No longer. I am here at the summons of the Council, to aid Haven during this crisis. I do not intend to stay."

He felt her attempt to probe his thoughts, and did his best to shield himself from her scrutiny. He'd forgotten how powerful his master was. "You've found a woman," she said softly. "A mortal."

He turned away from her to face the door leading into the room that served as both library and Council chamber. "Aye."

"She is aware of what you are."

It took him a moment to draw the courage to respond. "Aye."

"There will be questions asked, Joshua. You know the rules."

"Catherine is no danger to the Community. I have her loyalty."

"Then you've taken control of her." When he didn't respond to her statement, he felt a flash of anger from her. "Have you learned nothing from your last such encounter?"

"I remember that lesson only too well," he said sharply. "I do not feel inclined to explain my relationship with Catherine to you or anyone else. It is none of your concern. I will protect her from harm, even to my last ounce of strength."

"Your feelings for her must be deep if you're willing to risk retribution."

He spun around and faced her with his anger, knowing full well he could not resist her superior strength if she decided to use it. "As I said, she is none of your concern. I do not wish to discuss her with you, or anyone else."

"Well, you'll have to," she countered, a sharp glitter in her onyx eyes, "but right now, the Community has worse things to worry about. You're tired from your journey. Go take your rest. We meet at sunset."

With a curt nod, he shouldered his bag and headed up the wide marble staircase to the windowless second floor and took the first vacant room he came to. He dropped his bag on the chair, kicked off his shoes, and laid himself on top of the bed. His last thoughts were of Catherine as he twined his fingers into the stitching of his scarf and surrendered to his rest.

* * * *

"It is not yet certain the extent of this threat," Trey said, his deep voice booming through the Council chamber. "Our first task will be to set up surveillance in the woods and gather any information we can. If the person, or persons, responsible for our destruction can be discovered, they must be captured and brought before the Council for examination. We must learn how many enemies we face, and how far this threat reaches."

"That sounds reasonable," Rudy said with a respectful nod, "but we should not go out alone. We will work in teams, and keep constant mental communication open so we don't lose any more friends."

"Well spoken," Antonia said. "That is, in fact, the plan. You'll all be paired up and sent to checkpoints. We have the manpower to cover Haven's Realm, including Fulcrum and Carrington."

"Be extra diligent in your observations," Trey added tightly. "You will set out at dusk every night, and return for a meeting every morning, one hour before dawn, to compare any information gathered. Are there any questions?"

"Has there been any progress in procuring vests, or any other form of protection?" Stephan asked.

"Dragon-skin vests are being ordered, but it is difficult to fill as large a request as we need without raising undue attention. They will be issued as they arrive, but I don't expect the first to be available at least until next week. In the mean time, your complete attention to your surroundings will be your best defense. You're all dismissed to your assignments. Return here at the end of the night."

Joshua felt relieved Antonia had not brought the subject of Catherine to the attention of the Council. He hadn't realized he was mentally holding his breath in suspense at the prospect of having to face them with his news. He had received a welcome, if, he felt certain, short-lived reprieve. Vincent approached him as he rose from his seat. "Somehow, I have the feeling you'll be more comfortable in my company just now. Shall we go?" He nodded, clasped his friend on the arm and felt the man's hand firmly grip his in return, then turned to leave the mansion.

* * * *

Katie quickly realized there was something wrong with her, but she kept her discomfort to herself. She woke each evening feeling worse than she had the previous day. She had very little appetite and had to force herself to eat, but she felt her strength beginning to wane. Occasional bouts of mild nausea became gut-wrenching cramps that robbed her of sleep. Dizzy spells kept her head throbbing painfully. She found she had to force herself out of bed each night, unwilling to give her watchful companions the impression she was giving in to depression again.

Alex did his best to tend to her needs, and Carl paid frequent visits. She endured countless evenings of games and visits, grateful for the company and the sound of another human voice each time Carl came, but the strain of keeping up her act was quickly catching up with her.

During one of Carl's visits, three weeks after Joshua's departure, she felt a sharp pain lance through her chest. She screamed and sank to the floor, clutching her chest and gasping for breath. "Katie, what's wrong?" Carl asked, instantly at her side.

"I don't know," she cried. "Oh, God this hurts!"

"I'll call an ambulance."

"No!" she exclaimed. The pain eased and she pulled herself weakly upright. "No, I'm okay. It's not that bad now."

Carl helped her to Joshua's easy chair and raised her feet. "Are you sure you're all right?"

"Yeah, thank you," she answered weakly as she rubbed the still-throbbing ache beneath her left breast. "Maybe it was a cramp. Something I ate."

Carl nodded doubtfully, but from that night on, his visits came more frequently. In the days that followed, her condition continued to worsen until Carl spoke up again. "I think you need to see a doctor."

"No doctor," she argued weakly. "I can't take the risk."

He knelt beside her, deep concern on his face. "Tell me what's wrong."

With a deep breath, more to steady herself than for any other reason, she told him what happened between herself and Joshua the night before he left. "I can't take the chance this has something to do with him," she concluded. "If the doctor finds anything out of the ordinary, anything I can't explain…."

"I think I understand, Katie. Really. But you can't risk your health like this. Joshua would want you to get help. Look at you! Have you even been eating?"

"I'm having a hard time keeping food down," she admitted, then straightened in the chair and tried to look strong. "I'll be fine. Joshua will be back any time. He promised. After I've had a chance to talk to him, if he agrees there's no risk, I'll go."

"All right," he agreed reluctantly, "but if you don't get better soon, I'll take you to the hospital myself, even if I have to tie you down to do it. And to hell with the consequences."

* * * *

She sat in the chair by the fire late one night two weeks later, sipping gingerly at a cup of tea Alex had made for her and wishing desperately for Joshua's return. Five weeks had passed, and she didn't know if she would survive a sixth. She hadn't had the energy to take a shower in over a week, and spent most of her time in bed. Another wave of nausea, and the accompanying dizziness, made her lower her head between her knees. Her belly cramped painfully, and she did her best to breathe deeply until the pain passed. When she raised her head again, she saw a woman standing in front of her. She was too weak to feel even mild surprise.

"You look like hell."

"Th-thanks." She forced herself upright and looked at her unexpected visitor. The woman might have been Nicole's older sister. Her hair was the color of the midnight sky, and fell straight and sleek to her lower back. Her black, almond-shaped eyes glittered like onyx, and were strikingly set into a pale, delicately carved face. Her thin, shapely figure belonged on the cover of an exclusive fashion magazine. She wore a sleeveless black satin tunic over a pair of skin-tight black leather pants. The dark clothes accentuated her smooth pale skin, skin that had an unnatural glow. A lump formed in her throat she suspected was her heart. "Antonia."

"So he's told you of me." The woman sounded impatient. "Don't be afraid, Catherine. I haven't come to hurt you."

She nodded, swallowing down her fear with a couple of short gasps. "Joshua…?"

"He is…not here."

"He's in trouble, isn't he?"

Before Antonia responded, another cramp twisted her middle. She groaned loudly, collapsed to the floor, and curled in a tight fetal position beside a pair of stiletto-clad feet. The creaking of leather told her Antonia had knelt beside her before she felt her strong hands lift her shoulders. She opened her eyes and gazed at her pleadingly. "Help me," she whispered.

"What's wrong with you?" she asked more sympathetically.

"Don't know. I've been sick. I…I think I'm dying." She took a couple of short, painful breaths. "Can you…please…don't let me die."

When she looked up again, she saw the woman understood what she was asking. Before her eyes, Antonia's face took on the expected change. Her eyes went from jet black to feral yellow. When she parted her full, red lips, a pair of delicate fangs glinted in the firelight. "You willingly offer me your complete trust?"

She swallowed hard and nodded, closed her eyes, and gave herself over to the vampire's will. As Antonia pulled her easily into her arms, she did her best to relax and surrender to the power she felt rush through her, power much more intense than anything she'd felt from Joshua. She accepted the woman's mind and felt a surge of emotional calm overtake her. Antonia's cool breath brushed her neck before her tongue gently moistened the skin at the base of her throat. The sharp points of her fangs pressed against her skin, but then she paused for a moment and backed away. A look of uncertainty darkened her face. She was surprised when, instead of taking her blood, Antonia sank her fangs into her own wrist.

"Drink," she said tightly, holding that wrist to her lips. "Come, now," she scolded when she hesitated. "It's not as if you haven't taken blood before."

She felt surprised and embarrassed at the knowledge Antonia had obviously found in her mind. "Just once," she whispered. "I thought that might be what's wrong with me."

"You're mistaken, Catherine," Antonia said, her tone patently impatient. "You must have faced grave illness or some other need that drove Joshua to feed you. A vampire can always sense if, and how often, a mortal has fed. Now, drink."

Suddenly everything that had happened to her since that night in the hospital made perfect sense. The strange bond that had formed between her and Joshua, the heightened senses, all of it, had to have been his doing, but she knew down deep inside he'd never have done such a thing unless he had no other choice. He had said at the time he'd believed she would die. She found just enough strength to wonder why he'd never told her.

She sighed in resignation and parted her lips to accept Antonia's blood, and swallowed more from reflex than will when the cool, rich liquid flowed down her throat. Her stomach settled down almost instantly. She drew gently against the woman's wrist and swallowed again, and shot a surprised look at Antonia as the nausea eased.

"Don't be shy," Antonia said, her voice more gentle, like that of a mother nursing a reluctant child. "You need it more than I do right now." She pulled again at the wound and closed her eyes as, with every swallow, more of the pain in her belly eased. Her dizziness faded. Strength slowly returned to her limbs. By the time Antonia pulled her wrist away and helped her back into the chair, she felt much better.

"What's wrong with me?" she asked as she watched Alex offer a bandage to Antonia. "Am I turning into a vampire?"

Antonia chuckled as she taped the bandage to her wrist. "No, Catherine. It takes more than a little blood to bring someone across."

"Then why...?"

"Why didn't I bring you across?" She nodded once to confirm the question. Antonia sighed, a wholly theatrical gesture. "I sense things in you that concern me, but I don't want to say anything until I'm sure."

Alex gestured to her briefly with a look of grave concern. "Yes, Alex. I'm feeling better." He gestured again and turned to Antonia with a look of respect in his eyes. He held his wrist to the woman solemnly, and Antonia looked at him in surprise. "Alex wishes to express his thanks for helping me," she said quietly.

Antonia nodded once and accepted Alex's offer, and Katie watched the woman drink in the same way Joshua had taken him. Then she helped her out of the chair and down the hall to her bedroom. "You should clean yourself up," she observed. "Do you need help?"

She tested her own legs, wobbled slightly, and shook her head. "I think I can manage."

Antonia considered her for a moment longer, then nodded curtly. "I have some phone calls to make. I'd advise you to hurry. You will soon need to sleep." She gave her a puzzled look. "There's no time to explain," Antonia told her as she moved to the door. "Shower and go to bed. I'll look in on you later."

* * * *

When Antonia returned to the front of the house, Alex gestured to her, a look of deep concern on his face. She raised her hand and shook her head. "I don't understand you," she told him, "but Catherine will live." Alex lowered his hands and nodded, though he didn't look very reassured. Antonia heard the sound of water running and felt a measure of satisfaction in knowing the girl had made it into her shower. "I need a phone," she told him. He pointed to the kitchen and she nodded. "I'll be staying for a day or two. Where may I rest?" Alex headed down the hall and into the back bedroom. When he saw her behind him, he pushed his finger on part of the wallpaper and motioned to the dark chamber beyond the panel.

Antonia nodded again. "Very well. I think you should get some sleep. I'll wake you before sunrise." He nodded reluctantly and left for his room. She turned to examine Joshua's hiding place. It wasn't large, but it was free of dust. The twin-sized bed happily had all the appropriate trimmings. She was glad he was a modern vampire. Some of the more archaic types preferred punishing themselves by resting in coffins, or worse. Satisfied, she returned to the kitchen and picked up the phone.

She had forgotten how much she detested telephones until she heard the tinny tone coming from the handset. She dialed the number she'd known for many years, and listened to the irritating tone confirming the connection. "I need to speak to Dr. Carter," she said when she heard a woman's voice at the other end. "Yes, I know what time it is. Tell him it's an emergency." Antonia tapped impatiently on the counter top with one manicured nail while the sleepy woman went to wake the doctor.

"This is Carter," a groggy man's voice mumbled.

"I'm sorry to wake you, Gale, but I had no choice. I need your help."

"Antonia, is that you? What's wrong?"

"How fast can you get to Washington State?"

He groaned tiredly into the phone. "What are you doing all the way out there?"

"I came to see Joshua MacAaron's woman. She's seriously ill, Gale.

She almost died."

"What are her symptoms?"

Antonia described the condition she'd found the young mortal in. "I fed her my blood. It was all I could think to do at the time. She's stable for the moment, sleeping it off. Gale, I need you to examine her. I think we have a difficult situation on our hands."

"What kind of situation?"

"It is possible Joshua's seed has taken hold. I don't want to say for sure until you've looked at her."

"I see," he said. "Have you told her?"

"Not yet. She's too weak to stand the news. I don't know what to do for her, and I'm certainly not going to stay here and tend to her myself."

"All right," he said with a sigh. "I'll see if I can contact Joe Rogers. I think he's still running his charter service. What airport do I need to come to?"

Antonia groaned inwardly and thumbed through the phone book. After a minute, she answered, "It looks like there's one in Centralia."

"All right. Let me see what I can arrange, and I'll call you back. What's Joshua's number?"

Antonia read him the number printed above the telephone's touch pad. "I'll find someone to meet you. Just let me know when." She hung up the phone, and slipped into Catherine's room to find her sleeping deeply, probably, from the looks of her, for the first time in many days. She laid a cool hand on her forehead and noted with satisfaction there was no fever. The harsh sound of the phone ringing jangled her already frayed nerves, and she hurried to answer it before the sound drove her mad.

"I got in touch with Rogers," Gale said, sounding more awake. "He's prepping his fastest jet. I'll be leaving as soon as I can pack my medical bag and get to the airport. It will probably be around seven tomorrow morning before I arrive."

"Thank you, Gale," she said, feeling a measure of relief. "Someone will be there to meet you."

She went into Alex's room. "Wake up," she said, shaking his shoulder. He raised his head and blinked groggily at her. "I've called my doctor," she told him. He smiled and nodded. "I need you to go to the airport in Centralia and meet him. He arrives around seven tomorrow morning." Alex frowned and began gesturing. Antonia shook her head. "I don't understand," she told him. "You can't drive?" He shook his head and ran to his dresser. From his wallet, he gave her a battered business card. "Carl Foster? Is he a friend of Joshua's?" Alex rolled his eyes and flapped his hands, and she nodded her understanding. "All right. Thank you. Go back to bed."

Carl Foster sounded just as reluctant to be brought out of bed in the middle of the night. "Who did you say you are?" he asked, gruff annoyance in his tone.

"Antonia," she repeated sharply.

"Antonia?" She heard a hint of recognition in the man's voice as he repeated her name. "What can I do for you?"

"I'm at Joshua's house. His woman is ill. I've sent for my doctor, but he won't arrive until morning. Can you get him?"

"Of course. When does he arrive?" Antonia relayed the flight information with barely contained patience. "I'll have him there as quick as I can."

Antonia hung up the phone impatiently. "Mortals," she rasped to herself. She looked in on the girl one more time, and paced the house thoughtfully until the rising sun drove her into Joshua's shelter.

Chapter Eighteen

Katie woke to the sensation of someone pulling on her arm. She groaned and opened her eyes, gasped and struggled to free herself from the strange man's grasp. "Easy, girl," he told her. "I'm Dr. Gale Carter. I'm here to help you."

She stopped her struggles to glare at the middle-aged man with gray at his temples and kindness in his eyes. Out of the corner of her eye, she saw Alex and Carl standing in her doorway. "I don't want a doctor," she grumbled. "Go away." She weakly dropped back against her pillow.

"You're fortunate Antonia chose this time to visit," he said with a slight smile as he removed the blood pressure cuff. "You don't know just how close you were. If she hadn't helped you when she did, you wouldn't be alive to fight with me."

She eyed him suspiciously. "You know Antonia?"

He paused to rub the base of his throat meaningfully. "For a very long time. Whatever's wrong with you, I assure you I'm the most qualified doctor in the country to help you."

She let herself relax. A vampire doctor. Who knew? "What *is* wrong with me?"

"Well, your blood pressure is low. Haven't been eating well, have you? Hmmm. You're probably a bit anemic. I'll need to do a blood workup on you." She nodded and obliged the doctor with the use of her arm. After he'd taken several small bottles and stashed them in his bag, he smiled nervously. "I, uh," he paused to clear his throat. "I need to examine you. I know this is a little unorthodox. I don't have a nurse with me to chaperone."

She nodded uncomfortably, cast a glance at Alex and Carl and made a weak dismissal gesture with her eyes. Carl took Alex by the arm and they left the room, closing the door behind them. "Whatever you need to do, doctor."

"Right, then." He reached into his bag for a glove and some ointment, and gently pulled back her covers. After palpitating her abdomen, he cleared his throat again. "I need you to lift your knee some." When she complied self-consciously, he nodded. "That's it. Now, relax for me.

Okay?" She felt his finger enter her, and closed her eyes. He pressed against her belly again, then pulled his hand away with a frown. "When was your last monthly flow, my dear?"

She felt her face grow hot as she tried hard to remember. How had the time gone by so quickly, when every night without Joshua had felt like an eternity? "I don't know. Two weeks before Joshua left, I think." Her eyes widened. "I'm not...no. That's not possible," she argued. "He told me he...that it couldn't happen."

"Well, apparently he was wrong, unless this child is not his."

The look she gave the doctor was fierce. "I love Joshua. I'd never betray him." A tear fell unexpectedly down her cheek, and she dashed it away angrily, then the implications of her condition struck home. "Oh, God," she cried. "How can I tell him? He won't believe it's his. He'll think I...." she choked down a sob. "He's been hurt so badly. If he believes I betrayed his trust..."

"I'm sure, once we explain things to him, he'll believe you."

She shook her head. "You don't understand. You don't know him."

"I think I can guess," he said sympathetically. "The jealous type, I'll bet. Betrayed once or twice before?" She nodded miserably. "Well, it may help you to know that while this kind of thing is rare, it's not unheard of. I've never seen one myself, but there are tales. Have you ever heard the word 'damphere'?" She shook her head. "It's a word used to describe a creature born of a mortal and a vampire." He smiled wryly. "It's a good thing Antonia didn't bring you across when you asked. It might have complicated things."

She considered his words for a moment. "What happens now?"

"Well, I can prescribe something to help with the nausea. You'll need to eat well and take a vitamin supplement rich in iron. Your discomfort should ease quickly."

"Will I...do I have to drink blood?"

He frowned. "I shouldn't think so. Your baby will take from your body all the nutrients it needs to grow. You may need to alter your diet to include foods higher in protein and iron, and your blood chemistry should be monitored to make sure your own health doesn't suffer. Too little is known about this sort of thing. I'll need to do some more research." He picked up his bag, "I want you to get some rest. I'll check on you again before I leave."

She nodded and watched the doctor leave her room. Her hand found its way to the lowest part of her belly, where she thought she felt a slight hardening in her womb. Images of tiny baby things she'd seen in the mall swam past her mind as she drifted back to sleep.

* * * *

Antonia rose quickly that evening and hurried to find Dr. Carter. He was sitting on the sofa studying a thick book. "So, it's true," Antonia said, reading the man's thoughts easily.

"Good evening, Antonia," Dr. Carter said warmly. "Yes, I'm afraid it's true. What's more, she insists the child can only be Joshua's." He rose from the chair to take her hand affectionately. "It's good to see you again. It's been quite some time."

Antonia smiled and favored the doctor with a warm embrace, and remembered a time when they were once lovers. "Too long. You really should visit Haven more often."

"Well, my practice keeps me busy, even if I am a semi-retired country doctor now," he told her. "Now, about Catherine. I think we should consider moving her to Haven. She'll need better looking after than she can get here. And I'll need to have her closer to my clinic where I can keep an eye on her progress. She'll need someone to deliver the baby when the time comes, and an uninitiated pediatrician might raise too much fuss."

Antonia nodded thoughtfully. "There's something you should know, Gale. Joshua has disappeared. We believe he's been destroyed. Not one of us has sensed him in almost two weeks."

"Does she know?"

"She was near death when I found her. I came to give her the news, but, well, how could I tell her something like that in her condition?"

"Then moving her to Haven becomes even more necessary."

Antonia frowned. "It could be dangerous for her there. Jason is…" A brief stab of pain flickered through her heart and caught in her throat. "We're concerned about Jason's recovery. We don't know what to expect from him when he finally rises."

Carter raised his eyebrows. "Is he feeding?"

She shook her head. "He doesn't respond. We've been forcing our own blood down his throat in an attempt to strengthen him. His body is healing slowly, but I'm afraid his mind might be lost. We won't know for sure until he wakes, and that can be any day now, or years down the road. If he's lost his mind…"

"…you'll need to destroy him," Carter finished. "The last thing any of us needs is another rogue vampire on the loose."

"It will be difficult," she agreed. "He is, after all, the oldest of all of us. Before this happened, he was a powerful friend." She paced to the fireplace and jabbed at the cold wood with the poker, flicked her mind at it and brought it to life. "The others will guard Jason," she said after some thought. "He won't rise during the day, not if he has any instinct at all. Our servants will be about to make sure nothing happens to Catherine while we rest. Once the others understand her condition, they may be motivated to protect her. The child must be raised to trust us."

"Have you ever met a damphere?"

"Once. In the old country, centuries ago. His mother hated his father, and taught their child everything he needed to know to destroy our kind. Imagine a creature with the strengths and abilities of a vampire, but able to walk in the daylight." She shook her head. "A lot of good friends died before he was taken down. I hope none of the others feel it's too much of a risk, bringing another damphere into the world. Some might decide it best to destroy the woman and her unborn child before it has the chance to act against us."

* * * *

Katie heard the quiet conversation taking place in the outer room, and forced herself out of bed. She reached the end of the hall as Antonia made her last statements. "Joshua won't let anyone hurt me." Gale and Antonia turned together to see her leaning weakly against the hallway entrance.

"Young lady, you should be in bed," Dr. Carter admonished.

"You told me to eat. What's this about someone wanting to kill me?"

Gale helped her to one of the dining room chairs and nodded at Alex, who had come from the hall. She looked up at Alex and managed a couple of quick signs. He headed for the kitchen with a smile on his face. Then she turned to the doctor and Antonia and demanded, "Answer me."

"You'll do well to mind your manners, mortal," Antonia said, clearly ruffled at her tone. But then she deflated, gave the doctor an uncomfortable look and sat down at the opposite end of the table and affected a sigh. "I suppose you have the right to know. The child you bear poses a very real threat to the vampire Community. If it is not raised carefully, it could grow to become a formidable enemy. There may be those among us who will not be willing to take that risk."

She felt the blood drain from her face. "Joshua wouldn't let anyone hurt me," she said again, though her words didn't sound convincing, even to herself.

"I know you think highly of him," Antonia said tightly, "but you should know he is among our youngest members. He is no match for older, much stronger vampires. If it's decided you must not be allowed to deliver this child, no one, not even Joshua, will be able to protect you."

"No," she whispered, tears welling in her eyes. Alex placed a bowl of chicken soup before her, and she ignored it. "Please," she cried, looking desperately at Antonia. "Can't you do something? You've already hurt him enough. If I die, it will destroy him. Don't let him be hurt again."

Antonia's dark eyes glittered dangerously. "Have a care, Catherine, of what you accuse me. I will not be judged by the likes of you."

Heat rushed to her cheeks. "He loved you very much."

She saw by the look in her eyes Antonia understood what she was talking about. "He only thought he did."

"He believed you were in love with him. When he found you with someone else, it broke his heart."

"He was mistaken. Catherine, you have to understand. He expected more of me than I was able to give. Vampires don't engage in permanent alliances. That level of fidelity is not possible for immortal beings to endure."

"Sometimes they do," she countered, her eyes pinned squarely on Antonia's.

The vampiress held her firm gaze for a full minute before she whispered, "You took the Vow."

She nodded slowly. "Controlled or not, I belong to him for the rest of my life," she said in confirmation, "and he belongs to me."

Antonia pulled in a deep breath and let it out slowly. "That gives you…certain rights."

"You saved my life. Joshua will thank you for that favor. Please don't waste this opportunity to make up for the pain you caused him by letting anything happen to me."

She turned to the doctor and said, "I must call a meeting. The Council needs to know. Can you stay a couple of days?"

"Yes, I think I can arrange that. I need to wait on the lab work anyway."

Antonia nodded decisively. "I'll leave right away." She rose and put a reassuring hand on Katie's shoulder. "I'll see what can be done," she told her more gently. "This is not a decision I can make on my own. We must all be in complete agreement on how to handle this."

"Tell them," she began, chocking back another sob. "Tell them I mean them no harm. I'll teach my baby to respect you all, I swear it."

"I'll contact you in a day or so," Antonia said. "Try not to worry." Dr. Carter escorted her to the door, where they exchanged glances before she left.

He returned to the table, pushed the soup in front of her and said, "You need to eat this. You'll need your strength."

"Why? So they'll have more of a challenge when they come to kill me?"

Dr. Carter pulled out a chair, swung it around and thrust it between his knees, sat, and folded both arms over the back. "You don't know who you have on your side," he said with a twinkle in his eyes. "Second to Jason, she's probably the oldest vampire in known existence. She is a well-respected member of the Council of Elders. Not only that," he added, the twinkle in his eyes becoming a gleam, "she still cares for Joshua more than she's willing to admit."

"She's not the jealous type, is she?"

He laughed out loud. "Antonia? Not a chance. She plays around more than a she-cat in heat." The look on his face softened when he added, "She cares a great deal for those she takes to heart, immortal or not. I know her very well, Catherine. She's seen into your heart. She understands all she needs to know about you, or she wouldn't be willing to help you."

She took an uncertain sip at her soup. Her stomach was feeling touchy again, more from distress than illness. "She's not the one who gets to decide."

He put a reassuring hand on her arm. "Try not to worry. For now, the best you can do is to take care of yourself, for the sake of your baby, and for Joshua."

She nodded and put another spoonful of soup in her mouth. She closed her eyes and wished desperately for her beloved forest guardian to come to her rescue.

* * * *

The telephone rang in the middle of the night, bringing Katie out of sleep with a jolt. By the time she was able to drag herself out of bed, Dr. Carter had answered the phone. She heard him speak quietly to whoever was on the other end, but clearly heard only the words, "Yes, I understand." He hung up the phone, ran his hand through his hair, and turned. His surprise at seeing her standing in the hall behind him was obvious.

"It was them, wasn't it?" Her voice sounded very small.

"Catherine, you shouldn't be up. You're still weak."

"Tell me, damn it!" she said with a stomp of her foot. "Quit patronizing me. I'm not a child."

He studied her eyes for a moment, then lowered his own. "There's to be a tribunal. We're to leave for Georgia as soon as possible."

She felt the starch go out of her knees and reached to the wall for support. "A tribunal? You mean a trial? For my life?"

"Essentially."

"Is…is Joshua there?"

"They didn't say."

She shook her head. "No. I won't go. I can't."

"I'm afraid you have no choice. If you don't, they're sure to view it as rebellion. They'll hunt you down."

"I'll…I'll run away. Hide. Please…" Desperation brought tears to her eyes.

"I can't help you, Catherine, not with this. As much as I'd like to do so, I answer to them. There is nowhere you can go. You can't hope to hide from them, because they will find you. And when they do, there will be no second chance."

What would Joshua want me to do? He'd taught her to face up to challenges, to participate in her fate instead of becoming a victim of it. Besides, he was taking her to Haven, closer to Joshua. She nodded reluctantly. "All right. When do we leave?"

He sighed heavily. "Go back to bed. I'll make arrangements for our flight to Atlanta. I'll have Alex pack you a bag."

Chapter Nineteen

Dr. Carter, Alex and Katie arrived at the Chehalis/Centralia Airport shortly after dawn, where a private pilot waited to take them to Atlanta. Her first airplane trip should have been an adventure, but her situation and state of health prevented her from enjoying the novelty. She tried to make the most of the flight, but as she sat and stared out the window at the passing clouds, she dwelled more and more on her situation. The isolated life she'd led left her ill equipped to deal with the dangers she now faced.

She had no idea how to face dangerous situations diplomatically. Since the day her father died, she'd withdrawn from the world, clinging to her mother and avoiding social interactions that might lead her to feel close to someone else–someone who might leave her the way her father had. She'd thrown herself into chores and studies, spending most of what free time she'd had reading books from the school library. She hadn't learned how to deal with people, let alone vampires, on anything more than a passive level. Until Joshua stepped into her life.

He'd taught her how to find the strength hidden deep inside herself, to be brave when her instincts told her to withdraw, to stand up for herself and what she believed was right. He'd made her feel safe. But she wasn't safe anymore. She was once again alone, and faced with a situation she could deal with in one of two ways–she could withdraw to passive resistance, as she had all her life, and become the victim of her fate, or she could stand up for herself and her baby.

The first option would more than likely get her killed because she'd give in and allow whatever the Community decided. The second was, in many ways, worse. She would stand up for herself, draw on the courage Joshua had shown her how to find, and show the Community she was too strong-willed and defiant. Her inexperience with diplomacy would ultimately anger them and get her killed. She grappled with the impossibility of her situation as the miles fell behind her. Before she knew it, they were landing in Atlanta.

She had never seen a city as big as Atlanta before. She watched the tall buildings float past in a tired daze, then the landscape became wooded and hilly. "Where are we going?" she asked weakly.

"To my house in Fulcrum," Dr. Carter replied. "It doubles as my clinic. We can rest there until they send for us."

"Will it be long?"

"We'll probably be called on just after sunset." He patted her knee gently. "We have a few hours yet."

His home-slash-clinic looked to her like one of those old antebellum guesthouses pictured in history books. It was much larger than Joshua's house in the woods. Grand columns graced the front of a wide porch. White rockers sat at the ready on both sides of the front door. The whitewashed exterior looked weathered but well tended. A heavy stand of live oaks sheltered most of it from the sun. He led her to the side of the house, where a shingle reading, "Dr. G. Carter, MD, General Practitioner," hung above the door. "Helen?" A portly middle-aged woman in a nurse's uniform entered the office from somewhere deeper in the house. "I need a room. No, not here," he decided when she started for the treatment rooms. "We'll put her upstairs in one of the bedrooms."

Helen nodded, cast a concerned glance in her direction, and left the clinic. "Does she know?" she asked quietly.

"Helen has been with me for many years. Trey brought her to me after my last nurse died of sudden heart failure. She's a servant. Like me."

"Trey?"

He shook his head with an abashed smile as he led her toward the stairs. "I'm sorry. I assumed Joshua might have told you about the Council. Did he tell you nothing of your new culture?"

"He was good at giving vampire lectures. Every time I missed an assumption, he'd council me for hours. He never spoke of Haven until the night he left, though I remember hearing words like 'Council,' 'Community,' and…" She paused to swallow her dread. "…'Enforcers.' He told me about Antonia, of course, and I met Vincent the night we spoke our Vow. I know about Devon and Jason, but he didn't have time to tell me more."

He was quiet for a moment. "You really took the Vow with him." It wasn't a question.

"Why is everyone so surprised?"

He chuckled softly. "Because it's so rarely done."

She nodded her understanding. "What happens now?"

"Well first, I'm getting you to bed. That trip was hard on you, and you'll need to be at your best tonight. I'll have a good supper ready for you before sunset."

He led her into the bedroom Helen had prepared for her. She looked around at the pristine white Swiss eyelet and deep burgundy accents and sighed away her reluctance. With sad resignation, she allowed them to help her to bed. Dr. Carter produced a syringe and began swabbing her arm. "No," she said, pulling her arm away in protest. "I don't need that."

"This is just something to help you relax. You need to sleep. It's going to be a long night for you, I'm afraid." Reluctantly, she allowed the doctor to administer the contents of the syringe, and instantly fell asleep.

Hours later, Helen came to get her dressed. She brushed her hair and gently fastened a gold barrette to each side. "There. You're as pretty as a picture." After a quick knock, Alex entered with a tray containing what smelled like savory beef stew. "There's your dinner. Dr. Carter wants you to eat well. You'll need your strength."

She nodded and lifted the spoon to her lips. The stew was surprisingly mild in flavor and easy on her touchy stomach. "What's in this," she asked between bites. "It tastes different."

"I used to study the ways of the old healers. There are herbs in that stew that can calm the worst stomach problems."

She stuffed another spoonful into her mouth and sighed. Before long, she'd finished the entire meal, bread and all, and felt better than she had in a long time. She was about to say so when Dr. Carter appeared at the door. Antonia was behind him. Helen excused herself abruptly and left the room with the empty tray. The bottom dropped out of her stomach. "It's time, isn't it?"

Without explanation or ceremony, Antonia knelt beside her, captured her eyes, and commanded in a stern but gentle voice, "Submit to me." Fear clenched her heart, but she no longer had a choice. She opened her mind. Antonia pinned her gaze and issued a mental command that she had to obey.

* * * *

"Catherine, wake up," Dr. Carter ordered. She opened her eyes slowly, then sat upright with a start. "We'll be arriving in a few minutes," he told her. "There are some things I need to say to you."

She looked out the windshield and saw they were deep in the woods. It was very dark outside. Only that part of the woods lit by the car's headlights was visible. "Where are we?"

"Catherine, pay attention," he said sharply. She looked at him in surprise. "This is the only help I can offer you. For your own sake, listen to me."

"All right," she said slowly. "I'm listening."

"Don't let yourself give in to fear. Vampires view fear as weakness. You can't afford to give them any reason to doubt you. And don't resist them. Do whatever they ask."

"What...what will they do to me?"

He glanced at her uncomfortably for a moment, and turned his attention back to the rough road in front of them. "Your courage will serve you well. Remember that. But don't confuse courage with foolish bravado. Don't give them any reason to believe you will turn against them." The road abruptly curved around to the left, the trees parted, and a huge stone building loomed before them. Carter pulled the car to a stop in front of the mansion and killed the engine. "Look, I don't know what you can expect in there," he told her more softly. "Try to remember all you have learned from Joshua, and everything I just said."

She swallowed hard and nodded. "Let's get this over with."

In the darkness, Haven was a foreboding structure. The rough-cut stones comprising the front walk gave the mansion a medieval feel, and the pair of heavy wood doors felt to her like the doors of a prison. When Dr. Carter opened the door for her to enter, she took a deep breath, squared her shoulders, and stepped inside.

She was surprised to find how luxurious the place was. Chandeliers dripping with long, elegant crystals hung at intervals from the high ceiling. Electricity had to have been added many years after construction, if it had been there as long as Joshua had said, but the modifications had been made with the greatest care and discretion, so as not to detract from the mansion's graceful beauty. Rich tapestries and paintings adorned the walls. Brightly polished white, gray, and black marble tiles were set into the floor in a pattern that gave the impression of three-dimensional cubes. At the far end of the massive entry hall, a wide staircase of white marble flanked by gleaming gilded banisters fanned out from the top landing. Hallways opened darkly on either side of the long second-floor balcony. She wasn't sure what she expected of a vampire mansion, but extraordinary opulence was not even close.

Dr. Carter slipped his arm around her waist and conducted her off to the right, to another pair of heavy, intricately carved doors. She heard the sound of quiet conversation coming from beyond them. After gently squeezing her shoulder in reassurance, he pushed the doors open. She set her jaw and entered the room, the doctor and Alex close behind her.

The room became very still. She found herself in a room big enough to require three chandeliers. Every available bit of wall space was covered in heavy bookcases, all of them well stocked. Deep burgundy draperies richly embroidered in gold hung over the two plate glass windows. A matching sofa rested near the opposite wall. Overstuffed chairs were arranged throughout the room beside small tables.

Occupying the room was not a dozen, but perhaps as many as fifty people. All of them, she was sure, were vampires. There seemed to be people from every nationality present. She remembered Joshua saying they had been summoned from all over the country. They looked at her appraisingly, giving her the uncomfortable feeling she was a sheep that had wandered into a den of hungry wolves.

"You know why you are here," a man with blond hair and a thick French accent said.

"Of course," she answered with a solemn nod. She swept the room with her eyes, wishing Joshua were among the fiends before her. The only ones she recognized were Antonia, who stood to the back of the room with an inscrutable look on her face, and Vincent, who was watching her with an odd mixture of respect and sorrow.

"So, this is the mortal everyone's so worried about," a strikingly handsome male with thick, curly blond hair said as he moved toward her. "She doesn't look like much of a threat to me." He raised his hand to touch a lock of her hair. "No threat at all." She allowed herself to look into his strange, violet eyes, and was instantly trapped by his gaze. She felt him reach into her mind, and nervously opened herself to his scrutiny. The world faded away under his intense control. *Give yourself to me, pretty one. Surrender and I'll protect you.* He stroked her face tenderly, tipped it to his. When his lips touched hers, she pulled herself together, backed away sharply, and slapped him with all the strength she had. The effort cost her. She staggered and would've fallen to the floor if not for Alex's quick support.

"I belong to Joshua! Don't do that again." She heard amused chuckles from the crowd. The vampire in front of her responded more violently. His eyes glowed with the same red malice she'd seen only once before. He bared his fangs and hissed as he moved toward her. A stab of pure panic clenched her heart.

"Enough, Stephan," a very large, very black man boomed to her great relief. "You cannot find fault in her loyalty. Go find some other mortal to toy with." Another round of chuckles followed. She didn't know whether that was a good sign or not. The black man made his way to the front of the room, brushed the one called Stephan aside, and considered her carefully. "You have a lot of courage for one so small," he said sternly, his voice deep and powerful. "One might even call you reckless."

She found she had to struggle to meet his gaze. This man stood at least head and shoulders taller than anyone she'd ever met before. His skin was almost as dark as his midnight black hair and eyes. He was probably the biggest, meanest looking character she'd ever seen in her life. "What else have I got?" she asked carefully.

He moved closer and captured her eyes with his own dark orbs. "Fear," he said after a moment. "You don't trust us." His statement sounded like a verdict.

"I don't have reason to. You're the ones who are to decide whether I live or die."

"Bravely said, small one," he said, looking amused. She thought he might have a nice smile, if he ever did smile. To her surprise, the corners of his mouth lifted. He'd heard her thoughts. Then she felt his mind probe hers. After what had just happened, she was reluctant to give in. She shook her head and attempted to block him, but his strength made it difficult for her to concentrate. He sensed her reluctance immediately, as well as the reason for it. "I have no sexual interest in you, mortal," he told her sternly. "We must know your heart. Your child is a threat we cannot easily dismiss. If it is, in fact, a damphere you carry, it can grow to destroy us all."

She swallowed hard against the terror rising to her throat. "I'll teach it to respect you. I swear it. The baby won't be a danger to you."

"If we could be certain of that, none of this would be necessary. Open yourself to me."

She shifted nervously on her feet for a moment, then something Joshua had told her came to mind, and her indecision changed to wary determination. She raised her arm to him defiantly. "Blood is more than sustenance. All that I am is written there, like a blueprint for my life."

The look on his face was one of complete surprise. She wasn't sure if he was surprised at her knowledge, or that she dared to challenge him. "This is so," he answered. "Joshua has taught you well."

"Then drink, vampire, if you're willing to take the risk."

He took her wrist in his hand and stroked the pad of his thumb gently along her smooth skin. "You are a bold one." More amusement was showing in his eyes and evident in his voice. "Tell me, why do you prefer I drink from you? Reading your mind is so much less invasive."

Some of her bold courage faded from her heart. "You'll learn more from me this way."

The expression on his face softened even as his eyes changed from black to the feral yellow she'd come to expect. "Don't be afraid." he told her gently. His fangs peeked from behind his lips as he spoke. "I need not cause you pain."

"Trey, take care," she heard Antonia warn. "She's been very ill. She's too weak to stand much loss."

She closed her eyes and let the vampire put his lips to the underside of her wrist. She felt the influence of his mind sweep over her a moment before his fangs broke her skin. She didn't feel the intensely erotic sensations she expected from Joshua. Instead, a feeling of comfort swept through her at the vampire's bite, making her realize the effects of the bite might be greatly influenced by the vampire's mood. She reached up with her other hand for the support of his shoulder while he drank from her, and he slipped a strong arm around her. Then the floor spun out from under her and the library vanished.

When she was able to open her eyes again, she found herself seated in the deep, soft sofa, still surrounded by a roomful of vampires. She groaned and weakly pulled herself upright. The vampire called Trey studied her from one of the chairs, a look of deep concentration on his face. Dr. Carter handed her a glass of water with a look of awe and approval.

"Tell us of your relationship with Joshua," Trey commanded quietly. The others nodded, some whispered words like 'yes' and 'tell us.' She looked around until she saw Vincent, and gave him a questioning look. He responded by nodding once, an unreadable look on his face.

She took a deep breath and spent the better part of an hour telling them everything, starting with her first encounter with him when she was eight. "He's all I've got," she concluded sadly. "We've pledged our lives to each other." At her final words, surprised gasps and whispers floated around the room.

"So what Antonia told us is true," an older vampire with a German accent commented.

"I was witness to the event," Vincent confirmed, breaking his silence at long last and stepping to the front of the gathering. "They have indeed shared the Vow. Joshua wished only for me to know until such time as Catherine's safety became threatened."

The room fell to quiet conversation for a moment before a beautiful Asian female said tightly, "Your fear of him was great. What made you submit to his Vow?"

"Love," she said softly, opening her heart to her audience. "My fear was instinctual and uncontrollable. I had to face up to it or lose him, and that would have killed me." She touched her throat gently as the memory of his first sip filled her mind. She hoped that memory was visible to the preternatural jury now examining her. "It was just as hard for him to trust me. I think he was afraid of history repeating itself."

"Meaning his experience with Jeanette," Trey commented.

She nodded. "He told me that if you…if he didn't take control of me and you found out…" She realized she was stammering and paused to collect her thoughts while sweeping her eyes over the group. Her eyes found and held Antonia's, and she said in judgment, "You hurt him, you…and Jeanette. That pain was still fresh in his heart. He was afraid the same thing would happen with me. Taking the Vow with him was the only way I could convince him of my dedication."

"He loved you that much, that he would sacrifice the rest of eternity to your care?" the German man asked. There was deep surprise on his face.

When she nodded, Vincent said, "There is truth in her words. Joshua would not have taken her into his heart easily." To her, he added, "I know Joshua well. I was not the one who killed Jeanette or her assassins, but I was there to help him after her attack. It took him months to recover his injuries, and in that time I watched him build an impenetrable wall around his heart. After that, he went into seclusion. He vowed never again to pair himself with anyone, vampire or mortal."

Silence dominated the room for several minutes. "You fear us even now," the Asian woman observed.

She looked up at the faces studying her intently. "I know what you are. I know what you can do to me, especially if I make you mad enough. But that's not what scares me."

"What then, mortal?" yet another asked.

She considered her answer carefully. "I think I'd be afraid of anyone who placed themselves in the position of judge, jury, and executioner against me. I find myself forced to defend my right to live and give life to my child, and the only crime I'm guilty of is my complete love and devotion to a man who just happens to be a vampire." She swept a pleading gaze at the crowd of faces looking at her with mild disapproval. "Please. I…I want to be with Joshua and give him this child. I know from the talks we've had that he regrets not being able to father a child of his own. I'm sure he will be pleased when he learns I carry his baby."

A murmur rose from the crowd. She heard one distinct voice say, "Joshua is gone. Who here will pledge to spend their next years to babysitting this mortal and her little monster?"

"What do you mean 'gone?'" she asked timidly. The murmuring

quieted instantly. "Tell me," she asserted more loudly. "Where's Joshua?"

Antonia stepped forward at last and sat next to her. "Catherine, Joshua hasn't returned from the mission we sent him on. Vincent was with him that night. No one has sensed him for two weeks. We think..." she lowered her eyes sadly. "We think he has been destroyed, along with several others who've failed to return."

Her jaw dropped open, then she shook her head in defiance. "He's not dead," she said with certainty. "I'd know it if he was."

"We hold no hope for his survival," Vincent stated. He moved forward and knelt before her. "Joshua was more than willing to participate in the search for our enemies. His abilities with wildlife gave him an advantage many of us lack. He thought if he couldn't sense the hunters, perhaps he could read their presence in the minds of the animals. We were searching the woods south of here when he was struck down."

He paused to take a deep breath, and she thought she saw a hint of pain in his eyes. "I was in mental contact with him when he disappeared. I sensed...I felt the sudden shock of his pain, then I lost contact. I searched for him—we all did—but there was no sign of him anywhere. There is nowhere out there he could have found shelter that we haven't explored. I'm truly sorry."

Her hand rose automatically to her own breast. "Pain," she whispered. "Sharp, searing pain, lancing through his chest, reaching for his heart."

"You felt it as well?" Antonia asked.

She nodded and felt hot tears drip down her cheeks. "I can still feel it, like a dull, throbbing ache. Sometimes, especially at night, it still sends sharp edges through my nerves. I've been getting weaker ever since."

"I should've expected this," Vincent said sadly. "Your life force is connected to his through the power of your Vow. It will kill you eventually, unless you can come to terms with his death."

"But he can't be dead," she insisted. "Why else would I still be feeling his pain?"

"What you're feeling is an echo of his last moments," Antonia said gently. "Perhaps you are able to sense his spirit remaining near you. You have to let him go if you want him to be at peace."

She felt her whole world fall out from under her. "Why didn't you tell me?" she asked quietly. The realization that she was now very dependent upon these immortal strangers for her survival left her feeling utterly alone in the world. "Oh, God."

"Do not entreat His mercy," Trey told her sternly. "You'll find no help from that quarter, not where our kind is concerned."

Her soul was fast becoming a desolate wasteland. Despair was settling heavily in her heart. "What will happen to me?"

Antonia's expression remained sympathetic for a moment longer, then reverted to her inscrutable state. She looked up at Dr. Carter and said, "Take her upstairs, Gale." She cast another look at Katie, rose and turned away.

With an uncomfortable nod, Dr. Carter reached his hand to her. "Come with me." He led her upstairs to a windowless bedroom and turned on the light. "You'll be staying here," he told her, his tone resolute. "I must return to the meeting, in case they need information from me." She glanced around the room quickly and received the feeling it was not the sort of room reserved for guests. Although it was big by her standards, it was much smaller than the one she'd had in Joshua's home. The bed was smaller, the end tables much less sturdy. The dresser on the opposite wall was half the size, and lacked a mirror. A door to the rear led to a small bathroom. She felt as though it were nothing more than a prison cell. "Don't do anything foolish, Catherine. Your fate is not yet sealed. Don't let them believe you will fight them."

"How long am I gonna have to stay here?"

"Until it's decided what to do about you, I'm afraid. You may as well go to bed. I'll let you know what they decide as soon as I can." With that, he left the room. She heard a key turn in the lock and quickly ran to test the door. When she found she couldn't open it, she sank into one of the two overstuffed chairs flanking the dresser and covered her womb protectively with her hands. "He's not dead, little one," she insisted softly. "They're wrong, they have to be. He can't be dead."

Chapter Twenty

Katie paced her room through the long hours and waited for the judgment of the Community. Servants arrived at intervals to bring her food, which she ate indifferently. In the silence between meals, she examined every inch of her room, familiarized herself with every piece of furniture, every fiber in the carpeting. She knelt to examine the lock on her door. The house was ancient; she should've realized the locks would be simple ones. She peered through the keyhole, listened intently, but neither saw nor sensed a guard. Apparently, they believed there was no danger in her escaping.

Indeed, her prospects for freedom seemed bleak. She needed a tool to work the bolt on that lock, and there was no sign of anything in her room that would serve. The dresser was empty except for the paper lining the old drawers and her own clothing, which she put in herself after one of the servants delivered her suitcase. There were no metal objects at all in the bathroom, not even a nail file. She sat down and thought for a long time about her predicament, feeling certain there had to be something she overlooked. With a tired sigh, she went to bed.

More hours passed. She heard another servant enter her room quietly, and the smell of grilled steak and baked potato brought an uncomfortable grumble to her stomach. When she felt a tender hand on her shoulder, she rolled over to see Alex looking down at her with deep concern. She was in his arms in an instant and felt him hold her close with all the tenderness of a brother. Then she stepped back to look in his eyes. "Did they hurt you? Are you okay?"

I'm fine. Just tired, he signed before guiding her to a chair and putting the dinner tray in her lap. *Master Trey had a lot of questions.*

She grimly ate every edible crumb and drop of fluid from the tray while Alex watched in silent satisfaction. When she finished, he rose to take her dishes away. "Stay with me," she said quietly. "I can be brave if I'm not alone."

Alex shook his head sadly and guided her to the bed. *I'm not allowed to stay long,* he signed.

She put a hand on his arm, and he looked at her with sympathy. "Can you at least stay with me until I go back to sleep? Please?" He nodded, and when she curled up on her side and closed her eyes, she felt him climb in behind her and put a comforting arm around her waist. His solid warmth gave her enough security to help her drift off to sleep.

Still more hours passed, how many she couldn't guess. Yet another servant entered the room to bring in some fresh towels, linens, and some magazines, and turned silently to leave.

"Wait, please," she said before the girl reached the door. "Has the Community started their meeting again?"

"Yes miss, over an hour ago," the girl answered nervously. With that, she quickly left the room.

Once again she was left to pace her room in solitude. How much longer would she have to wait? With a frustrated sigh, she curled up on the bed again and stared at the wall.

After another very long wait, her door opened again. She turned to see who was there, expecting yet another servant. She sat upright with a jerk when she saw Dr. Carter enter her room. He looked haggard, but gave no other indication by his appearance as to what news he brought her. Yet another servant waited outside the door, and when the doctor entered the room and closed the door, it was locked from the outside. He sat down in one of the chairs and steepled his fingers in front of his face. She couldn't stand his silence, but was afraid to ask.

"They've been aware of your actions," he said at last. "Your willingness to cooperate helped save your life."

"They're not going to kill me?" she asked quietly.

The doctor sighed. "Your life will be spared. Antonia and Vincent both pled earnestly for your sake."

"And the baby?"

He cleared his throat. Deep sorrow filled his eyes. "I've been instructed to terminate your pregnancy as soon as possible."

"Why?"

"I'm afraid they feel the absence of the child's natural father's love and guidance makes it too great a threat to the others. They've also asked me to ensure you can no longer conceive."

"Why don't I like the sound of that?" she asked, her voice barely a whisper.

Dr. Carter shrugged uncomfortably. "Very few women are capable of nurturing a vampire's seed as you have. They want to be certain it won't happen again. As soon as I can make the arrangements, I will be performing what is known as a partial hysterectomy."

Her heart sank uncomfortably low in her abdomen. "You can't do that to me," she whispered. "You're a doctor. You swore an oath to do no harm."

He gave her a look that was not altogether unsympathetic. "I must do as they command me, even to put aside my mortal vows. Catherine, I'm sure you understand that few mortals are aware of the existence of vampires. Those that know must be controlled. They own me. I don't have any choice in the matter."

"No. I won't let you," she said firmly. "Joshua…"

He frowned at her. "Joshua is gone, Catherine. Accept it."

She shook her head defiantly. "I can still feel him. He's close; I know it. He's hurt, weak, and alone. He needs my help."

"You have to let him go. You're only harming yourself by continuing to deny the truth."

"It's not the truth until I see proof. Right now, he's just missing, and I've got to believe that until someone can convince me otherwise, show me evidence of his death."

"Weren't you paying attention to what Vincent said? If you don't let him go, your own life will end."

Fresh tears flowed down her cheeks. "I don't care," she whispered. "If he is dead, then his spirit is still somewhere close, waiting for me to join him. I can feel his presence as strongly as if he were sitting right here beside me."

"The Community will not allow you to succumb to this kind of suicide. I've been charged with your well being, and I'll do anything in my power to make sure nothing happens to you."

"Why do they care?"

"Joshua vowed centuries ago never again to allow anyone close enough to hurt him. He preferred his life of solitude. No one, not even Antonia, was welcome in his presence for long. His visits to Haven were infrequent at best. I've never met him myself, since he hasn't visited during my lifetime, at least not that I know of. I only know the stories they tell. Because he chose to trust his heart to you after all this time, the others know you must be special.

"Because of this, and in respect for his memory and his obvious faith in you, they plan to offer you a choice. You'll be afforded the opportunity to join them, once you've recovered from surgery. They'll even let you choose your master, if you have a preference. Once you're brought across, and properly instructed on how to care for yourself, you'll be free to go as you will."

"And if I refuse?"

"They'll likely take you in thrall, as they've done all the others. Like me."

She thought for a moment, and shook her head. "No. There has to be another way." He shook his head in sad disagreement. "Without Joshua or my baby, I have no reason to live. They will only be condemning me to an eternity of misery. I can't be alone like that. I just…can't!"

"The Community is not without sympathy and compassion, Catherine. They've asked my opinion on ways to make this ordeal as easy on you as possible. I have a treatment plan in mind that will minimize your suffering. That's all I can tell you, but, believe me, I do have your best interests at heart."

He rose from the chair and moved to put his arms around her, but she shrugged away from his touch. "It won't be as bad as you think. There are those who have become quite fond of you, Trey for one. I think that hefty slap you gave to Stephan impressed him."

She looked up nervously. "Is…is he still mad at me?"

"He's annoyed, for the most part. You stung his pride, but he didn't do it to get you into his bed. He wanted to prove to the others you could be easily led. He was testing the strength of your loyalty to Joshua."

"I think I proved my point," she said dryly.

"I dare say," he agreed. "Your courage does you justice. They respect you for it. You sure surprised me the way you stood up for yourself."

She sniffed loudly in an attempt to keep her tears under control. "How long do we have?"

"I'll need at least a week to set things up. Maybe more. I can't do this in my clinic. I'll need a fully staffed operating room. That won't be an easy trick. My attendants will have to be hand selected and properly controlled. We don't want any uncomfortable questions raised."

A smile tempted her lips. "So, there's still time for Joshua to return."

He placed his hand gently on her shoulder. "I know you want to believe he's still alive," he said softly. "The sooner you accept reality, the better it will be for all of us."

She frowned and turned away from him. "Go away," she told him, her voice thick with unshed tears. "Leave me alone."

He rose and rapped twice on the door. "I'll be around to look in on you. Don't do anything stupid."

She ignored the sharp tone in his voice. When she heard the key turn once more in the lock, she put her hand on her abdomen again, feeling the need to assure herself the baby was still in there. She peered through the lock, and discovered to her surprise the key had been left in the keyhole.

She stood up abruptly; her heart pounded in her chest. Quickly, she pulled her mental disciplines into play and shielded her thoughts as Joshua had instructed. She pondered the problem carefully. She had to get her hands on that key, but she had absolutely no idea how to do it. All the knowledge locked in her brain had come from the minds of her teachers, and from the textbooks and occasional fictions she'd read. But teachers instructed while drawing on their own experiences, didn't they? And wouldn't the writers of all those books draw on their experiences and research?

She looked again at the key. There had to be a way. She paced her room anxiously, examining its contents again. She opened a dresser drawer, fingered through her clothes and picked at the paper lining. Something she read in a mystery novel too many years ago came to mind. She quickly pulled the paper from the drawer and held it in front of her. No, she thought. The solution was too simple to work. Still, she had to try.

She knelt down by the door and placed the paper flat on the floor. She paused for a minute to listen carefully, and felt certain no one was in the hallway. She pushed the paper under the door until an inch was left in her room. She looked in the keyhole again, reached up to scratch her head in thought and discovered the barrettes she had forgotten she still wore. She pulled one off and studied it, then ripped the tension bar out of it. With trembling fingers, she worked the bar into the lock and wiggled it. After several long minutes, and just as she was ready give up, the key slipped from the lock and dropped to the floor. She heard it hit the paper.

For one frightening moment, she considered the possibility the key might've bounced off the paper or was laying on the edge, taunting her. She took a deep breath in an attempt to calm the racing of her heart and gently pulled the paper back. When she heard the key come in contact with the door, she felt a surge of relief followed by a feeling of dismay. There wasn't enough space between the door and the floor to allow the key to pass. She sat up for a moment to think, and dug her fingers into the carpeting.

"That's it," she said out loud. The carpet was thick. That meant it would compress. She crouched low and pressed her finger under the door. With a nod of satisfaction, she cast the paper aside and carefully worked her finger over to where the key lay. She had to twist her hand at a painful angle to force her finger over the key, and it took several attempts, but she successfully nudged the key under the door. She almost laughed in triumph. "Careful," she reminded herself. "You can't afford to be too hasty." She moved back to the bed and sat down again to think.

It was an hour before sunrise, by her estimate. She didn't think she could escape until the vampires were resting. Most of the servants would probably turn in as well. She remembered her breakfast had been brought to her around nine the previous morning. That could mean the daytime servants might still be sleeping. The crack of dawn was probably the best time to make her attempt.

She fingered the key absently for a few more minutes. What was it Vincent had said? They were south of the mansion when Joshua disappeared? That was the direction she'd take if she managed to escape. She needed to find out for herself if he was dead or hiding somewhere, waiting for her to discover him. There had to be evidence somewhere to prove his fate. It will take time though, she thought, maybe days. She'd need to keep warm, and feed herself and the baby. The nights will probably be cold, and it's not likely she'll be able to forage for enough food to survive. She still felt weak from her illness.

She pocketed the key, went through her clothing again, and put on two extra sweaters. She stripped the cases off her pillows and arranged the bedspread to cover them up again, thus hiding, if only for a few minutes, her intent. She pressed her ear against the door and listened until she thought she heard activity in the hall, and waited for that activity to die down again. After another cautious peek through the keyhole, she fished the key from her pocket and slowly drew back the latch. She listened at the door again, her heart beating so loud in her chest she thought someone might hear it, but the hallway sounded deserted. She closed her eyes, closed off her thoughts with all the discipline she could muster, and gently eased open the door.

The hallway was indeed deserted. She slipped silently from her room, locked the door behind her, then pulled off her shoes and padded as silently as possible to the opening at the beginning of the hall and peered around the corner at the grand stairway before her. It looked deserted, but the wide-open space made her too nervous. She turned her eyes to the far end of the hall. Wouldn't there be a back staircase? There was in one of the historical mysteries she borrowed from her mother. She tiptoed quickly to the other end of the long hall, and was relieved to find the narrow servant's stair that probably led to the service areas of the house. She started down them, pausing once when a board gave an uncomfortably loud creak to listen for any sign someone heard, and safely made it to the ground floor of the mansion.

The kitchen was remarkably easy to find, but not vacant as she'd hoped. She had to wait several minutes for her chance to plunder the food stores. A bowl of fruit sat on a long table in the center of the room. Without a second thought, she emptied it into one of her pillowcases. In the pantry, she discovered some dried meat and bottles of juice. She took all she could carry, and helped herself to several freshly baked rolls. When she heard voices returning to the kitchen, she quickly closed everything she'd opened and darted for the back door. She barely managed her escape, and paused against the cool exterior of the mansion to collect her wits. She slipped shoes back on, and with a final, desperate burst of energy, dashed for the relative cover of the forest.

She ran for several minutes until her lungs burned and her sides ached. She stopped to catch her breath in the cover of some bushes, and waited. When she heard no sign of pursuit, she heaved a sigh of relief and looked around. Now, she thought, she needed to head south. The sun was not yet high enough in the sky to tell through the trees which direction it was rising from. She would have to draw on what knowledge she had about nature to guide her. *Come on, Katie, think.*

Horticulture class! Her teacher had mentioned that moss grows on the north side of trees. She studied several trunks carefully. Although the moss was thick, it did seem to be, primarily, on one side of the trees. She started her long search southward, breathing deep the fresh forest air and tasting at last the sweet flavor of freedom.

Chapter Twenty-One

Katie dreaded the coming of each night, and sought shelter before each sunset. With her mind carefully shielded, she waited the coming dawn and prayed desperately she wouldn't be discovered. Her lack of sleep was catching up with her, and she was forced to take short naps during the day, which slowed her progress considerably. After little more than a week, with her carefully rationed food supply nearly spent and exhaustion taking its toll, she lost hope of finding any sign of Joshua. She'd wrinkled her nose more than once at the things her horticulture teacher had said were edible–dandelion leaves, shepherd's purse and other weeds, *worms*. She realized she'd have to set aside her squeamishness once her more familiar forms of sustenance were gone.

Late on the tenth day she came upon a clearing where she sat down to rest. She munched her last piece of fruit while resting against a tree, then stretched out to rest on a pile of dry leaves. Her hand touched something soft and she pulled at it to see what she'd found. The sight of the scarf she'd made for Joshua brought hot tears to her eyes. She shook the dried debris from the wool, looped it loosely around her neck, and held it close. The thought that he'd had it with him during his last moments brought the sting of overwhelming grief to her heart.

She reasoned he must have dropped the scarf when he was attacked. She began a careful search northward, assuming he would've tried to return to Haven, certain she was close to her goal. She didn't stop when night fell, but kept on in stubborn resolve. When her energy failed her, she dared to call to him with her mind. If he was nearby, maybe he could give her some kind of sign. She waited; her mind open to any sound, any stray, alien thought at all that might come from Joshua. Several long, tense minutes passed before she allowed herself to relax.

She was about to give up for the night and seek shelter when she heard a rustling sound in the trees. She froze, half afraid of discovery and half hopeful the sound was coming from Joshua himself. The vampire who stepped into her sight considered her for only a moment before she found herself pinned against a tree. He hissed at her, his eyes glowing blood red in the gloom. Panicked, she struggled to break free from his grasp and cried out in terror. "Don't hurt me!"

He forced her harder against the tree and made a move to drive his fangs into her throat. She missed the quiet hiss of the arrow that struck her attacker, but the results of that shot were obvious. The vampire gave an anguished howl and fell to the ground.

It took several seconds for her to shake off the raw terror she'd felt. When she saw another silhouette standing deep in the shadows, a fresh surge of panic ripped through her. Before she had a chance to scream, a woman asked sharply, "What are you doing out here alone?"

"Who are you?" she countered. She gestured to the fallen vampire. "Did you do this?"

"I saved your life. You should thank me for not allowing you to become that evil creature's evening meal."

Realization set in that the woman standing within a few feet from her was one of the hunters the Community had been searching for. "They're not all evil."

"You know of them?" the woman asked in surprise.

"I married one," she admitted tightly.

"Then you're a bigger fool than I take you for. They're cold-blooded killers."

"You're wrong," she argued, taking a step forward and forcing herself to calm down. "The ones I've met have morals. Codes of conduct. This one," she pointed to the fallen man, "wasn't at all like the ones I know."

"Your perceptions are clouded by your association with them."

"You wouldn't say that if you knew what I know. My husband is a good and gentle man. He'd never hurt anyone that didn't deserve it." Sudden hope surged through her. "Were you here, in this area, about three weeks ago?"

"I hunt the woods often," she answered.

"Did you...are you the one who..." She took a deep, calming breath. "Have you seen my husband?"

After a moment, the woman asked, "What did he look like?" She gave Joshua's description. "I saw that one," she confirmed tightly. "Not far from here."

"No," she cried softly. "Is he...did you kill him?"

"You're better off without him," the woman said coldly, retreating from sight. "Get out of these woods before something else happens to you."

The woman vanished so quickly she couldn't follow, and she realized she hadn't gotten a good look at her. In shock, she wandered from the area, clutching the scarf and facing the fact that Joshua might be dead after all. Stephan's sudden appearance took her completely by surprise.

"You've become more trouble than you're worth," he proclaimed, his eyes glowing menacingly. She backed away from him. "Don't resist me this time," he warned evenly. "You'll only make things harder on yourself."

"What are you going to do?"

He smiled, showing his fangs to their best advantage. "That should be obvious, my dear."

Her hand flew to her throat. "No, please."

Stephan had her by the shoulders before she had the chance to think about turning to run. When he leaned toward her, she whimpered a weak protest and closed her eyes. He released her suddenly, and she was almost afraid to open her eyes to discover why. She was relieved to see Vincent holding Stephan aloft by the throat. "Do you intend to take Community matters into your own hands?" he hissed.

"The woman is trouble. She disobeyed the orders of the Council. I was acting for the safety of our race."

"Did you think to ask her the reason for her disobedience before you blindly decided she deserves to die?" Vincent's voice sounded dangerously close to outrage.

"Doesn't she?" he asked defensively.

"Her fate is for the Council to decide," Vincent said, releasing Stephan abruptly. "You will adhere to their wishes in all things, or I will hold you accountable."

Stephan shook himself and cast a quick glance at her. "As you wish," he said more quietly. Then he was gone.

Vincent turned to her, his eyes still glowing with anger. "Well?"

Still shocked by her terror, she opened and closed her mouth dumbly for several seconds. "Please, Vincent. I didn't mean any harm."

"You should not have wandered out here alone," he scolded. The fire in his eyes flickered and went out. "We've already searched this area. Joshua is not here. Now, will you submit yourself to me willingly, or must I take you by force?"

While she was trying to decide on her answer, he noticed the downed vampire. He knelt to study the man carefully. "I don't know him," he muttered. "He may have been a rogue." He looked up at her with concern in his eyes. "Did he hurt you?"

"No," she answered quietly. "He almost…"

"Did you see who did this?" he asked, indicating the arrow protruding from the vampire's back.

"Sh-she was here," she stuttered. "I talked to her."

"She?" He rose quickly to his feet and took hold of her upper arms. "What did she look like? Did you get a good look at her?"

"No. She stayed in the shadows."

Disappointment swept his features. "What did you talk about?"

Tears came to her eyes. "She said she saw Joshua. Vincent, she believes all vampires are like that one. I tried to convince her otherwise, but she wouldn't listen."

"This part of the forest isn't safe," he said tightly. "Rogues roam the forest at night. You're lucky you survived this long." His eyes fell to the scarf hanging loosely over her shoulders and frowned. He lifted one end in his hand and clutched it tightly. "Joshua was never without this. Where did you find it?"

"That way," she answered, pointing in the direction she'd come from.

"Show me." She led him southward through the woods to the clearing and watched him examine the area carefully. "This way," he said at last, following a trail farther south than she had gone. They walked slowly for several minutes in silence until they came upon another clearing. He knelt to the ground and carefully examined the soil. "He fell here," he said at last. Then, to her surprise, he dropped to his seat and issued one short, quiet sob.

She was on her knees beside him in an instant. "Tell me. I need to know."

He looked up at her, the deep pain in his eyes unmistakable. "He died here, Catherine. Look." She studied the ground where he indicated and saw fine traces of white ash. "This spot is not protected from the sun. I can only hope he was dead before it found him."

She remembered the vivid description Joshua had given her of what would happen if he were caught in the sun's rays. She could only imagine the agony. "Are...are you sure he was here?" she asked, her voice barely a whisper.

He nodded and forced himself to his feet. "His ashes must have been scattered by the wind. There can be no mistake now."

She stared at the spot as sorrow overtook her. "Joshua," she whispered, choking on the lump forming in her throat. "Oh, Joshua..." She rested her trembling hand tenderly over the ashes.

"Are you satisfied?" he asked gently.

She had no choice but to agree. She closed her eyes tight and nodded. "Do you have a handkerchief?"

"Yeah," she heard him whisper. She took the handkerchief he offered, and with tender care, transferred as much of the white powder as she could onto the center of the soft cloth and folded it neatly into a roll which she knotted and tucked under her bra, close to her own heart.

He stood watch while she dealt reverently with the remains. "I share your grief, Catherine," he said thickly. "Joshua was more than my friend. We were brothers, in the fashion of our ways. We shared a master, and so a bloodline."

She nodded, feeling like she understood some of his sentiment. She put her hand against the ground to push herself onto her feet, and felt an odd lump under the leaves. "What's this?" she asked, picking up a stick with shredded feathers clinging to one end.

"It looks like the broken shaft of an arrow," he said, taking the artifact from her grasp. "The Council will want to examine it." He pocketed the find and turned his eyes to her once more. "Will you surrender to me now?"

She looked at him, tears pooling in her eyes. "What will you do to me?"

He sighed heavily and made a visible attempt to shake off his grief. "I'll take you back to Haven. It is for the Council to decide your fate."

"What if I refuse?"

He gave her a look that was plainly a non-verbal plea. "You really don't want to find out, do you?"

She took the ends of Joshua's scarf in her hands and clutched it tight to her middle. She couldn't resist them, even if she tried with all the strength she had left. She could not hope to hide from them for long; they would eventually find her anywhere she went. And, as Dr. Carter had warned, there would be no second chance. Her only hope depended on her cooperation with them from this moment on. "No, I suppose not," she whispered. Without another word, she allowed him to gather her in his arms. She closed her eyes tightly when they rose into the air and headed back to Haven.

Chapter Twenty-Two

Katie found herself once again locked in her room to await the judgment of the Community. Vincent had handed her over to a servant, and turned away in silence to join the vampires who were gathering in the library without giving her a second glance. Still too stunned by her discovery, she'd followed the servant to her room in silence. She peered through the keyhole and saw a guard outside her door, and knew she would be given no further opportunities to escape. She paced her room nervously, wishing she'd been allowed to speak with them in her own defense.

Not too much time passed before Alex was admitted to her room. She looked at him for only an instant before rushing to his arms. He held her for several minutes and allowed her to cry on his shoulder, then seated them both on the bed. "Oh, Alex," she sniffed. "He's gone. Joshua is really gone. I didn't want to believe it!" She pulled her precious package from her chest and cradled it tenderly in her hands. "We found the place where he died."

He signed that he couldn't believe it either, and told her he'd believed his master would always be there for him.

"I've lost everyone I've ever been close to," she told him sadly. "I thought Joshua was the only one I would ever have in my life who could never leave me."

He shook his head sadly and asked about the baby.

"I don't know, Alex. I don't think they're going to let me keep it. And after I disobeyed them, I don't think they're going to let me live either. Stephan..." she chocked back a sob. "He was right, I'm too much trouble. They're not going to want to keep me here, and they can't let me go."

You still have me, he signed with a caring look on his face. *I'll take care of you like I did Joshua.*

She was touched deeply by his devotion. They huddled together, cradling each other while the tears of overwhelming grief poured from both of them. After several long and painful minutes, she pulled back to dry her eyes, and decided to take a shower. "Will you wait for me?" she asked. "I need to clean up." He smiled and stretched himself on her bed while she turned to the bathroom.

She emerged a few minutes later, cleaner, but still feeling miserable. He quickly guided her to a chair and put a tray in her lap. She poked at the steaming bowl of stew with her spoon, but couldn't bring herself to put any of the nourishment into her mouth. "I'm too upset to eat," she said, lifting the tray to her dresser. She sat on the bed and folded her legs in front of her, and pulled the end of the scarf across her lap. "Help me clean this up, Alex." He nodded, and the two of them sat for a while picking forest debris carefully from the wool and silently sharing their sorrow.

A quiet knock at the door drew her from her task, and when she looked up, she saw Trey's impressive form filling the doorway of her room. The look on his face was as inscrutable as ever. Alex rose reluctantly, cast one more pained glance at her, and retreated from the room.

Trey entered the room, and surprised her by sitting next to her on the bed. "I am heartened to see you have found someone with whom you can share your grief. Please know that you and Alex are not the only ones deeply affected by Joshua's death."

"I didn't want to believe…"

"I know," he said gently. "We all know how you feel."

She risked looking into his midnight eyes, and saw the barest hint of the sorrow she heard in his voice. "I…I didn't mean to make you angry with me."

"You don't need to explain yourself, Catherine, though I must admit your courage and ingenuity surprised even me, who should know you better than any other." He sighed in pause, and she received the impression he was trying to control his own feelings. "Vincent spoke for you, though the effort cost him dearly. He has closed himself in his room to deal with his grief in private.

"Make no mistake, the Council is not happy with the way you've conducted yourself to this point. Escaping Haven and traipsing off through the forest alone was not only foolhardy, it was extraordinarily dangerous. You placed yourself at great risk, as you well know. You're lucky to still be alive to await our judgment."

"I'm sorry," she whispered. "I had to know."

"Catherine, you allowed yourself to trust me the night you arrived, at least enough to give me your blood. Do you think you can trust me a little further?" She looked at him in disbelief. "I need you to open your mind to me. I must see what you saw in the forest tonight. I know you didn't see the woman clearly, but there may be something of her you failed to notice."

She considered his request very carefully. If she allowed herself to trust Trey, would that, perhaps, strengthen the Council's opinion of her? The idea gave her hope. She nodded slowly.

"Close your eyes," he said gently. "I won't hurt you." She did as he asked, and felt the expected hypnotic sensation as his mind swept hers. With tenderness she found hard to believe him capable, he slipped his arm around her and supported her when she grew dizzy from his influence. "Think of the woman," he whispered. Instantly, visions of her interaction with the hunter filled her mind. Her voice, the way she moved, every detail of every moment came back to her with crystal clarity. Trey released his hold on her mind and shook his head. "She was too deep in the shadows. Your mortal perceptions were not able to record much more than we've already learned. I caught a wisp of scent and something of her vocal qualities. It's not much to go on." He sighed heavily. "Thank you for cooperating with me."

Fresh tears filled her eyes and slid unhindered down her pale cheeks. "What…what has the Council decided to do with me?"

Trey closed his eyes for a long moment before speaking. "We have the highest regard for you, Catherine MacAaron." His manner of speech told her she was hearing the words of the Council, that Trey was one of its members. "As for me personally, I…well," he cleared his throat. "You shared yourself with me. That was no small favor. You were right to remind me of the risk. Your essence has had a profound effect on me. It runs through me still. I understand fully why Joshua favored you as he did. You're a rare and special young lady."

"I wish I could say the feeling is mutual."

He took her hand and held it tightly. "I understand your devotion to Joshua. He was dear to all of us. That he was willing to assist us in our time of need, even to leaving one such as you behind, was a rare and wonderful favor, no doubt a result of your influence over him. He will be sorely missed."

She felt tears threaten her eyes again and struggled to push them back. "He was all I had."

He squeezed her hand. "I know you're feeling alone right now, but given time, you will find the strength to go on without him. Treasure your memories of the times you shared, keep within you all that was good about him, but let go of the past and allow yourself to look to the future. The Council is willing, under the circumstances, to overlook your transgression. We all feel your loss. We will continue with our plans as originally decided. Once all of this unpleasantness is behind you, you'll be free to explore new horizons. You should give careful consideration to our offer to join us. Perhaps, in time, you will find someone new to fill the void in your heart. Joshua would've wanted it that way."

"I pledged my life to him," she said tightly. "I'll have no other, even if I live to see the end of the earth."

"Would he want you to be unhappy, Catherine? I'm sure he'd be honored by your fidelity, but consider this–he's gone. Your Vow to him has been absolved. How do you think he would feel if he knew how miserable you are? Don't you think he might be comforted by the fact you went on with your life? Perhaps even learned to care for another immortal?"

She shook her head at the hope she saw in his dark gaze. "I don't think I ever can. Joshua was very special to me. He taught me things about myself I never knew. We were bonded to each other before we took the Vow."

He brushed the tear from her face and smiled gently. "There are many who are willing to teach you, although I'm not sure any of us can offer you the devotion you shared with Joshua. Unions such as yours are rare. We were all surprised to learn you had pledged your lives to each other." The look on his face softened in awe as he added, "Eternity is a long time to spend with one person. It takes a very special couple to make that kind of relationship work."

"Joshua never asked me for eternity," she said sadly, "but I think I might've been willing to take the chance. We were so happy together. I can't imagine that would've ever changed."

"I'm sure it wouldn't have," he told her. "Joshua was a private man. It couldn't have been easy for him to lose his heart to you. Once given, it would be even more difficult for him to take it back. I know the devotion he was capable of and why he held it so jealously to himself. You see, it was I who dispatched Jeanette all those years ago."

"You?" A million thoughts rushed through her head as she realized the implications of his words. "He didn't...I'm not..." She struggled against the panic welling up inside. "He told me it was against the rules to leave me uncontrolled. He warned me what would happen if...if you found out."

"You spend your fear needlessly. When you accepted his Vow and understood its meaning, you became bound to him much more deeply than if he had only taken you in thrall. He should have realized this the moment the Vow was spoken." He paused to touch her hair with tenderness, easing away her fear. "This is why we wish for you to join us. I would be greatly honored to take you myself, if that is of your choosing. None of us will force you. You may have the time you need to mend these wounds to your soul."

She met his gaze fully and without fear, as Joshua had instructed, and saw recognition and surprise glowing in his eyes. "I know you're trying to convince me going along with all this is in my best interest. And you're probably all very sure I'll eventually give in to you. But I can't see that happening. Joshua is gone. I know that now, but I'm still having trouble accepting it. We had a connection I was only beginning to understand, but I can still feel him, in here," she said, pressing her closed fist over her heart. "I'm not ready to let that go.

"You've sentenced his child to death for crimes it may never commit. I will never accept your belief this is· for the good of all concerned. It would be an injustice I can't live with, and will never accept." She paused to wipe her face on her sleeve. "I know I can't fight you, but I can't cooperate with you either. I won't be a party to murder. My conscience won't allow it. My child, any child, is rare and precious, and deserves a chance at life. This baby is all the family I have left. If you take that from me, I won't have anything left to live for. I swear I will hate all of you to my last breath."

Trey laid a strong, gentle hand on the side of her head. "You'll feel differently in time," he said gently. "I'm a patient man, but my patience has its limits. The sooner you accept your fate, the better it will be for all of us." With that, he rose and left the room. She stared at the wall for a long time after he left and contemplated every word he'd had said to her. After a while, she closed her eyes and hummed a simple, melancholy tune.

* * * *

Gale entered the library, sat heavily on the sofa, and dropped his medical bag to the floor at his feet. "I've finished my examination."

"What is her condition?" Antonia asked.

"Her excursion into the forest weakened her. She's suffering from exhaustion and malnutrition. She may also be developing a good case of clinical depression. She denies it, of course." He tried to smile, but it felt more like a grimace. "She is strong-willed, and I can't say I blame her for not wanting to trust me. When I tried to give her a vitamin shot, she refused to cooperate until I gave myself an injection first. I think she was afraid it was a sedative, and we were ready to proceed with the operation."

"I'm afraid we can expect more resistance from Catherine until after her surgery," Trey said quietly. "I find myself understanding her more than I want to."

"I think we should give her some consideration," Antonia said. "After all, she's lost more in her young life than any mortal should have to endure."

"I have the operating room on standby," Gale reported grimly. "I told the administrator at the hospital the young woman was suffering from a rare form of uterine cancer, but was also allergic to sunlight." When the vampires in the room shot him a surprised look, he shrugged and added, "There've been known cases like this. It was all I could think of to explain why I needed the room prepped so late at night."

"You cover for us very well," Antonia said softly.

"It wasn't easy," he said with a tired sigh. "I called Sly Parker, our computer hacker contact in Atlanta, and set Miss Catherine Mills up with a detailed medical record, right down to when her tonsils were removed. He double-checked for existing records with the state of Washington, and I worked in a convincing string of entries leading up to her current condition. Took me all night and six pots of coffee to write it all up," he concluded with a yawn.

"Is she ready for surgery?" she asked.

"I'm concerned about her general state of health. I would much rather wait until she regains her strength, but of course, the longer we wait, the more difficult the procedure will be. Still, she is far too weak to withstand the physical stress of an operation, and if her condition worsens…"

"You must make certain she eats," Trey said firmly. "Catherine will be made to survive her ordeal."

"I'll do what I can to help her, but it might not be enough, especially if she continues to hold on to this obsession she has with Joshua."

"She's going to have to let go soon," Antonia said sadly. "I can sense her life force draining from her."

"Catherine's pain runs deep," Tray said tightly. "I do not wish her to suffer any more than she must at the loss of her child."

"I've given that some thought," Gale said. "I can remove her womb vaginally. It will be quite a trick, enlarged as it is, but I believe I can manage it. That will improve her healing time and minimize scaring that will remind her of what she's lost. I can keep her in a drug-induced coma until her body recovers, though I think a vampire-induced one might be better for her at this point. The real trick is getting her to the hospital in the first place. She's likely to put up a fight."

"Simple enough," Antonia said, taking a weary seat next to the doctor. "One of us can pay her a visit before sunup that day. We...we'll tell her we are concerned about her weakened state, and give her blood. She will likely agree to that, after her experience with me when we first met. Once she sleeps, we'll give her a command that will keep her asleep until after the surgery is over."

"That would be the simplest solution," Trey said softly. "I suggest feeding her earlier, though. It wouldn't hurt her to sleep that long, not as tired as she is." He scratched his chin and smiled. "I'll do it. I think she will be more likely to trust me as anyone here."

"You could be right," Antonia agreed. "There is also Vincent. I think I sensed a certain connection forming between those two, perhaps because of their shared experience in the woods. They understand each other, although I doubt either of them realizes that."

"He was close to Joshua," Trey offered. "They were very much alike– both jealously guarding their hearts."

"It's possible he could be led to take her under his wing out of brotherly responsibility," Antonia mused quietly. "On the other hand, he is also a private creature, and his heart is...otherwise committed. I suppose only time will tell."

"Well," Gale said, rising to his feet, "I need to get going. It's been a long day. I'll come back tomorrow to check on her again." He picked up his medical bag tiredly, and cast one last glance in Antonia's direction before turning to leave.

"Gale," she said before he left the room, "plan to stay until it's over. I want you closer."

"As you wish," he replied without turning.

* * * *

Katie did her best to eat the food brought to her, but found it harder to force anything down until at last she stopped trying. All she wanted was sleep, but her mind refused to give her the peace she needed. She turned her senses inward in an attempt at communion with her unborn child, and grieved that she would never see its face.

Would it have Joshua's eyes? His smile? She wondered if it sensed its impending fate...if it had any of Joshua's mental abilities. Even in an undeveloped state, it might have a certain amount of cognitive awareness. With that thought in mind, she talked to the baby, extolling its father's virtues. She read aloud, knowing that if it couldn't understand the words, the cadence of her voice might comfort it. This would be the one chance she would ever have to be a mother. She decided to make the best of the short time she had left.

She took out the handkerchief containing Joshua's remains, gently untied the bundle and touched the soft white powder. The memory of his smile, the soft looks he gave her with those beautiful chocolate eyes, the tender love he'd made with her, all flooded back in a wash of fresh grief. She choked back a sob and carefully folded the memento into a tight square. After a moment's thought, she pulled one of her softest sweaters from the dresser and sat on the bed to work at the stitching.

Without a pair of scissors, she had a hard time unraveling the cashmere, and had to use her teeth to cut off the length she pulled from the sleeve. She looped the yarn tightly around the bundle and worked it into a braided rope, and tied it off with a bow over the folded handkerchief. She looped it around her neck and felt the weight of her new pendant settle low on her chest, near to her heart.

Catherine.

She raised her head and listened, certain she'd just heard Joshua's soft whisper calling her name. "Joshua, is that you?" she asked quietly. "Are you near?" She opened her mind wide to the memory of their bond and waited, but received no sense of him. With a determined sigh, she mentally called his name, giving all her strength to the effort. She was rewarded by a brief sense of him, vague enough it could've been her own wishful thinking, but it gave her a certain comfort to believe he was thinking of her. Feeling satisfied, she curled up on her bed and cradled his scarf in her arms.

Alex began making frequent visits in an attempt to support her and lighten her mood. The deeply troubled look in his light eyes made her feel sorry her plight was causing him pain. Servants came at intervals to change her bedding and bring her fresh towels, and provided her with books from the library. She did her best to pass the time, praying with every breath for some kind of miracle.

When Stephan was admitted by one of her ever-present guards, she eyed him warily as he took a seat. "Don't be afraid, Catherine. I won't hurt the smallest hair on your head."

"Why are you here?"

He chuckled. "Still reckless. It suits you." He shifted his position in the chair and sobered. "Actually, I came to apologize for the way I treated you. I've been listening to the others speak of you, and I think I understand you better now. Do you think you can forgive me?"

"I don't know. It took months for me to learn to trust Joshua after he frightened me, and he wasn't trying to kill me."

He shook his head. "I am sorry, please believe that. I'm not normally so impetuous. I understand you much better than I did. I think you'll find life in Haven can be more than pleasant if you give us a chance."

She shook her head sadly. "I'm sorry. You are all mistaken to think I will ever get over this. It hurts too much. I can't handle it anymore." Tears sprung to her eyes once again and she turned her head away. "Please leave."

"As you wish," he said, rising from his chair. "But know their wishes will be followed. They would be much happier if you accept their offer." He left the room. She instantly burst into tears.

* * * *

"You don't understand," Gale explained later that evening. "She wants to die. There's not much I can do to snap her out it."

"She must eat," Trey said sharply. "Ever since her return from the forest, she's refused everything the servants have tried to do for her."

"She won't listen to me! I don't have any influence over her. Not anymore. I suggest you do something." He suddenly found himself sailing across the room, an explosion of pain erupting on the side of his face. He looked at Trey in surprise and fear as the big man loomed over him, his eyes glowing with all the fire in his soul.

"Let that be a reminder, mortal," he hissed. "Fail us, and you'll know pain the likes of which you can only imagine." He turned and stalked out of the library.

Antonia watched Trey leave, then knelt by the doctor's side. "You're lucky all you got was a slap," she said, not unsympathetically. "Gale, you know better."

"He's being unreasonable, and you know it." He gingerly touched his cheek. The bruise was beginning to swell. He gave her a look that was plainly a plea. "What do I do? She won't let me talk to her."

She shrugged and pulled him to his feet. "Try again. Threaten her. She must learn obedience."

"Antonia, has the thought ever occurred to any of you that treating her this way will only make matters worse? What's the harm in letting her keep the child? You can keep them here and watch them. If the damphere begins to show signs of rebellion, there will be plenty of time to dispatch it later."

"The decision's been made." She paced the floor sullenly for a moment. "I don't like it any more than you do. The woman wants to hold on to some piece of Joshua. I find I understand how she feels. We'll have to hope that, in time, she finds a new path for her life." She looked at him sadly. "You'd better go to her, Gale. See what you can do."

He winced, nodded and turned for the stairs reluctantly. "I'll try," he muttered, mostly to himself.

* * * *

Katie didn't blink her eyes when she heard the lock turn in her door. It opened and closed silently and she sensed she was no longer alone. She continued to stare blankly at the wall, even when the doctor appeared from around the bed. When he placed himself in her line of sight, she deliberately closed her eyes.

"Catherine, for God's sake!" he pleaded. "Can't you see I'm trying to help you?" When she failed to respond, he pulled her sharply upright and shook her. "Look at me, damn you!" he hissed. She opened her eyes and noticed the deep, fresh bruise on his cheek, but did not allow herself to show the slightest hint of reaction. "You're not hurting yourself anymore. When they kill me, it won't be quick and painless. They have ways of making a man wish for death. Don't you care?"

"No."

He released her and sank into a chair. "Ah, Catherine, have mercy. It won't be as bad as you imagine." He touched his swollen eye experimentally with the tips of his fingers. "They can be as kind as they can harsh," he told her more quietly. "For who knows what reason, they value you enough to want you to remain. Some are even sorry about the baby. Others are beginning to feel more than tender concern for your welfare. Can't you give them a chance?"

"What chance have they given my baby?" she asked, her voice sounding hollow and defeated.

"At least try to eat," he begged as he pulled himself to his feet. "If you don't, I'll have you strapped down and fed intravenously." When she looked at him in surprise, he added, "Don't think I won't. You must be strong enough to withstand your surgery. I've been warned to keep you alive."

She turned away to bury her face in her pillow. "Get away from me."

"Remember what I said, Catherine. Eat. Take better care of yourself, or I'll be forced to take more drastic measures." He left the room, leaving her feeling more defeated than she ever had in her life.

The following morning, one of the stronger servants brought her a breakfast tray. He set it down purposefully, crossed his meaty arms across his chest and waited for her response. Reluctantly, she pulled herself off the bed and sat down in front of the food. When she picked up the fork and put a bite of the soufflé in her mouth, he relaxed his stance, but made it clear by his continued presence he intended to watch her swallow every morsel. She complied silently, and watched him take the empty tray from the room with a look of grim satisfaction.

That evening after dinner, she heard a light tap at her door. She threw the book she was reading at it. It struck the sill and dropped heavily to the floor. "Leave me alone!"

"Catherine, admit me," Trey's deep voice called from the other side of the door. When she hesitated, she heard him say, "Please."

"All right, Trey," she said with a heavy sigh. When the big man entered the room, she saw the pain in his eyes. He studied her in silence for several long minutes before he spoke.

"Gale has finalized the arrangements for your operation," he said once he had taken a seat next to her on the bed. "The surgery will take place late tomorrow night when the hospital will be the least crowded." A tear slid unheeded down her cheek, but she didn't reply. He winced and raised a finger to wipe the moisture from her cheek. "I feel your pain," he told her. "Your tears call to me, even in my daily rest. Can I offer you no comfort?"

She lowered her gaze to her hands, passively resisting his control. "The only thing I want is the one thing you won't let me have."

"I've been talking with some of the others. I'm afraid their decision stands. Too many remember the last time a damphere threatened their existence. It's too much to ask that they risk that kind of danger again."

Another tear rolled silently down her cheek. "Leave me," she whispered. "Let me die in peace."

"Your life is not in jeopardy. You will survive this."

She sat silently for almost a minute before answering. "The baby and my Vow to Joshua are all I have," she said thickly. "I will not release my hold on Joshua if I can't keep his child. You can't force me to give up on everything that will ever mean anything to me. If my link with him is killing me, I'll let it. I know he's waiting for me. I can feel him, and I want to be with him. I'll never forgive your precious Community, and I won't accept any kind of life in Haven. Even if you do take control of me, you won't control my spirit. Before a year goes by, if I survive that long, I'll find a way to end my life, or make one of you mad enough to end it for me."

Fathomless sorrow filled his eyes as he asked, "Do you feel no kindness for any of us?"

"I don't know," she answered, looking at him with sympathy. "Some of those I've met aren't unlikable. Under better circumstances, I might've been glad, even proud, to call some of you friends." She shook her head and put a hand on his arm. "I feel closer to you and Vincent than to any of the others. Maybe the blood I took from Antonia has formed a weak bond between us. I still don't quite understand how that works. But I'll never feel for anyone what I had with Joshua, not ever."

Deep pain darkened the big man's eyes. "You're right, of course. The patience of the Community has limits. We are all affected by the pain in your heart. It will not go unanswered long." She felt the weight of his gaze as he sat studying her in silent contemplation. "Do you trust me still?" he asked softly. She nodded silently in response. He traced her jaw with the outside of his thumb and sighed. "Are you willing to give your life to me?"

"I won't let you bring me across," she told him. "I don't want to live forever. Not without Joshua. I can't take it."

"That's not my intention," he said solemnly. "I can put your spirit to rest if you permit me to do so. Will you surrender your life to me?"

Understanding brought a surge of anxiety to her heart. "Do they know you're here?" she asked, her voice a mere whisper.

He held her gaze without flinching. "I was sent to feed you my blood, to strengthen you for your surgery tomorrow. I was to leave you with a command that would keep you asleep until after it is done," he answered her. "The others will be angry, to be certain, but I can be much more reasonable, and merciful, when I choose to be. Your pain does not honor the memory of your beloved. I will end it for you here and now, if that is your wish. Again I ask, for I will not take your life from you without your leave."

Her anxiety at the prospect of dying was tempered by concern. "Won't they punish you?"

He chuckled. "Joshua was right when he said you give of yourself unselfishly. Even now, at the darkest hour of your life, you are unwilling to risk my discomfort. Yes," he answered as he brushed her hair back from her neck. "There will be retribution, of that I have no doubt, but nothing the Council can do will be as difficult for me to bear as your despair has been."

She swallowed hard. Her heart hammered heavily in her chest. "All right. Take me then," she whispered. "I won't fight you."

"I can feel your fear, Catherine. Are you certain?"

Another tear dripped from her cheek. "Yes," she said, forcing a smile. "But I want you to make me a promise first."

"If I can," he answered softly.

"Alex," she had to pause to swallow a lump forming in her throat. "He's going to need looking after. He cared for Joshua like a devoted son."

"I'll take care of him."

"No, give him to Vincent. I think he'll be more comfortable that way. Vincent will appreciate the kind of loyalty Alex will give him."

He nodded his understanding. "I'll make sure it is done."

"There's a man in Washington, an attorney named Carl Foster. Alex knows how to contact him. He took care of all of Joshua's financial and legal needs, and he's become like a father to me. I would like him released from his obligation and given Joshua's estate. I think he would've liked that."

"I'll see to it personally."

"There's one more thing." She brushed a tear from her cheek and heaved a shaky sigh. "I want my...my body cremated, and my ashes sprinkled in the woods over the place where Joshua died so I can rest closest to him. Vincent knows the spot. You'll take care of that, won't you?"

He stroked the side of her face and gave her a smile filled with sorrow. "You have my word."

"Okay, then. I'm ready." He gathered her in his strong arms and cradled her as he would a child. He looked deeply into her eyes, capturing them with his own. She reached up with one hand and touched his face. "Thank you," she whispered with all gratitude and trust she felt in her heart.

"Think of happier times, small one," he said sadly. "You will feel no pain."

She felt the influence of his mind sweep through her and surrendered to him. Her mind filled with calm serenity. She drowned herself the feeling and followed his spell to a place where she imagined herself lying in Joshua's arms. She held on to that image and closed her eyes when she felt the cool touch of his lips on her throat.

Chapter Twenty-Three

Gale rose from the sofa and crossed the library to stare out at the dark woods. "I still wish there was some other way."

Antonia rose to move up behind him and placed a hand gently on his arm to turn him toward her. "I feel as bad about this as you do. Spend this night with me. Let us console each other."

He smiled sadly. "Can you still find me attractive, Antonia? I'm old enough now to be your father. Older, maybe."

She responded by pressing her lips against his and running one hand down the front of his shirt, then farther. "What has age to do with matters of the heart?" she asked gently.

He pulled her tightly against him and took possession of her mouth. His arms closed around her while he kissed her hungrily. "It's been so long," he said against her lips. She pressed her body against his and returned his passion with her own. When she pulled away abruptly and turned toward the entry hall, he almost collapsed to his knees. "What is it?" he asked, frustration and caution mixed in his voice.

"I heard something." She cocked her head. Her whole body was tense and still, like a wild tigress sensing danger.

Then he heard it too–the sound of someone trying to open the front door. "Do you sense anyone?" he whispered.

"No."

"Someone's trying to get in." They heard the distinctive sound of someone sliding down the door and hitting the ground with a thud. A low male groan followed.

"Sounds like someone's hurt," she said more loudly as she rushed to open the door. A man lay at the threshold, moaning softly. "Help me get him inside," she ordered. They pulled him onto the marble floor. Gale quickly closed the door while she examined him. When she turned him onto his back, he weakly pulled his blood-encrusted coat open. The broken end of a wooden shaft protruded from his chest.

"My God," Gale said, kneeling beside him. The fact that the stranger was a vampire was not missed in the doctor's scrutiny. His pale, translucent skin was a dead giveaway for someone who knew what to look for. "Is he one of ours?"

She nodded silently as she brushed his hair from his face. "The arrow..." the man whispered weakly, "...barbed."

He looked up at one of the servants who appeared from the back of the house. "My med kit is in the back seat of my car," he said loudly enough for the servant to understand his meaning. As she ran for the car, he turned to Antonia. "I'll need help."

She pulled her eyes away from the injured man and sent a mental call that was instantly answered. Several people, vampires and servants alike, appeared from all corners of the house. "The table in the kitchen is long enough," she suggested, urgency in her voice. Four of the men picked up the injured man and carried him quickly into the kitchen. When they laid him on the table, he groaned loudly. "Hang on," she told him tightly.

* * * *

Trey pressed the tips of his fangs against the skin of Katie's throat, then jerked his head away. She looked up at him in dazed surprise as he jumped from the bed, his eyes focused beyond the confines of the bedroom. "There is trouble," he said, a tight edge in his voice. "A call for help has been issued." He looked down at her, his eyes once again the color of coal. "I must go."

"No, please," she begged weakly. "Finish this."

"There's no time. This call is urgent. I will return for you before sunrise," he promised as he quickly left her room.

With his mental influence still clogging her mind, the best she could do was lie back on the pillow, confusion and disappointment filling her every pore. She touched the spot where she'd felt his fangs graze her skin, and tears filled her eyes. He'd been so close, she thought. Her ordeal had almost come to a final end. Fearing that someone else might sense her plan, she resolutely closed her mind. She closed her eyes and prayed he would remember his promise.

* * * *

Deep in his solitude, Vincent also heard Antonia's call for help. "No," he growled, putting his hands unnecessarily to his ears in an attempt to shield himself from the call. He sensed the urgency of the call rise and become entwined with additional voices and shook his head. "Leave me in peace!" He rose to pace the confines of his room. Urgency became desperation as more and more voices echoed in his mind, growing in insistence until it became a loud roar he could not close himself to. The atmosphere of the great house became so emotionally charged he would have no rest until he discovered the cause. With a grunt of irritation, he jerked open his door and left his room.

* * * *

"Get his clothes off," Gale ordered. "I've got to see what I'm dealing with." Two servants quickly cut off his clothing while another brought water from the sink and gingerly sponged at the wound to remove the clots of blood-soaked dirt. The doctor fished through the contents of his medical bag, withdrew a thin metal probe and leaned over the man's chest. After carefully testing the depth of the wound, he shook his head. "He's right. It's the same kind of arrow that killed Devon. It won't come out the way it went in, not easily, but it's resting against his heart. If I push it through…"

"You'll kill him," Antonia cried. "Gale, do something!"

More people gathered in the kitchen to see what was happening. "I need you all to clear out. Give me room to work," he ordered. Most of them backed out of the room obediently, concern deeply engraved on their faces. He turned to his bag and arranged instruments on the table beside the man's body.

Trey filled the doorway of the kitchen, and when he saw the man lying on the table, he called his name with a wild combination of emotions in his voice. "Joshua!" Gale's head snapped instantly to his patient's face. *So this is Joshua!* The implications of the man's identity flooded his mind, making him feel more determined than ever to save him. Trey took his place beside Antonia at his head. "Can you help him?" The tone of his voice reflected the emotions that were coursing through the other occupants of the mansion.

"I'll try my best," he answered tightly. "Someone better knock him out. This is gonna hurt like hell."

Before Trey turned focus his power on Joshua, Alex skidded through the door. When he saw his master, tears sprang to his eyes. Unfortunately, Joshua caught sight of his servant as well and struggled to pull himself upright. "Alex," he exclaimed weakly. "What in bloody hell are you doing here?" He tried to rise from the table and several hands pushed him down. "Where's Catherine?"

"We don't have time for this," Gale growled.

Trey placed his hand firmly on the younger vampire's forehead.

"Sleep."

Joshua resisted Trey's command with strength Gale knew he couldn't afford. "What have you done with her?"

"I said sleep, fledgling," Trey boomed, putting all his mental energy into the command. Joshua was too weak to resist the order. His head fell to the side. His body, heretofore clenched against the pain, fell deathly limp.

Vincent found his way to the kitchen by that time and saw Joshua lying on the table. "By the *Gods!*" He moved to the foot of the table, his firm control over his emotions all but lost. "Does he live?"

"Barely," Gale said absently as he picked up a scalpel. "I'm going to widen this wound and make a clean path to get the arrow out." He looked up at Trey. "I need someone with strong fingers to hold his ribs apart. It's lodged in there pretty tight."

Trey moved obediently to the opposite side of the table and watched as the doctor made a neat incision between Joshua's ribs. When he'd made a large enough opening, he pointed to a spot three inches to the side of the arrow. "Here. Any closer and we risk breaking his ribs." Trey slid both his index fingers between the ribs and pulled with sufficient force to part them. "I need more light," he grumbled. A servant instantly produced a flashlight and shone it into the wound. He cut a careful path along the shaft of the arrow. "It missed his lung," he muttered. "Good thing he packed the wound, though. It kept him from bleeding out." When he reached the arrowhead, he said, "Someone clean out this hole. There's a syringe on the table. Quickly!"

Antonia picked up the syringe and siphoned blood from the wound. Gale nodded and worked at the arrowhead grimly. "Damn. Looks like the tip pierced his heart." Sweat started trickling down the side of his face. The servant girl who had been aiding him picked up some gauze and wiped it off. "Thanks," he said absently. He pulled both of his lips between his teeth and bit down hard in concentration, poked some gauze into the wound and tucked it carefully around the head of the arrow. "Okay, here we go," he whispered. With mind-numbing slowness, he eased the arrow out of the wound. "A little wider, Trey. That's it." He dropped the broken shaft onto the table.

"I'm not done yet," he said sharply when the others sighed their relief. "Someone thread me a needle." He was quickly handed a needle threaded with fine silk, and he grabbed a pair of forceps. He stitched the heart closed, then watched to make sure he'd sealed it properly. His needlework held, but then the heart fluttered to a halt. "His heart's stopped!" he cried. "He's lost too much blood. His arteries are collapsing!"

"Gale," Antonia began, her eyes filling with tears.

Her wishes found their way easily into his mind. He quickly grabbed a length of sterile tubing and cut sharp wedges on both ends. He pressed the tip of his scalpel into Joshua's throat and fed one end into the artery. Then with equal precision, he plied his scalpel to the underside of her arm and inserted the other end. She closed her eyes in concentration as her blood flowed into Joshua's body. One of the stronger servants moved behind her and wrapped his arms around her for support.

Desperately, Gale thrust his fingers into the wound and started working at the stilled heart. "Come on, damn you." More sweat ran down his face, and the girl swabbed his brow once more. "Come on, now," he repeated tensely. "Live, damn it." He stilled, his fingers resting against the heart, his whole attention focused on what he thought he'd felt there. One tentative pulsation vibrated against his fingers. Another. A third. The heart settled in to a weak but stable rhythm. "Good boy," he sighed. "Let's keep it that way, shall we?"

When he nodded at Antonia, she removed the tubing and allowed the servant to pull her onto his lap on one of the chairs behind them. He cradled her and offered his wrist, which she accepted with tired gratitude.

Stitching the wound closed took a small eternity. Everyone seemed to be holding his or her breath until he knotted the last stitch. A collective sigh swept the room. "Thank the stars you people don't suffer from infection," he said as he cleaned the wound site. He put the arrow in a plastic bag and handed it to Trey, who accepted it with a grim nod. When he finished taping a pressure bandage to the wound, he looked up at Trey again. "Wake him. He's lost a lot of blood...."

Trey nodded in understanding and released Joshua from his mental hold before the doctor finished his statement. Just as quickly, servants lined up to act as donors for the downed vampire. Alex took the lead, pushing the other servants away and putting his hand on Joshua's arm possessively.

* * * *

Joshua parted his eyelids slowly. "Catherine," he breathed weakly.

Alex pressed his wrist against Joshua's lips. When he didn't respond, Trey once again forced his will on him. "Drink," he said firmly. Reluctantly, he took Alex's wrist with his fangs. In his weakened state, he was neither able to soothe the minds of his donors nor judge how much he was taking. His conscience was mollified when Trey took charge of servants. When one had donated to the point of weakness, he pulled him away and motioned for the next. Stephan and Vincent cared for those servants who had given their aid, offering them juice and muffins somewhere beyond his feet. Several servants cleansed his body and hair while he continued to feed. By the time he was cleaned and a robe produced, he was able to sit upright with assistance. He swung his legs over the side of the table.

"No more," he said weakly as he waved off yet another servant. "I've had my fill for now." He searched in his mind for Catherine while the robe was fitted over his arms and around his body. What he found appalled him. He called to her mentally but her mind was too tightly closed to hear him. "What have you done to my wife?" he asked angrily.

"She is here," Trey confirmed when the others wouldn't speak. "There are things you should know before you go to her. Things it will not be easy for you to hear."

"I'll rip your heart out," he threatened.

Trey chuckled softly. "You're welcome to try, though I might advise you to wait until you're stronger."

"You've destroyed her spirit."

"Catherine will recover, now that you've returned," he said gently. "She is the most remarkable creature I've ever had the pleasure of sinking my teeth into; strong willed and stubborn to the last."

He stared at him in disbelief. "You drank from her?"

"She offered herself to me during the tribunal. She said things to me you must've taught her. There is a lot of courage in that one."

More anger flared in his mind, bringing with it the unique sharpening of his vision that told him his eyes were beginning to glow. "You put her on trial? Why?"

"Joshua," Antonia began, "we had much to consider when we brought her here. There was much at stake." When he turned his angry gaze on her, she continued quickly. "Understand, we thought you were lost to us. We had to act for the safety of the Community."

"You know me," he said hotly. "You know how hard it was for me to let Catherine into my heart, yet leave her uncontrolled. I trust her more than you can possibly imagine. She is no threat to you." When he moved off the table, many hands reached out to support him. He was helped into one of the kitchen chairs, though he thought he'd made it clear he had another destination in mind.

Antonia knelt beside him and met his angry gaze. "When it was determined you had met with disaster, I went to her. I meant only to tell her what had become of you, so she could move on with her life." She lowered her eyes when she added, "After all we've meant to each other, I couldn't let her sit for the rest of her life wondering your fate. When I found her, she was near death. She recognized me for what I am and asked me to bring her across. Instead I fed her enough to sustain her and called Dr. Carter to her aid."

He stared at her in stunned silence for several long moments. "Why bring her here? I don't understand."

Gale cleared his throat. "Joshua, she's carrying your child."

He gaped openly at the doctor, then darkness filled his heart as old wounds reopened. "That's not possible. She lied to you."

"It's not only possible, I'm afraid it's true," Antonia told him. He shook his head with a frown.

"The child is indeed yours," Trey interjected. "I tasted its nature in Catherine's blood. She carries a damphere in her womb."

His confusion drew his brows into a deeper frown. "A what?"

"A vampire-human hybrid," Gale explained.

"You're too young to know of such things, darling," Antonia told him. "The fault is mine for not telling you about them a long time ago." She rose to her feet and leaned back against the counter. "It is rare. None of us has created one, at least not that we are aware of. The circumstances had to be just right for conception to take place."

He considered her words carefully. "The night before I left her…" He looked up at Antonia feeling bemused. "She wished to feel my power. She insisted I not hold myself back when we made love. She was not prepared for my intensity, nor did she fully understand the danger she faced when I abandoned control. The strain nearly ruptured her heart. I made her drink. I thought to give her my strength so she might endure my passion. The pleasure was almost more than I myself could bear. I thought my entire being would spill into her."

"The power you subjected her to, and the intensity you describe, was enough to give the required strength to your seed," she said with a nod. "And, her womb was probably at its most receptive. It had to have happened very quickly."

He stared at the floor in silence for a few moments, then looked squarely into her eyes. "Why did you consider her a threat?"

She tried to break the hold he had on her gaze without success. "The child she bears can grow up to become a formidable enemy to our kind. It will likely have all of our powers, all of our strengths, but without our weaknesses to hold it back. Imagine a creature that can sense our presence, can mask its own, and can hunt us with all the power of a vampire while we sleep." She shook her head. "We argued the matter at great length. It was decided that the child was too great a risk."

"What are you saying?" he asked coldly.

"I've been ordered to terminate the pregnancy," Gale told him uncomfortably. "The procedure will take place tomorrow night."

Up until that moment, he hadn't believed he could be made to feel more miserable. The knowledge of the distress Catherine would've felt and the strength of her despair weighed down his heart as if his blood had turned to molten lead. "Take me to her," he demanded, a dangerous edge in his voice.

"There is one more thing you should know," Trey said, looking somewhat abashed. "Catherine is not well. When we first brought her to Haven and told her what we believed was the truth about you, she escaped and set out to search the forest for you on her own. It took us over a week to find her."

"We found evidence of your death," Vincent said. "I saw...there were ashes. I thought...we all believed..."

"I'll explain everything later," Joshua said tightly.

"She is ready to die" Trey continued, bringing a hush to the room. "We believed the bond you shared was draining her life force, and all of us tried our best to convince her to let you go, but she is quite stubborn. We've all taken steps to sustain her life, even to forcing food on her. Her pain became more than I could bear. The influence of her blood offering affects me still. I was in her room tonight. When Antonia called us to your aid, I was...preparing to end her life." Gasps of surprise and outrage rippled through the occupants of the kitchen. "She surrendered herself to me willingly," he said to his own defense. "She desired an end to her pain. I could no longer deny her." He reluctantly met Antonia's gaze. "Had you been any longer in calling out..."

Joshua sank into himself for a moment, the visions inspired by Trey's words flitting painfully in his mind. He gave Trey a look he knew reflected his almost fathomless grief. "She must trust you deeply."

Trey moved to place a gentle hand on his shoulder. "Her loyalty to you is unshaken, my friend. We can all attest to that. She was offered the opportunity to join us. Any one of us would've been honored to take her. She remained steadfast in her refusal to give in to us. She would not release her Vow to you, even when it was certain you were no more. Without you, she's lost. She vowed to me she would never love another."

Joshua rose to his feet, groaned, and put a hand over his heart. "You'll start to bleed again," Gale scolded.

He pulled himself painfully to his own full height, and even so had to look up to meet Trey's uncomfortable gaze. "Take me to her," he said in a voice that was a low, dangerous growl. "Now."

* * * *

In the long hours that passed, Katie paced her room anxiously and waited for Trey's return. She had the chance to think about what he was prepared do for her, and knew it was what she wanted. There was a certain amount of peace in the decision. She felt unusually weak, tired down deep to her core, so she returned to her bed. Sleep took her so suddenly she didn't realize it happened until she woke with the startling sensation of someone brushing her mind with their own. Reflexively, she snapped closed the hard shell of her control, protecting her vulnerable thoughts with the suddenness of a startled clam, but not before she thought she heard Joshua's voice calling to her once more. The pain that shot through her heart didn't feel like her own. Was it his spirit she sensed? Was he hovering near, watching over her? The thought gave her some comfort. Wherever he was, he was lonely, she felt sure of that.

She curled up tight on her bed and thought of the soft white satin she'd slept under contentedly with Joshua by her side. Those happier times were lost to her forever, but she wanted those tender moments to be among the last things she thought about. She dozed off again, carried gently away on the wind of her memories. When she heard Trey's knock on her door, she sat up sleepily. Without waiting for a response, he entered her room, the look on his face unreadable. She nodded solemnly to indicate she was ready for him.

He took one step away from the door to admit Dr. Carter, and she instantly felt betrayed. Suddenly filled with dread, she kicked her feet until her back was pressed firmly against the headboard. Before she had a chance to gather her voice for protest, he stepped back, admitting Vincent. Joshua was leaning heavily on his shoulder.

At first, she did not believe what she was seeing. The man leaning against Vincent bore very little resemblance to the Joshua she had known. "No, I'm dreaming." She closed her eyes for a second, and when she opened them again, he was still there.

He looked worse than he had when he'd burned his back. His complexion was beyond pale, the expression on his face one of extreme exhaustion. Three weeks of beard growth accentuated his haggard appearance. In his eyes, she saw pain deeper and more profound than the pain she'd caused him with her fear. "Catherine," he whispered at last.

The sound of his voice broke her from her stunned paralysis. She slid shakily from of the bed and went to him, gathering momentum as she moved, tears streaming down her face. Trey had to catch her before she collided with him. "Carefully, small one. He's been injured."

Joshua closed the gap between them and gathered her gingerly in his arms. "I am so sorry," he said into her hair. "Ah, Catherine, my love, forgive me. I didn't know."

She buried her face in his shoulder and released all the grief and despair she'd held tight inside her, and clung to him, afraid he would vanish like a mirage. His hands stroked her back and head, and she felt him press his face deeper into her hair. "I thought you were dead," she whispered between sobs.

"I almost was. Do you mean to finish the job by drowning me in your tears?" She heaved a shaky sigh and did her best to calm her tears.

She turned her face to him, and their lips connected with a shared moan. She stroked his face with her fingertips. "Are you really here?"

"Aye, love. You are not imagining me."

"You look terrible."

He brushed the hair from her face and studied her, and she saw in his eyes he didn't like what he saw. "I can say the same of you. What have they done to you?"

"Nothing," she said quietly. "I've been sick ever since you left. They did their best to take care of me." She lowered her eyes and whispered, "I haven't been very cooperative."

"They understand," he said softly. "Had I known the reason for your distress, I would've tried harder to return to you."

She pulled away far enough to move the front of his robe aside, and gasped at the thick bandage taped to his chest. With trembling fingers, she touched him, then moved her hand to her own breast. "I felt it," she whispered. "I felt your pain. I didn't know what it meant."

"This bond we share," he said softly. "I didn't realize you felt it so strongly you would know of my injury from so great a distance. I was aware of your sorrow and your fear, but I believed it was only because by my absence. I had to close myself to your feelings to better concentrate on the matters at hand. I should've realized you are not strong enough to be apart from me for too long. Our Vow is far too powerful, and not meant for the fragility of the mortal heart. I'll never leave your side again."

She reached inside her sweater and removed the homemade pendant she wore. "When we found your ashes…and the broken arrow shaft…"

He took the pendant from her and let it drop to the floor with an air of dismissal. "I know how hard it's been for you. 'Tis all over now."

His knees weakened and Trey hurried to his side. "You need to lie down, my friend. Catherine…" She was already moving to pull back the covers on her bed. Trey helped Joshua onto the bed and arranged the covers over him while she took her place on the other side. Joshua put his hand on Trey's arm, and they looked at each other in silent communion for a moment. Trey nodded almost imperceptibly and rounded the bed to sit beside her. He pulled out a penknife and pressed it into his wrist, then applied pressure to the wound with his thumb and held it to her. "Drink."

She shook her head and looked at Joshua uncertainly. "Do as he asks," he told her weakly.

She stared at him a moment, uncertain as to how much the others had told him about her condition. "Joshua…?"

"Please, Catherine. Take from him the help I am not strong enough to offer you myself."

She looked back at Trey reluctantly. Her dawning understanding of the risks of this kind of sharing, and the strange bonds that resulted, made her question his offer further. It had been one thing to trust Trey when she believed Joshua was gone, but another issue entirely now that he had returned. If a bond formed between herself and the dark giant sitting beside her, would it conflict with her Vow? Or was he still following the wishes of the Community?

"It's all right," Trey said, his voice soft and deep, his eyes reflecting his understanding of her concerns. "You have need of the strength I can provide." She took his wrist with one trembling hand, and a silent tear dripped onto his skin as she closed her mouth over the wound. Trey cradled her with his other arm while she took him, and Joshua took her other hand and held it tight. His blood had the same profound effect on her as Antonia's had before, but this time it felt much stronger. She trembled under the force of the big man's awesome power.

When she'd taken all she could hold, he released her and bound his wrist. She felt his blood rushing through her system and a bond she couldn't define build between them. She met his gaze and saw confirmation burning there. She swallowed hard at the lump forming in her throat. "Trey…" she whispered.

He put his arms around her and held her tenderly against him for a moment. "Be at peace, little sister," he whispered. "No action will be taken against you this day." She gaped at him in confusion while he moved to the door to follow her other visitors out of the room. Dark clouds were quickly filling her head, bringing the same warm-velvet drowsiness she'd felt after Antonia's gift.

"Trey," Joshua said before he left the room, "tell the others to meet with me after sunset. I will tell the Community all that I know, and..." he added with a sharp tone in his voice, "we *will* revisit the matter of Catherine's child." Trey nodded his understanding and closed the door.

"Joshua," she began nervously.

"Quiet, love. The time for explanations will come. Lay beside me. Let me feel your warmth while I take my rest."

She quickly shrugged out of her clothing and slid under the covers. He pulled open his robe, and she stretched herself along his side and rested her head on his shoulder. He put his arm around her as if he were afraid she would vanish once his eyes were closed. "If I seem to die, please don't be alarmed. I must enter a very deep sleep if I am to mend. Do you understand?" She nodded her head gently against him. He turned his thoughts on the light, and when the room fell to darkness, she sighed contentedly and surrendered to her own deep rest.

Chapter Twenty-Four

Katie woke to the cool touch of Joshua's hand on her ribs but kept still and allowed herself to enjoy the sweet sensation of his touch. She felt better, stronger, than she had in weeks. Was it Trey's gift that had fortified her, or the realization of Joshua's renewing strength? Maybe it was a little of both. He slid his hand tenderly along her skin until it came to rest on her hip and she felt his gentle pressure guiding her onto her back. She sighed and allowed him to move her, and his hand settled on the lowest part of her abdomen where his fingers gently explored her hardened womb. "You're still here," she commented sleepily.

"Were you afraid I would leave you?" he asked quietly.

"No. I was afraid it was all a dream." She put her hand over his. "I didn't know how to tell you. You were so sure you couldn't give me a baby. I thought…"

He moved his hand away to press a finger to her lips. "It was not easy for me to accept the possibility that I could, in fact, be responsible for such a miracle," he told her candidly. "I'm ashamed to admit that, for a moment, I allowed myself to believe the worst of you. The others were most diligent in their efforts to improve my lacking education in this matter. They were very convincing, especially Trey."

"Trey?"

He shielded her eyes and brought the light on with a quick mental command, and smoothed her hair away from her face. "He told me how you offered yourself to him when your loyalty and motives were at question. You remembered the lessons I taught you very well. He said he tasted the babe's presence in your blood. He convinced me the child you carry is no mere mortal. I also learned of your bold escape, and your determination to learn for yourself what had happened to me, even against the wishes of the Council. Catherine, you've held up under the most difficult circumstances any mortal can endure, with bravery beyond anything I might've expected. I must admit to feeling a certain measure of pride when they described it all to me."

"I had to be strong," she told him uncomfortably, still squinting against the light. "Dr. Carter told me I couldn't afford to let myself be afraid."

"True enough," he said. "Still, defying them the way you did took a lot of courage. You placed yourself in grave danger."

"I'm sorry," she said with a sigh. "I had to know. I still felt you. I couldn't take their word that you were gone. It didn't feel right."

"You're lucky you survived. You don't know how dangerous these woods can be, especially at night."

"Oh, believe me, I do. I was attacked by a rogue…"

His body tensed beside her. "He didn't hurt you?"

She shook her head. "A hunter was there. She killed him before he had a chance to do more than frighten me."

"You saw her?"

"She was in the shadows. I didn't see much. Joshua, she thought all vampires are like the one she killed. She doesn't understand. She's got to be stopped."

"I know," he said gently. "We're trying." He pulled her back into his arms. "You've been through so much. I swore I would never hurt you, yet you've suffered greatly at my hand. How can I ever make it up to you?"

"It wasn't your fault," she whispered. "You couldn't have known what was happening to me. Just promise me, whatever happens, we'll always be together."

"You'll have a hard time getting rid of me from now on," he answered with a halfhearted chuckle. His hand strayed once more to her womb. "I can feel the child's life force. Though right now it is not much more than a collection of cells, it is very strong. I think it will take after its mother. And," he added more tenderly, "it is resting much more comfortably. I'm sorry you were ill."

"I almost died."

"I know. Why didn't you go to a doctor?"

"I didn't know what was wrong with me. After what we did, after you shared your power, and your blood, I was afraid a doctor might find something I couldn't explain. I needed to protect your secrets."

"When are you going consider yourself first?" he asked in quiet admonishment. "You might've at least considered how your death would've affected me."

"I was hoping you'd come back before it was too late."

He raised himself up onto his elbow, and from the look on his face, she was in for another one of his vampire lectures. "The unique properties in vampire blood dissipate quickly in the mortal digestive system. Your doctors would've found nothing unusual. It has the power to lesson illness and give strength when it's needed, though I'm not sure if it can cure serious diseases such as your AIDS virus. For obvious reasons, we don't share ourselves in this manner often, so little is known of long-term effects. If there had been any chance my blood could do you harm, I would never have allowed you to take it."

"Why does it make me so sleepy?"

"Depending on the severity of the need, it causes you to experience, in the closest way a mortal can, the vampire's unique kind of rest. Your system devotes all but the most critical resources to your recovery."

She thought for a moment. "When I woke up after our last night together, I still felt weak. If your blood makes me stronger, why did I get sick?"

"I made you drink that night because the intensity of my passion threatened to kill you. You didn't take enough to do more than allow you to withstand it. You probably became ill, at least initially, as a result of conception, as most mortal women would."

She nodded thoughtfully. "Okay, I get it. But what about the baby? Once the doctors realized it wasn't normal…"

"I'm certain nothing in your chemistry would betray the nature of the child. Unless tests were done on the baby itself, they would not have found anything out of the ordinary."

She thought about his words for a moment, compared them with things she'd learned in her short time with the Community. "Joshua, Antonia told me she could tell you'd given me your blood before that night. I think I understand some of the things I've been feeling ever since I woke up in the hospital. Up until that time, I didn't understand the bond I felt with you, or the strange way my senses changed. Why didn't you tell me, after I knew the truth?"

"I was afraid you would believe I was attempting to unduly influence your attraction to me. I wanted to earn your love and trust, not force it on you. Once I realized the affects my blood had on you, I was tempted to let you go, but Vincent convinced me I'd already had your heart or you would not have so easily accepted our connection." He paused to give her a soft, lingering kiss, melting her into the mattress. "You came close to dying in that hospital. I sensed you had mere moments of life remaining and simply couldn't bear to lose you that way. I considered bringing you across, but was unwilling to change on you without your understanding and permission. I suspected my blood would have certain side effects, but I was willing to risk almost anything to preserve your life."

"I'd have understood. You should've trusted me."

After a brief knock at the door, a servant entered with a breakfast tray. "Breakfast has arrived," he said as he tugged his robe around himself and rose from the bed. She scooted herself up against the headboard, shielding her own body from view with the bedclothes. The servant placed a food tray in her lap and she smiled gratefully at the ham and cheese omelet and coffee it held. Then he turned, bared his wrist, and offered himself to Joshua. Joshua sat on the edge of the bed and accepted his wrist, stroked it gently while meeting his gaze, and drank.

When he finished with the man, another servant, a young girl, entered the room with fresh clothing for the couple. Joshua allowed the girl to sit in his lap. He touched the side of her face gently and put his arms around her as he fastened his mouth to her throat. Rapture swept the girl's face, giving Katie an unexpected pang of jealousy. When he released her, he said, "Thank you, my dear. Have the others risen?"

"Yes, sir," she answered shyly.

"Good. Tell them we'll be down shortly." She nodded, cast an embarrassed look at Katie, and retreated from the room.

She sat staring at him, stricken, the contents of her plate as yet untouched. He smiled, shrugged his shoulders, and said, "They know I'm not yet strong enough to hunt."

"Why did you, I mean…?"

"Catherine," he interrupted, "the servants here are well cared for. True, they're all enthralled. Still, not one of them is here against their will. Most of them feel honored to offer themselves to me in that manner. They do me a great service. Do not begrudge them what small pleasure I can easily give them in return."

"That girl…"

"…knows she will not find herself in my bed," he finished for her. "She is satisfied with what I've given her. I do not take favors I cannot repay. None of us ever will. Tell me, did you not feel pleasure when Trey took you?"

She felt a blush rising to her cheeks. "Not pleasure, but it wasn't bad—more a feeling of comfort. I'm sorry," she said as she cut off a portion of the omelet in her lap. "I'm being stupid."

"No, your reaction is normal, all things considered. There is much yet you do not understand. You'll learn in time." He tipped her face so she had to meet his gaze. "If it bothers you so, I will no longer feed from the women. I belong to you. I share with you pleasures no other creature will ever learn from me."

She felt his meaning clearly, and gave him a mischievous smile.

"And, uh…what pleasures are you referring to?"

He growled happily and rose to his feet. "When we have more time, I'll remind you, wife. Now, finish your breakfast. The others are waiting." He carefully removed the bandage from his chest to examine his wound. A pink, puckered line cut across his heart from the center of his chest all the way to his side, a scar she knew would fade quickly. He gently pressed against the widest part of the wound with his fingers and winced, but seemed satisfied.

She turned her attention to her omelet while he grabbed his clothing and went into her closet-sized bathroom. She listened reverently to the sounds of him taking a shower, shaving, and making use of her blow drier, common, every-day sounds she thought she'd never hear again. When he emerged, he looked more like the sweet, gentle, powerful man she'd fallen in love with. Still, although he appeared much stronger than he had the night before, it could be some time before he felt like his old self again.

After she had finished her breakfast and gotten dressed, he brushed the snarls from of her hair. "I can't tell you how much I've missed you," he said softly. "All I could think about was how lonely you had to be. I was afraid I wouldn't survive long enough to find the help I needed. Thinking of you helped keep me alive."

Tears threatened to spill down her cheeks. "I was so afraid I'd lost you."

"I know." He helped her to her feet and put his arms around her, pulled her close. "This trial hasn't been easy for either of us, but we survived it. It'll never happen again, I promise you." He paused at the knock on the door, and sighed. "We still have one more little matter to see to. Are you ready?" She brushed his smooth cheek gently with her fingertips and nodded. "Let's go, then. We don't want to keep the Council waiting any longer."

Chapter Twenty-Five

Antonia rose quickly the moment the sun had set and walked the halls of Haven thoughtfully. Everyone in the great house had suffered profoundly from Catherine's distress. Tensions ran high. The servants sensed the tension rising in their vampire hosts and became equally afflicted. She realized she couldn't blame Trey for offering to end the girl's pain. If she had been the one to enter her room last night, she might've done the same thing.

The atmosphere of the great house changed profoundly the moment Catherine set eyes on Joshua. As she watched the others rise, she saw the change. They joked with each other, laughed as they once had. There was an ease about them that hadn't been there the night before. Visiting members of the Community were ready to move on. It was dangerous for so many vampires to be together for too long. They all knew that. It was clear a new strategy was needed if they were to stop the slaughter of the civilized Community. It was mutually understood that no vampire would go abroad alone.

When they gathered at last in the library to wait for the couple to arrive, they talked amongst themselves in quiet earnest. Antonia saw Trey smile at something one of the servants said to him. It was the first time the big man's face had lit up in more than two weeks. As she surveyed the gathering, she couldn't help but smile herself.

* * * *

Katie noticed the change in the atmosphere of Haven the moment she left her room with Joshua at her side. Servants who had always eyed her warily now smiled openly as they passed by. He put his arm around her protectively and led her down the wide staircase. When she hesitated nervously in front of the heavy, carved doors she'd faced once before, he gently tipped her face to his.

"We must accept whatever they decide, Catherine. You know that now, don't you?" She nodded reluctantly. "I'll plead our case as strongly as I can. I never thought to have a child of my own. I can't tell you how pleased and how very proud I am. If they allow us to keep the child, we must accept any limitations or provisions they require. But if there is to be no future for our child, we'll still have each other. We'll leave this place and return to Washington, and never look back. Whatever happens in there, I'll be right by your side. Don't be afraid." She took a deep breath, nodded her understanding, and put her hand on the door.

The assembly fell silent when the doors swung open to admit them. Those who had been sitting rose respectfully. He paused inside the entrance and she saw his gaze sweep briefly around the room. "May we sit?" he asked quietly, and she saw nods of consent from his peers. He led her to the sofa where they sat down and he pulled her protectively against him.

For the longest time, no one spoke. She found herself looking from face to face and remembering with vivid clarity the last time she had faced the Community. She felt Joshua willing her his strength and found courage in the support of his arms. Vincent walked stoically to where the couple sat and offered his hand to Joshua. They clasped arms in silent acknowledgement, and he knelt before them. "Joshua, Catherine found your scarf in the forest. I knew you wouldn't have left it behind. I saw traces of ash where...I believed that...Brother, how is it you survived?"

"I believe our mental communication drew the woman to me," Joshua explained. "She came out of nowhere. At first, I was not aware of her presence. I received a brief flash, little more, but 'twas enough to gather information that may be of use." He drew in a deep breath and released it slowly before continuing.

"I received no sense the woman was not acting alone. My first impression was a strong feeling of pain. I came to understand her motives may be of a personal nature." He cast a glance at Antonia and added, "Hers is the pain of loss, a feeling with which I am well acquainted." Antonia's eyes lowered, but the inscrutable expression she wore didn't otherwise waver.

"She is a mortal, but her mental disciplines are uncanny. She possesses the ability to sense our presence and mask her own, but the reason for her knowledge of us was not communicated to me during that brief contact. It is possible she is one of these creatures you so greatly fear, but I know so little of the nature of this hybrid you describe I cannot say with any certainty that it is, in fact, a damphere we are dealing with.

"I caught sight of her crossbow just as she released the trigger. I remember grabbing at the arrow in an attempt to stop its progress and feeling the pain of my failure. I fell and felt the end of it break off over my fist. She started to approach me, for what reason I cannot fathom, but when I moved she became alarmed and fled. I tried to go after her, but the pain was too great. I lay on that spot for some time. When I realized I was bleeding to death, I packed dirt around the arrow and started for Haven."

"Then the ash we found was nothing more than your blood the sun claimed," Vincent said, beginning to understand.

Joshua nodded his agreement. "Aye. I could barely stand, let alone walk, which is why it took me so long to return. I remember stumbling several times. That's probably how I lost my scarf. The best I could do was find shelter before dawn each day and continue my journey with each sunset."

"We searched for you," Vincent argued, grief and confusion evident in his voice. "I checked every possible shelter for signs of your presence. How is it we were unable to find you?"

"The woman can sense our presence. I was afraid if I called for help, or even opened my mind to your calls, she'd come back for me and kill anyone who came to my aid. I needed to protect myself and the knowledge I had gained. I was forced to block my presence with all the strength I could manage. I hid in the most unlikely places, took hidden paths where no one would think to look."

Katie stared at him in open-mouthed disbelief. "How did you survive?"

He smiled tenderly at her. "All that kept me going was my love for you. There were times, when I thought all my energy was spent, I believed I felt you calling to me. My feelings for you gave me the strength to go on. Perhaps it was our connection that gave me the will to keep moving."

"I felt myself getting weaker after I felt..." she put her hand over her heart and realized the dull ache was gone. "I think maybe, even with all those miles between us, you were drawing on my strength to keep you alive."

"Perhaps I was without realizing it. I couldn't exercise my most trivial powers. I did not dare to draw animals to my aid, for fear of attracting the wrong kind of attention. But I always felt you with me. I never dreamed our bond could be so powerful." He paused to trace the track of a tear that had dripped down her cheek with the tip of his index finger. "Had I known you'd been brought here, if I had known of your peril, I would have been more willing to risk summoning rescue."

The library fell to silence for several long minutes while everyone in the room processed in their own minds the ordeal Joshua had survived. Even the look Vincent wore on his face betrayed his deep feelings. She sensed an overwhelming surge of sympathy and regret flowing from the gathering. Joshua himself broke the silence. "What of the child?"

"We've given the matter much thought," Antonia said, her voice betraying no hint of her intent.

"Wait. Before you tell us, there's something I need to say," Katie said, drawing the attention of the gathering. She glanced at Joshua nervously, and when he nodded for her to proceed, she cleared her throat nervously. "When I was brought to Haven, I was afraid. I think I had every right to be. I felt threatened by you because I knew you were here to pass judgment on me. These past two weeks have been hell for all of us." A murmur of agreement passed briefly through the gathering.

"I know I haven't been behaving like a model Haven citizen, but I won't apologize for the way I acted. I know you understand my reasons for defying you. I was in pain, physically as well as emotionally. I think I started hating all of you for putting me through this. Some of you feel I'm too willful. I've been stubborn and uncooperative since the moment I arrived. I promise I won't give you any more trouble, no matter what is decided tonight.

"I have a lot to learn," she continued, feeling bolder. "There are things about your ways that still confuse me, but I'm not afraid anymore, not with Joshua here to help me. I want you to know I've always had a hard time holding a grudge. I don't hate any of you anymore. In fact, there are some of you I think I might even like."

She sniffed back a tear and swept her eyes pleadingly over the crowd. "Joshua once told me he believed I had a destiny he had no right to interfere with. I've had a lot of time to think about the path my life has taken, and I strongly feel he was wrong. Since the first, destiny has played a role in bringing us together. I believe I was meant to be with him and bring this special child into the world. Some of you know my heart. Surely you must understand that the gifts Joshua so strongly values in me, my ability to love and to give, will be passed down to our child, along with Joshua's gentle nature and devotion. Please don't deny our child the chance to discover its own destiny."

Then she squared her shoulders and showed some of the bold character that had amused them in the past. "I've been told you have certain codes of conduct, that you don't take life unless it's absolutely necessary, and yet you've passed judgment on a life that hasn't had the chance to commit any crime or pose any danger, because it has the potential to do so. I want you to think for a moment where any of you would be today if some fortune-telling fanatic predicted your destiny to become vampires and executed your mothers before you were born."

She paused to watch the faces of the Community members and saw some of them lower their eyes in understanding, or maybe, she hoped, in shame. Joshua gave her a gentle squeeze, letting her know he approved. "I love Joshua with my whole heart," she concluded. "I don't think that fact has ever been in doubt. With him at my side, and with your approval, I will raise our child to understand and appreciate the need to respect all life, mortal or not. We will teach it your values, your laws, help it learn not to fear or hate you. I'm confident you will see it as no threat to you."

"You've all warned me of the dangers of bringing a damphere into existence," Joshua added sternly. "Have you not also considered the benefits of having such a creature on our side? Imagine, if you will, having someone in our camp who is able to protect us with all the powers we have at our disposal when we are not in a position to do so, a creature with the power to aid in our control of the rogues at times when they can be caught at a disadvantage. You have within your grasp a potentially powerful ally. I'd advise you to consider this strongly before you waste this opportunity."

A quiet murmur rippled through the room, the combined voices making their words and intent unintelligible to her ears, but she sensed a strong feeling of consideration in the crowd. She looked up in surprise at Joshua and whispered, "I wish I had thought of that."

"Your feelings had you otherwise occupied," he told her knowingly.

"There's one more thing I need you to know," she said more loudly, regaining the attention of the gathering. "I've given this a lot of thought too, and I've decided I want to join you. I…" She glanced at Joshua and saw the surprise in his eyes. More quietly, she said, "I never really understood what loneliness was until I thought I'd lost you. I couldn't stand it for two months. I can't imagine what it must've been like for you before we met. You've been alone too long, been hurt too deeply. I don't want you to ever be lonely again, and I can't stand the thought of ever leaving you." She returned her gaze to the others. "If you allow us to keep the baby, I'll wait until it is old enough to understand this is something I want. My choice. When it's ready and we all can agree the timing is right, I'll ask Joshua to bring me across."

A louder murmur rose in the room as each member of the Community voiced their concerns. "That is a very bold idea." Antonia spoke loudly to bring the room to order again. "But not altogether wise." She started to protest, but Antonia raised her hand and continued. "Joshua is among our youngest members. There are a few younger, but most of us are much more experienced. The trick of bringing someone over is an art that takes some practice. Joshua has never made the attempt. If he should fail, the child would surely resent him for ending your life and robbing him of his mother. If you wish to pursue this course of action, you must choose another, more powerful master." Agreement spread through the crowd.

She looked to Joshua for help, and he met her gaze with a serious one of his own. "Be very careful, Catherine," he warned. "Are you certain this is what you want?" When she nodded, he pulled her closer and cupped her face in his hand. "I might have been willing to try before, but now I must agree with them. The risk is too great, there's too much at stake now. If I lost you, I'd never be able to forgive myself."

She felt her throat closing. "Our Vow…"

"…will not be compromised," he assured her quietly. More loudly, and in a much more assertive voice, he added, "Whoever accepts this responsibility will be well aware of the limitations of their control over you."

She shook her head. "I want to belong to you."

"If you want to keep the child, you must accept their conditions," he reminded her. "When the time comes, if this is truly what you want, you must be willing to surrender yourself to someone else." His gaze swept the gathering again as he said, "The Vow we gave to each other is among our most sacred laws. No one here will violate it. But if it means that, in the end, you will be able to stay with me forever, sharing your loyalty with another will be a small price to pay."

"Do you trust them that much?"

"No, love," he answered softly. "I trust you that much."

She looked around at the vampires who were now watching her with interest. "Who do you want me to chose," she whispered. The soft chuckling she heard from the group told her they'd heard her, and she felt her face flush.

His smile was heartbreaking. "The choice is yours alone to make. Most mortals who make the decision to accept this gift are not offered the opportunity to choose their master. You will become of that vampire's bloodline. A part of you may change to reflect the relationship. You will have a bond with him, or her, for the rest of eternity. You must consider that carefully before you make your decision."

"Do I need to decide now?" she asked softly.

"They expect you to," he said gently. "Once your consent is given and accepted, you, and they, will be honor bound to abide by it when your time comes." He stroked her face with the backs of his fingers. "I trust your judgment. You should know some of them well enough."

She looked at Antonia and remembered hearing somewhere that, beside the still-sleeping Jason, she was the oldest vampire known. "Antonia is the one who brought you over. You are of her bloodline."

"That's right."

She rose from the sofa and stepped boldly closer to Antonia. "I know I'm still very naïve about all of this," she began to the agreement of her audience. "I drank from you. I think a bond of some kind has formed between us because of it." Antonia nodded her head once, her face as inscrutable as ever. "You saved my life that night. I'm ashamed to admit I resented you for it. If I offended you, I am sorry."

"I understand how you felt," Antonia said tightly. "I've put the matter to rest. I suggest you do the same."

She nodded solemnly. "You are strong, confident in your powers and abilities, and, unfortunately, very firmly set in your ways. I think…no, I'm sure, I'm too strong willed to match myself with you. I'd like to think we could become great friends, but a stronger relationship might turn out badly. Sometimes women like us clash." Her comment won her a round of laughter and eased some of the anxiety still cramping her heart.

Antonia laughed as well and placed a companionable hand on her shoulder. "Bravely said, Catherine. You are probably correct." She glanced again at Joshua, and though his face was solemn, there was a glow of pride and approval in his eyes.

Her eyes moved from one expectant face to the next as she slowly walked across the room, and nodded or smiled at the creatures she had become acquainted with. When she looked at Stephan, he smiled winningly at her and raised his eyebrows. She rolled her eyes dramatically and said, "Oh, please," in a tone of sarcasm that won her another round of laughter.

When she faced Vincent, she took his hand in recognition of the feelings they shared and considered him carefully. "You and Joshua are alike in many ways," she said softly. "I know your relationship is closer than that of any mortal brotherly bond, and that you'd honor our Vow out of family respect. But I sense more from you that bothers me." She put her hand gently on his shoulder and gave him a sad smile. "Your emotions are deep and very tightly controlled. I suspect you have a temper I may risk bringing to the surface. But you're also hiding inside you a pain so private I doubt anyone knows its cause. If I surrendered some of my loyalty to you I might become tempted to help you, and that would put both of our relationships with Joshua at risk. I can't take that chance, and I don't think you'd want to either."

Vincent gave her a brief yet firm embrace. "Joshua chose his mate well. You should be proud of her, my brother," he said more loudly. "She is worthy of your trust."

"Of that, I am certain," she heard Joshua say behind her. She turned to take his hand and give it a gentle squeeze before she returned her attention to the rest of the room's occupants.

When her eyes touched on Trey's, she felt a ripple pass through her in recognition of the bond she'd felt forming between them. "Trey," she whispered, suddenly at a loss for words. He moved to the front of the crowd and knelt in front of her, making it easier for her to face him. "I gave you my blood. You know my heart better than anyone else except for Joshua. I think that's what made you side with me when no one else would dare, when I thought I had no hope left in the world."

"The blood I gave you in turn has forged a bond between us. I do not wish this to influence your decision. You know I will take no liberties with you that are not freely offered. Please consider carefully, small one, before you ask."

She turned to look at Joshua again, but his mind and expression were unreadable. He was holding his feelings to himself, waiting for her to make up her own mind without his influence. She looked again into Trey's midnight gaze and saw his understanding and acceptance. "I will be a challenge," she said uncertainly. "Do you think you can be patient with me?"

"Your courage honors me," he said gently. He rose to his full height, towering over her until she felt the overpowering weight of his gaze soften her knees. She had to struggle to match herself to his scrutiny. After a long pause, he chuckled softly, took her chin in his hand and captured her gaze, sealing her fate forever into his care. "You are uncommonly bold for a mortal. I accept your challenge and will endeavor to make myself worthy of your trust." To Joshua, he said, "When the time comes, I will take her. I will help you teach her our ways with all the tender dignity of a brother. You need never fear I will betray the relationship the two of you share."

Joshua moved to put his arms around her from behind. "Do you understand what you have just done?" he asked, his voice filled with concern. "You feared me at my worst, and I am yet a fledgling compared to this one. Trey may not be the oldest vampire known, but his power is without equal. His anger, once aroused, cannot be easily mollified. Even Jason has never dared to oppose him."

She leaned against his supporting embrace. "I'll try not to hold that against him," she said softly, winning her yet another round of soft laughter from the gathering.

"I hope your child will come to think of me as a favorite uncle," Trey said lightly. "I will show it all the love I've come to feel for you, small one."

She gasped in surprise. "Then...then we can keep it?"

He paused for one long, suspenseful moment, then favored her with the first real smile she'd seen on his dark face. "That decision was concluded the moment Joshua's arms came around you. We all felt the change in your heart, the sense of joy and completion coming from you both. The love bond the two of you share is stronger than any other consideration. We believe it will be enough."

She threw her arms around his neck, not an easy task, but he stooped quickly to put his strong arms around her and lift her into his embrace. "Thank you," she whispered to him. After he released her, she returned to Joshua's arms and turned her gaze to the rest of the Community. "Thank you all."

"Joshua," Trey said more firmly, "you will be required to remain with us, at least for the first, most formative years of the child's development. I'm afraid you will have to give up your self-imposed solitude."

She felt his entire body wince behind her and turned in his embrace to offer him a reassuring smile. "It will be okay," she said softly. "Where we live isn't that important, is it?"

He nodded his reluctant, but respectful, agreement in Trey's direction.

"I would prefer it if you became a permanent resident of Haven," Trey told her. "The day you take your family away will be a dark one indeed. You have a fine woman, my friend," he added to Joshua.

"Aye," he answered, his eyes reflecting a great deal of pride as he looked at her. "That she is, and so very much more."

"A suite of rooms has been prepared for your use, and preparations have already begun to convert the connecting room into a nursery. If there are any belongings you need from your home in Washington, some of us are willing to help you collect them."

"That won't be necessary. With your permission, Catherine and I will return to Washington as soon as she is strong enough to travel. Briefly," he stressed, "so we may help my attorney close up our home." He smiled lovingly at her. "Carl can retire and settle here with us. I'm sure your adopted father will enjoy watching his grandchild grow." She smiled her approval, then watched his eyes darken mischievously. "Now if you all will excuse us, my wife and I would like to become...reacquainted."

"Are you sure you're up to it?" she asked, hoping her concern for his health was evident in her voice, and not her sudden surge of anticipation.

He responded by giving her a deep, possessive kiss, seemingly unconcerned of the audience watching them with amused smiles. "Ask me again in the morning," he whispered against her lips.

Trey laughed a deep, hearty sound that rumbled around the room, and clapped Joshua on the shoulder. Some of the others responded to Trey's good humor, bringing the hottest blush ever to her face. She couldn't bring herself to look at any of them while Joshua led her out of the library and up the marble stairs.

THE END

About The Author

Tamara Monteau was born and raised in Washington State, graduated from Hudson's Bay High School in 1978, and joined the Air Force the following year, where she met her husband Mike. After traveling parts of Europe, and an extended stay in Louisiana, they have settled in Middle Georgia where Mike retired from the Air Force in 2004. They have four children and one grandchild.

Tamara has always been a dreamer, her head more often in the clouds than in reality. She discovered early in life the pleasures to be found between the covers of a well-written book, and is a strong advocate for reading. She began exploring her writing talents in 1992, and registered her first completed novel in 2003. Although a devoted Christian, she has always had a fascination for the macabre in general, and the vampire mystique in particular, and tries to reflect her values in her writings whenever possible.

Secret Cravings Publishing
www.secretcravingspublishing.com